F. Scott Fitzgerald

THE RICH BOY
and other stories

Selected by MATTHEW J. BRUCCOLI

PHŒNIX

A PHOENIX PAPERBACK

First published in 1998
by Phoenix, a division of Orion Books Ltd
Orion House, 5 Upper St Martin's Lane, London WC2H 9EA

A CIP catalogue record for this book
is available from the British Library.

ISBN 0 75380 444 1

Typeset by Deltatype Ltd, Birkenhead, Merseyside
Printed in Great Britain by
The Guernsey Press Co. Ltd., Guernsey, C. I.

Contents

Note on the Author and Editor

FRANCIS SCOTT KEY FITZGERALD was born in St Paul, Minnesota, in September 1896. He attended Princeton University, but did not graduate; he served in the US Army during the First World War, but was not sent overseas. After the great popularity of his first novel, *This Side of Paradise* (1920), he married Zelda Sayre of Montgomery, Alabama, and published two volumes of stories and a second novel, *The Beautiful and Damned*, during the next two years. Scott and Zelda, who led a life of dissipation and intermittent hard work in America and Europe, seemed to epitomize the glamorous spirit of the Jazz Age. In 1925 Fitzgerald published *The Great Gatsby*, which was made into a successful stage play, and took his first writing job in Hollywood in 1927. During another two-year spree in France, Zelda had a period of balletomania and suffered her first mental breakdown in 1930. She was in and out of mental asylums for the rest of her life.

After leading a luxurious life in the 1920s, Fitzgerald found that his popularity had suddenly declined, and he plunged into poverty and alcoholism in the 1930s. He struggled with *Tender is the Night*, his most ambitious novel, for nine years and finally published it in 1934. He spent his last few years as an unsuccessful screenwriter in Hollywood, where he met the gossip columnist Sheilah Graham, who became his devoted companion. He was working on his uncompleted Hollywood novel, *The Love of the Last Tycoon*, when he died of a heart attack in December 1940. Though neglected and nearly forgotten for the last decade of his life, Fitzgerald, helped by the posthumously published *The Crack-up* (1945) and several other collections of his work, experienced an astonishing resurgence after the Second World War. He is now considered, with Hemingway and Faulkner, one of the triumvirate of major American novelists of the twentieth century. *The Great Gatsby* continues to sell 300,000 copies a year.

MATTHEW J. BRUCCOLI is the leading authority on F. Scott Fitzgerald and is the author of *Some Sort of Epic Grandeur*, the standard biography of Fitzgerald. He is the author of nine books and editor of thirty-three volumes on or by Fitzgerald. Bruccoli is the Emily Brown Jefferies Professor of English at the University of South Carolina.

Introduction

The 1996 centenary of F. Scott Fitzgerald's birth was celebrated in the United States with more activity than has been accorded to the centenary of any other American author. The commemorations elicited speculation about how important Fitzgerald's work truly is when separated from the circumstances and legends of his life. Quite possibly, no American wrote better prose. That does not mean that Fitzgerald is the best or greatest American fiction writer: only that, as John O'Hara told John Steinbeck, 'Scott Fitzgerald was a better just plain writer than all of us put together. Just words writing.' Fitzgerald's prose provides rare pleasure. It looks rich on the page; it sounds rich to readers who hear what they are reading.

The qualities that identify a Fitzgerald paragraph are beyond style or technique. The recognizable voice of his prose conveys warmth: an emotional commitment to his material combined with a concern for his readers. Fitzgerald was probably referring to his novels when he wrote: 'Taking things hard ... That's the stamp that goes into my books so that people can read blind like brail.' The statement also applies to his best stories. Raymond Chandler testified that Fitzgerald 'had one of the rarest qualities in all literature ... the word is charm – charm as Keats would have used it. Who has it today? It's not a matter of pretty writing or clear style. It's a kind of subdued magic, controlled and exquisite, the sort of thing you get from good string quartets.' There is something else in the stories Fitzgerald wrote during the Twenties – call it buoyancy or ebullience.

Brilliant writing is not enough to generate endurance. Fitzgerald's fiction compulsively examines the themes of aspiration and disillusionment (disenchantment, failure) – which are often concomitants. Lionel Trilling observed that Fitzgerald 'was perhaps the last notable writer to affirm the Romantic fantasy, descended from the Renaissance, of personal ambition or heroism, of life committed to, or thrown away for, some ideal of self'. Perfect – except for the word *fantasy*.

Lasting fiction is remembered for its characters. All great fiction is great social history. The memorable characters in this edition – Gordon Sterrett, Anson Hunter, Dexter Green, Ailie Calhoun, Nicole and Nelson Kelly, Charlie Wales – are time-and-place specific. Experience was inseparable from setting for Fitzgerald. Malcolm Cowley commented that Fitzgerald wrote as though he worked in a room full of clocks and calendars. The clocks were always running, and Fitzgerald's characters are defeated by mutability. See the conclusion of 'Winter Dreams'.

Fitzgerald's stories are not outdated. Although he is identified with the Twenties – when most of his stories were written – his fiction attracts new readers generation after generation who recognize themselves in his people. Nor is this intensely American author reserved for his compatriots. Fitzgerald has reached a prodigious public outside the USA for fifty years. One of the modern gauges of a classic author's influence is his availability at airports; Fitzgerald scores high on the Gatwick/Heathrow test.

Fitzgerald's stories were long deprecated by critics as potboilers or hack work because most of the 160 stories were published in high-paying mass-circulation magazines. Professionals write for money. They also write for other reasons, but they can't write without money. The price was high because the stories really were crowd-pleasers: Fitzgerald's name on covers sold magazines during the years before TV when the racks were populated with competing fiction periodicals. Satisfying the expectations of his market was hard work; the stories were not scribbled between parties. The enduring ones are commercial masterpieces.

Fitzgerald wrote just three novellas – 'May Day', 'The Diamond as Big as the Ritz' and 'The Rich Boy' – which are now classics that are read for pleasure. 'The Rich Boy' is the only novella that appeared in a mass-circulation periodical, but Fitzgerald always wrote for a wide public. All the short stories included here initially appeared in popular magazines. Two of his most anthologized stories – 'The Last of the Belles' and 'Babylon Revisited' – were published in *The Saturday Evening Post*, which had a weekly circulation of 2,750,000.

'The Rich Boy' provides an opportunity to comment on Fitzgerald's most-cited sentences: 'Let me tell you about the very rich. They are different from you and me.' Ernest Hemingway misquoted this statement in 'The Snows of Kilimanjaro' (1936) and then supplied an apocryphal interpretation: '... someone had said to Scott, Yes they have more money. But that was not humorous to Scott. He thought they were a special glamorous race and when he found they weren't it wrecked him just as much as any other thing that wrecked him.' This fictive exchange became one of the most-repeated American anecdotes, cited to establish Fitzgerald's fatuous worship of wealth and Hemingway's tough-minded superiority to the money that bought his boat, his finca, his safaris and his suites at the Paris Ritz. Yet Fitzgerald complexly assessed the effects of money – and the lack of money – on character. (See the rest of the 'very rich' paragraph in 'The Rich Boy'.) That, among other concerns, is what *The Great Gatsby* and *Tender Is the Night* are about. That is what six of the stories in this edition are about. That is what much of American and British fiction is about. But it was open season on Fitzgerald during the Thirties because he depicted the attractions as well as the corruptions of wealth.

After *The Great Gatsby*, while he was working on *Tender Is the Night*, Fitzgerald increasingly denigrated his stories because he resented the time they took away from novel-writing. We do not know how many novels F. Scott Fitzgerald might have written instead of stories; but we can judge the best of his stories and award them a secure place among the valuable achievements in American fiction.

MATTHEW J. BRUCCOLI

Note on the Text

The stories that Fitzgerald revised for his own collections are published here in those texts. The others are reprinted from their original magazine appearances. Typographical errors, misspellings and punctuation have been silently corrected. Editorial word emendations are stipulated.

THE RICH BOY
and other stories

May Day
(1920)

Fitzgerald provided this comment when the story was collected in Tales of the Jazz Age *(1922):*

> *This somewhat unpleasant tale . . . relates a series of events which took place in the spring of the previous year. Each of the three events made a great impression upon me. In life they were unrelated, except by the general hysteria of that spring, which inaugurated the Age of Jazz, but in my story I have tried, unsuccessfully I fear, to weave them into a pattern – a pattern which would give the effect of those months in New York as they appeared to at least one member of what was then the younger generation.*

There had been a war fought and won and the great city of the conquering people was crossed with triumphal arches and vivid with thrown flowers of white, red, and rose. All through the long spring days the returning soldiers marched up the chief highway behind the strump of drums and the joyous, resonant wind of the brasses, while merchants and clerks left their bickerings and figurings and, crowding to the windows, turned their white-bunched faces gravely upon the passing battalions.

Never had there been such splendor in the great city, for the victorious war had brought plenty in its train, and the merchants had flocked thither from the South and West with their households to taste of all the luscious feasts and witness the lavish entertainments prepared – and to buy for their women furs against the next winter and bags of golden mesh and varicolored slippers of silk and silver and rose satin and cloth of gold.

So gaily and noisily were the peace and prosperity impending hymned by the scribes and poets of the conquering people that more and more spenders had gathered from the provinces to drink the wine of excitement, and faster and faster did the merchants dispose of their trinkets and slippers until they sent up a mighty cry for more trinkets and more slippers in order that

they might give in barter what was demanded of them. Some
even of them flung up their hands helplessly, shouting:

'Alas! I have no more slippers! and alas! I have no more
trinkets! May Heaven help me, for I know not what I shall do!'

But no one listened to their great outcry, for the throngs were
far too busy – day by day, the foot-soldiers trod jauntily the
highway and all exulted because the young men returning were
pure and brave, sound of tooth and pink of cheek, and the young
women of the land were virgins and comely both of face and of
figure.

So during all this time there were many adventures that
happened in the great city, and, of these, several – or perhaps one
– are here set down.

1

At nine o'clock on the morning of the first of May, 1919, a young
man spoke to the room clerk at the Biltmore Hotel, asking if Mr
Philip Dean were registered there, and if so, could he be
connected with Mr Dean's rooms. The inquirer was dressed in a
well-cut, shabby suit. He was small, slender, and darkly handsome; his eyes were framed above with unusually long eyelashes
and below with the blue semicircle of ill health, this latter effect
heightened by an unnatural glow which colored his face like a
low, incessant fever.

Mr Dean was staying there. The young man was directed to a
telephone at the side.

After a second his connection was made; a sleepy voice hello'd
from somewhere above.

'Mr Dean?' – this very eagerly – 'it's Gordon, Phil. It's Gordon
Sterrett. I'm down-stairs. I heard you were in New York and I
had a hunch you'd be here.'

The sleepy voice became gradually enthusiastic. Well, how
was Gordy, old boy! Well, he certainly was surprised and tickled!
Would Gordy come right up, for Pete's sake!

A few minutes later Philip Dean, dressed in blue silk pajamas,
opened his door and the two young men greeted each other with
a half-embarrassed exuberance. They were both about twenty-
four, Yale graduates of the year before the war; but there the

resemblance stopped abruptly. Dean was blond, ruddy, and rugged under his thin pajamas. Everything about him radiated fitness and bodily comfort. He smiled frequently, showing large and prominent teeth.

'I was going to look you up,' he cried enthusiastically. 'I'm taking a couple of weeks off. If you'll sit down a sec I'll be right with you. Going to take a shower.'

As he vanished into the bathroom his visitor's dark eyes roved nervously around the room, resting for a moment on a great English travelling bag in the corner and on a family of thick silk shirts littered on the chairs amid impressive neckties and soft woollen socks.

Gordon rose and, picking up one of the shirts, gave it a minute examination. It was of very heavy silk, yellow, with a pale blue stripe – and there were nearly a dozen of them. He stared involuntarily at his own shirt-cuffs – they were ragged and linty at the edges and soiled to a faint gray. Dropping the silk shirt, he held his coat-sleeves down and worked the frayed shirt-cuffs up till they were out of sight. Then he went to the mirror and looked at himself with listless, unhappy interest. His tie, of former glory, was faded and thumb-creased – it served no longer to hide the jagged button-holes of his collar. He thought, quite without amusement, that only three years before he had received a scattering vote in the senior elections at college for being the best-dressed man in his class.

Dean emerged from the bathroom polishing his body.

'Saw an old friend of yours last night,' he remarked. 'Passed her in the lobby and couldn't think of her name to save my neck. That girl you brought up to New Haven senior year.'

Gordon started.

'Edith Bradin? That whom you mean?'

"At's the one. Damn good looking. She's still sort of a pretty doll – you know what I mean: as if you touched her she'd smear.'

He surveyed his shining self complacently in the mirror, smiled faintly, exposing a section of teeth.

'She must be twenty-three anyway,' he continued.

'Twenty-two last month,' said Gordon absently.

'What? Oh, last month. Well, I imagine she's down for the Gamma Psi dance. Did you know we're having a Yale Gamma Psi dance to-night at Delmonico's? You better come up, Gordy. Half of New Haven'll probably be there. I can get you an invitation.'

Draping himself reluctantly in fresh underwear, Dean lit a cigarette and sat down by the open window, inspecting his calves and knees under the morning sunshine which poured into the room.

'Sit down, Gordy,' he suggested, 'and tell me all about what you've been doing and what you're doing now and everything.'

Gordon collapsed unexpectedly upon the bed; lay there inert and spiritless. His mouth, which habitually dropped a little open when his face was in repose, became suddenly helpless and pathetic.

'What's the matter?' asked Dean quickly.

'Oh, God!'

'What's the matter?'

'Every God damn thing in the world,' he said miserably. 'I've absolutely gone to pieces, Phil. I'm all in.'

'Huh?'

'I'm all in.' His voice was shaking.

Dean scrutinized him more closely with appraising blue eyes.

'You certainly look all shot.'

'I am. I've made a hell of a mess of everything.' He paused. 'I'd better start at the beginning – or will it bore you?'

'Not at all; go on.' There was, however, a hesitant note in Dean's voice. This trip East had been planned for a holiday – to find Gordon Sterrett in trouble exasperated him a little.

'Go on,' he repeated, and then added half under his breath, 'Get it over with.'

'Well,' began Gordon unsteadily, 'I got back from France in February, went home to Harrisburg for a month, and then came down to New York to get a job. I got one – with an export company. They fired me yesterday.'

'Fired you?'

'I'm coming to that, Phil. I want to tell you frankly. You're about the only man I can turn to in a matter like this. You won't mind if I just tell you frankly, will you, Phil?'

Dean stiffened a bit more. The pats he was bestowing on his knees grew perfunctory. He felt vaguely that he was being unfairly saddled with responsibility; he was not even sure he

wanted to be told. Though never surprised at finding Gordon
Sterrett in mild difficulty, there was something in this present
misery that repelled him and hardened him, even though it
excited his curiosity.

'Go on.'

'It's a girl.'

'Hm.' Dean resolved that nothing was going to spoil his trip. If
Gordon was going to be depressing, then he'd have to see less of
Gordon.

'Her name is Jewel Hudson,' went on the distressed voice from
the bed. 'She used to be "pure," I guess, up to about a year ago.
Lived here in New York – poor family. Her people are dead now
and she lives with an old aunt. You see it was just about the time
I met her that everybody began to come back from France in
droves – and all I did was to welcome the newly arrived and go
on parties with 'em. That's the way it started, Phil, just from
being glad to see everybody and having them glad to see me.'

'You ought to've had more sense.'

'I know,' Gordon paused, and then continued listlessly. 'I'm on
my own now, you know, and Phil, I can't stand being poor. Then
came this darn girl. She sort of fell in love with me for a while
and, though I never intended to get so involved, I'd always seem
to run into her somewhere. You can imagine the sort of work I
was doing for those exporting people – of course, I always
intended to draw; do illustrating for magazines; there's a pile of
money in it.'

'Why didn't you? You've got to buckle down if you want to
make good,' suggested Dean with cold formalism.

'I tried, a little, but my stuff's crude. I've got talent, Phil; I can
draw – but I just don't know how. I ought to go to art school and
I can't afford it. Well, things came to a crisis about a week ago.
Just as I was down to about my last dollar this girl began
bothering me. She wants some money; claims she can make
trouble for me if she doesn't get it.'

'Can she?'

'I'm afraid she can. That's one reason I lost my job – she kept
calling up the office all the time, and that was sort of the last
straw down there. She's got a letter all written to send to my

family. Oh, she's got me, all right. I've got to have some money for her.'

There was an awkward pause. Gordon lay very still, his hands clenched by his side.

'I'm all in,' he continued, his voice trembling. 'I'm half crazy, Phil. If I hadn't known you were coming East, I think I'd have killed myself. I want you to lend me three hundred dollars.'

Dean's hands, which had been patting his bare ankles, were suddenly quiet – and the curious uncertainty playing between the two became taut and strained.

After a second Gordon continued:

'I've bled the family until I'm ashamed to ask for another nickel.'

Still Dean made no answer.

'Jewel says she's got to have two hundred dollars.'

'Tell her where she can go.'

'Yes, that sounds easy, but she's got a couple of drunken letters I wrote her. Unfortunately she's not at all the flabby sort of person you'd expect.'

Dean made an expression of distaste.

'I can't stand that sort of woman. You ought to have kept away.'

'I know,' admitted Gordon wearily.

'You've got to look at things as they are. If you haven't got money you've got to work and stay away from women.'

'That's easy for you to say,' began Gordon, his eyes narrowing. 'You've got all the money in the world.'

'I most certainly have not. My family keep darn close tab on what I spend. Just because I have a little leeway I have to be extra careful not to abuse it.'

He raised the blind and let in a further flood of sunshine.

'I'm no prig, Lord knows,' he went on deliberately. 'I like pleasure – and I like a lot of it on a vacation like this, but you're – you're in awful shape. I never heard you talk just this way before. You seem to be sort of bankrupt – morally as well as financially.'

'Don't they usually go together?'

Dean shook his head impatiently.

'There's a regular aura about you that I don't understand. It's a sort of evil.'

'It's an air of worry and poverty and sleepless nights,' said Gordon, rather defiantly.

'I don't know.'

'Oh, I admit I'm depressing. I depress myself. But, my God, Phil, a week's rest and a new suit and some ready money and I'd be like – like I was. Phil, I can draw like a streak, and you know it. But half the time I haven't had the money to buy decent drawing materials – and I can't draw when I'm tired and discouraged and all in. With a little ready money I can take a few weeks off and get started.'

'How do I know you wouldn't use it on some other woman?'

'Why rub it in?' said Gordon quietly.

'I'm not rubbing it in. I hate to see you this way.'

'Will you lend me the money, Phil?'

'I can't decide right off. That's a lot of money and it'll be darn inconvenient for me.'

'It'll be hell for me if you can't – I know I'm whining, and it's all my own fault but – that doesn't change it.'

'When could you pay it back?'

This was encouraging. Gordon considered. It was probably wisest to be frank.

'Of course, I could promise to send it back next month, but – I'd better say three months. Just as soon as I start to sell drawings.'

'How do I know you'll sell any drawings?'

A new hardness in Dean's voice sent a faint chill of doubt over Gordon. Was it possible that he wouldn't get the money?

'I supposed you had a little confidence in me.'

'I did have – but when I see you like this I begin to wonder.'

'Do you suppose if I wasn't at the end of my rope I'd come to you like this? Do you think I'm enjoying it?' He broke off and bit his lip, feeling that he had better subdue the rising anger in his voice. After all, he was the suppliant.

'You seem to manage it pretty easily,' said Dean angrily. 'You put me in the position where, if I don't lend it to you, I'm a sucker – oh, yes, you do. And let me tell you it's no easy thing for me to get hold of three hundred dollars. My income isn't so big but that a slice like that won't play the deuce with it.'

He left his chair and began to dress, choosing his clothes

carefully. Gordon stretched out his arms and clenched the edges of the bed, fighting back a desire to cry out. His head was splitting and whirring, his mouth was dry and bitter and he could feel the fever in his blood resolving itself into innumerable regular counts like a slow dripping from a roof.

Dean tied his tie precisely, brushed his eyebrows, and removed a piece of tobacco from his teeth with solemnity. Next he filled his cigarette case, tossed the empty box thoughtfully into the waste basket, and settled the case in his vest pocket.

'Had breakfast?' he demanded.

'No; I don't eat it any more.'

'Well, we'll go out and have some. We'll decide about that money later. I'm sick of the subject. I came East to have a good time.

'Lets go over to the Yale Club,' he continued moodily, and then added with an implied reproof: 'You've given up your job. You've got nothing else to do.'

'I'd have a lot to do if I had a little money,' said Gordon pointedly.

'Oh, for Heaven's sake drop the subject for a while! No point in glooming on my whole trip. Here, here's some money.'

He took a five-dollar bill from his wallet and tossed it over to Gordon, who folded it carefully and put it in his pocket. There was an added spot of color in his cheeks, an added glow that was not fever. For an instant before they turned to go out their eyes met and in that instant each found something that made him lower his own glance quickly. For in that instant they quite suddenly and definitely hated each other.

2

Fifth Avenue and Forty-fourth Street swarmed with the noon crowd. The wealthy, happy sun glittered in transient gold through the thick windows of the smart shops, lighting upon mesh bags and purses and strings of pearls in gray velvet cases; upon gaudy feather fans of many colors; upon the laces and silks of expensive dresses; upon the bad paintings and the fine period furniture in the elaborate show rooms of interior decorators.

Working-girls, in pairs and groups and swarms, loitered by

these windows, choosing their future boudoirs from some resplendent display which included even a man's silk pajamas laid domestically across the bed. They stood in front of the jewelry stores and picked out their engagement rings, and their wedding rings and their platinum wrist watches, and then drifted on to inspect the feather fans and opera cloaks; meanwhile digesting the sandwiches and sundaes they had eaten for lunch.

All through the crowd were men in uniform, sailors from the great fleet anchored in the Hudson, soldiers with divisional insignia from Massachusetts to California, wanting fearfully to be noticed, and finding the great city thoroughly fed up with soldiers unless they were nicely massed into pretty formations and uncomfortable under the weight of a pack and rifle.

Through this medley Dean and Gordon wandered; the former interested, made alert by the display of humanity at its frothiest and gaudiest; the latter reminded of how often he had been one of the crowd, tired, casually fed, overworked, and dissipated. To Dean the struggle was significant, young, cheerful; to Gordon it was dismal, meaningless, endless.

In the Yale Club they met a group of their former classmates who greeted the visiting Dean vociferously. Sitting in a semicircle of lounges and great chairs, they had a highball all around.

Gordon found the conversation tiresome and interminable. They lunched together *en masse*, warmed with liquor as the afternoon began. They were all going to the Gamma Psi dance that night – it promised to be the best party since the war.

'Edith Bradin's coming,' said some one to Gordon. 'Didn't she used to be an old flame of yours? Aren't you both from Harrisburg?'

'Yes.' He tried to change the subject. 'I see her brother occasionally. He's sort of a socialistic nut. Runs a paper or something here in New York.'

'Not like his gay sister, eh?' continued his eager informant. 'Well, she's coming to-night with a junior named Peter Himmel.'

Gordon was to meet Jewel Hudson at eight o'clock – he had promised to have some money for her. Several times he glanced nervously at his wrist watch. At four, to his relief, Dean rose and announced that he was going over to Rivers Brothers to buy some collars and ties. But as they left the Club another of the party joined them, to Gordon's great dismay. Dean was in a jovial mood now, happy, expectant of the evening's party, faintly hilarious. Over in Rivers' he chose a dozen neckties, selecting each one after long consultations with the other man. Did he think narrow ties were coming back? And wasn't it a shame that Rivers couldn't get any more Welch Margetson collars? There never was a collar like the 'Covington.'

Gordon was in something of a panic. He wanted the money immediately. And he was now inspired also with a vague idea of attending the Gamma Psi dance. He wanted to see Edith – Edith whom he hadn't met since one romantic night at the Harrisburg Country Club just before he went to France. The affair had died, drowned in the turmoil of the war and quite forgotten in the arabesque of these three months, but a picture of her, poignant, debonnaire, immersed in her own inconsequential chatter, recurred to him unexpectedly and brought a hundred memories with it. It was Edith's face that he had cherished through college with a sort of detached yet affectionate admiration. He had loved to draw her – around his room had been a dozen sketches of her – playing golf, swimming – he could draw her pert, arresting profile with his eyes shut.

They left Rivers' at five-thirty and paused for a moment on the sidewalk.

'Well,' said Dean genially, 'I'm all set now. Think I'll go back to the hotel and get a shave, haircut, and massage.'

'Good enough,' said the other man, 'I think I'll join you.'

Gordon wondered if he was to be beaten after all. With difficulty he restrained himself from turning to the man and snarling out, 'Go on away, damn you!' In despair he suspected that perhaps Dean had spoken to him, was keeping him along in order to avoid a dispute about the money.

They went into the Biltmore – a Biltmore alive with girls – mostly from the West and South, the stellar débutantes of many cities gathered for the dance of a famous fraternity of a famous university. But to Gordon they were faces in a dream. He gathered together his forces for a last appeal, was about to come out with he knew not what, when Dean suddenly excused himself to the other man and taking Gordon's arm led him aside.

'Gordy,' he said quickly, 'I've thought the whole thing over carefully and I've decided that I can't lend you that money. I'd like to oblige you, but I don't feel I ought to – it'd put a crimp in me for a month.'

Gordon, watching him dully, wondered why he had never before noticed how much those upper teeth projected.

'– I'm mighty sorry, Gordon,' continued Dean, 'but that's the way it is.'

He took out his wallet and deliberately counted out seventy-five dollars in bills.

'Here,' he said, holding them out, 'here's seventy-five; that makes eighty all together. That's all the actual cash I have with me, besides what I'll actually spend on the trip.'

Gordon raised his clenched hand automatically, opened it as though it were a tongs he was holding, and clenched it again on the money.

'I'll see you at the dance,' continued Dean. 'I've got to get along to the barber shop.'

'So long,' said Gordon in a strained and husky voice.

'So long.'

Dean began to smile, but seemed to change his mind. He nodded briskly and disappeared.

But Gordon stood there, his handsome face awry with distress, the roll of bills clenched tightly in his hand. Then, blinded by sudden tears, he stumbled clumsily down the Biltmore steps.

3

About nine o'clock of the same night two human beings came out of a cheap restaurant in Sixth Avenue. They were ugly, ill-nourished, devoid of all except the very lowest form of intelligence, and without even that animal exuberance that in itself brings color into life; they were lately vermin-ridden, cold, and hungry in a dirty town of a strange land; they were poor, friendless; tossed as driftwood from their births, they would be tossed as driftwood to their deaths. They were dressed in the uniform of the United States Army, and on the shoulder of each was the insignia of a drafted division from New Jersey, landed three days before.

The taller of the two was named Carrol Key, a name hinting

that in his veins, however thinly diluted by generations of degeneration, ran blood of some potentiality. But one could stare endlessly at the long, chinless face, the dull, watery eyes, and high cheek-bones, without finding a suggestion of either ancestral worth or native resourcefulness.

His companion was swart and bandy-legged, with rat-eyes and a much-broken hooked nose. His defiant air was obviously a pretense, a weapon of protection borrowed from that world of snarl and snap, of physical bluff and physical menace, in which he had always lived. His name was Gus Rose.

Leaving the café they sauntered down Sixth Avenue, wielding toothpicks with great gusto and complete detachment.

'Where to?' asked Rose, in a tone which implied that he would not be surprised if Key suggested the South Sea Islands.

'What you say we see if we can getta holda some liquor?' Prohibition was not yet. The ginger in the suggestion was caused by the law forbidding the selling of liquor to soldiers.

Rose agreed enthusiastically.

'I got an idea,' continued Key, after a moment's thought, 'I got a brother somewhere.'

'In New York?'

'Yeah. He's an old fella.' He meant that he was an elder brother. 'He's a waiter in a hash joint.'

'Maybe he can get us some.'

'I'll say he can!'

'B'lieve me, I'm goin' to get this darn uniform off me to-morra. Never get me in it again, neither. I'm goin' to get me some regular clothes.'

'Say, maybe I'm not.'

As their combined finances were something less than five dollars, this intention can be taken largely as a pleasant game of words, harmless and consoling. It seemed to please both of them, however, for they reinforced it with chuckling and mention of personages high in biblical circles, adding such further emphasis as 'Oh, boy!' 'You know!' and 'I'll say so!' repeated many times over.

The entire mental pabulum of these two men consisted of an offended nasal comment extended through the years upon the institution – army, business, or poorhouse – which kept them alive, and toward their immediate superior in that institution. Until that very morning the institution had been the 'government' and the immediate superior had been the 'Cap'n' – from these two they had glided out and were now in the vaguely uncomfortable state before they should adopt their next bondage. They were uncertain, resentful, and somewhat ill at ease. This they hid by pretending an elaborate relief at being out of the army, and by assuring each other that military discipline should never again rule their stubborn, liberty-loving wills. Yet, as a matter of fact, they would have felt more at home in a prison than in this new-found and unquestionable freedom.

Suddenly Key increased his gait. Rose, looking up and following his glance, discovered a crowd that was collecting fifty yards down the street. Key chuckled and began to run in the direction of the crowd; Rose thereupon also chuckled and his short bandy legs twinkled beside the long, awkward strides of his companion.

Reaching the outskirts of the crowd they immediately became an indistinguishable part of it. It was composed of ragged civilians somewhat the worse for liquor, and of soldiers representing many divisions and many stages of sobriety, all clustered around a gesticulating little Jew with long black whiskers, who was waving his arms and delivering an excited but succinct harangue. Key and Rose, having wedged themselves into the approximate parquet, scrutinized him with acute suspicion, as his words penetrated their common consciousness.

'– What have you got outa the war?' he was crying fiercely. 'Look arounja, look arounja! Are you rich? Have you got a lot of money offered you? – no; you're lucky if you're alive and got both your legs; you're lucky if you came back an' find your wife ain't gone off with some other fella that had the money to buy himself out of the war! That's when you're lucky! Who got anything out of it except J. P. Morgan an' John D. Rockerfeller?'

At this point the little Jew's oration was interrupted by the hostile impact of a fist upon the point of his bearded chin and he toppled backward to a sprawl on the pavement.

'God damn Bolsheviki!' cried the big soldier-blacksmith who had delivered the blow. There was a rumble of approval; the crowd closed in nearer.

The Jew staggered to his feet, and immediately went down again before a half-dozen reaching-in fists. This time he stayed down, breathing heavily, blood oozing from his lip where it was cut within and without.

There was a riot of voices, and in a minute Rose and Key found themselves flowing with the jumbled crowd down Sixth Avenue under the leadership of a thin civilian in a slouch hat and the brawny soldier who had summarily ended the oration. The crowd had marvellously swollen to formidable proportions and a stream of more non-committal citizens followed it along the sidewalks lending their moral support by intermittent huzzas.

'Where we goin'?' yelled Key to the man nearest him.

His neighbor pointed up to the leader in the slouch hat.

'That guy knows where there's a lot of 'em! We're goin' to show 'em!'

'We're goin' to show 'em!' whispered Key delightedly to Rose, who repeated the phrase rapturously to a man on the other side.

Down Sixth Avenue swept the procession joined here and there by soldiers and marines, and now and then by civilians, who came up with the inevitable cry that they were just out of the army themselves, as if presenting it as a card of admission to a newly formed Sporting and Amusement Club.

Then the procession swerved down a cross street and headed for Fifth Avenue and the word filtered here and there that they were bound for a Red meeting at Tolliver Hall.

'Where is it?'

The question went up the line and a moment later the answer floated back. Tolliver Hall was down on Tenth Street. There was a bunch of other sojers who was goin' to break it up and was down there now!

But Tenth Street had a faraway sound and at the word a general groan went up and a score of the procession dropped out. Among these were Rose and Key, who slowed down to a saunter and let the more enthusiastic sweep on by.

'I'd rather get some liquor,' said Key as they halted and made their way to the sidewalk amid cries of 'Shell hole!' and 'Quitters!'

'Does your brother work around here?' asked Rose, assuming the air of one passing from the superficial to the eternal.

'He oughta,' replied Key. 'I ain't seen him for a coupla years. I been out to Pennsylvania since. Maybe he don't work at night anyhow. It's right along here. He can get us some o'right if he ain't gone.'

They found the place after a few minutes' patrol of the street – a shoddy tablecloth restaurant between Fifth Avenue and Broadway. Here Key went inside to inquire for his brother George, while Rose waited on the sidewalk.

'He ain't here no more,' said Key emerging. 'He's a waiter up to Delmonico's.'

Rose nodded wisely, as if he'd expected as much. One should not be surprised at a capable man changing jobs occasionally. He knew a waiter once – there ensued a long conversation as they walked as to whether waiters made more in actual wages than in tips – it was decided that it depended on the social tone of the joint wherein the waiter labored. After having given each other vivid pictures of millionaires dining at Delmonico's and throwing away fifty-dollar bills after their first quart of champagne, both men thought privately of becoming waiters. In fact, Key's narrow brow was secreting a resolution to ask his brother to get him a job.

'A waiter can drink up all the champagne those fellas leave in bottles,' suggested Rose with some relish, and then added as an afterthought, 'Oh, boy!'

By the time they reached Delmonico's it was half past ten, and they were surprised to see a stream of taxis driving up to the door one after the other and emitting marvelous, hatless young ladies, each one attended by a stiff young gentleman in evening clothes.

'It's a party,' said Rose with some awe. 'Maybe we better not go in. He'll be busy.'

'No, he won't. He'll be o'right.'

After some hesitation they entered what appeared to them to be the least elaborate door and, indecision falling upon them immediately, stationed themselves nervously in an inconspicuous corner of the small dining-room in which they found themselves. They took off their caps and held them in their hands. A cloud of gloom fell upon them and both started when a door at one end of the room crashed open, emitting a comet-like waiter who streaked across the floor and vanished through another door on the other side.

There had been three of these lightning passages before the
seekers mustered the acumen to hail a waiter. He turned, looked
at them suspiciously, and then approached with soft, catlike
steps, as if prepared at any moment to turn and flee.

'Say,' began Key, 'say do you know my brother? He's a waiter
here.'

'His name is Key,' annotated Rose.

Yes, the waiter knew Key. He was up-stairs, he thought. There
was a big dance going on in the main ballroom. He'd tell him.

Ten minutes later George Key appeared and greeted his brother
with the utmost suspicion; his first and most natural thought
being that he was going to be asked for money.

George was tall and weak chinned, but there his resemblance
to his brother ceased. The waiter's eyes were not dull, they were
alert and twinkling, and his manner was suave, in-door, and
faintly superior. They exchanged formalities. George was married
and had three children. He seemed fairly interested, but not
impressed by the news that Carrol had been abroad in the army.
This disappointed Carrol.

'George,' said the younger brother, these amenities having
been disposed of, 'we want to get some booze, and they won't sell
us none. Can you get us some?'

George considered.

'Sure. Maybe I can. It may be half an hour, though.'

'All right,' agreed Carrol, 'we'll wait.'

At this Rose started to sit down in a convenient chair, but was
hailed to his feet by the indignant George.

'Hey! Watch out, you! Can't sit down here! This room's all set
for a twelve o'clock banquet.'

'I ain't goin' to hurt it,' said Rose resentfully. 'I been through
the delouser.'

'Never mind,' said George sternly, 'if the head waiter seen me
here talkin' he'd romp all over me.'

'Oh.'

The mention of the head waiter was full explanation to the
other two; they fingered their overseas caps nervously and waited
for a suggestion.

'I tell you,' said George, after a pause, 'I got a place you can
wait; you just come here with me.'

They followed him out the far door, through a deserted pantry and up a pair of dark winding stairs, emerging finally into a small room chiefly furnished by piles of pails and stacks of scrubbing brushes, and illuminated by a single dim electric light. There he left them, after soliciting two dollars and agreeing to return in half an hour with a quart of whiskey.

'George is makin' money, I bet,' said Key gloomily as he seated himself on an inverted pail. 'I bet he's making fifty dollars a week.'

Rose nodded his head and spat.

'I bet he is, too.'

'What'd he say the dance was of?'

'A lot of college fellas. Yale College.'

They both nodded solemnly at each other.

'Wonder where that crowda sojers is now?'

'I don't know. I know that's too damn long to walk for me.'

'Me too. You don't catch me walkin' that far.'

Ten minutes later restlessness seized them.

'I'm goin' to see what's out here,' said Rose, stepping cautiously toward the other door.

It was a swinging door of green baize and he pushed it open a cautious inch.

'See anything?'

For answer Rose drew in his breath sharply.

'Doggone! Here's some liquor I'll say!'

'Liquor?'

Key joined Rose at the door, and looked eagerly.

'I'll tell the world that's liquor,' he said, after a moment of concentrated gazing.

It was a room about twice as large as the one they were in – and in it was prepared a radiant feast of spirits. There were long walls of alternating bottles set along two white covered tables; whiskey, gin, brandy, French and Italian vermouths, and orange juice, not to mention an array of syphons and two great empty punch bowls. The room was as yet uninhabited.

'It's for this dance they're just starting,' whispered Key; 'hear the violins playin'? Say, boy, I wouldn't mind havin' a dance.'

They closed the door softly and exchanged a glance of mutual comprehension. There was no need of feeling each other out.

'I'd like to get my hands on a coupla those bottles,' said Rose emphatically.

'Me too.'

'Do you suppose we'd get seen?'

Key considered.

'Maybe we better wait till they start drinking' 'em. They got 'em all laid out now, and they know how many of them there are.'

They debated this point for several minutes. Rose was all for getting his hands on a bottle now and tucking it under his coat before any one came into the room. Key, however, advocated caution. He was afraid he might get his brother in trouble. If they waited till some of the bottles were opened it'd be all right to take one, and everybody'd think it was one of the college fellas.

While they were still engaged in argument George Key hurried through the room and, barely grunting at them, disappeared by way of the green baize door. A minute later they heard several corks pop, and then the sound of cracking ice and splashing liquid. George was mixing the punch.

The soldiers exchanged delighted grins.

'Oh, boy!' whispered Rose.

George reappeared.

'Just keep low, boys,' he said quickly. 'I'll have your stuff for you in five minutes.'

He disappeared through the door by which he had come.

As soon as his footsteps receded down the stairs, Rose, after a cautious look, darted into the room of delights and reappeared with a bottle in his hand.

'Here's what I say,' he said, as they sat radiantly digesting their first drink. 'We'll wait till he comes up, and we'll ask him if we can't just stay here and drink what he brings us – see. We'll tell him we haven't got any place to drink it – see. Then we can sneak in there whenever there ain't nobody in that there room and tuck a bottle under our coats. We'll have enough to last us a coupla days – see?'

'Sure,' agreed Rose enthusiastically. 'Oh boy! And if we want to we can sell it to sojers any time we want to.

They were silent for a moment thinking rosily of this idea. Then Key reached up and unhooked the collar of his O. D. coat.

'It's hot in here, ain't it?'

Rose agreed earnestly.

'Hot as hell.'

4

She was still quite angry when she came out of the dressing-room and crossed the intervening parlor of politeness that opened onto the hall – angry not so much at the actual happening which was, after all, the merest commonplace of her social existence, but because it had occurred on this particular night. She had no quarrel with herself. She had acted with that correct mixture of dignity and reticent pity which she always employed. She had succinctly and deftly snubbed him.

It had happened when their taxi was leaving the Biltmore – hadn't gone half a block. He had lifted his right arm awkwardly – she was on his right side – and attempted to settle it snugly around the crimson fur-trimmed opera cloak she wore. This in itself had been a mistake. It was inevitably more graceful for a young man attempting to embrace a young lady of whose acquiescence he was not certain, to first put his far arm around her. It avoided that awkward movement of raising the near arm.

His second *faux pas* was unconscious. She had spent the afternoon at the hairdresser's; the idea of any calamity overtaking her hair was extremely repugnant – yet as Peter made his unfortunate attempt the point of his elbow had just faintly brushed it. That was his second *faux pas*. Two were quite enough.

He had begun to murmur. At the first murmur she had decided that he was nothing but a college boy – Edith was twenty-two, and anyhow, this dance, first of its kind since the war, was reminding her, with the accelerating rhythm of its associations, of something else – of another dance and another man, a man for whom her feelings had been little more than a sad-eyed, adolescent mooniness. Edith Bradin was falling in love with her recollection of Gordon Sterrett.

So she came out of the dressing-room at Delmonico's and stood for a second in the doorway looking over the shoulders of a black dress in front of her at the groups of Yale men who flitted like dignified black moths around the head of the stairs. From the

room she had left drifted out the heavy fragrance left by the
passage to and fro of many scented young beauties – rich
perfumes and the fragile memory-laden dust of fragrant powders.
This odor drifting out acquired the tang of cigarette smoke in the
hall, and then settled sensuously down the stairs and permeated
the ballroom where the Gamma Psi dance was to be held. It was
an odor she knew well, exciting, stimulating, restlessly sweet –
the odor of a fashionable dance.

She thought of her own appearance. Her bare arms and
shoulders were powdered to a creamy white. She knew they
looked very soft and would gleam like milk against the black
backs that were to silhouette them tonight. The hairdressing had
been a success; her reddish mass of hair was piled and crushed
and creased to an arrogant marvel of mobile curves. Her lips
were finely made of deep carmine; the irises of her eyes were
delicate, breakable blue, like china eyes. She was a complete,
infinitely delicate, quite perfect thing of beauty, flowing in an
even line from a complex coiffure to two small slim feet.

She thought of what she would say to-night at this revel,
faintly prestiged already by the sounds of high and low laughter
and slippered footsteps, and movements of couples up and down
the stairs. She would talk the language she had talked for many
years – her line – made up of the current expressions, bits of
journalese and college slang strung together into an intrinsic
whole, careless, faintly provocative, delicately sentimental. She
smiled faintly as she heard a girl sitting on the stairs near her say:
'You don't know the half of it, dearie!'

And as she smiled her anger melted for a moment, and closing
her eyes she drew in a deep breath of pleasure. She dropped her
arms to her side until they were faintly touching the sleek sheath
that covered and suggested her figure. She had never felt her own
softness so much nor so enjoyed the whiteness of her own arms.

'I smell sweet,' she said to herself simply, and then came
another thought – 'I'm made for love.'

She liked the sound of this and thought it again; then in
inevitable succession came her new-born riot of dreams about
Gordon. The twist of her imagination which, two months before,
had disclosed to her her unguessed desire to see him again,
seemed now to have been leading up to this dance, this hour.

For all her sleek beauty, Edith was a grave, slow-thinking girl. There was a streak in her of that same desire to ponder, of that adolescent idealism that had turned her brother socialist and pacifist. Henry Bradin had left Cornell, where he had been an instructor in economics, and had come to New York to pour the latest cures for incurable evils into the columns of a radical weekly newspaper.

Edith, less fatuously, would have been content to cure Gordon Sterrett. There was a quality of weakness in Gordon that she wanted to take care of; there was a helplessness in him that she wanted to protect. And she wanted someone she had known a long while, someone who had loved her a long while. She was a little tired; she wanted to get married. Out of a pile of letters, half a dozen pictures and as many memories, and this weariness, she had decided that next time she saw Gordon their relations were going to be changed. She would say something that would change them. There was this evening. This was her evening. All evenings were her evenings.

Then her thoughts were interrupted by a solemn undergraduate with a hurt look and an air of strained formality who presented himself before her and bowed unusually low. It was the man she had come with, Peter Himmel. He was tall and humorous, with horned-rimmed glasses and an air of attractive whimsicality. She suddenly rather disliked him – probably because he had not succeeded in kissing her.

'Well,' she began, 'are you still furious at me?'

'Not at all.'

She stepped forward and took his arm.

'I'm sorry,' she said softly. 'I don't know why I snapped out that way. I'm in a bum humor to-night for some strange reason. I'm sorry.'

'S'all right,' he mumbled, 'don't mention it.'

He felt disagreeably embarrassed. Was she rubbing in the fact of his late failure?

'It was a mistake,' she continued, on the same consciously gentle key. 'We'll both forget it.' For this he hated her.

A few minutes later they drifted out on the floor while the dozen swaying, sighing members of the specially hired jazz

orchestra informed the crowded ballroom that 'if a saxophone
and me are left alone why then two is compan-ee!'

A man with a mustache cut in.

'Hello,' he began reprovingly. 'You don't remember me.'

'I can't just think of your name,' she said lightly – 'and I know
you so well.'

'I met you up at –' His voice trailed disconsolately off as a man
with very fair hair cut in. Edith murmured a conventional
'Thanks, loads – cut in later,' to the *inconnu*.

The very fair man insisted on shaking hands enthusiastically.
She placed him as one of the numerous Jims of her acquaintance
– last name a mystery. She remembered even that he had a
peculiar rhythm in dancing and found as they started that she
was right.

'Going to be here long?' he breathed confidentially.

She leaned back and looked up at him.

'Couple of weeks.'

'Where are you?'

'Biltmore. Call me up some day.'

'I mean it,' he assured her. 'I will. We'll go to tea.'

'So do I – Do.'

A dark man cut in with intense formality.

'You don't remember me, do you?' he said gravely.

'I should say I do. Your name's Harlan.'

'No-ope. Barlow.'

'Well, I knew there were two syllables anyway. You're the boy
that played the ukulele so well up at Howard Marshall's house
party.'

'I played – but not—'

A man with prominent teeth cut in. Edith inhaled a slight
cloud of whiskey. She liked men to have had something to drink;
they were so much more cheerful, and appreciative and compli-
mentary – much easier to talk to.

'My name's Dean, Philip Dean,' he said cheerfully. 'You don't
remember me, I know, but you used to come up to New Haven
with a fellow I roomed with senior year, Gordon Sterrett.'

Edith looked up quickly.

'Yes, I went up with him twice – to the Pump and Slipper and
the Junior prom.'

'You've seen him, of course,' said Dean carelessly. 'He's here to-night. I saw him just a minute ago.'

Edith started. Yet she had felt quite sure he would be here.

'Why, no, I haven't—'

A fat man with red hair cut in.

'Hello, Edith,' he began.

'Why – hello there—'

She slipped, stumbled lightly.

'I'm sorry, dear,' she murmured mechanically.

She had seen Gordon – Gordon very white and listless, leaning against the side of a doorway, smoking and looking into the ballroom. Edith could see that his face was thin and wan – that the hand he raised to his lips with a cigarette was trembling. They were dancing quite close to him now.

'– They invite so darn many extra fellas that you –' the short man was saying.

'Hello, Gordon,' called Edith over her partner's shoulder. Her heart was pounding wildly.

His large dark eyes were fixed on her. He took a step in her direction. Her partner turned her away – she heard his voice bleating—

'– but half the stags get lit and leave before long, so—'

Then a low tone at her side.

'May I, please?'

She was dancing suddenly with Gordon; one of his arms was around her; she felt it tighten spasmodically; felt his hand on her back with the fingers spread. Her hand holding the little lace handkerchief was crushed in his.

'Why Gordon,' she began breathlessly.

'Hello, Edith.'

She slipped again – was tossed forward by her recovery until her face touched the black cloth of his dinner coat. She loved him – she knew she loved him – then for a minute there was silence while a strange feeling of uneasiness crept over her. Something was wrong.

Of a sudden her heart wrenched, and turned over as she realized what it was. He was pitiful and wretched, a little drunk, and miserably tired.

'Oh—' she cried involuntarily.

His eyes looked down at her. She saw suddenly that they were blood-streaked and rolling uncontrollably.

'Gordon,' she murmured, 'we'll sit down; I want to sit down.'

They were nearly in mid-floor, but she had seen two men start toward her from opposite sides of the room, so she halted, seized Gordon's limp hand and led him bumping through the crowd, her mouth tight shut, her face a little pale under her rouge, her eyes trembling with tears.

She found a place high up on the soft-carpeted stairs, and he sat down heavily beside her.

'Well,' he began, staring at her unsteadily, 'I certainly am glad to see you, Edith.'

She looked at him without answering. The effect of this on her was immeasurable. For years she had seen men in various stages of intoxication, from uncles all the way down to chauffeurs, and her feelings had varied from amusement to disgust, but here for the first time she was seized with a new feeling – an unutterable horror.

'Gordon,' she said accusingly and almost crying, 'you look like the devil.'

He nodded. 'I've had trouble, Edith.'

'Trouble?'

'All sorts of trouble. Don't you say anything to the family, but I'm all gone to pieces. I'm a mess, Edith.'

His lower lip was sagging. He seemed scarcely to see her.

'Can't you – can't you,' she hesitated, 'can't you tell me about it, Gordon? You know I'm always interested in you.'

She bit her lip – she had intended to say something stronger, but found at the end that she couldn't bring it out.

Gordon shook his head dully. 'I can't tell you. You're a good woman. I can't tell a good woman the story.'

'Rot,' she said, defiantly. 'I think it's a perfect insult to call any one a good woman in that way. It's a slam. You've been drinking, Gordon.'

'Thanks.' He inclined his head gravely. 'Thanks for the information.'

'Why do you drink?'

'Because I'm so damn miserable.'

'Do you think drinking's going to make it any better?'

'What you doing – trying to reform me?'

'No; I'm trying to help you, Gordon. Can't you tell me about it?'

'I'm in awful mess. Best thing you can do is to pretend not to know me.'

'Why, Gordon?'

'I'm sorry I cut in on you – it's unfair to you. You're pure woman – and all that sort of thing. Here, I'll get some one else to dance with you.'

He rose clumsily to his feet, but she reached up and pulled him down beside her on the stairs.

'Here, Gordon. You're ridiculous. You're hurting me. You're acting like a – like a crazy man—'

'I admit it. I'm a little crazy. Something's wrong with me, Edith. There's something left me. It doesn't matter.'

'It does, tell me.'

'Just that. I was always queer – little bit different from other boys. All right in college, but now it's all wrong. Things have been snapping inside me for four months like little hooks on a dress, and it's about to come off when a few more hooks go. I'm very gradually going loony.'

He turned his eyes full on her and began to laugh, and she shrank away from him.

'What *is* the matter?'

'Just me,' he repeated. 'I'm going loony. This whole place is like a dream to me – this Delmonico's—'

As he talked she saw he had changed utterly. He wasn't at all light and gay and careless – a great lethargy and discouragement had come over him. Revulsion seized her, followed by a faint, surprising boredom. His voice seemed to come out of a great void.

'Edith,' he said, 'I used to think I was clever, talented, an artist. Now I know I'm nothing. Can't draw, Edith. Don't know why I'm telling you this.'

She nodded absently.

'I can't draw, I can't do anything. I'm poor as a church mouse.' He laughed, bitterly and rather too loud. 'I've become a damn beggar, a leech on my friends. I'm a failure. I'm poor as hell.'

Her distaste was growing. She barely nodded this time, waiting for her first possible cue to rise.

Suddenly Gordon's eyes filled with tears.

'Edith,' he said, turning to her with what was evidently a strong effort at self-control, 'I can't tell you what it means to me to know there's one person left who's interested in me.'

He reached out and patted her hand, and involuntarily she drew it away.

'It's mighty fine of you,' he repeated.

'Well,' she said slowly, looking him in the eye, 'any one's always glad to see an old friend – but I'm sorry to see you like this, Gordon.'

There was a pause while they looked at each other, and the momentary eagerness in his eyes wavered. She rose and stood looking at him, her face quite expressionless.

'Shall we dance?' she suggested, coolly.

– Love is fragile – she was thinking – but perhaps the pieces are saved, the things that hovered on lips, that might have been said. The new love words, the tendernesses learned, are treasured up for the next lover.

5

Peter Himmel, escort to the lovely Edith, was unaccustomed to being snubbed; having been snubbed, he was hurt and embarrassed, and ashamed of himself. For a matter of two months he had been on special delivery terms with Edith Bradin, and knowing that the one excuse and explanation of the special delivery letter is its value in sentimental correspondence, he had believed himself quite sure of his ground. He searched in vain for any reason why she should have taken this attitude in the matter of a simple kiss.

Therefore when he was cut in on by the man with the mustache he went out into the hall and, making up a sentence, said it over to himself several times. Considerably deleted, this was it:

'Well, if any girl ever led a man on and then jolted him, she did – and she has no kick coming if I go out and get beautifully boiled.'

So he walked through the supper room into a small room adjoining it, which he had located earlier in the evening. It was a room in which there were several large bowls of punch flanked by many bottles. He took a seat beside the table which held the bottles.

At the second highball, boredom, disgust, the monotony of time, the turbidity of events, sank into a vague background before which glittering cobwebs formed. Things became reconciled to themselves, things lay quietly on their shelves; the troubles of the day arranged themselves in trim formation and at his curt wish of dismissal, marched off and disappeared. And with the departure of worry came brilliant, permeating symbolism. Edith became a flighty, negligible girl, not to be worried over; rather to be laughed at. She fitted like a figure of his own dream into the surface world forming about him. He himself became in a measure symbolic, a type of the continent bacchanal, the brilliant dreamer at play.

Then the symbolic mood faded and as he sipped his third highball his imagination yielded to the warm glow and he lapsed into a state similar to floating on his back in pleasant water. It was at this point that he noticed that a green baize door near him was open about two inches, and that through the aperture a pair of eyes were watching him intently.

'Hm,' murmured Peter calmly.

The green door closed – and then opened again – a bare half inch this time.

'Peek-a-boo,' murmured Peter.

The door remained stationary and then he became aware of a series of tense intermittent whispers.

'One guy.'

'What's he doin'?'

'He's sittin' lookin'.'

'He better beat it off. We gotta get another li'l' bottle.'

Peter listened while the words filtered into his consciousness.

'Now this,' he thought, 'is most remarkable.'

He was excited. He was jubilant. He felt that he had stumbled upon a mystery. Affecting an elaborate carelessness he arose and walked around the table – then, turning quickly, pulled open the green door, precipitating Private Rose into the room.

Peter bowed.

'How do you do?' he said.

Private Rose set one foot slightly in front of the other, poised for fight, flight, or compromise.

'How do you do?' repeated Peter politely.

'I'm o'right.'

'Can I offer you a drink?'

Private Rose looked at him searchingly, suspecting possible sarcasm.

'O'right,' he said finally.

Peter indicated a chair.

'Sit down.'

'I got a friend,' said Rose, 'I got a friend in there.' He pointed to the green door.

'By all means let's have him in.'

Peter crossed over, opened the door and welcomed in Private Key, very suspicious and uncertain and guilty. Chairs were found and the three took their seats around the punch bowl. Peter gave them each a highball and offered them a cigarette from his case. They accepted both with some diffidence.

'Now,' continued Peter easily, 'may I ask why you gentlemen prefer to lounge away your leisure hours in a room which is chiefly furnished, as far as I can see, with scrubbing brushes. And when the human race has progressed to the stage where seventeen thousand chairs are manufactured on every day except Sunday—' he paused. Rose and Key regarded him vacantly. 'Will you tell me,' went on Peter, 'why you choose to rest yourselves on articles intended for the transportation of water from one place to another?'

At this point Rose contributed a grunt to the conversation.

'And lastly,' finished Peter, 'will you tell me why, when you are in a building beautifully hung with enormous candelabra, you prefer to spend these evening hours under one anemic electric light?'

Rose looked at Key; Key looked at Rose. They laughed; they laughed uproariously; they found it was impossible to look at each other without laughing. But they were not laughing with this man – they were laughing at him. To them a man who talked after this fashion was either raving drunk or raving crazy.

'You are Yale men, I presume,' said Peter, finishing his highball and preparing another.

They laughed again.

'Na-ah.'

'So? I thought perhaps you might be members of that lowly section of the university known as the Sheffield Scientific School.'

'Na-ah.'

'Hm. Well, that's too bad. No doubt you are Harvard men, anxious to preserve your incognito in this – this paradise of violet blue, as the newspapers say.'

'Na-ah,' said Key scornfully, 'we was just waitin' for somebody.'

'Ah,' exclaimed Peter, rising and filling their glasses, 'very interestin'. Had a date with a scrublady, eh?'

They both denied this indignantly.

'It's all right,' Peter reassured them, 'don't apologize. A scrublady's as good as any lady in the world. Kipling says "Any lady and Judy O'Grady under the skin."'

'Sure,' said Key, winking broadly at Rose.

'My case, for instance,' continued Peter, finishing his glass. 'I got a girl up here that's spoiled. Spoildest darn girl I ever saw. Refused to kiss me; no reason whatsoever. Led me on deliberately to think sure I want to kiss you and then plunk! Threw me over! What's the younger generation comin' to?'

'Say tha's hard luck,' said Key – 'that's awful hard luck.'

'Oh, boy!' said Rose.

'Have another?' said Peter.

'We got in a sort of fight for a while,' said Key after a pause, 'but it was too far away.'

'A fight? – tha's stuff!' said Peter, seating himself unsteadily. 'Fight 'em all! I was in the army.'

'This was with a Bolshevik fella.'

'Tha's stuff!' exclaimed Peter, enthusiastic. 'That's what I say! Kill the Bolshevik! Exterminate 'em!'

'We're Americuns,' said Rose, implying a sturdy, defiant patriotism.

'Sure,' said Peter. 'Greatest race in the world! We're all Americuns! Have another.'

They had another.

6

At one o'clock a special orchestra, special even in a day of special
orchestras, arrived at Delmonico's, and its members, seating
themselves arrogantly around the piano, took up the burden of
providing music for the Gamma Psi Fraternity. They were headed
by a famous flute-player, distinguished throughout New York for
his feat of standing on his head and shimmying with his
shoulders while he played the latest jazz on his flute. During his
performance the lights were extinguished except for the spotlight
on the flute-player and another roving beam that threw flickering
shadows and changing kaleidoscopic colors over the massed
dancers.

Edith had danced herself into that tired, dreamy state habitual
only with débutantes, a state equivalent to the glow of a noble
soul after several long highballs. Her mind floated vaguely on the
bosom of her music; her partners changed with the unreality of
phantoms under the colorful shifting dusk, and to her present
coma it seemed as if days had passed since the dance began. She
had talked on many fragmentary subjects with many men. She
had been kissed once and made love to six times. Earlier in the
evening different undergraduates had danced with her, but now,
like all the more popular girls there, she had her own entourage –
that is, half a dozen gallants had singled her out or were
alternating her charms with those of some other chosen beauty;
they cut in on her in regular, inevitable succession.

Several times she had seen Gordon – he had been sitting a long
time on the stairway with his palm to his head, his dull eyes fixed
at an infinite speck on the floor before him, very depressed,
he looked, and quite drunk – but Edith each time had averted
her glance hurriedly. All that seemed long ago; her mind was
passive now, her senses were lulled to trance-like sleep; only
her feet danced and her voice talked on in hazy sentimental
banter.

But Edith was not nearly so tired as to be incapable of moral
indignation when Peter Himmel cut in on her, sublimely and
happily drunk. She gasped and looked up at him.

'Why, *Peter*!'

'I'm a li'l' stewed, Edith.'

'Why, Peter, you're a *peach*, you are! Don't you think it's a bum way of doing – when you're with me?'

Then she smiled unwillingly, for he was looking at her with owlish sentimentality varied with a silly spasmodic smile.

'Darlin' Edith,' he began earnestly, 'you know I love you, don't you?'

'You tell it well.'

'I love you – and I merely wanted you to kiss me,' he added sadly.

His embarrassment, his shame, were both gone. She was a mos' beautiful girl in whole worl'. Mos' beautiful eyes, like stars above. He wanted to 'pologize – firs', for presuming try to kiss her; second, for drinking – but he'd been so discouraged 'cause he had thought she was mad at him –

The red-fat man cut in, and looking up at Edith smiled radiantly.

'Did you bring any one?' she asked.

No. The red-fat man was a stag.

'Well, would you mind – would it be an awful bother for you to – to take me home to-night?' (this extreme diffidence was a charming affectation on Edith's part – she knew that the red-fat man would immediately dissolve into a paroxysm of delight).

'Bother? Why, good Lord, I'd be darn glad to! You know I'd be darn glad to.'

'Thanks *loads!* You're awfully sweet.'

She glanced at her wrist-watch. It was half-past one. And, as she said 'half-past one' to herself, it floated vaguely into her mind that her brother had told her at luncheon that he worked in the office of his newspaper until after one-thirty every evening.

Edith turned suddenly to her current partner.

'What street is Delmonico's on, anyway?'

'Street? Oh, why Fifth Avenue, of course.'

'I mean, what cross street?'

'Why – let's see – it's on Forty-fourth Street.'

This verified what she had thought. Henry's office must be across the street and just around the corner, and it occurred to her immediately that she might slip over for a moment and surprise him, float in on him, a shimmering marvel in her new crimson opera cloak and 'cheer him up.' It was exactly the sort of thing Edith revelled in doing – an unconventional, jaunty thing. The idea reached out and gripped at her imagination – after an instant's hesitation she had decided.

'My hair is just about to tumble entirely down,' she said pleasantly to her partner; 'would you mind if I go and fix it?'

'Not at all.'

'You're a peach.'

A few minutes later, wrapped in her crimson opera cloak, she flitted down a side-stairs, her cheeks glowing with excitement at her little adventure. She ran by a couple who stood at the door – a weak-chinned waiter and an over-rouged young lady, in hot dispute – and opening the outer door stepped into the warm May night.

7

The over-rouged young lady followed her with a brief, bitter glance – then turned again to the weak-chinned waiter and took up her argument.

'You better go up and tell him I'm here,' she said defiantly, 'or I'll go up myself.'

'No, you don't!' said George sternly.

The girl smiled sardonically.

'Oh, I don't, don't I? Well, let me tell you I know more college fellas and more of 'em know me, and are glad to take me out on a party, than you ever saw in your whole life.'

'Maybe so—'

'Maybe so,' she interrupted. 'Oh, it's all right for any of 'em like that one that just ran out – God knows where *she* went – it's all right for them that are asked here to come or go as they like – but when I want to see a friend they have some cheap, ham-slinging, bring-me-a-doughnut waiter to stand here and keep me out.'

'See here,' said the elder Key indignantly, 'I can't lose my job. Maybe this fella you're talkin' about doesn't want to see you.'

'Oh, he wants to see me all right.'

'Anyways, how could I find him in all that crowd?'

'Oh, he'll be there,' she asserted confidently. 'You just ask anybody for Gordon Sterrett and they'll point him out to you. They all know each other, those fellas.'

She produced a mesh bag, and taking out a dollar bill handed it to George.

'Here,' she said, 'here's a bribe. You find him and give him my message. You tell him if he isn't here in five minutes I'm coming up.'

George shook his head pessimistically, considered the question for a moment, wavered violently, and then withdrew.

In less than the allotted time Gordon came down-stairs. He was drunker than he had been earlier in the evening and in a different way. The liquor seemed to have hardened on him like a crust. He was heavy and lurching – almost incoherent when he talked.

''Lo, Jewel,' he said thickly. 'Came right away. Jewel, I couldn't get that money. Tried my best.'

'Money nothing!' she snapped. 'You haven't been near me for ten days. What's the matter?'

He shook his head slowly.

'Been very low, Jewel. Been sick.'

'Why didn't you tell me if you were sick. I don't care about the money that bad. I didn't start bothering you about it at all until you began neglecting me.'

Again he shook his head.

'Haven't been neglecting you. Not at all.'

'Haven't! You haven't been near me for three weeks, unless you been so drunk you didn't know what you were doing.'

'Been sick, Jewel,' he repeated, turning his eyes upon her wearily.

'You're well enough to come and play with your society friends here all right. You told me you'd meet me for dinner, and you said you'd have some money for me. You didn't even bother to ring me up.'

'I couldn't get any money.'

'Haven't I just been saying that doesn't matter? I wanted to see *you*, Gordon, but you seem to prefer your somebody else.'

He denied this bitterly.

'Then get your hat and come along,' she suggested.

Gordon hesitated – and she came suddenly close to him and slipped her arms around his neck.

'Come on with me, Gordon,' she said in a half whisper. 'We'll

go over to Devineries' and have a drink, and then we can go up
to my apartment.'

'I can't, Jewel,—'

'You can,' she said intensely.

'I'm sick as a dog!'

'Well, then, you oughtn't to stay here and dance.'

With a glance around him in which relief and despair were
mingled, Gordon hesitated; then she suddenly pulled him to her
and kissed him with soft, pulpy lips.

'All right,' he said heavily. 'I'll get my hat.'

8

When Edith came out into the clear blue of the May night she
found the Avenue deserted. The windows of the big shops were
dark; over their doors were drawn great iron masks until they
were only shadowy tombs of the late day's splendor. Glancing
down toward Forty-second Street she saw a commingled blur of
lights from the all-night restaurants. Over on Sixth Avenue the
elevated, a flare of fire, roared across the street between the
glimmering parallels of light at the station and streaked along
into the crisp dark. But at Forty-fourth Street it was very quiet.

Pulling her cloak close about her Edith darted across the
Avenue. She started nervously as a solitary man passed her and
said in a hoarse whisper – 'Where bound, kiddo?' She was
reminded of a night in her childhood when she had walked
around the block in her pajamas and a dog had howled at her
from a mystery-big back yard.

In a minute she had reached her destination, a two-story,
comparatively old building on Forty-fourth, in the upper window
of which she thankfully detected a wisp of light. It was bright
enough outside for her to make out the sign beside the window –
the *New York Trumpet*. She stepped inside a dark hall and after a
second saw the stairs in the corner.

Then she was in a long, low room furnished with many desks
and hung on all sides with file copies of newspapers. There were
only two occupants. They were sitting at different ends of the
room, each wearing a green eye-shade and writing by a solitary
desk light.

For a moment she stood uncertainly in the doorway, and then both men turned around simultaneously and she recognized her brother.

'Why, Edith!' He rose quickly and approached her in surprise, removing his eye-shade. He was tall, lean, and dark, with black, piercing eyes under very thick glasses. They were far-away eyes that seemed always fixed just over the head of the person to whom he was talking.

He put his hands on her arms and kissed her cheek.

'What is it?' he repeated in some alarm.

'I was at a dance across at Delmonico's, Henry,' she said excitedly, 'and I couldn't resist tearing over to see you.'

'I'm glad you did.' His alertness gave way quickly to a habitual vagueness. 'You oughtn't to be out alone at night though, ought you?'

The man at the other end of the room had been looking at them curiously, but at Henry's beckoning gesture he approached. He was loosely fat with little twinkling eyes, and, having removed his collar and tie, he gave the impression of a Middle-Western farmer on a Sunday afternoon.

'This is my sister,' said Henry. 'She dropped in to see me.'

'How do you do?' said the fat man, smiling. 'My name's Bartholomew, Miss Bradin. I know your brother has forgotten it long ago.'

Edith laughed politely.

'Well,' he continued, 'not exactly gorgeous quarters we have here, are they?'

Edith looked around the room.

'They seem very nice,' she replied. 'Where do you keep the bombs?'

'The bombs?' repeated Bartholomew, laughing. 'That's pretty good – the bombs. Did you hear her, Henry? She wants to know where we keep the bombs. Say, that's pretty good.'

Edith swung herself onto a vacant desk and sat dangling her feet over the edge. Her brother took a seat beside her.

'Well,' he asked, absent-mindedly, 'how do you like New York this trip?'

'Not bad. I'll be over at the Biltmore with the Hoyts until Sunday. Can't you come to luncheon to-morrow?'

He thought a moment.

'I'm especially busy,' he objected, 'and I hate women in groups.'

'All right,' she agreed, unruffled. 'Let's you and me have luncheon together.'

'Very well.'

'I'll call for you at twelve.'

Bartholomew was obviously anxious to return to his desk, but apparently considered that it would be rude to leave without some parting pleasantry.

'Well' – he began awkwardly.

They both turned to him.

'Well, we – we had an exciting time earlier in the evening.'

The two men exchanged glances.

'You should have come earlier,' continued Bartholomew, somewhat encouraged. 'We had a regular vaudeville.'

'Did you really?'

'A serenade,' said Henry. 'A lot of soldiers gathered down there in the street and began to yell at the sign.'

'Why?' she demanded.

'Just a crowd,' said Henry, abstractedly. 'All crowds have to howl. They didn't have anybody with much initiative in the lead, or they'd probably have forced their way in here and smashed things up.'

'Yes,' said Bartholomew, turning again to Edith, 'you should have been here.'

He seemed to consider this a sufficient cue for withdrawal, for he turned abruptly and went back to his desk.

'Are the soldiers all set against the Socialists?' demanded Edith of her brother. 'I mean do they attack you violently and all that?'

Henry replaced his eye-shade and yawned.

'The human race has come a long way,' he said casually; 'but most of us are throw-backs; the soldiers don't know what they want, or what they hate, or what they like. They're used to acting in large bodies, and they seem to have to make demonstrations. So it happens to be against us. There've been riots all over the city to-night. It's May Day, you see.'

'Was the disturbance here pretty serious?'

'Not a bit,' he said scornfully. 'About twenty-five of them

stopped in the street about nine o'clock, and began to bellow at
the moon.'

'Oh' – She changed the subject. 'You're glad to see me, Henry?'

'Why, sure.'

'You don't seem to be.'

'I am.'

'I suppose you think I'm a – a waster. Sort of the World's
Worst Butterfly.'

Henry laughed.

'Not at all. Have a good time while you're young. Why? Do I
seem like the priggish and earnest youth?'

'No –' She paused, '– but somehow I began thinking how
absolutely different the party I'm on is from – from all your
purposes. It seems sort of – of incongruous, doesn't it? – me being
at a party like that, and you over here working for a thing that'll
make that sort of party impossible ever any more, if your ideas
work.'

'I don't think of it that way. You're young, and you're acting
just as you were brought up to act. Go ahead – have a good
time?'

Her feet, which had been idly swinging, stopped and her voice
dropped a note.

'I wish you'd – you'd come back to Harrisburg and have a
good time. Do you feel sure that you're on the right track—'

'You're wearing beautiful stockings,' he interrupted. 'What on
earth are they?'

'They're embroidered,' she replied, glancing down. 'Aren't they
cunning?' She raised her skirts and uncovered slim, silk-sheathed
calves. 'Or do you disapprove of silk stockings?'

He seemed slightly exasperated, bent his dark eyes on her
piercingly.

'Are you trying to make me out as criticizing you in any way,
Edith?'

'Not at all—'

She paused. Bartholomew had uttered a grunt. She turned and
saw that he had left his desk and was standing at the window.

'What is it?' demanded Henry.

'People,' said Bartholomew, and then after an instant: 'Whole
jam of them. They're coming from Sixth Avenue.'

'People?'

The fat man pressed his nose to the pane.

'Soldiers, by God!' he said emphatically. 'I had an idea they'd come back.'

Edith jumped to her feet, and running over joined Bartholomew at the window.

'There's a lot of them!' she cried excitedly. 'Come here, Henry!'

Henry readjusted his shade, but kept his seat.

'Hadn't we better turn out the lights?' suggested Bartholomew.

'No. They'll go away in a minute.'

'They're not,' said Edith, peering from the window. 'They're not even thinking of going away. There's more of them coming. Look – there's a whole crowd turning the corner of Sixth Avenue.'

By the yellow glow and blue shadows of the street lamp she could see that the sidewalk was crowded with men. They were mostly in uniform, some sober, some enthusiastically drunk, and over the whole swept an incoherent clamor and shouting.

Henry rose, and going to the window exposed himself as a long silhouette against the office lights. Immediately the shouting became a steady yell, and a rattling fusillade of small missiles, corners of tobacco plugs, cigarette-boxes, and even pennies beat against the window. The sounds of the racket now began floating up the stairs as the folding doors revolved.

'They're coming up!' cried Bartholomew.

Edith turned anxiously to Henry.

'They're coming up, Henry.'

From down-stairs in the lower hall their cries were now quite audible.

'– God damn Socialists!'

'Pro-Germans! Boche-lovers!'

'Second floor, front! Come on!'

'We'll get the sons—'

The next five minutes passed in a dream. Edith was conscious that the clamor burst suddenly upon the three of them like a cloud of rain, that there was a thunder of many feet on the stairs, that Henry had seized her arm and drawn her back toward the rear of the office. Then the door opened and an overflow of men were forced into the room – not the leaders, but simply those who happened to be in front.

'Hello, Bo!'

'Up late, ain't you?'

'You an' your girl. Damn *you!*'

She noticed that two very drunken soldiers had been forced to the front, where they wobbled fatuously – one of them was short and dark, the other was tall and weak of chin.

Henry stepped forward and raised his hand.

'Friends!' he said.

The clamor faded into a momentary stillness, punctuated with mutterings.

'Friends!' he repeated, his far-away eyes fixed over the heads of the crowd, 'you're injuring no one but yourselves by breaking in here to-night. Do we look like rich men? Do we look like Germans? I ask you in all fairness—'

'Pipe down!'

'I'll say you do!'

'Say, who's your lady friend, buddy?'

A man in civilian clothes, who had been pawing over a table, suddenly held up a newspaper.

'Here it is!' he shouted. 'They wanted the Germans to win the war!'

A new overflow from the stairs was shouldered in and of a sudden the room was full of men all closing around the pale little group at the back. Edith saw that the tall soldier with the weak chin was still in front. The short dark one had disappeared.

She edged slightly backward, stood close to the open window, through which came a clear breath of cool night air.

Then the room was a riot. She realized that the soldiers were surging forward, glimpsed the fat man swinging a chair over his head – instantly the lights went out, and she felt the push of warm bodies under rough cloth, and her ears were full of shouting and trampling and hard breathing.

A figure flashed by her out of nowhere, tottered, was edged sideways, and of a sudden disappeared helplessly out through the open window with a frightened, fragmentary cry that died staccato on the bosom of the clamor. By the faint light streaming from the building backing on the area Edith had a quick impression that it had been the tall soldier with the weak chin.

Anger rose astonishingly in her. She swung her arms wildly, edged blindly toward the thickest of the scuffling. She heard grunts, curses, the muffled impact of fists.

'Henry!' she called frantically, 'Henry!'

Then, it was minutes later, she felt suddenly that there were other figures in the room. She heard a voice, deep, bullying, authoritative; she saw yellow rays of light sweeping here and there in the fracas. The cries became more scattered. The scuffling increased and then stopped.

Suddenly the lights were on and the room was full of policemen, clubbing left and right. The deep voice boomed out:

'Here now! Here now! Here now!'

And then:

'Quiet down and get out! Here now!'

The room seemed to empty like a wash-bowl. A policeman fast-grappled in the corner released his hold on his soldier antagonist and started him with a shove toward the door. The deep voice continued. Edith perceived now that it came from a bull-necked police captain standing near the door.

'Here now! This is no way! One of your own sojers got shoved out of the back window an' killed hisself!'

'Henry!' called Edith, 'Henry!'

She beat wildly with her fists on the back of the man in front of her; she brushed between two others; fought, shrieked, and beat her way to a very pale figure sitting on the floor close to a desk.

'Henry,' she cried passionately, 'what's the matter? What's the matter? Did they hurt you?'

His eyes were shut. He groaned and then looking up said disgustedly –

'They broke my leg. My God, the fools!'

'Here now!' called the police captain. 'Here now! Here now!'

9

'Childs', Fifty-ninth Street,' at eight o'clock of any morning differs from its sisters by less than the width of their marble tables or the degree of polish on the frying-pans. You will see there a crowd of poor people with sleep in the corners of their eyes, trying to look straight before them at their food so as not to see the other poor people. But Childs', Fifty-ninth, four hours earlier is quite unlike any Childs' restaurant from Portland, Oregon, to Portland, Maine. Within its pale but sanitary walls one finds a noisy medley of chorus girls, college boys, débutantes, rakes, *filles de joie* – a not unrepresentative mixture of the gayest of Broadway, and even of Fifth Avenue.

In the early morning of May the second it was unusually full. Over the marble-topped tables were bent the excited faces of flappers whose fathers owned individual villages. They were eating buckwheat cakes and scrambled eggs with relish and gusto, an accomplishment that it would have been utterly impossible for them to repeat in the same place four hours later.

Almost the entire crowd were from the Gamma Psi dance at Delmonico's except for several chorus girls from a midnight revue who sat at a side table and wished they'd taken off a little more make-up after the show. Here and there a drab, mouse-like figure, desperately out of place, watched the butterflies with a weary, puzzled curiosity. But the drab figure was the exception. This was the morning after May Day, and celebration was still in the air.

Gus Rose, sober but a little dazed, must be classed as one of the drab figures. How he had got himself from Forty-fourth Street to Fifty-ninth Street after the riot was only a hazy half-memory. He had seen the body of Carrol Key put in an ambulance and driven off, and then he had started up town with two or three soldiers. Somewhere between Forty-fourth Street and Fifty-ninth Street the other soldiers had met some women and disappeared. Rose had wandered to Columbus Circle and chosen the gleaming lights of Childs' to minister to his craving for coffee and doughnuts. He walked in and sat down.

All around him floated airy, inconsequential chatter and high-pitched laughter. At first he failed to understand, but after a puzzled five minutes he realized that this was the aftermath of some gay party. Here and there a restless, hilarious young man wandered fraternally and familiarly between the tables, shaking hands indiscriminately and pausing occasionally for a facetious chat, while excited waiters, bearing cakes and eggs aloft, swore at him silently, and bumped him out of the way. To Rose, seated at the most inconspicuous and least crowded table, the whole scene was a colorful circus of beauty and riotous pleasure.

He became gradually aware, after a few moments, that the couple seated diagonally across from him, with their backs to the crowd, were not the least interesting pair in the room. The man was drunk. He wore a dinner coat with a dishevelled tie and shirt swollen by spillings of water and wine. His eyes, dim and bloodshot, roved unnaturally from side to side. His breath came short between his lips.

'He's been on a spree!' thought Rose.

The woman was almost if not quite sober. She was pretty, with dark eyes and feverish high color, and she kept her active eyes fixed on her companion with the alertness of a hawk. From time to time she would lean and whisper intently to him, and he would answer by inclining his head heavily or by a particularly ghoulish and repellent wink.

Rose scrutinized them dumbly for some minutes, until the woman gave him a quick, resentful look; then he shifted his gaze to two of the most conspicuously hilarious of the promenaders who were on a protracted circuit of the tables. To his surprise he recognized in one of them the young man by whom he had been so ludicrously entertained at Delmonico's. This started him thinking of Key with a vague sentimentality, not unmixed with awe. Key was dead. He had fallen thirty-five feet and split his skull like a cracked cocoanut.

'He was a darn good guy,' thought Rose mournfully. 'He was a darn good guy, o'right. That was awful hard luck about him.'

The two promenaders approached and started down between Rose's table and the next, addressing friends and strangers alike with jovial familiarity. Suddenly Rose saw the fair-haired one with the prominent teeth stop, look unsteadily at the man and girl opposite, and then begin to move his head disapprovingly from side to side.

The man with the blood-shot eyes looked up.

'Gordy,' said the promenader with the prominent teeth, 'Gordy.'

'Hello,' said the man with the stained shirt thickly.

Prominent Teeth shook his finger pessimistically at the pair, giving the woman a glance of aloof condemnation.

'What'd I tell you Gordy?'

Gordon stirred in his seat.

'Go to hell!' he said.

Dean continued to stand there shaking his finger. The woman began to get angry.

'You go way!' she cried fiercely. 'You're drunk, that's what you are!'

'So's he,' suggested Dean, staying the motion of his finger and pointing it at Gordon.

Peter Himmel ambled up, owlish now and oratorically inclined.

'Here now,' he began as if called upon to deal with some petty dispute between children. 'Wha's all trouble?'

'You take your friend away,' said Jewel tartly. 'He's bothering us.'

'What's 'at?'

'You heard me!' she said shrilly. 'I said to take your drunken friend away.'

Her rising voice rang out above the clatter of the restaurant and a waiter came hurrying up.

'You gotta be more quiet!'

'That fella's drunk,' she cried. 'He's insulting us.'

'Ah-ha, Gordy,' persisted the accused. 'What'd I tell you.' He turned to the waiter. 'Gordy an' I friends. Been tryin' help him, haven't I, Gordy?'

Gordy looked up.

'Help me? Hell, no!'

Jewel rose suddenly, and seizing Gordon's arm assisted him to his feet.

'Come on, Gordy!' she said, leaning toward him and speaking in a half whisper. 'Let's us get out of here. This fella's got a mean drunk on.'

Gordon allowed himself to be urged to his feet and started toward the door. Jewel turned for a second and addressed the provoker of their flight.

'I know all about *you!*' she said fiercely. 'Nice friend, you are, I'll say. He told me about you.'

Then she seized Gordon's arm, and together they made their
way through the curious crowd, paid their check, and went out.

'You'll have to sit down,' said the waiter to Pete after they had
gone.

'What's 'at? Sit down?'

'Yes – or get out.'

Peter turned to Dean.

'Come on,' he suggested. 'Let's beat up this waiter.'

'All right.'

They advanced toward him, their faces grown stern. The
waiter retreated.

Peter suddenly reached over to a plate on the table beside him
and picking up a handful of hash tossed it into the air. It
descended as a languid parabola in snowflake effect on the heads
of those near by.

'Hey! Ease up!'

'Put him out!'

'Sit down, Peter!'

'Cut out that stuff!'

Peter laughed and bowed.

'Thank you for your kind applause, ladies and gents. If some
one will lend me some more hash and a tall hat we will go on
with the act.'

The bouncer bustled up.

'You've gotta get out!' he said to Peter.

'Hell, no!'

'He's my friend!' put in Dean indignantly.

A crowd of waiters were gathering. 'Put him out!'

'Better go, Peter.'

There was a short struggle and the two were edged and pushed
toward the door.

'I got a hat and a coat here!' cried Peter.

'Well, go get 'em and be spry about it!'

The bouncer released his hold on Peter, who, adopting a
ludicrous air of extreme cunning, rushed immediately around to
the other table, where he burst into derisive laughter and
thumbed his nose at the exasperated waiters.

'Think I just better wait a l'il' longer,' he announced.

The chase began. Four waiters were sent around one way and

four another. Dean caught hold of two of them by the coat, and another struggle took place before the pursuit of Peter could be resumed; he was finally pinioned after overturning a sugar-bowl and several cups of coffee. A fresh argument ensued at the cashier's desk, where Peter attempted to buy another dish of hash to take with him and throw at policemen.

But the commotion upon his exit proper was dwarfed by another phenomenon which drew admiring glances and a prolonged involuntary 'Oh-h-h!' from every person in the restaurant.

The great plate-glass front had turned to a deep creamy blue, the color of a Maxfield Parrish moonlight – a blue that seemed to press close upon the pane as if to crowd its way into the restaurant. Dawn had come up in Columbus Circle, magical, breathless dawn, silhouetting the great statue of the immortal Christopher, and mingling in a curious and uncanny manner with the fading yellow electric light inside.

10

Mr In and Mr Out are not listed by the census-taker. You will search for them in vain through the social register or the births, marriages, and deaths, or the grocer's credit list. Oblivion has swallowed them and the testimony that they ever existed at all is vague and shadowy, and inadmissible in a court of law. Yet I have it upon the best authority that for a brief space Mr In and Mr Out lived, breathed, answered to their names and radiated vivid personalities of their own.

During the brief span of their lives they walked in their native garments down the great highway of a great nation; were laughed at, sworn at, chased, and fled from. Then they passed and were heard of no more.

They were already taking form dimly, when a taxicab with the top open breezed down Broadway in the faintest glimmer of May dawn. In this car sat the souls of Mr In and Mr Out discussing with amazement the blue light that had so precipitately colored the sky behind the statue of Christopher Columbus, discussing with bewilderment the old, gray faces of the early risers which skimmed palely along the street like blown bits of paper on a gray lake. They were agreed on all things, from the absurdity of the bouncer in Childs' to the absurdity of the business of life. They were dizzy with the extreme maudlin happiness that the morning had awakened in their glowing souls. Indeed, so fresh and vigorous was their pleasure in living that they felt it should be expressed by loud cries.

'Ye-ow-ow!' hooted Peter, making a megaphone with his hands – and Dean joined in with a call that, though equally significant and symbolic, derived its resonance from its very inarticulateness.

'Yo-ho! Yea! Yoho! Yo-buba!'

Fifty-third Street was a bus with a dark, bobbed-hair beauty atop; Fifty-second was a street cleaner who dodged, escaped, and sent up a yell of, 'Look where you're aimin'!' in a pained and grieved voice. At Fiftieth Street a group of men on a very white sidewalk in front of a very white building turned to stare after them, and shouted:

'Some party, boys!'

At Forty-ninth Street Peter turned to Dean. 'Beautiful morning,' he said gravely, squinting up his owlish eyes.

'Probably is.'

'Go get some breakfast, hey?'

Dean agreed – with additions.

'Breakfast and liquor.'

'Breakfast and liquor,' repeated Peter, and they looked at each other, nodding. 'That's logical.'

Then they both burst into loud laughter.

'Breakfast and liquor! Oh, gosh!'

'No such thing,' announced Peter.

'Don't serve it? Ne'mind. We force 'em serve it. Bring pressure bear.'

'Bring logic bear.'

The taxi cut suddenly off Broadway, sailed along a cross street, and stopped in front of a heavy tomb-like building in Fifth Avenue.

'What's idea?'

The taxi-driver informed them that this was Delmonico's.

This was somewhat puzzling. They were forced to devote

several minutes to intense concentration, for if such an order had been given there must have been a reason for it.

'Somep'm 'bouta coat,' suggested the taxi-man.

That was it. Peter's overcoat and hat. He had left them at Delmonico's. Having decided this, they disembarked from the taxi and strolled toward the entrance arm in arm.

'Hey!' said the taxi-driver.

'Huh?'

'You better pay me.'

They shook their heads in shocked negation.

'Later, not now – we give orders, you wait.'

The taxi-driver objected; he wanted his money now. With the scornful condescension of men exercising tremendous self-control they paid him.

Inside Peter groped in vain through a dim, deserted check-room in search of his coat and derby.

'Gone, I guess. Somebody stole it.'

'Some Sheff student.'

'All probability.'

'Never mind,' said Dean, nobly. 'I'll leave mine here too – then we'll both be dressed the same.'

He removed his overcoat and hat and was hanging them up when his roving glance was caught and held magnetically by two large squares of cardboard tacked to the two coat-room doors. The one on the left-hand door bore the word 'In' in big black letters, and the one on the right-hand door flaunted the equally emphatic word 'Out.'

'Look!' he exclaimed happily –

Peter's eyes followed his pointing finger.

'What?'

'Look at the signs. Let's take 'em.'

'Good idea.'

'Probably pair very rare an' valuable signs. Probably come in handy.'

Peter removed the left-hand sign from the door and endea-vored to conceal it about his person. The sign being of considerable proportions, this was a matter of some difficulty. An idea flung itself at him, and with an air of dignified mystery he turned his back. After an instant he wheeled dramatically around, and stretching out his arms displayed himself to the admiring Dean. He had inserted the sign in his vest, completely covering his shirt front. In effect, the word 'In' had been painted upon his shirt in large black letters.

'Yoho!' cheered Dean. 'Mister In.'

He inserted his own sign in like manner.

'Mister Out!' he announced triumphantly. 'Mr In meet Mr Out.'

They advanced and shook hands. Again laughter overcame them and they rocked in a shaken spasm of mirth.

'Yoho!'

'We probably get a flock of breakfast.'

'We'll go – go to the Commodore.'

Arm in arm they sallied out the door, and turning east in Forty-fourth Street set out for the Commodore.

As they came out a short dark soldier, very pale and tired, who had been wandering listlessly along the sidewalk, turned to look at them.

He started over as though to address them, but as they immediately bent on him glances of withering unrecognition, he waited until they had started unsteadily down the street, and then followed at about forty paces, chuckling to himself and saying 'Oh, boy!' over and over under his breath, in delighted, anticipatory tones.

Mr In and Mr Out were meanwhile exchanging pleasantries concerning their future plans.

'We want liquor; we want breakfast. Neither without the other. One and indivisible.'

'We want both 'em!'

'Both 'em!'

It was quite light now, and passers-by began to bend curious eyes on the pair. Obviously they were engaged in a discussion, which afforded each of them intense amusement, for occasionally a fit of laughter would seize upon them so violently that, still with their arms interlocked, they would bend nearly double.

Reaching the Commodore, they exchanged a few spicy epigrams with the sleepy-eyed doorman, navigated the revolving door with some difficulty, and then made their way through a thinly populated but startled lobby to the dining-room, where a puzzled waiter showed them an obscure table in a corner. They

studied the bill of fare helplessly, telling over the items to each
other in puzzled mumbles.

'Don't see any liquor here,' said Peter reproachfully.

The waiter became audible but unintelligible.

'Repeat,' continued Peter, with patient tolerance, 'that there
seems to be unexplained and quite distasteful lack of liquor upon
bill of fare.'

'Here!' said Dean confidently, 'let me handle him.' He turned to
the waiter – 'Bring us – bring us –' he scanned the bill of fare
anxiously. 'Bring us a quart of champagne and a – a – probably
ham sandwich.'

The waiter looked doubtful.

'Bring it!' roared Mr In and Mr Out in chorus.

The waiter coughed and disappeared. There was a short wait
during which they were subjected without their knowledge to a
careful scrutiny by the headwaiter. Then the champagne arrived,
and at the sight of it Mr In and Mr Out became jubilant.

'Imagine their objecting to us having champagne for breakfast
– jus' imagine.'

They both concentrated upon the vision of such an awesome
possibility, but the feat was too much for them. It was impossible
for their joint imaginations to conjure up a world where any one
might object to any one else having champagne for breakfast.
The waiter drew the cork with an enormous *pop* – and their
glasses immediately foamed with pale yellow froth.

'Here's health, Mr In.'

'Here's same to you, Mr Out.'

The waiter withdrew; the minutes passed; the champagne
became low in the bottle.

'It's – it's mortifying,' said Dean suddenly.

'Wha's mortifying?'

'The idea their objecting us having champagne breakfast.'

'Mortifying?' Peter considered. 'Yes, tha's word – mortifying.'

Again they collapsed into laughter, howled, swayed, rocked
back and forth in their chairs, repeating the word 'mortifying'
over and over to each other – each repetition seeming to make it
only more brilliantly absurd.

After a few more gorgeous minutes they decided on another
quart. Their anxious waiter consulted his immediate superior,

and this discreet person gave implicit instructions that no more champagne should be served. Their check was brought.

Five minutes later, arm in arm, they left the Commodore and made their way through a curious, staring crowd along Forty-second Street, and up Vanderbilt Avenue to the Biltmore. There, with sudden cunning, they rose to the occasion and traversed the lobby, walking fast and standing unnaturally erect.

Once in the dining-room they repeated their performance. They were torn between intermittent convulsive laughter and sudden spasmodic discussions of politics, college, and the sunny state of their dispositions. Their watches told them that it was now nine o'clock, and a dim idea was born in them that they were on a memorable party, something that they would remember always. They lingered over the second bottle. Either of them had only to mention the word 'mortifying' to send them both into riotous gasps. The dining-room was whirring and shifting now; a curious lightness permeated and rarefied the heavy air.

They paid their check and walked out into the lobby.

It was at this moment that the exterior doors revolved for the thousandth time that morning, and admitted into the lobby a very pale young beauty with dark circles under her eyes, attired in a much-rumpled evening dress. She was accompanied by a plain stout man, obviously not an appropriate escort.

At the top of the stairs this couple encountered Mr In and Mr Out.

'Edith,' began Mr In, stepping toward her hilariously and making a sweeping bow, 'darling, good morning.'

The stout man glanced questioningly at Edith, as if merely asking her permission to throw this man summarily out of the way.

''Scuse familiarity,' added Peter, as an afterthought. 'Edith, good-morning.'

He seized Dean's elbow and impelled him into the foreground. 'Meet Mr In, Edith, my bes' frien'. Inseparable. Mr In and Mr Out.'

Mr Out advanced and bowed; in fact, he advanced so far and bowed so low that he tipped slightly forward and only kept his balance by placing a hand lightly on Edith's shoulder.

'I'm Mr Out, Edith,' he mumbled pleasantly, 'S'misterin Misterout.'

''Smisterinanout,' said Peter proudly.

But Edith stared straight by them, her eyes fixed on some infinite speck in the gallery above her. She nodded slightly to the stout man, who advanced bull-like and with a sturdy brisk gesture pushed Mr In and Mr Out to either side. Through this alley he and Edith walked.

But ten paces farther on Edith stopped again – stopped and pointed to a short, dark soldier who was eying the crowd in general, and the tableau of Mr In and Mr Out in particular, with a sort of puzzled, spell-bound awe.

'There,' cried Edith. 'See there!'

Her voice rose, became somewhat shrill. Her pointing finger shook slightly.

'There's the soldier who broke my brother's leg.'

There were a dozen exclamations; a man in a cutaway coat left his place near the desk and advanced alertly; the stout person made a sort of lightning-like spring toward the short, dark soldier, and then the lobby closed around the little group and blotted them from the sight of Mr In and Mr Out.

But to Mr In and Mr Out this event was merely a particolored iridescent segment of a whirring, spinning world.

They heard loud voices; they saw the stout man spring; the picture suddenly blurred.

Then they were in an elevator bound skyward.

'What floor, please?' said the elevator man.

'Any floor,' said Mr In.

'Top floor,' said Mr Out.

'This is the top floor,' said the elevator man.

'Have another floor put on,' said Mr Out.

'Higher,' said Mr In.

'Heaven,' said Mr Out.

11

In a bedroom of a small hotel just off Sixth Avenue Gordon Sterrett awoke with a pain in the back of his head and a sick throbbing in all his veins. He looked at the dusky gray shadows in the corners of the room and at a raw place on a large leather chair in the corner where it had long been in use. He saw clothes, dishevelled, rumpled clothes on the floor and he smelt stale cigarette smoke and stale liquor. The windows were tight shut. Outside the bright sunlight had thrown a dust-filled beam across the sill – a beam broken by the head of the wide wooden bed in which he had slept. He lay very quiet – comatose, drugged, his eyes wide, his mind clicking wildly like an unoiled machine.

It must have been thirty seconds after he perceived the sunbeam with the dust on it and the rip on the large leather chair that he had the sense of life close beside him, and it was another thirty seconds after that before that he realized that he was irrevocably married to Jewel Hudson.

He went out half an hour later and bought a revolver at a sporting goods store. Then he took a taxi to the room where he had been living on East Twenty-seventh Street, and leaning across the table that held his drawing materials, fired a cartridge into his head just behind the temple.

Winter Dreams
(1922)

Some of the caddies were poor as sin and lived in one-room houses with a neurasthenic cow in the front yard, but Dexter Green's father owned the second best grocery-store in Black Bear – the best one was 'The Hub,' patronized by the wealthy people from Sherry Island – and Dexter caddied only for pocket-money.

In the fall when the days became crisp and gray, and the long Minnesota winter shut down like the white lid of a box, Dexter's skis moved over the snow that hid the fairways of the golf course. At these times the country gave him a feeling of profound melancholy – it offended him that the links should lie in enforced fallowness, haunted by ragged sparrows for the long season. It was dreary, too, that on the tees where the gay colors fluttered in summer there were now only the desolate sand-boxes knee-deep in crusted ice. When he crossed the hills the wind blew cold as misery, and if the sun was out he tramped with his eyes squinted up against the hard dimensionless glare.

In April the winter ceased abruptly. The snow ran down into Black Bear Lake scarcely tarrying for the early golfers to brave the season with red and black balls. Without elation, without an interval of moist glory, the cold was gone.

Dexter knew that there was something dismal about this Northern spring, just as he knew there was something gorgeous about the fall. Fall made him clinch his hands and tremble and repeat idiotic sentences to himself, and make brisk abrupt gestures of command to imaginary audiences and armies. October filled him with hope which November raised to a sort of ecstatic triumph, and in this mood the fleeting brilliant impressions of the summer at Sherry Island were ready grist to his mill. He became a golf champion and defeated Mr T. A. Hedrick in a marvellous match played a hundred times over the fairways of his imagination, a match each detail of which he changed about untiringly – sometimes he won with almost laughable ease, sometimes he came up magnificently from behind. Again, stepping from a Pierce-Arrow automobile, like Mr Mortimer Jones, he strolled frigidly into the lounge of the Sherry Island Golf Club – or perhaps, surrounded by an admiring crowd, he gave an exhibition of fancy diving from the spring-board of the club raft . . . Among those who watched him in open-mouthed wonder was Mr Mortimer Jones.

And one day it came to pass that Mr Jones – himself and not his ghost – came up to Dexter with tears in his eyes and said that Dexter was the —— best caddy in the club, and wouldn't he decide not to quit if Mr Jones made it worth his while, because every other —— caddy in the club lost one ball a hole for him – regularly –

'No, sir,' said Dexter decisively, 'I don't want to caddy any more.' Then, after a pause: 'I'm too old.'

'You're not more than fourteen. Why the devil did you decide just this morning that you wanted to quit? You promised that next week you'd go over to the State tournament with me.'

'I decided I was too old.'

Dexter handed in his 'A Class' badge, collected what money was due him from the caddy master, and walked home to Black Bear Village.

'The best —— caddy I ever saw,' shouted Mr Mortimer Jones over a drink that afternoon. 'Never lost a ball! Willing! Intelligent! Quiet! Honest! Grateful!'

The little girl who had done this was eleven – beautifully ugly as little girls are apt to be who are destined after a few years to be inexpressibly lovely and bring no end of misery to a great number of men. The spark, however, was perceptible. There was a general ungodliness in the way her lips twisted down at the corners when she smiled, and in the – Heaven help us! – in the almost passionate quality of her eyes. Vitality is born early in such women. It was utterly in evidence now, shining through her thin frame in a sort of glow.

She had come eagerly out on to the course at nine o'clock with a white linen nurse and five small new golf-clubs in a white canvas bag which the nurse was carrying. When Dexter first saw her she was standing by the caddy house, rather ill at ease and trying to conceal the fact by engaging her nurse in an obviously

unnatural conversation graced by startling and irrelevant grima-
ces from herself.

'Well, it's certainly a nice day, Hilda,' Dexter heard her say.
She drew down the corners of her mouth, smiled, and glanced
furtively around, her eyes in transit falling for an instant on
Dexter.

Then to the nurse:

'Well, I guess there aren't very many people out here this
morning, are there?'

The smile again – radiant, blatantly artificial – convincing.

'I don't know what we're supposed to do now,' said the nurse,
looking nowhere in particular.

'Oh, that's all right. I'll fix it up.'

Dexter stood perfectly still, his mouth slightly ajar. He knew
that if he moved forward a step his stare would be in her line of
vision – if he moved backward he would lose his full view of her
face. For a moment he had not realized how young she was. Now
he remembered having seen her several times the year before – in
bloomers.

Suddenly, involuntarily, he laughed, a short abrupt laugh –
then, startled by himself, he turned and began to walk quickly
away.

'Boy!'

Dexter stopped.

'Boy—'

Beyond question he was addressed. Not only that, but he was
treated to that absurd smile, that preposterous smile – the
memory of which at least a dozen men were to carry into middle
age.

'Boy, do you know where the golf teacher is?'

'He's giving a lesson.'

'Well, do you know where the caddy-master is?'

'He isn't here yet this morning.'

'Oh.' For a moment this baffled her. She stood alternately on
her right and left foot.

'We'd like to get a caddy,' said the nurse. 'Mrs Mortimer Jones
sent us out to play golf, and we don't know how without we get a
caddy.'

Here she was stopped by an ominous glance from Miss Jones, followed immediately by the smile.

'There aren't any caddies here except me,' said Dexter to the nurse, 'and I got to stay here in charge until the caddy-master gets here.'

'Oh.'

Miss Jones and her retinue now withdrew, and at a proper distance from Dexter became involved in a heated conversation, which was concluded by Miss Jones taking one of the clubs and hitting it on the ground with violence. For further emphasis she raised it again and was about to bring it down smartly upon the nurse's bosom, when the nurse seized the club and twisted it from her hands.

'You damn little mean old *thing*!' cried Miss Jones wildly.

Another argument ensued. Realizing that the elements of the comedy were implied in the scene, Dexter several times began to laugh, but each time restrained the laugh before it reached audibility. He could not resist the monstrous conviction that the little girl was justified in beating the nurse.

The situation was resolved by the fortuitous appearance of the caddy-master, who was appealed to immediately by the nurse.

'Miss Jones is to have a little caddy, and this one says he can't go.'

'Mr McKenna said I was to wait here till you came,' said Dexter quickly.

'Well, he's here now.' Miss Jones smiled cheerfully at the caddy-master. Then she dropped her bag and set off at a haughty mince toward the first tee.

'Well?' The caddy-master turned to Dexter. 'What you standing there like a dummy for? Go pick up the young lady's clubs.'

'I don't think I'll go out to-day,' said Dexter.

'You don't—'

'I think I'll quit.'

The enormity of his decision frightened him. He was a favorite caddy, and the thirty dollars a month he earned through the summer were not to be made elsewhere around the lake. But he had received a strong emotional shock, and his perturbation required a violent and immediate outlet.

It is not so simple as that, either. As so frequently would be the

case in the future, Dexter was unconsciously dictated to by his
winter dreams.

2

Now, of course, the quality and the seasonability of these winter
dreams varied, but the stuff of them remained. They persuaded
Dexter several years later to pass up a business course at the
State university – his father, prospering now, would have paid his
way – for the precarious advantage of attending an older and
more famous university in the East, where he was bothered by
his scanty funds. But do not get the impression, because his
winter dreams happened to be concerned at first with musings on
the rich, that there was anything merely snobbish in the boy. He
wanted not association with glittering things and glittering
people – he wanted the glittering things themselves. Often he
reached out for the best without knowing why he wanted it –
and sometimes he ran up against the mysterious denials and
prohibitions in which life indulges. It is with one of those denials
and not with his career as a whole that this story deals.

He made money. It was rather amazing. After college he went
to the city from which Black Bear Lake draws its wealthy
patrons. When he was only twenty-three and had been there not
quite two years, there were already people who liked to say: 'Now
there's a boy –' All about him rich men's sons were peddling
bonds precariously, or investing patrimonies precariously, or
plodding through the two dozen volumes of the 'George Washington Commercial Course,' but Dexter borrowed a thousand
dollars on his college degree and his confident mouth, and
bought a partnership in a laundry.

It was a small laundry when he went into it but Dexter made a
specialty of learning how the English washed fine woollen golf-
stockings without shrinking them, and within a year he was
catering to the trade that wore knickerbockers. Men were
insisting that their Shetland hose and sweaters go to his laundry
just as they had insisted on a caddy who could find golf-balls. A
little later he was doing their wives' lingerie as well – and
running five branches in different parts of the city. Before he was
twenty-seven he owned the largest string of laundries in his

section of the country. It was then that he sold out and went to New York. But the part of his story that concerns us goes back to the days when he was making his first big success.

When he was twenty-three Mr Hart – one of the gray-haired men who like to say 'Now there's a boy' – gave him a guest card to the Sherry Island Golf Club for a week-end. So he signed his name one day on the register, and that afternoon played golf in a foursome with Mr Hart and Mr Sandwood and Mr T. A. Hedrick. He did not consider it necessary to remark that he had once carried Mr Hart's bag over this same links, and that he knew every trap and gully with his eyes shut – but he found himself glancing at the four caddies who trailed them, trying to catch a gleam or gesture that would remind him of himself, that would lessen the gap which lay between his present and his past.

It was a curious day, slashed abruptly with fleeting, familiar impressions. One minute he had the sense of being a trespasser – in the next he was impressed by the tremendous superiority he felt toward Mr T. A. Hedrick, who was a bore and not even a good golfer any more.

Then, because of a ball Mr Hart lost near the fifteenth green, an enormous thing happened. While they were searching the stiff grasses of the rough there was a clear call of 'Fore!' from behind a hill in their rear. And as they all turned abruptly from their search a bright new ball sliced abruptly over the hill and caught Mr T. A. Hedrick in the abdomen.

'By Gad!' cried Mr T. A. Hedrick, 'they ought to put some of these crazy women off the course. It's getting to be outrageous.'

A head and a voice came up together over the hill:

'Do you mind if we go through?'

'You hit me in the stomach!' declared Mr Hedrick wildly.

'Did I?' The girl approached the group of men. 'I'm sorry. I yelled "Fore!"'

Her glance fell casually on each of the men – then scanned the fairway for her ball.

'Did I bounce into the rough?'

It was impossible to determine whether this question was ingenuous or malicious. In a moment, however, she left no doubt, for as her partner came up over the hill she called cheerfully:

'Here I am! I'd have gone on the green except that I hit something.'

As she took her stance for a short mashie shot, Dexter looked at her closely. She wore a blue gingham dress, rimmed at throat and shoulders with a white edging that accentuated her tan. The quality of exaggeration, of thinness, which had made her passionate eyes and down-turning mouth absurd at eleven, was gone now. She was arrestingly beautiful. The color in her cheeks was centered like the color in a picture – it was not a 'high' color, but a sort of fluctuating and feverish warmth, so shaded that it seemed at any moment it would recede and disappear. This color and the mobility of her mouth gave a continual impression of flux, of intense life, of passionate vitality – balanced only partially by the sad luxury of her eyes.

She swung her mashie impatiently and without interest, pitching the ball into a sand-pit on the other side of the green. With a quick, insincere smile and a careless 'Thank you!' she went on after it.

'That Judy Jones!' remarked Mr Hedrick on the next tee, as they waited – some moments – for her to play on ahead. 'All she needs is to be turned up and spanked for six months and then to be married off to an old-fashioned cavalry captain.'

'My God, she's good-looking!' said Mr Sandwood, who was just over thirty.

'Good-looking!' cried Mr Hedrick contemptuously, 'she always looks as if she wanted to be kissed! Turning those big cow-eyes on every calf in town!'

It was doubtful if Mr Hedrick intended a reference to the maternal instinct.

'She'd play pretty good golf if she'd try,' said Mr Sandwood.

'She has no form,' said Mr Hedrick solemnly.

'She has a nice figure,' said Mr Sandwood.

'Better thank the Lord she doesn't drive a swifter ball,' said Mr Hart, winking at Dexter.

Later in the afternoon the sun went down with a riotous swirl of gold and varying blues and scarlets, and left the dry, rustling night of Western summer. Dexter watched from the veranda of the Golf Club, watched the even overlap of the waters in the little wind, silver molasses under the harvest-moon. Then the moon

held a finger to her lips and the lake became a clear pool, pale
and quiet. Dexter put on his bathing-suit and swam out to the
farthest raft, where he stretched dripping on the wet canvas of
the springboard.

There was a fish jumping and a star shining and the lights
around the lake were gleaming. Over on a dark peninsula a piano
was playing the songs of last summer and of summers before that
– songs from 'Chin-Chin' and 'The Count of Luxemburg' and 'The
Chocolate Soldier' – and because the sound of a piano over a
stretch of water had always seemed beautiful to Dexter he lay
perfectly quiet and listened.

The tune the piano was playing at that moment had been gay
and new five years before when Dexter was a sophomore at
college. They had played it at a prom once when he could not
afford the luxury of proms, and he had stood outside the
gymnasium and listened. The sound of the tune precipitated in
him a sort of ecstasy and it was with that ecstasy he viewed what
happened to him now. It was a mood of intense appreciation, a
sense that, for once, he was magnificently attune to life and that
everything about him was radiating a brightness and a glamor
he might never know again.

A low, pale oblong detached itself suddenly from the darkness
of the Island, spitting forth the reverberate sound of a racing
motor-boat. Two white streamers of cleft water rolled themselves
out behind it and almost immediately the boat was beside him,
drowning out the hot tinkle of the piano in the drone of its spray.
Dexter raising himself on his arms was aware of a figure standing
at the wheel, of two dark eyes regarding him over the
lengthening space of water – then the boat had gone by and was
sweeping in an immense and purposeless circle of spray round
and round in the middle of the lake. With equal eccentricity one
of the circles flattened out and headed back toward the raft.

'Who's that?' she called, shutting off her motor. She was so
near now that Dexter could see her bathing-suit, which consisted
apparently of pink rompers.

The nose of the boat bumped the raft, and as the latter tilted
rakishly he was precipitated toward her. With different degrees of
interest they recognized each other.

'Aren't you one of those men we played through this afternoon?' she demanded.

He was.

'Well, do you know how to drive a motor-boat? Because if you do I wish you'd drive this one so I can ride on the surf-board behind. My name is Judy Jones' – she favored him with an absurd smirk – rather, what tried to be a smirk, for, twist her mouth as she might, it was not grotesque, it was merely beautiful – 'and I live in a house over there on the Island, and in that house there is a man waiting for me. When he drove up at the door I drove out of the dock because he says I'm his ideal.'

There was a fish jumping and a star shining and the lights around the lake were gleaming. Dexter sat beside Judy Jones and she explained how her boat was driven. Then she was in the water, swimming to the floating surf-board with a sinuous crawl. Watching her was without effort to the eye, watching a branch waving or a sea-gull flying. Her arms, burned to butternut, moved sinuously among the dull platinum ripples, elbow appearing first, casting the forearm back with a cadence of falling water, then reaching out and down, stabbing a path ahead.

They moved out into the lake; turning, Dexter saw that she was kneeling on the low rear of the now uptilted surf-board.

'Go faster,' she called, 'fast as it'll go.'

Obediently he jammed the lever forward and the white spray mounted at the bow. When he looked around again the girl was standing up on the rushing board, her arms spread wide, her eyes lifted toward the moon.

'It's awful cold,' she shouted. 'What's your name?'

He told her.

'Well, why don't you come to dinner to-morrow night?'

His heart turned over like the fly-wheel of the boat, and, for the second time, her casual whim gave a new direction to his life.

3

Next evening while he waited for her to come down-stairs, Dexter peopled the soft deep summer room and the sun-porch that opened from it with the men who had already loved Judy Jones. He knew the sort of men they were – the men who when he first went to college had entered from the great prep schools with graceful clothes and the deep tan of healthy summers. He had seen that, in one sense, he was better than these men. He was newer and stronger. Yet in acknowledging to himself that he wished his children to be like them he was admitting that he was but the rough, strong stuff from which they eternally sprang.

When the time had come for him to wear good clothes, he had known who were the best tailors in America, and the best tailors in America had made him the suit he wore this evening. He had acquired that particular reserve peculiar to his university, that set it off from other universities. He recognized the value to him of such a mannerism and he had adopted it; he knew that to be careless in dress and manner required more confidence than to be careful. But carelessness was for his children. His mother's name had been Krimslich. She was a Bohemian of the peasant class and she had talked broken English to the end of her days. Her son must keep to the set patterns.

At a little after seven Judy Jones came down-stairs. She wore a blue silk afternoon dress, and he was disappointed at first that she had not put on something more elaborate. This feeling was accentuated when, after a brief greeting, she went to the door of a butler's pantry and pushing it open called: 'You can serve dinner, Martha.' He had rather expected that a butler would announce dinner, that there would be a cocktail. Then he put these thoughts behind him as they sat down side by side on a lounge and looked at each other.

'Father and mother won't be here,' she said thoughtfully.

He remembered the last time he had seen her father, and he was glad the parents were not to be here to-night – they might wonder who he was. He had been born in Keeble, a Minnesota village fifty miles farther north, and he always gave Keeble as his home instead of Black Bear Village. Country towns were well enough to come from if they weren't inconveniently in sight and used as footstools by fashionable lakes.

They talked of his university, which she had visited frequently during the past two years, and of the near-by city which supplied Sherry Island with its patrons, and whither Dexter would return next day to his prospering laundries.

During dinner she slipped into a moody depression which gave

Dexter a feeling of uneasiness. Whatever petulance she uttered in her throaty voice worried him. Whatever she smiled at – at him, at a chicken liver, at nothing – it disturbed him that her smile could have no root in mirth, or even in amusement. When the scarlet corners of her lips curved down, it was less a smile than an invitation to a kiss.

Then, after dinner, she led him out on the dark sun-porch and deliberately changed the atmosphere.

'Do you mind if I weep a little?' she said.

'I'm afraid I'm boring you,' he responded quickly.

'You're not. I like you. But I've just had a terrible afternoon. There was a man I cared about, and this afternoon he told me out of a clear sky that he was poor as a church-mouse. He'd never even hinted it before. Does this sound horribly mundane?'

'Perhaps he was afraid to tell you.'

'Suppose he was,' she answered. 'He didn't start right. You see, if I'd thought of him as poor – well, I've been mad about loads of poor men, and fully intended to marry them all. But in this case, I hadn't thought of him that way, and my interest in him wasn't strong enough to survive the shock. As if a girl calmly informed her fiancé that she was a widow. He might not object to widows, but–'

'Let's start right,' she interrupted herself suddenly. 'Who are you, anyhow?'

For a moment Dexter hesitated. Then:

'I'm nobody,' he announced. 'My career is largely a matter of futures.'

'Are you poor?'

'No,' he said frankly, 'I'm probably making more money than any man my age in the Northwest. I know that's an obnoxious remark, but you advised me to start right.'

There was a pause. Then she smiled and the corners of her mouth drooped and an almost imperceptible sway brought her closer to him, looking up into his eyes. A lump rose in Dexter's throat, and he waited breathless for the experiment, facing the unpredictable compound that would form mysteriously from the elements of their lips. Then he saw – she communicated her excitement to him, lavishly, deeply, with kisses that were not a promise but a fulfillment. They aroused in him not hunger

demanding renewal but surfeit that would demand more surfeit
... kisses that were like charity, creating want by holding back
nothing at all.

It did not take him many hours to decide that he had wanted
Judy Jones ever since he was a proud, desirous little boy.

4

It began like that – and continued, with varying shades of
intensity, on such a note right up to the dénouement. Dexter
surrendered a part of himself to the most direct and unprincipled
personality with which he had ever come in contact. Whatever
Judy wanted, she went after with the full pressure of her charm.
There was no divergence of method, no jockeying for position or
premeditation of effects – there was very little mental side to any
of her affairs. She simply made men conscious to the highest
degree of her physical loveliness. Dexter had no desire to change
her. Her deficiencies were knit up with a passionate energy that
transcended and justified them.

When, as Judy's head lay against his shoulder that first night,
she whispered, 'I don't know what's the matter with me. Last
night I thought I was in love with a man and to-night I think I'm
in love with you—' – it seemed to him a beautiful and romantic
thing to say. It was the exquisite excitability that for the moment
he controlled and owned. But a week later he was compelled to
view this same quality in a different light. She took him in her
roadster to a picnic supper, and after supper she disappeared,
likewise in her roadster, with another man. Dexter became
enormously upset and was scarcely able to be decently civil to the
other people present. When she assured him that she had not
kissed the other man, he knew she was lying – yet he was glad
that she had taken the trouble to lie to him.

He was, as he found before the summer ended, one of a
varying dozen who circulated about her. Each of them had at one
time been favored above all others – about half of them still
basked in the solace of occasional sentimental revivals. Whenever one showed signs of dropping out through long neglect, she
granted him a brief honeyed hour, which encouraged him to tag
along for a year or so longer. Judy made these forays upon the

helpless and defeated without malice, indeed half unconscious that there was anything mischievous in what she did.

When a new man came to town every one dropped out – dates were automatically cancelled.

The helpless part of trying to do anything about it was that she did it all herself. She was not a girl who could be 'won' in the kinetic sense – she was proof against cleverness, she was proof against charm; if any of these assailed her too strongly she would immediately resolve the affair to a physical basis, and under the magic of her physical splendor the strong as well as the brilliant played her game and not their own. She was entertained only by the gratification of her desires and by the direct exercise of her own charm. Perhaps from so much youthful love, so many youthful lovers, she had come, in self-defense, to nourish herself wholly from within.

Succeeding Dexter's first exhilaration came restlessness and dissatisfaction. The helpless ecstasy of losing himself in her was opiate rather than tonic. It was fortunate for his work during the winter that those moments of ecstasy came infrequently. Early in their acquaintance it had seemed for a while that there was a deep and spontaneous mutual attraction – that first August, for example – three days of long evenings on her dusky veranda, of strange wan kisses through the late afternoon, in shadowy alcoves or behind the protecting trellises of the garden arbors, of mornings when she was fresh as a dream and almost shy at meeting him in the clarity of the rising day. There was all the ecstasy of an engagement about it, sharpened by his realization that there was no engagement. It was during those three days that, for the first time, he had asked her to marry him. She said 'maybe some day,' she said 'kiss me,' she said 'I'd like to marry you,' she said 'I love you' – she said – nothing.

The three days were interrupted by the arrival of a New York man who visited at her house for half September. To Dexter's agony, rumor engaged them. The man was the son of the president of a great trust company. But at the end of a month it was reported that Judy was yawning. At a dance one night she sat all evening in a motor-boat with a local beau, while the New Yorker searched the club for her frantically. She told the local beau that she was bored with her visitor, and two days later he

left. She was seen with him at the station, and it was reported
that he looked very mournful indeed.

On this note the summer ended. Dexter was twenty-four, and
he found himself increasingly in a position to do as he wished. He
joined two clubs in the city and lived at one of them. Though he
was by no means an integral part of the stag-lines at these clubs,
he managed to be on hand at dances where Judy Jones was likely
to appear. He could have gone out socially as much as he liked –
he was an eligible young man, now, and popular with downtown fathers. His confessed devotion to Judy Jones had rather
solidified his position. But he had no social aspirations and rather
despised the dancing men who were always on tap for the
Thursday or Saturday parties and who filled in at dinners with
the younger married set. Already he was playing with the idea of
going East to New York. He wanted to take Judy Jones with him.
No disillusion as to the world in which she had grown up could
cure his illusion as to her desirability.

Remember that – for only in the light of it can what he did for
her be understood.

Eighteen months after he first met Judy Jones he became
engaged to another girl. Her name was Irene Scheerer, and her
father was one of the men who had always believed in Dexter.
Irene was light-haired and sweet and honorable, and a little
stout, and she had two suitors whom she pleasantly relinquished
when Dexter formally asked her to marry him.

Summer, fall, winter, spring, another summer, another fall – so
much he had given of his active life the incorrigible lips of Judy
Jones. She had treated him with interest, with encouragement,
with malice, with indifference, with contempt. She had inflicted
on him the innumerable little slights and indignities possible in
such a case – as if in revenge for having ever cared for him at all.
She had beckoned him and yawned at him and beckoned him
again and he had responded often with bitterness and narrowed
eyes. She had brought him ecstatic happiness and intolerable
agony of spirit. She had caused him untold inconvenience and
not a little trouble. She had insulted him, and she had ridden
over him, and she had played his interest in her against his
interest in his work – for fun. She had done everything to him
except to criticise him – this she had not done – it seemed to him

only because it might have sullied the utter indifference she manifested and sincerely felt toward him.

When autumn had come and gone again it occurred to him that he could not have Judy Jones. He had to beat this into his mind but he convinced himself at last. He lay awake at night for a while and argued it over. He told himself the trouble and the pain she had caused him, he enumerated her glaring deficiencies as a wife. Then he said to himself that he loved her, and after a while he fell asleep. For a week, lest he imagine her husky voice over the telephone or her eyes opposite him at lunch, he worked hard and late, and at night he went to his office and plotted out his years.

At the end of a week he went to a dance and cut in on her once. For almost the first time since they had met he did not ask her to sit out with him or tell her that she was lovely. It hurt him that she did not miss these things – that was all. He was not jealous when he saw that there was a new man to-night. He had been hardened against jealousy long before.

He stayed late at the dance. He sat for an hour with Irene Scheerer and talked about books and about music. He knew very little about either. But he was beginning to be master of his own time now, and he had a rather priggish notion that he – the young and already fabulously successful Dexter Green – should know more about such things.

That was in October, when he was twenty-five. In January, Dexter and Irene became engaged. It was to be announced in June, and they were to be married three months later.

The Minnesota winter prolonged itself interminably, and it was almost May when the winds came soft and the snow ran down into Black Bear Lake at last. For the first time in over a year Dexter was enjoying a certain tranquility of spirit. Judy Jones had been in Florida, and afterward in Hot Springs, and somewhere she had been engaged, and somewhere she had broken it off. At first, when Dexter had definitely given her up, it had made him sad that people still linked them together and asked for news of her, but when he began to be placed at dinner next to Irene Scheerer people didn't ask him about her any more – they told him about her. He ceased to be an authority on her.

May at last. Dexter walked the streets at night when the

darkness was damp as rain, wondering that so soon, with so little done, so much of ecstasy had gone from him. May one year black had been marked by Judy's poignant, unforgivable, yet forgiven turbulence – it had been one of those rare times when he fancied she had grown to care for him. That old penny's worth of happiness he had spent for this bushel of content. He knew that Irene would be no more than a curtain spread behind him, a hand moving among gleaming tea-cups, a voice calling to children . . . fire and loveliness were gone, the magic of nights and the wonder of the varying hours and seasons . . . slender lips, down-turning, dropping to his lips and bearing him up into a heaven of eyes. . . . The thing was deep in him. He was too strong and alive for it to die lightly.

In the middle of May when the weather balanced for a few days on the thin bridge that led to deep summer he turned in one night at Irene's house. Their engagement was to be announced in a week now – no one would be surprised at it. And to-night they would sit together on the lounge at the University Club and look on for an hour at the dancers. It gave him a sense of solidity to go with her – she was so sturdily popular, so intensely 'great.'

He mounted the steps of the brownstone house and stepped inside.

'Irene,' he called.

Mrs Scheerer came out of the living-room to meet him.

'Dexter,' she said, 'Irene's gone up-stairs with a splitting headache. She wanted to go with you but I made her go to bed.'

'Nothing serious, I—'

'Oh, no. She's going to play golf with you in the morning. You can spare her for just one night, can't you, Dexter?'

Her smile was kind. She and Dexter liked each other. In the living-room he talked for a moment before he said good-night.

Returning to the University Club, where he had rooms, he stood in the doorway for a moment and watched the dancers. He leaned against the door-post, nodded at a man or two – yawned.

'Hello, darling.'

The familiar voice at his elbow startled him. Judy Jones had left a man and crossed the room to him – Judy Jones, a slender enamelled doll in cloth of gold: gold in a band at her head, gold in two slipper points at her dress's hem. The fragile glow of her face seemed to blossom as she smiled at him. A breeze of warmth and light blew through the room. His hands in the pockets of his dinner-jacket tightened spasmodically. He was filled with a sudden excitement.

'When did you get back?' he asked casually.

'Come here and I'll tell you about it.'

She turned and he followed her. She had been away – he could have wept at the wonder of her return. She had passed through enchanted streets, doing things that were like provocative music. All mysterious happenings, all fresh and quickening hopes, had gone away with her, come back with her now.

She turned in the doorway.

'Have you a car here? If you haven't, I have.'

'I have a coupé.'

In then, with a rustle of golden cloth. He slammed the door. Into so many cars she had stepped – like this – like that – her back against the leather, so – her elbow resting on the door – waiting. She would have been soiled long since had there been anything to soil her – except herself – but this was her own self outpouring.

With an effort he forced himself to start the car and back into the street. This was nothing, he must remember. She had done this before, and he had put her behind him, as he would have crossed a bad account from his books.

He drove slowly down-town and, affecting abstraction, traversed the deserted streets of the business section, peopled here and there where a movie was giving out its crowd or where consumptive or pugilistic youth lounged in front of pool halls. The clink of glasses and the slap of hands on the bars issued from saloons, cloisters of glazed glass and dirty yellow light.

She was watching him closely and the silence was embarrassing, yet in this crisis he could find no casual word with which to profane the hour. At a convenient turning he began to zigzag back toward the University Club.

'Have you missed me?' she asked suddenly.

'Everybody missed you.'

He wondered if she knew of Irene Scheerer. She had been back only a day – her absence had been almost contemporaneous with his engagement.

'What a remark!' Judy laughed sadly – without sadness. She looked at him searchingly. He became absorbed in the dashboard.

'You're handsomer than you used to be,' she said thoughtfully. 'Dexter, you have the most rememberable eyes.'

He could have laughed at this, but he did not laugh. It was the sort of thing that was said to sophomores. Yet it stabbed at him.

'I'm awfully tired of everything, darling.' She called every one darling, endowing the endearment with careless, individual comraderie. 'I wish you'd marry me.'

The directness of this confused him. He should have told her now that he was going to marry another girl, but he could not tell her. He could as easily have sworn that he had never loved her.

'I think we'd get along,' she continued, on the same note, 'unless probably you've forgotten me and fallen in love with another girl.'

Her confidence was obviously enormous. She had said, in effect, that she found such a thing impossible to believe, that if it were true he had merely committed a childish indiscretion – and probably to show off. She would forgive him, because it was not a matter of any moment but rather something to be brushed aside lightly.

'Of course you could never love anybody but me,' she continued. 'I like the way you love me. Oh, Dexter, have you forgotten last year?'

'No, I haven't forgotten.'

'Neither have I!'

Was she sincerely moved – or was she carried along by the wave of her own acting?

'I wish we could be like that again,' she said, and he forced himself to answer:

'I don't think we can.'

'I suppose not. . . . I hear you're giving Irene Scheerer a violent rush.'

There was not the faintest emphasis on the name, yet Dexter was suddenly ashamed.

'Oh, take me home,' cried Judy suddenly; 'I don't want to go back to that idiotic dance – with those children.'

Then, as he turned up the street that led to the residence

district, Judy began to cry quietly to herself. He had never seen her cry before.

The dark street lightened, the dwellings of the rich loomed up around them, he stopped his coupé in front of the great white bulk of the Mortimer Joneses house, somnolent, gorgeous, drenched with the splendor of the damp moonlight. Its solidity startled him. The strong walls, the steel of the girders, the breadth and beam and pomp of it were there only to bring out the contrast with the young beauty beside him. It was sturdy to accentuate her slightness – as if to show what a breeze could be generated by a butterfly's wing.

He sat perfectly quiet, his nerves in wild clamor, afraid that if he moved he would find her irresistibly in his arms. Two tears had rolled down her wet face and trembled on her upper lip.

'I'm more beautiful than anybody else,' she said brokenly, 'why can't I be happy?' Her moist eyes tore at his stability – her mouth turned slowly downward with an exquisite sadness: 'I'd like to marry you if you'll have me, Dexter. I suppose you think I'm not worth having, but I'll be so beautiful for you, Dexter.'

A million phrases of anger, pride, passion, hatred, tenderness fought on his lips. Then a perfect wave of emotion washed over him, carrying off with it a sediment of wisdom, of convention, of doubt, of honor. This was his girl who was speaking, his own, his beautiful, his pride.

'Won't you come in?' He heard her draw in her breath sharply. Waiting.

'All right,' his voice was trembling, 'I'll come in.'

5

It was strange that neither when it was over nor a long time afterward did he regret that night. Looking at it from the perspective of ten years, the fact that Judy's flare for him endured just one month seemed of little importance. Nor did it matter that by his yielding he subjected himself to a deeper agony in the end and gave serious hurt to Irene Scheerer and to Irene's parents, who had befriended him. There was nothing sufficiently pictorial about Irene's grief to stamp itself on his mind.

Dexter was at bottom hard-minded. The attitude of the city on

his action was of no importance to him, not because he was
going to leave the city, but because any outside attitude on the
situation seemed superficial. He was completely indifferent to
popular opinion. Nor, when he had seen that it was no use, that
he did not possess in himself the power to move fundamentally or
to hold Judy Jones, did he bear any malice toward her. He loved
her, and he would love her until the day he was too old for loving
– but he could not have her. So he tasted the deep pain that is
reserved only for the strong, just as he had tasted for a little while
the deep happiness.

Even the ultimate falsity of the grounds upon which Judy
terminated the engagement that she did not want to 'take him
away' from Irene – Judy, who had wanted nothing else – did not
revolt him. He was beyond any revulsion or any amusement.

He went East in February with the intention of selling out his
laundries and settling in New York – but the war came to
America in March and changed his plans. He returned to the
West, handed over the management of the business to his
partner, and went into the first officers' training-camp in late
April. He was one of those young thousands who greeted the war
with a certain amount of relief, welcoming the liberation from
webs of tangled emotion.

6

This story is not his biography, remember, although things creep
into it which have nothing to do with those dreams he had when
he was young. We are almost done with them and with him
now. There is only one more incident to be related here, and it
happens seven years farther on.

It took place in New York, where he had done well – so well
that there were no barriers too high for him. He was thirty-two
years old, and, except for one flying trip immediately after the
war, he had not been West in seven years. A man named Devlin
from Detroit came into his office to see him in a business way,
and then and there this incident occurred, and closed out, so to
speak, this particular side of his life.

'So you're from the Middle West,' said the man Devlin with
careless curiosity. 'That's funny – I thought men like you were

probably born and raised on Wall Street. You know – wife of one of my best friends in Detroit came from your city. I was an usher at the wedding.'

Dexter waited with no apprehension of what was coming.

'Judy Simms,' said Devlin with no particular interest; 'Judy Jones she was once.'

'Yes, I knew her.' A dull impatience spread over him. He had heard, of course, that she was married – perhaps deliberately he had heard no more.

'Awfully nice girl,' brooded Devlin meaninglessly, 'I'm sort of sorry for her.'

'Why?' Something in Dexter was alert, receptive, at once.

'Oh, Lud Simms has gone to pieces in a way. I don't mean he ill-uses her, but he drinks and runs around—'

'Doesn't she run around?'

'No. Stays at home with her kids.'

'Oh.'

'She's a little too old for him,' said Devlin.

'Too old!' cried Dexter. 'Why, man, she's only twenty-seven.'

He was possessed with a wild notion of rushing out into the streets and taking a train to Detroit. He rose to his feet spasmodically.

'I guess you're busy,' Devlin apologized quickly. 'I didn't realize—'

'No, I'm not busy,' said Dexter, steadying his voice. 'I'm not busy at all. Not busy at all. Did you say she was – twenty-seven? No, I said she was twenty-seven.'

'Yes, you did,' agreed Devlin dryly.

'Go on, then. Go on.'

'What do you mean?'

'About Judy Jones.'

Devlin looked at him helplessly.

'Well, that's – I told you all there is to it. He treats her like the devil. Oh, they're not going to get divorced or anything. When he's particularly outrageous she forgives him. In fact, I'm inclined to think she loves him. She was a pretty girl when she first came to Detroit.'

A pretty girl! The phrase struck Dexter as ludicrous.

'Isn't she – a pretty girl, any more?'

'Oh, she's all right.'

'Look here,' said Dexter, sitting down suddenly, 'I don't understand. You say she was a "pretty girl" and now you say she's "all right." I don't understand what you mean – Judy Jones wasn't a pretty girl, at all. She was a great beauty. Why, I knew her, I knew her. She was—'

Devlin laughed pleasantly.

'I'm not trying to start a row,' he said. 'I think Judy's a nice girl and I like her. I can't understand how a man like Lud Simms could fall madly in love with her, but he did.' Then he added: 'Most of the women like her.'

Dexter looked closely at Devlin, thinking wildly that there must be a reason for this, some insensitivity in the man or some private malice.

'Lots of women fade just like *that*,' Devlin snapped his fingers. 'You must have seen it happen. Perhaps I've forgotten how pretty she was at her wedding. I've seen her so much since then, you see. She has nice eyes.'

A sort of dullness settled down upon Dexter. For the first time in his life he felt like getting very drunk. He knew that he was laughing loudly at something Devlin had said, but he did not know what it was or why it was funny. When, in a few minutes, Devlin went he lay down on his lounge and looked out the window at the New York sky-line into which the sun was sinking in dull lovely shades of pink and gold.

He had thought that having nothing else to lose he was invulnerable at last – but he knew that he had just lost something more, as surely as if he had married Judy Jones and seen her fade away before his eyes.

The dream was gone. Something had been taken from him. In a sort of panic he pushed the palms of his hands into his eyes and tried to bring up a picture of the waters lapping on Sherry Island and the moonlit veranda, and gingham on the golf-links and the dry sun and the gold color of her neck's soft down. And her mouth damp to his kisses and her eyes plaintive with melancholy and her freshness like new fine linen in the morning. Why, these things were no longer in the world! They had existed and they existed no longer.

For the first time in years the tears were streaming down his face. But they were for himself now. He did not care about mouth and eyes and moving hands. He wanted to care, and he could not care. For he had gone away and he could never go back any more. The gates were closed, the sun was gone down, and there was no beauty but the gray beauty of steel that withstands all time. Even the grief he could have borne was left behind in the country of illusion, of youth, of the richness of life, where his winter dreams had flourished.

'Long ago,' he said, 'long ago, there was something in me, but now that thing is gone. Now that thing is gone, that thing is gone. I cannot cry. I cannot care. That thing will come back no more.'

The Diamond as Big as the Ritz
(1922)

Before H. L. Mencken accepted it for The Smart Set, *this classic novelette – originally entitled 'The Diamond in the Sky' – was rejected by magazine editors who found it baffling, blasphemous, or objectionably satiric about wealth. Fitzgerald was discouraged by the editorial reaction to a story 'into which I put three weeks real enthusiasm. . . . But by God + Lorimer [editor of* The Saturday Evening Post] *I'm going to make a fortune yet'. When he collected it in* Tales of the Jazz Age *Fitzgerald explained that 'Diamond':*

> *. . . was designed utterly for my own amusement. I was in a mood characterized by a perfect craving for luxury, and the story began as an attempt to feed that craving on imaginary foods.*

John T. Unger came from a family that had been well known in Hades – a small town on the Mississippi River – for several generations. John's father had held the amateur golf championship through many a heated contest; Mrs Unger was known 'from hot-box to hot-bed,' as the local phrase went, for her political addresses; and young John T. Unger, who had just turned sixteen, had danced all the latest dances from New York before he put on long trousers. And now, for a certain time, he was to be away from home. That respect for a New England education which is the bane of all provincial places, which drains them yearly of their most promising young men, had seized upon his parents. Nothing would suit them but that he should go to St Midas' School near Boston – Hades was too small to hold their darling and gifted son.

Now in Hades – as you know if you ever have been there – the names of the more fashionable preparatory schools and colleges mean very little. The inhabitants have been so long out of the world that, though they make a show of keeping up to date in dress and manners and literature, they depend to a great extent on hearsay, and a function that in Hades would be considered elaborate would doubtless be hailed by a Chicago beef-princess as 'perhaps a little tacky.'

John T. Unger was on the eve of departure. Mrs Unger, with maternal fatuity, packed his trunks full of linen suits and electric fans, and Mr Unger presented his son with an asbestos pocket-book stuffed with money.

'Remember, you are always welcome here,' he said. 'You can be sure, boy, that we'll keep the home fires burning.'

'I know,' answered John huskily.

'Don't forget who you are and where you come from,' continued his father proudly, 'and you can do nothing to harm you. You are an Unger – from Hades.'

So the old man and the young shook hands and John walked away with tears streaming from his eyes. Ten minutes later he had passed outside the city limits, and he stopped to glance back for the last time. Over the gates the old-fashioned Victorian motto seemed strangely attractive to him. His father had tried time and time again to have it changed to something with a little more push and verve about, such as 'Hades – Your Opportunity,' or else a plain 'Welcome' sign set over a hearty handshake pricked out in electric lights. The old motto was a little depressing, Mr Unger had thought – but now. . . .

So John took his look and then set his face resolutely toward his destination. And, as he turned away, the lights of Hades against the sky seemed full of a warm and passionate beauty.

St Midas' School is half an hour from Boston in a Rolls-Pierce motorcar. The actual distance will never be known, for no one, except John T. Unger, had ever arrived there save in a Rolls-Pierce and probably no one ever will again. St Midas' is the most expensive and the most exclusive boys' preparatory school in the world.

John's first two years there passed pleasantly. The fathers of all the boys were money-kings and John spent his summers visiting at fashionable resorts. While he was very fond of all the boys he visited, their fathers struck him as being much of a piece, and in his boyish way he often wondered at their exceeding sameness. When he told them where his home was they would ask jovially, 'Pretty hot down there?' and John would muster a faint smile and answer, 'It certainly is.' His response would have been heartier had they not all made this joke – at best varying it with, 'Is it hot enough for you down there?' which he hated just as much.

In the middle of his second year at school, a quiet, handsome boy named Percy Washington had been put in John's form. The newcomer was pleasant in his manner and exceedingly well dressed even for St Midas', but for some reason he kept aloof from the other boys. The only person with whom he was intimate was John T. Unger, but even to John he was entirely uncommunicative concerning his home or his family. That he was wealthy went without saying, but beyond a few such deductions John knew little of his friend, so it promised rich confectionery for his curiosity when Percy invited him to spend the summer at his home 'in the West.' He accepted, without hesitation.

It was only when they were in the train that Percy became, for the first time, rather communicative. One day while they were eating lunch in the dining-car and discussing the imperfect characters of several of the boys at school, Percy suddenly changed his tone and made an abrupt remark.

'My father,' he said, 'is by far the richest man in the world.'

'Oh,' said John, politely. He could think of no answer to make to this confidence. He considered 'That's very nice,' but it sounded hollow and was on the point of saying, 'Really?' but refrained since it would seem to question Percy's statement. And such an astounding statement could scarcely be questioned.

'By far the richest,' repeated Percy.

'I was reading in the *World Almanac*,' began John, 'that there was one man in America with an income of over five million a year and four men with incomes of over three million a year, and—'

'Oh, they're nothing.' Percy's mouth was a half-moon of scorn. 'Catch-penny capitalists, financial small-fry, petty merchants and money-lenders. My father could buy them out and not know he'd done it.'

'But how does he—'

'Why haven't they put down *his* income tax? Because he doesn't pay any. At least he pays a little one – but he doesn't pay any on his *real* income.'

'He must be very rich,' said John simply. 'I'm glad. I like very rich people.

'The richer a fella is, the better I like him.' There was a look of passionate frankness upon his dark face. 'I visited the Schnlitzer-Murphys last Easter. Vivian Schnlitzer-Murphy had rubies as big as hen's eggs, and sapphires that were like globes with lights inside them—'

'I love jewels,' agreed Percy enthusiastically. 'Of course I wouldn't want any one at school to know about it, but I've got quite a collection myself. I used to collect them instead of stamps.'

'And diamonds,' continued John eagerly. 'The Schnlitzer-Murphys had diamonds as big as walnuts—'

'That's nothing.' Percy had leaned forward and dropped his voice to a low whisper. 'That's nothing at all. My father has a diamond bigger than the Ritz-Carlton Hotel.'

2

The Montana sunset lay between two mountains like a gigantic bruise from which dark arteries spread themselves over a poisoned sky. An immense distance under the sky crouched the village of Fish, minute, dismal, and forgotten. There were twelve men, so it was said, in the village of Fish, twelve somber and inexplicable souls who sucked a lean milk from the almost literally bare rock upon which a mysterious populatory force had begotten them. They had become a race apart, these twelve men of Fish, like some species developed by an early whim of nature, which on second thought had abandoned them to struggle and extermination.

Out of the blue-black bruise in the distance crept a long line of moving lights upon the desolation of the land, and the twelve men of Fish gathered like ghosts at the shanty depot to watch the passing of the seven o'clock train, the Transcontinental Express from Chicago. Six times or so a year the Transcontinental Express, through some inconceivable jurisdiction, stopped at the village of Fish, and when this occurred a figure or so would disembark, mount into a buggy that always appeared from out of the dusk, and drive off toward the bruised sunset. The observation of this pointless and preposterous phenomenon had become a sort of cult among the men of Fish. To observe, that was all; there remained in them none of the vital quality of illusion which would make them wonder or speculate, else a religion might have grown up around these mysterious visitations. But the men of Fish were beyond all religion – the barest and most savage tenets of even Christianity could gain no foothold on that barren rock – so there was no altar, no priest, no sacrifice; only each night at seven the silent concourse by the shanty depot, a congregation who lifted up a prayer of dim, anæmic wonder.

On this June night, the Great Brakeman, whom, had they deified any one, they might well have chosen as their celestial protagonist, had ordained that the seven o'clock train should leave its human (or inhuman) deposit at Fish. At two minutes after seven Percy Washington and John T. Unger disembarked, hurried past the spellbound, the agape, the fearsome eyes of the twelve men of Fish, mounted into a buggy which had obviously appeared from nowhere, and drove away.

After half an hour, when the twilight had coagulated into dark, the silent negro who was driving the buggy hailed an opaque body somewhere ahead of them in the gloom. In response to his cry, it turned upon them a luminuous disk which regarded them like a malignant eye out of the unfathomable night. As they came close, John saw that it was the tail-light of an immense automobile, larger and more magnificent than any he had ever seen. Its body was gleaming metal richer than nickel and lighter than silver, and the hubs of the wheels were studded with irridescent geometric figures of green and yellow – John did not dare to guess whether they were glass or jewel.

Two negroes, dressed in glittering livery such as one sees in pictures of royal processions in London, were standing at attention beside the car and as the two young men dismounted from the buggy they were greeted in some language which the guest could not understand, but which seemed to be an extreme form of the Southern negro's dialect.

'Get in,' said Percy to his friend, as their trunks were tossed to the ebony roof of the limousine. 'Sorry we had to bring you this far in that buggy, but of course it wouldn't do for the people on the train or those Godforsaken fellas in Fish to see this automobile.'

'Gosh! What a car!' This ejaculation was provoked by its interior. John saw that the upholstery consisted of a thousand minute and exquisite tapestries of silk, woven with jewels and embroideries, and set upon a back-ground of cloth of gold. The two armchair seats in which the boys luxuriated were covered with stuff that resembled duvetyn, but seemed woven in numberless colors of the ends of ostrich feathers.

'What a car!' cried John again, in amazement.

'This thing?' Percy laughed. 'Why, it's just an old junk we use for a station wagon.'

By this time they were gliding along through the darkness toward the break between the two mountains.

'We'll be there in an hour and a half,' said Percy, looking at the clock. 'I may as well tell you it's not going to be like anything you ever saw before.'

If the car was any indication of what John would see, he was prepared to be astonished indeed. The simple piety prevalent in Hades has the earnest worship of and respect for riches as the first article of its creed – had John felt otherwise than radiantly humble before them, his parents would have turned away in horror at the blasphemy.

They had now reached and were entering the break between the two mountains and almost immediately the way became much rougher.

'If the moon shone down here, you'd see that we're in a big gulch,' said Percy, trying to peer out of the window. He spoke a few words into the mouthpiece and immediately the footman turned on a search-light and swept the hillsides with an immense beam.

'Rocky, you see. An ordinary car would be knocked to pieces in half an hour. In fact, it's take a tank to navigate it unless you knew the way. You notice we're going uphill now.'

They were obviously ascending, and within a few minutes the car was crossing a high rise, where they caught a glimpse of a pale moon newly risen in the distance. The car stopped suddenly and several figures took shape out of the dark beside it – these were negroes also. Again the two young men were saluted in the same dimly recognizable dialect; then the negroes set to work and four immense cables dangling from overhead were attached with hooks to the hubs of the great jeweled wheels. At a resounding 'Hey-yah!' John felt the car being lifted slowly from the ground – up and up – clear of the tallest rocks on both sides – then higher, until he could see a wavy, moonlit valley stretched out before him in sharp contrast to the quagmire of rocks that they had just left. Only on one side was there still rock – and then suddenly there was no rock beside them or anywhere around.

It was apparent that they had surmounted some immense knife-blade of stone, projecting perpendicularly into the air. In a moment they were going down again, and finally with a soft bump they were landed upon the smooth earth.

'The worst is over,' said Percy, squinting out the window. 'It's only five miles from here, and our own road – tapestry brick – all the way. This belongs to us. This is where the United States ends, father says.'

'Are we in Canada?'

'We are not. We're in the middle of the Montana Rockies. But you are now on the only five square miles of land in the country that's never been surveyed.'

'Why hasn't it? Did they forget it?'

'No,' said Percy, grinning, 'they tried to do it three times. The first time my grandfather corrupted a whole department of the State survey; the second time he had the official maps of the United States tinkered with – that held them for fifteen years. The last time was harder. My father fixed it so that their compasses were in the strongest magnetic field ever artificially set up. He had a whole set of surveying instruments made with a slight defection that would allow for this territory not to appear, and he substituted them for the ones that were to be used. Then he had a river deflected and he had what looked like a village built up on its banks – so that they'd see it, and think it was a town ten miles farther up the valley. There's only one thing my father's afraid of,' he concluded, 'only one thing in the world that could be used to find us out.'

'What's that?'

Percy sank his voice to a whisper.

'Aeroplanes,' he breathed. 'We've got half a dozen anti-aircraft guns and we've arranged it so far – but there've been a few deaths and a great many prisoners. Not that we mind *that*, you know, father and I, but it upsets mother and the girls, and there's always the chance that some time we won't be able to arrange it.'

Shreds and tatters of chinchilla, courtesy clouds in the green moon's heaven, were passing the green moon like precious Eastern stuffs paraded for the inspection of some Tartar Khan. It seemed to John that it was day, and that he was looking at some lads sailing above him in the air, showering down tracts and patent medicine circulars, with their messages of hope for despairing, rockbound hamlets. It seemed to him that he could see them look down out of the clouds and stare – and stare at whatever there was to stare at in this place whither he was bound – What then? Were they induced to land by some insidious device there to be immured far from patent medicines and from tracts until the judgment day – or, should they fail to fall into the trap, did a quick puff of smoke and the sharp round of a splitting shell bring them drooping to earth – and 'upset' Percy's mother and sisters. John shook his head and the wraith of a hollow laugh issued silently from his parted lips. What desperate transaction lay hidden here? What a moral expedient of a bizarre Croesus? What terrible and golden mystery? . . .

The chinchilla clouds had drifted past now and outside the Montana night was bright as day. The tapestry brick of the road was smooth to the tread of the great tires as they rounded a still, moonlit lake; they passed into darkness for a moment, a pine grove, pungent and cool; then they came out into a broad avenue of lawn and John's exclamation of pleasure was simultaneous with Percy's taciturn 'We're home.'

Full in the light of the stars, an exquisite château rose from the borders of the lake, climbed in marble radiance half the height of an adjoining mountain, then melted in grace, in perfect symmetry, in translucent feminine languor, into the massed darkness of a forest of pine. The many towers, the slender tracery of the sloping parapets, the chiselled wonder of a thousand yellow windows with their oblongs and hectagons and triangles of golden light, the shattered softness of the intersecting planes of star-shine and blue shade, all trembled on John's spirit like a chord of music. On one of the towers, the tallest, the blackest at its base, an arrangement of exterior lights at the top made a sort of floating fairyland – and as John gazed up in warm enchantment the faint acciaccare sound of violins drifted down in a rococo harmony that was like nothing he had ever heard before. Then in a moment the car stopped before wide, high marble steps around which the night air was fragrant with a host of flowers. At the top of the steps two great doors swung silently open and amber light flooded out upon the darkness, silhouetting the figure of an exquisite lady with black, high-piled hair, who held out her arms toward them.

'Mother,' Percy was saying, 'this is my friend, John Unger, from Hades.'

Afterward John remembered that first night as a daze of many colors, of quick sensory impressions, of music soft as a voice in love, and of the beauty of things, lights and shadows, and motions and faces. There was a white-haired man who stood drinking a many-hued cordial from a crystal thimble set on a golden stem. There was a girl with a flowery face, dressed like Titania with braided sapphires in her hair. There was a room where the solid, soft gold of the walls yielded to the pressure of his hand, and a room that was like a platonic conception of the ultimate prism* – ceiling, floor, and all, it was lined with an unbroken mass of diamonds, diamonds of every size and shape, until, lit with tall violet lamps in the corners, it dazzled the eyes with a whiteness that could be compared only with itself, beyond human wish or dream.

Through a maze of these rooms the two boys wandered. Sometimes the floor under their feet would flame in brilliant patterns from lighting below, patterns of barbaric clashing colors, of pastel delicacy, of sheer whiteness, or of subtle and intricate mosaic, surely from some mosque on the Adriatic Sea. Sometimes beneath layers of thick crystal he would see blue or green water swirling, inhabited by vivid fish and growths of rainbow foliage. Then they would be treading on furs of every texture and color or along corridors of palest ivory, unbroken as though carved complete from the gigantic tusks of dinosaurs extinct before the age of man. . . .

* In his own copy of *Tales of the Jazz Age* Fitzgerald emended 'prison' to 'prisym'.

Then a hazily remembered transition, and they were at dinner – where each plate was of two almost imperceptible layers of solid diamond between which was curiously worked a filigree of emerald design, a shaving sliced from green air. Music, plangent and unobtrusive, drifted down through far corridors – his chair, feathered and curved insidiously to his back, seemed to engulf and overpower him as he drank his first glass of port. He tried drowsily to answer a question that had been asked him, but the honeyed luxury that clasped his body added to the illusion of sleep – jewels, fabrics, wines, and metals blurred before his eyes into a sweet mist. . . .

'Yes,' he replied with a polite effort, 'it certainly is hot enough for me down there.

He managed to add a ghostly laugh; then, without movement, without resistance, he seemed to float off and away, leaving an iced dessert that was pink as a dream. . . . He fell asleep.

When he awoke he knew that several hours had passed. He was in a great quiet room with ebony walls and a dull illumination that was too faint, too subtle, to be called a light. His young host was standing over him.

'You fell asleep at dinner,' Percy was saying. 'I nearly did, too – it was such a treat to be comfortable again after this year of school. Servants undressed and bathed you while you were sleeping.'

'Is this a bed or a cloud?' sighed John. 'Percy, Percy – before you go, I want to apologize.'

'For what?'

'For doubting you when you said you had a diamond as big as the Ritz-Carlton Hotel.'

Percy smiled.

'I thought you didn't believe me. It's that mountain, you know.'

'What mountain?'

'The mountain the château rests on. It's not very big, for a mountain. But except about fifty feet of sod and gravel on top it's solid diamond. *One* diamond, one cubic mile without a flaw. Aren't you listening? Say—'

But John T. Unger had again fallen asleep.

3

Morning. As he awoke he perceived drowsily that the room had at the same moment become dense with sunlight. The ebony panels of one wall had slid aside on a sort of track, leaving his chamber half open to the day. A large negro in a white uniform stood beside his bed.

'Good-evening,' muttered John, summoning his brains from the wild places.

'Good-morning, sir. Are you ready for your bath, sir? Oh, don't get up – I'll put you in, if you'll just unbutton your pajamas – there. Thank you sir.'

John lay quietly as his pajamas were removed – he was amused and delighted; he expected to be lifted like a child by this black Gargantua who was tending him, but nothing of the sort happened; instead he felt the bed tilt up slowly on its side – he began to roll, startled at first, in the direction of the wall, but when he reached the wall its drapery gave way, and sliding two yards farther down a fleecy incline he plumped gently into water the same temperature as his body.

He looked about him. The runway or rollway on which he had arrived had folded gently back into place. He had been projected into another chamber and was sitting in a sunken bath with his head just above the level of the floor. All about him, lining the walls of the room and the sides and bottom of the bath itself, was a blue aquarium, and gazing through the crystal surface on which he sat, he could see fish swimming among amber lights and even gliding without curiosity past his outstretched toes, which were separated from them only by the thickness of the crystal. From overhead, sunlight came down through sea-green glass.

'I suppose, sir, that you'd like hot rosewater and soapsuds this morning, sir – and perhaps cold salt water to finish.'

The negro was standing beside him.

'Yes,' agreed John, smiling inanely, 'as you please.' Any idea of ordering this bath according to his own meager standards of living would have been priggish and not a little wicked.

The negro pressed a button and a warm rain began to fall, apparently from overhead, but really, so John discovered after a moment, from a fountain arrangement near by. The water turned to a pale rose color and jets of liquid soap spurted into it from four miniature walrus heads at the corners of the bath. In a moment a dozen little paddle-wheels, fixed to the sides, had churned the mixture into a radiant rainbow of pink foam which enveloped him softly with its delicious lightness, and burst in shining, rosy bubbles here and there about him.

'Shall I turn on the moving-picture machine, sir?' suggested the negro deferentially. 'There's a good one-reel comedy in this machine to-day, or I can put in a serious piece in a moment, if you prefer it.'

'No, thanks,' answered John, politely but firmly. He was enjoying his bath too much to desire any distraction. But distraction came. In a moment he was listening intently to the sound of flutes from just outside, flutes dripping a melody that was like a waterfall, cool and green as the room itself, accompanying a frothy piccolo, in play more fragile than the lace of suds that covered and charmed him.

After a cold salt-water bracer and a cold fresh finish, he stepped out and into a fleecy robe, and upon a couch covered with the same material he was rubbed with oil, alcohol, and spice. Later he sat in a voluptuous chair while he was shaved and his hair was trimmed.

'Mr Percy is waiting in your sitting-room,' said the negro, when these operations were finished. 'My name is Gygsum, Mr Unger, sir. I am to see to Mr Unger every morning.'

John walked out into the brisk sunshine of his living-room, where he found breakfast waiting for him and Percy, gorgeous in white kid knickerbockers, smoking in an easy chair.

4

This is a story of the Washington family as Percy sketched it for John during breakfast.

The father of the present Mr Washington had been a Virginian, a direct descendant of George Washington, and Lord Baltimore. At the close of the Civil War he was a twenty-five-year-old Colonel with a played-out plantation and about a thousand dollars in gold.

Fitz-Norman Culpepper Washington, for that was the young Colonel's name, decided to present the Virginia estate to his younger brother and go West. He selected two dozen of the most faithful blacks, who, of course, worshipped him, and bought twenty-five tickets to the West, where he intended to take out land in their names and start a sheep and cattle ranch.

When he had been in Montana for less than a month and things were going very poorly indeed, he stumbled on his great discovery. He had lost his way when riding in the hills, and after a day without food he began to grow hungry. As he was without his rifle, he was forced to pursue a squirrel, and in the course of the pursuit he noticed that it was carrying something shiny in its mouth. Just before it vanished into its hole – for Providence did not intend that this squirrel should alleviate his hunger – it dropped its burden. Sitting down to consider the situation Fitz-Norman's eye was caught by a gleam in the grass beside him. In ten seconds he had completely lost his appetite and gained one hundred thousand dollars. The squirrel, which had refused with annoying persistence to become food, had made him a present of a large and perfect diamond.

Late that night he found his way to camp and twelve hours later all the males among his darkies were back by the squirrel hole digging furiously at the side of the mountain. He told them he had discovered a rhinestone mine, and, as only one or two of them had ever seen even a small diamond before, they believed him, without question. When the magnitude of his discovery became apparent to him, he found himself in a quandary. The mountain was *a* diamond – it was literally nothing else but solid diamond. He filled four saddle bags full of glittering samples and started on horseback for St Paul. There he managed to dispose of half a dozen small stones – when he tried a larger one a storekeeper fainted and Fitz-Norman was arrested as a public disturber. He escaped from jail and caught the train for New York, where he sold a few medium-sized diamonds and received in exchange about two hundred thousand dollars in gold. But he did not dare to produce any exceptional gems – in fact, he left New York just in time. Tremendous excitement had been created in jewelry circles, not so much by the size of his diamonds as by their appearance in the city from mysterious sources. Wild rumors became current that a diamond mine had been discovered in the Catskills, on the Jersey coast, on Long Island, beneath Washington Square. Excursion trains, packed with men carrying picks and shovels, began to leave New York hourly, bound for various neighboring El Dorados. But by that time young Fitz-Norman was on his way back to Montana.

By the end of a fortnight he had estimated that the diamond in the mountain was approximately equal in quantity to all the rest of the diamonds known to exist in the world. There was no valuing it by any regular computation, however, for it was *one solid diamond* – and if it were offered for sale not only would the bottom fall out of the market, but also, if the value should vary with its size in the usual arithmetical progression, there would not be enough gold in the world to buy a tenth part of it. And what could any one do with a diamond that size?

It was an amazing predicament. He was, in one sense, the richest man that ever lived – and yet was he worth anything at all? If his secret should transpire there was no telling to what measures the Government might resort in order to prevent a panic, in gold as well as in jewels. They might take over the claim immediately and institute a monopoly.

There was no alternative – he must market his mountain in secret. He sent South for his younger brother and put him in charge of his colored following – darkies who had never realized that slavery was abolished. To make sure of this, he read them a proclamation that he had composed, which announced that General Forrest had reorganized the shattered Southern armies and defeated the North in one pitched battle. The negroes believed him implicitly. They passed a vote declaring it a good thing and held revival services immediately.

Fitz-Norman himself set out for foreign parts with one hundred thousand dollars and two trunks filled with rough diamonds of all sizes. He sailed for Russia in a Chinese junk and six months after his departure from Montana he was in St Petersburg. He took obscure lodgings and called immediately upon the court jeweller, announcing that he had a diamond for the Czar. He remained in St Petersburg for two weeks, in constant danger of being murdered, living from lodging to lodging, and afraid to visit his trunks more than three or four times during the whole fortnight.

On his promise to return in a year with larger and finer stones, he was allowed to leave for India. Before he left, however, the Court Treasurers had deposited to his credit, in American banks, the sum of fifteen million dollars – under four different aliases.

He returned to America in 1868, having been gone a little over two years. He had visited the capitals of twenty-two countries and talked with five emperors, eleven kings, three princes, a shah, a khan, and a sultan. At that time Fitz-Norman estimated his own wealth at one billion dollars. One fact worked consistently against the disclosure of his secret. No one of his larger diamonds remained in the public eye for a week before being invested with a history of enough fatalities, amours, revolutions, and wars to have occupied it from the days of the first Babylonian Empire.

From 1870 until his death in 1900, the history of Fitz-Norman Washington was a long epic in gold. There were side issues, of course – he evaded the surveys, he married a Virginia lady, by whom he had a single son, and he was compelled, due to a series of unfortunate complications, to murder his brother, whose unfortunate habit of drinking himself into an indiscreet stupor had several times endangered their safety. But very few other murders stained these happy years of progress and expansion.

Just before he died he changed his policy, and with all but a few million dollars of his outside wealth bought up rare minerals in bulk, which he deposited in the safety vaults of banks all over the world, marked as bric-à-brac. His son, Braddock Tarleton Washington, followed this policy on an even more tensive scale. The minerals were converted into the rarest of all elements – radium – so that the equivalent of a billion dollars in gold could be placed in a receptacle no bigger than a cigar box.

When Fitz-Norman had been dead three years his son, Braddock, decided that the business had gone far enough. The amount of wealth that he and his father had taken out of the mountain was beyond all exact computation. He kept a note-book in cipher in which he set down the approximate quantity of radium in each of the thousand banks he patronized, and recorded the alias under which it was held. Then he did a very simple thing – he sealed up the mine.

He sealed up the mine. What had been taken out of it would

support all the Washingtons yet to be born in unparalleled luxury for generations. His one care must be the protection of his secret, lest in the possible panic attendant on its discovery he should be reduced with all the property-holders in the world to utter poverty.

This was the family among whom John T. Unger was staying. This was the story he heard in his silver-walled living-room the morning after his arrival.

5

After breakfast, John found his way out the great marble entrance, and looked curiously at the scene before him. The whole valley, from the diamond mountain to the steep granite cliff five miles away, still gave off a breath of golden haze which hovered idly above the fine sweep of lawns and lakes and gardens. Here and there clusters of elms made delicate groves of shade, contrasting strangely with the tough masses of pine forest that held the hills in a grip of dark-blue green. Even as John looked he saw three fawns in single file patter out from one clump about a half mile away and disappear with awkward gayety into the black-ribbed half-light of another. John would not have been surprised to see a goat-foot piping his way among the trees or to catch a glimpse of pink nymph-skin and flying yellow hair between the greenest of the green leaves.

In some such cool hope he descended the marble steps, disturbing faintly the sleep of two silky Russian wolfhounds at the bottom, and set off along a walk of white and blue brick that seemed to lead in no particular direction.

He was enjoying himself as much as he was able. It is youth's felicity as well as its insufficiency that it can never live in the present, but must always be measuring up the day against its own radiantly imagined future – flowers and gold, girls and stars, they are only prefigurations and prophecies of that incomparable, unattainable young dream.

John rounded a soft corner where the massed rose-bushes filled the air with heavy scent, and struck off across a park toward a patch of moss under some trees. He had never lain upon moss, and he wanted to see whether it was really soft enough to justify the use of its name as an adjective. Then he saw a girl coming toward him over the grass. She was the most beautiful person he had ever seen.

She was dressed in a white little gown that came just below her knees, and a wreath of mignonettes clasped with blue slices of sapphire bound up her hair. Her pink bare feet scattered the dew before them as she came. She was younger than John – not more than sixteen.

'Hello,' she cried softly, 'I'm Kismine.'

She was much more than that to John already. He advanced toward her, scarcely moving as he drew near lest he should tread on her bare toes.

'You haven't met me,' said her soft voice. Her blue eyes added, 'Oh, but you've missed a great deal!'... 'You met my sister, Jasmine, last night. I was sick with lettuce poisoning,' went on her soft voice, and her eyes continued, 'and when I'm sick I'm sweet – and when I'm well.'

'You have made an enormous impression on me,' said John's eyes, 'and I'm not so slow myself' – 'How do you do?' said his voice. 'I hope you're better this morning.' – 'You darling,' added his eyes tremulously.

John observed that they had been walking along the path. On her suggestion they sat down together upon the moss, the softness of which he failed to determine.

He was critical about women. A single defect – a thick ankle, a hoarse voice, a glass eye – was enough to make him utterly indifferent. And here for the first time in his life he was beside a girl who seemed to him the incarnation of physical perfection.

'Are you from the East?' asked Kismine with charming interest.

'No,' answered John simply. 'I'm from Hades.'

Either she had never heard of Hades, or she could think of no pleasant comment to make upon it, for she did not discuss it further.

'I'm going East to school this fall,' she said. 'D'you think I'll like it? I'm going to New York to Miss Bulge's. It's very strict, but you see over the weekends I'm going to live at home with the family in our New York house, because father heard that the girls had to go walking two by two.'

'Your father wants you to be proud,' observed John.

'We are,' she answered, her eyes shining with dignity. 'None of us has ever been punished. Father said we never should be. Once when my sister Jasmine was a little girl she pushed him downstairs and he just got up and limped away.

'Mother was – well, a little startled,' continued Kismine, 'when she heard that you were from – from where you *are* from, you know. She said that when she was a young girl – but then, you see, she's a Spaniard and old-fashioned.'

'Do you spend much time out here?' asked John, to conceal the fact that he was somewhat hurt by this remark. It seemed an unkind allusion to his provincialism.

'Percy and Jasmine and I are here every summer, but next summer Jasmine is going to Newport. She's coming out in London a year from this fall. She'll be presented at court.'

'Do you know,' began John hesitantly, 'you're much more sophisticated than I thought you were when I first saw you?'

'Oh, no, I'm not,' she exclaimed hurriedly. 'Oh, I wouldn't think of being. I think that sophisticated young people are *terribly* common, don't you? I'm not at all, really. If you say I am, I'm going to cry.'

She was so distressed that her lip was trembling. John was impelled to protest:

'I didn't mean that; I only said it to tease you.'

'Because I wouldn't mind if I *were*,' she persisted, 'but I'm *not*. I'm very innocent and girlish. I never smoke, or drink, or read anything except poetry. I know scarcely any mathematics or chemistry. I dress *very* simply – in fact, I scarcely dress at all. I think sophisticated is the last thing you can say about me. I believe that girls ought to enjoy their youths in a wholesome way.'

'I do, too,' said John heartily.

Kismine was cheerful again. She smiled at him, and a still-born tear dripped from the corner of one blue eye.

'I like you,' she whispered, intimately. 'Are you going to spend all your time with Percy while you're here, or will you be nice to me? Just think – I'm absolutely fresh ground. I've never had a boy in love with me in all my life. I've never been allowed even to *see* boys alone – except Percy. I came all the way out here into this grove hoping to run into you, where the family wouldn't be around.'

Deeply flattered, John bowed from the hips as he had been taught at dancing school in Hades.

'We'd better go now,' said Kismine sweetly. 'I have to be with mother at eleven. You haven't asked me to kiss you once. I thought boys always did that nowadays.'

John drew himself up proudly.

'Some of them do,' he answered, 'but not me. Girls don't do that sort of thing – in Hades.'

Side by side they walked back toward the house.

6

John stood facing Mr Braddock Washington in the full sunlight. The elder man was about forty with a proud, vacuous face, intelligent eyes, and a robust figure. In the mornings he smelt of horses – the best horses. He carried a plain walking-stick of gray birch with a single large opal for a grip. He and Percy were showing John around.

'The slaves' quarters are there.' His walking-stick indicated a cloister of marble on their left that ran in graceful Gothic along the side of the mountain. 'In my youth I was distracted for a while from the business of life by a period of absurd idealism. During that time they lived in luxury. For instance, I equipped every one of their rooms with a tile bath.'

'I suppose,' ventured John, with an ingratiating laugh, 'that they used the bathtubs to keep coal in. Mr Schnlitzer-Murphy told me that once he—'

'The opinions of Mr Schnlitzer-Murphy are of little importance, I should imagine,' interrupted Braddock Washington, coldly. 'My slaves did not keep coal in their bathtubs. They had orders to bathe every day, and they did. If they hadn't I might have ordered a sulphuric acid shampoo. I discontinued the baths for quite another reason. Several of them caught cold and died. Water is not good for certain races – except as a beverage.'

John laughed, and then decided to nod his head in sober agreement. Braddock Washington made him uncomfortable.

'All these negroes are descendants of the ones my father brought North with him. There are about two hundred and fifty now. You notice that they've lived so long apart from the world that their original dialect has become an almost indistinguishable patois. We bring a few of them up to speak English – my secretary and two or three of the house servants.

'This is the golf course,' he continued, as they strolled along the velvet winter grass. 'It's all a green, you see – no fairway, no rough, no hazards.'

He smiled pleasantly at John.

'Many men in the cage, father?' asked Percy suddenly.

Braddock Washington stumbled, and let forth an involuntary curse.

'One less than there should be,' he ejaculated darkly – and then added after a moment, 'We've had difficulties.'

'Mother was telling me,' exclaimed Percy, 'that Italian teacher—'

'A ghastly error,' said Braddock Washington angrily. 'But of course there's a good chance that we may have got him. Perhaps he fell somewhere in the woods or stumbled over a cliff. And then there's always the probability that if he did get away his story wouldn't be believed. Nevertheless, I've had two dozen men looking for him in different towns around here.'

'And no luck?'

'Some. Fourteen of them reported to my agent that they'd each killed a man answering to that description, but of course it was probably only the reward they were after—'

He broke off. They had come to a large cavity in the earth about the circumference of a merry-go-round and covered by a strong iron grating. Braddock Washington beckoned to John, and pointed his cane down through the grating. John stepped to the edge and gazed. Immediately his ears were assailed by a wild clamor from below.

'Come on down to Hell!'

'Hello, kiddo, how's the air up there?'

'Hey! Throw us a rope!'

'Got an old doughnut, Buddy, or a couple of second-hand sandwiches?'

'Say, fella, if you'll push down that guy you're with, we'll show you a quick disappearance scene.'

'Paste him one for me, will you?'

It was too dark to see clearly into the pit below, but John could tell from the coarse optimism and rugged vitality of the remarks and voices that they proceeded from middle-class Americans of the more spirited type. Then Mr Washington put out his cane and touched a button in the grass, and the scene below sprang into light.

'These are some adventurous mariners who had the misfortune to discover El Dorado,' he remarked.

Below them there had appeared a large hollow in the earth shaped like the interior of a bowl. The sides were steep and apparently of polished glass, and on its slightly concave surface stood about two dozen men clad in the half costume, half uniform, of aviators. Their upturned faces, lit with wrath, with malice, with despair, with cynical humor, were covered by long growths of beard, but with the exception of a few who had pined perceptibly away, they seemed to be a well-fed, healthy lot.

Braddock Washington drew a garden chair to the edge of the pit and sat down.

'Well, how are you, boys?' he inquired genially.

A chorus of execration in which all joined except a few too dispirited to cry out, rose up into the sunny air, but Braddock Washington heard it with unruffled composure. When its last echo had died away he spoke again.

'Have you thought up a way out of your difficulty?'

From here and there among them a remark floated up.

'We decided to stay here for love!'

'Bring us up there and we'll find us a way!'

Braddock Washington waited until they were again quiet. Then he said:

'I've told you the situation. I don't want you here. I wish to heaven I'd never seen you. Your own curiosity got you here, and any time that you can think of a way out which protects me and my interests I'll be glad to consider it. But so long as you confine your efforts to digging tunnels – yes, I know about the new one you've started – you won't get very far. This isn't as hard on you as you make it out, with all your howling for the loved ones at home. If you were the type who worried much about the loved ones at home, you'd never have taken up aviation.'

A tall man moved apart from the others, and held up his hand to call his captor's attention to what he was about to say.

'Let me ask you a few questions!' he cried. 'You pretend to be a fair-minded man.'

'How absurd. How could a man of *my* position be fair-minded toward *you*? You might as well speak of a Spaniard being fair-minded toward a piece of steak.'

At this harsh observation the faces of the two dozen steaks fell, but the tall man continued:

'All right!' he cried. 'We've argued this out before. You're not a humanitarian and you're not fair-minded, but you're human – at least you say you are – and you ought to be able to put yourself in our place for long enough to think how – how – how—'

'How what?' demanded Washington, coldly.

'– how unnecessary—'

'Not to me.'

'Well, – how cruel—'

'We've covered that. Cruelty doesn't exist where self-preservation is involved. You've been soldiers; you know that. Try another.'

'Well, then, how stupid.'

'There,' admitted Washington, 'I grant you that. But try to think of an alternative. I've offered to have all or any of you painlessly executed if you wish. I've offered to have your wives, sweethearts, children, and mothers kidnapped and brought out here. I'll enlarge your place down there and feed and clothe you the rest of your lives. If there was some method of producing permanent amnesia I'd have all of you operated on and released immediately, somewhere outside of my preserves. But that's as far as my ideas go.'

'How about trusting us not to peach on you?' cried some one.

'You don't proffer that suggestion seriously,' said Washington, with an expression of scorn. 'I did take out one man to teach my daughter Italian. Last week he got away.'

A wild yell of jubilation went up suddenly from two dozen throats and a pandemonium of joy ensued. The prisoners clog-danced and cheered and yodled and wrestled with one another in a sudden uprush of animal spirits. They even ran up the glass sides of the bowl as far as they could, and slid back to the bottom upon the natural cushions of their bodies. The tall man started a song in which they all joined –

> *'Oh, we'll hang the kaiser*
> *On a sour apple tree—'*

Braddock Washington sat in inscrutable silence until the song was over.

'You see,' he remarked, when he could gain a modicum of attention. 'I bear you no ill-will. I like to see you enjoying yourselves. That's why I didn't tell you the whole story at once. The man – what was his name? Critchtichiello? – was shot by some of my agents in fourteen different places.'

Not guessing that the places referred to were cities, the tumult of rejoicing subsided immediately.

'Nevertheless,' cried Washington with a touch of anger, 'he tried to run away. Do you expect me to take chances with any of you after an experience like that?'

Again a series of ejaculations went up.

'Sure!'

'Would your daughter like to learn Chinese?'

'Hey, I can speak Italian! My mother was a wop.'

'Maybe she'd like t'learna speak N'Yawk!'

'If she's the little one with the big blue eyes I can teach her a lot of things better than Italian.'

'I know some Irish songs – and I could hammer brass once't.'

Mr Washington reached forward suddenly with his cane and pushed the button in the grass so that the picture below went out instantly, and there remained only that great dark mouth covered dismally with the black teeth of the grating.

'Hey!' called a single voice from below, 'you ain't goin' away without givin' us your blessing?'

But Mr Washington, followed by the two boys, was already strolling on toward the ninth hole of the golf course, as though the pit and its contents were no more than a hazard over which his facile iron had triumphed with ease.

7

July under the lee of the diamond mountain was a month of blanket nights and of warm, glowing days. John and Kismine were in love. He did not know that the little gold football (inscribed with the legend *Pro deo et patria et St Mida*) which he had given her rested on a platinum chain next to her bosom. But it did. And she for her part was not aware that a large sapphire which had dropped one day from her simple coiffure was stowed away tenderly in John's jewel box.

Late one afternoon when the ruby and ermine music room was quiet, they spent an hour there together. He held her hand and she gave him such a look that he whispered her name aloud. She bent toward him – then hesitated.

'Did you say "Kismine"?' she asked softly, 'or—'

She had wanted to be sure. She thought, she might have misunderstood.

Neither of them had ever kissed before, but in the course of an hour it seemed to make little difference.

The afternoon drifted away. That night when a last breath of music drifted down from the highest tower, they each lay awake, happily dreaming over the separate minutes of the day. They had decided to be married as soon as possible.

8

Every day Mr Washington and the two young men went hunting or fishing in the deep forests or played golf around the somnolent course – games which John diplomatically allowed his host to win – or swam in the mountain coolness of the lake. John found Mr Washington a somewhat exacting personality – utterly uninterested in any ideas or opinions except his own. Mrs Washington was aloof and reserved at all times. She was apparently indifferent to her two daughters, and entirely absorbed in her son Percy, with whom she held interminable conversations in rapid Spanish at dinner.

Jasmine, the elder daughter, resembled Kismine in appearance – except that she was somewhat bow-legged, and terminated in large hands and feet – but was utterly unlike her in temperament. Her favorite books had to do with poor girls who kept house for widowed fathers. John learned from Kismine that Jasmine had never recovered from the shock and disappointment caused her by the termination of the World War, just as she was about to start for Europe as a canteen expert. She had even pined away for a time, and Braddock Washington had taken steps to promote a new war in the Balkans – but she had seen a photograph of some wounded Serbian soldiers and lost interest in the whole proceedings. But Percy and Kismine seemed to have inherited the arrogant attitude in all its harsh magnificence from their father. A chaste and consistent selfishness ran like a pattern through their every idea.

John was enchanted by the wonders of the château and the valley. Braddock Washington, so Percy told him, had caused to be kidnapped a landscape gardener, an architect, a designer of state settings, and a French decadent poet left over from the last century. He had put his entire force of negroes at their disposal, guaranteed to supply them with any materials that the world could offer, and left them to work out some ideas of their own. But one by one they had shown their uselessness. The decadent poet had at once begun bewailing his separation from the boulevards in spring – he made some vague remarks about spices, apes, and ivories, but said nothing that was of any practical value. The stage designer on his part wanted to make the whole valley a series of tricks and sensational effects – a state of things that the Washingtons would soon have grown tired of. And as for the architect and the landscape gardener, they thought only in terms of convention. They must make this like this and that like that.

But they had, at least, solved the problem of what was to be done with them – they all went mad early one morning after spending the night in a single room trying to agree upon the location of a fountain, and were now confined comfortably in an insane asylum at Westport, Connecticut.

'But,' inquired John curiously, 'who did plan all your wonderful reception rooms and halls, and approaches and bathrooms—?'

'Well,' answered Percy, 'I blush to tell you, but it was a moving-picture fella. He was the only man we found who was used to playing with an unlimited amount of money, though he did tuck his napkin in his collar and couldn't read or write.'

As August drew to a close John began to regret that he must soon go back to school. He and Kismine had decided to elope the following June.

'It would be nicer to be married here,' Kismine confessed, 'but of course I could never get father's permission to marry you at all. Next to that I'd rather elope. It's terrible for wealthy people to be married in America at present – they always have to send out bulletins to the press saying that they're going to be married in remnants, when what they mean is just a peck of old second-hand pearls and some used lace worn once by the Empress Eugénie.'

'I know,' agreed John fervently. 'When I was visiting the Schnlitzer-Murphys, the eldest daughter, Gwendolyn, married a man whose father owns half of West Virginia. She wrote home saying what a tough struggle she was carrying on on his salary as a bank clerk – and then she ended up by saying that "Thank God, I have four good maids anyhow, and that helps a little."'

'It's absurd,' commented Kismine. 'Think of the millions and millions of people in the world, laborers and all, who get along with only two maids.'

One afternoon late in August a chance remark of Kismine's changed the face of the entire situation, and threw John into a state of terror.

They were in their favorite grove, and between kisses John was indulging in some romantic forebodings which he fancied added poignancy to their relations.

'Sometimes I think we'll never marry,' he said sadly. 'You're too wealthy, too magnificent. No one as rich as you are can be like other girls. I should marry the daughter of some well-to-do wholesale hardware man from Omaha or Sioux City, and be content with her half-million.'

'I knew the daughter of a wholesale hardware man once,' remarked Kismine. 'I don't think you'd have been contented with her. She was a friend of my sister's. She visited here.'

'Oh, then you've had other guests?' exclaimed John in surprise.

Kismine seemed to regret her words.

'Oh, yes,' she said hurriedly, 'we've had a few.'

'But aren't you – wasn't your father afraid they'd talk outside?'

'Oh, to some extent, to some extent,' she answered. 'Let's talk about something pleasanter.'

But John's curiosity was aroused.

'Something pleasanter!' he demanded. 'What's unpleasant about that? Weren't they nice girls?'

To his great surprise Kismine began to weep.

'Yes – th – that's the – the whole t-trouble. I grew qu-quite attached to some of them. So did Jasmine, but she kept inviting them anyway. I couldn't under*stand* it.'

A dark suspicion was born in John's heart.

'Do you mean that they *told*, and your father had them – removed?'

'Worse than that,' she muttered brokenly. 'Father took no chances – and Jasmine kept writing them to come, and they had *such* a good time!'

She was overcome by a paroxysm of grief.

Stunned with the horror of this revelation, John sat there open-mouthed, feeling the nerves of his body twitter like so many sparrows perched upon his spinal column.

'Now, I've told you, and I shouldn't have,' she said, calming suddenly and drying her dark blue eyes.

'Do you mean to say that your father had them *murdered* before they left?'

She nodded.

'In August usually – or early in September. It's only natural for us to get all the pleasure out of them that we can first.'

'How abominable! How – why, I must be going crazy! Did you really admit that—'

'I did,' interrupted Kismine, shrugging her shoulders. 'We can't very well imprison them like those aviators, where they'd be a continual reproach to us every day. And it's always been made easier for Jasmine and me, because father had it done sooner than we expected. In that way we avoided any farewell scene—'

'So you murdered them! Uh!' cried John.

'It was done very nicely. They were drugged while they were asleep – and their families were always told that they died of scarlet fever in Butte.'

'But – I fail to understand why you kept on inviting them!'

'I didn't,' burst out Kismine. 'I never invited one. Jasmine did. And they always had a very good time. She'd give them the nicest presents toward the last. I shall probably have visitors too – I'll harden up to it. We can't let such an inevitable thing as death stand in the way of enjoying life while we have it. Think how lonesome it'd be out here if we never had *any* one. Why, father and mother have sacrificed some of their best friends just as we have.'

'And so,' cried John accusingly, 'and so you were letting me make love to you and pretending to return it, and talking about marriage, all the time knowing perfectly well that I'd never get out of here alive—'

'No,' she protested passionately. 'Not any more. I did at first. You were here. I couldn't help that, and I thought your last days might as well be pleasant for both of us. But then I fell in love with you, and – and I'm honestly sorry you're going to – going to be put away – though I'd rather you'd be put away than ever kiss another girl.'

'Oh, you would, would you?' cried John ferociously.

'Much rather. Besides, I've always heard that a girl can have more fun with a man whom she knows she can never marry. Oh, why did I tell you? I've probably spoiled your whole good time now, and we were really enjoying things when you didn't know it. I knew it would make things sort of depressing for you.'

'Oh, you did, did you?' John's voice trembled with anger. 'I've heard about enough of this. If you haven't any more pride and decency than to have an affair with a fellow that you know isn't much better than a corpse, I don't want to have any more to do with you!'

'You're not a corpse!' she protested in horror. 'You're not a corpse! I won't have you saying that I kissed a corpse!'

'I said nothing of the sort!'

'You did! You said I kissed a corpse!'

'I didn't!'

Their voices had risen, but upon a sudden interruption they both subsided into immediate silence. Footsteps were coming along the path in their direction, and a moment later the rose bushes were parted displaying Braddock Washington, whose intelligent eyes set in his good-looking vacuous face were peering in at them.

'Who kissed a corpse?' he demanded in obvious disapproval.

'Nobody,' answered Kismine quickly. 'We were just joking.'

'What are you two doing here, anyhow?' he demanded gruffly. 'Kismine, you ought to be – to be reading or playing golf with your sister. Go read! Go play golf! Don't let me find you here when I come back!'

Then he bowed at John and went up the path.

'See?' said Kismine crossly, when he was out of hearing. 'You've spoiled it all. We can never meet any more. He won't let me meet you. He'd have you poisoned if he thought we were in love.'

'We're not, any more!' cried John fiercely, 'so he can set his mind at rest upon that. Moreover, don't fool yourself that I'm going to stay around here. Inside of six hours I'll be over those mountains, if I have to gnaw a passage through them, and on my way East.'

They had both got to their feet, and at this remark Kismine came close and put her arm through his.

'I'm going, too.'

'You must be crazy—'

'Of course I'm going,' she interrupted impatiently.

'You most certainly are not. You—'

'Very well,' she said quietly, 'we'll catch up with father now and talk it over with him.'

Defeated, John mustered a sickly smile.

'Very well,' dearest,' he agreed, with pale and unconvincing affection, 'we'll go together.'

His love for her returned and settled placidly on his heart. She was his – she would go with him to share his dangers. He put his arms about her and kissed her fervently. After all she loved him; she had saved him, in fact.

Discussing the matter, they walked slowly back toward the château. They decided that since Braddock Washington had seen them together they had best depart the next night. Nevertheless, John's lips were unusually dry at dinner, and he nervously emptied a great spoonful of peacock soup into his left lung. He had to be carried into the turquoise and sable card-room and pounded on the back by one of the under-butlers, which Percy considered a great joke.

9

Long after midnight John's body gave a nervous jerk, and he sat suddenly upright, staring into the veils of somnolence that draped the room. Through the squares of blue darkness that were his open windows, he had heard a faint far-away sound that died upon a bed of wind before identifying itself on his memory, clouded with uneasy dreams. But the sharp noise that had succeeded it was nearer, was just outside the room – the click of a turned knob, a footstep, a whisper, he could not tell; a hard lump gathered in the pit of his stomach, and his whole body ached in the moment that he strained agonizingly to hear. Then one of the veils seemed to dissolve, and he saw a vague figure standing by the door, a figure only faintly limned and blocked in upon the darkness, mingled so with the folds of the drapery as to seem distorted, like a reflection seen in a dirty pane of glass.

With a sudden movement of fright or resolution John pressed the button by his bedside, and the next moment he was sitting in the green sunken bath of the adjoining room, waked into alterness by the shock of the cold water which half filled it.

He sprang out, and, his wet pajamas scattering a heavy trickle of water behind him, ran for the acquamarine door which he knew led out onto the ivory landing of the second floor. The door opened noiselessly. A single crimson lamp burning in a great dome above lit the magnificent sweep of the carved stairways with a poignant beauty. For a moment John hesitated, appalled by the silent splendor massed about him, seeming to envelop in its gigantic folds and contours the solitary drenched little figure shivering upon the ivory landing. Then simultaneously two things happened. The door of his own sitting-room swung open, precipitating three naked negroes into the hall – and, as John swayed in wild terror toward the stairway, another door slid back in the wall on the other side of the corridor, and John saw Braddock Washington standing in the lighted lift, wearing a fur coat and a pair of riding boots which reached to his knees and displayed, above, the glow of his rose-colored pajamas.

On the instant the three negroes – John had never seen any of them before, and it flashed through his mind that they must be the professional executioners – paused in their movement toward John, and turned expectantly to the man in the lift, who burst out with an imperious command:

'Get in here! All three of you! Quick as hell!'

Then, within the instant, the three negroes darted into the cage, the oblong of light was blotted out as the lift door slid shut, and John was again alone in the hall. He slumped weakly down against an ivory stair.

It was apparent that something portentous had occurred, something which, for the moment at least, had postponed his own petty disaster. What was it? Had the negroes risen in revolt? Had the aviators forced aside the iron bars of the grating? Or had the men of Fish stumbled blindly through the hills and gazed with bleak, joyless eyes upon the gaudy valley? John did not know. He heard a faint whir of air as the lift whizzed up again, and then, a moment later, as it descended. It was probable that Percy was hurrying to his father's assistance, and it occurred to John that this was his opportunity to join Kismine and plan an immediate escape. He waited until the lift had been silent for several minutes; shivering a little with the night cool that whipped in through his wet pajamas, he returned to his room and dressed himself quickly. Then he mounted a long flight of stairs and turned down the corridor carpeted with Russian sable which led to Kismine's suite.

The door of her sitting-room was open and the lamps were lighted. Kismine, in an angora kimono, stood near the window of the room in a listening attitude, and as John entered noiselessly she turned toward him.

'Oh, it's you!' she whispered, crossing the room to him. 'Did you hear them?'

'I heard your father's slaves in my—'

'No,' she interrupted excitedly. 'Aeroplanes!'

'Aeroplanes? Perhaps that was the sound that woke me.'

'There're at least a dozen. I saw one a few moments ago dead against the moon. The guard back by the cliff fired his rifle and that's what roused father. We're going to open on them right away.'

'Are they here on purpose?'

'Yes – it's that Italian who got away—'

Simultaneously with her last word, a succession of sharp cracks tumbled in through the open window. Kismine uttered a little cry, took a penny with fumbling fingers from a box on her dresser, and ran to one of the electric lights. In an instant the entire château was in darkness – she had blown out the fuse.

'Come on!' she cried to him. 'We'll go up to the roof garden, and watch it from there!'

Drawing a cape about her, she took his hand, and they found their way out the door. It was only a step to the tower lift, and as she pressed the button that shot them upward he put his arms around her in the darkness and kissed her mouth. Romance had come to John Unger at last. A minute later they had stepped out upon the star-white platform. Above, under the misty moon, sliding in and out of the patches of cloud that eddied below it, floated a dozen dark-winged bodies in a constant circling course. From here and there in the valley flashes of fire leaped toward them, followed by sharp detonations. Kismine clapped her hands with pleasure, which, a moment later, turned to dismay as the aeroplanes at some prearranged signal, began to release their bombs and the whole of the valley became a panorama of deep reverberate sound and lurid light.

Before long the aim of the attackers became concentrated upon the points where the anti-aircraft guns were situated, and one of them was almost immediately reduced to a giant cinder to lie smouldering in a park of rose bushes.

'Kismine,' begged John, 'you'll be glad when I tell you that this attack came on the eve of my murder. If I hadn't heard that guard shoot off his gun back by the pass I should now be stone dead—'

'I can't hear you!' cried Kismine, intent on the scene before her. 'You'll have to talk louder!'

'I simply said,' shouted John, 'that we'd better get out before they begin to shell the château!'

Suddenly the whole portico of the negro quarters cracked asunder, a geyser of flame shot up from under the colonnades, and great fragments of jagged marble were hurled as far as the borders of the lake.

'There go fifty thousand dollars' worth of slaves,' cried Kismine, 'at prewar prices. So few Americans have any respect for property.'

John renewed his efforts to compel her to leave. The aim of the aeroplanes was becoming more precise minute by minute, and only two of the anti-aircraft guns were still retaliating. It was obvious that the garrison, encircled with fire, could not hold out much longer.

'Come on!' cried John, pulling Kismine's arm, 'we've got to go. Do you realize that those aviators will kill you without question if they find you?'

She consented reluctantly.

'We'll have to wake Jasmine!' she said, as they hurried toward the lift. Then she added in a sort of childish delight: 'We'll be poor, won't we? Like people in books. And I'll be an orphan and utterly free. Free and poor! What fun!' She stopped and raised her lips to him in a delighted kiss.

'It's impossible to be both together,' said John grimly. 'People have found that out. And I should choose to be free as preferable of the two. As an extra caution you'd better dump the contents of your jewel box into your pockets.'

Ten minutes later the two girls met John in the dark corridor and they descended to the main floor of the château. Passing for the last time through the magnificence of the splendid halls, they stood for a moment out on the terrace, watching the burning negro quarters and the flaming embers of two planes which had fallen on the other side of the lake. A solitary gun was still keeping up a sturdy popping, and the attackers seemed timorous about descending lower, but sent their thunderous fireworks in a circle around it, until any chance shot might annihilate its Ethiopian crew.

John and the two sisters passed down the marble steps, turned sharply to the left, and began to ascend a narrow path that wound like a garter about the diamond mountain. Kismine knew a heavily wooded spot half-way up where they could lie concealed and yet be able to observe the wild night in the valley – finally to make an escape, when it should be necessary, along a secret path laid in a rocky gully.

10

It was three o'clock when they attained their destination. The obliging and phlegmatic Jasmine fell off to sleep immediately, leaning against the trunk of a large tree, while John and Kismine sat, his arm around her, and watched the desperate ebb and flow of the dying battle among the ruins of a vista that had been a garden spot that morning. Shortly after four o'clock the last remaining gun gave out a clanging sound and went out of action in a swift tongue of red smoke. Though the moon was down, they saw that the flying bodies were circling closer to the earth. When the planes had made certain that the beleaguered possessed no further resources, they would land and the dark and glittering reign of the Washingtons would be over.

With the cessation of the firing the valley grew quiet. The embers of the two aeroplanes glowed like the eyes of some monster crouching in the grass. The château stood dark and silent, beautiful without light as it had been beautiful in the sun, while the woody rattles of Nemesis filled the air above with a growing and receding complaint. Then John perceived that Kismine, like her sister, had fallen sound asleep.

It was long after four when he became aware of footsteps along the path they had lately followed, and he waited in breathless silence until the persons to whom they belonged had passed the vantage-point he occupied. There was a faint stir in the air now that was not of human origin, and the dew was cold; he knew that the dawn would break soon. John waited until the steps had gone a safe distance up the mountain and were inaudible. Then he followed. About half-way to the steep summit the trees fell away and a hard saddle of rock spread itself over the diamond beneath. Just before he reached this point he slowed down his pace, warned by an animal sense that there was life just ahead of him. Coming to a high boulder, he lifted his head gradually above its edge. His curiosity was rewarded; this is what he saw:

Braddock Washington was standing there motionless, silhouetted against the gray sky without sound or sign of life. As the dawn came up out of the east, lending a cold green color to the earth, it brought the solitary figure into insignificant contrast with the new day.

While John watched, his host remained for a few moments absorbed in some inscrutable contemplation; then he signalled to the two negroes who crouched at his feet to lift the burden which lay between them. As they struggled upright, the first yellow beam of the sun struck through the innumerable prisms of an immense and exquisitely chiselled diamond – and a white radiance was kindled that glowed upon the air like a fragment of the morning star. The bearers staggered beneath its weight for a moment – then their rippling muscles caught and hardened under the wet shine of the skins and the three figures were again motionless in their defiant impotency before the heavens.

After a while the white man lifted his head and slowly raised his arms in a gesture of attention, as one who would call a great crowd to hear – but there was no crowd, only the vast silence of the mountain and the sky, broken by faint bird voices down among the trees. The figure on the saddle of rock began to speak ponderously and with an inextinguishable pride.

'You out there –' he cried in a trembling voice. 'You – there—!' He paused, his arms still uplifted, his head held attentively as though he were expecting an answer. John strained his eyes to see whether there might be men coming down the mountain, but the mountain was bare of human life. There was only sky and a mocking flute of wind along the tree-tops. Could Washington be praying? For a moment John wondered. Then the illusion passed – there was something in the man's whole attitude antithetical to prayer.

'Oh, you above there!'

The voice was become strong and confident. This was no forlorn supplication. If anything, there was in it a quality of monstrous condescension.

'You there—'

Words, too quickly uttered to be understood, flowing one into the other. . . . John listened breathlessly, catching a phrase here and there, while the voice broke off, resumed, broke off again – now strong and argumentative, now colored with a slow, puzzled impatience. Then a conviction commenced to dawn on the single listener, and as realization crept over him a spray of quick blood rushed through his arteries. Braddock Washington was offering a bribe to God!

That was it – there was no doubt. The diamond in the arms of his slaves was some advance sample, a promise of more to follow.

That, John perceived after a time, was the thread running through his sentences. Prometheus Enriched was calling to witness forgotten sacrifices, forgotten rituals, prayers obsolete before the birth of Christ. For a while his discourse took the form of reminding God of this gift or that which Divinity had deigned to accept from men – great churches if he would rescue cities from the plague, gifts of myrrh and gold, of human lives and beautiful women and captive armies, of children and queens, of beasts of the forest and field, sheep and goats, harvests and cities, whole conquered lands that had been offered up in lust or blood for His appeasal, buying a meed's worth of alleviation from the Divine wrath – and now he, Braddock Washington, Emperor of Diamonds, king and priest of the age of gold, arbiter of splendor and luxury, would offer up a treasure such as princes before him had never dreamed of, offer it up not in suppliance, but in pride.

He would give to God, he continued, getting down to specifications, the greatest diamond in the world. This diamond would be cut with many more thousand facets than there were leaves on a tree, and yet the whole diamond would be shaped with the perfection of a stone no bigger than a fly. Many men would work upon it for many years. It would be set in a great dome of beaten gold, wonderfully carved and equipped with gates of opal and crusted sapphire. In the middle would be hollowed out a chapel presided over by an altar of iridescent, decomposing, ever-changing radium which would burn out the eyes of any worshipper who lifted up his head from prayer – and on this altar there would be slain for the amusement of the Divine Benefactor any victim He should choose, even though it should be the greatest and most powerful man alive.

In return he asked only a simple thing, a thing that for God would be absurdly easy – only that matters should be as they were yesterday at this hour and that they should so remain. So very simple! Let but the heavens open, swallowing these men and their aeroplanes – and then close again. Let him have his slaves once more, restored to life and well.

There was no one else with whom he had ever needed to treat or bargain.

He doubted only whether he had made his bribe big enough. God had His price, of course. God was made in man's image, so it had been said: He must have His price. And the price would be rare – no cathedral whose building consumed many years, no pyramid constructed by ten thousand workmen, would be like this cathedral, this pyramid.

He paused here. That was his proposition. Everything would be up to specifications and there was nothing vulgar in his assertion that it would be cheap at the price. He implied that Providence could take it or leave it.

As he approached the end his sentences became broken, became short and uncertain, and his body seemed tense, seemed strained to catch the slightest pressure or whisper of life in the spaces around him. His hair had turned gradually white as he talked, and now he lifted his head high to the heavens like a prophet of old – magnificently mad.

Then, as John stared in giddy fascination, it seemed to him that a curious phenomenon took place somewhere around him. It was as though the sky had darkened for an instant, as though there had been a sudden murmur in a gust of wind, a sound of far-away trumpets, a sighing like the rustle of a great silken robe – for a time the whole of nature round about partook of this darkness; the birds' song ceased; the trees were still, and far over the mountain there was a mutter of dull, menacing thunder.

That was all. The wind died along the tall grasses of the valley. The dawn and the day resumed their place in a time, and the risen sun sent hot waves of yellow mist that made its path bright before it. The leaves laughed in the sun, and their laughter shook the trees until each bough was like a girl's school in fairyland. God had refused to accept the bribe.

For another moment John watched the triumph of the day. Then, turning, he saw a flutter of brown down by the lake, then another flutter, then another, like the dance of golden angels alighting from the clouds. The aeroplanes had come to earth.

John slid off the boulder and ran down the side of the mountain to the clump of trees, where the two girls were awake and waiting for him. Kismine sprang to her feet, the jewels in her pockets jingling, a question on her parted lips, but instinct told John that there was no time for words. They must get off the mountain without losing a moment. He seized a hand of each, and in silence they threaded the tree-trunks, washed with light now and with the rising mist. Behind them from the valley came no sound at all, except the complaint of the peacocks far away and the pleasant undertone of morning.

When they had gone about half a mile, they avoided the park land and entered a narrow path that led over the next rise of ground. At the highest point of this they paused and turned around. Their eyes rested upon the mountainside they had just left – oppressed by some dark sense of tragic impendency.

Clear against the sky a broken, white-haired man was slowly descending the steep slope, followed by two gigantic and emotionless negroes, who carried a burden between them which still flashed and glittered in the sun. Half-way down two other figures joined them – John could see that they were Mrs Washington and her son, upon whose arm she leaned. The aviators had clambered from their machines to the sweeping lawn in front of the château, and with rifles in hand were starting up the diamond mountain in skirmishing formation.

But the little group of five which had formed farther up and was engrossing all the watchers' attention had stopped upon a ledge of rock. The negroes stooped and pulled up what appeared to be a trap-door in the side of the mountain. Into this they all disappeared, the white-haired man first, then his wife and son, finally the two negroes, the glittering tips of whose jeweled head-dresses caught the sun for a moment before the trap-door descended and engulfed them all.

Kismine clutched John's arm.

'Oh,' she cried wildly, 'where are they going? What are they going to do?'

'It must be some underground way of escape—'

A little scream from the two girls interrupted his sentence.

'Don't you see?' sobbed Kismine hysterically. 'The mountain is wired!'

Even as she spoke John put up his hands to shield his sight. Before their eyes the whole surface of the mountain had changed suddenly to a dazzling burning yellow, which showed up through the jacket of turf as light shows through a human hand. For a moment the intolerable glow continued, and then like an extinguished filament it disappeared, revealing a black waste from which blue smoke arose slowly, carrying off with it what remained of vegetation and of human flesh. Of the aviators there was left neither blood nor bone – they were consumed as completely as the five souls who had gone inside.

Simultaneously, and with an immense concussion, the château literally threw itself into the air, bursting into flaming fragments as it rose, and then tumbling back upon itself in a smoking pile that lay projecting half into the water of the lake. There was no fire – what smoke there was drifted off mingling with the sunshine, and for a few minutes longer a powdery dust of marble drifted from the great featureless pile that had once been the house of jewels. There was no more sound and the three people were alone in the valley.

11

At sunset John and his two companions reached the high cliff which had marked the boundaries of the Washingtons' dominion, and looking back found the valley tranquil and lovely in the dusk. They sat down to finish the food which Jasmine had brought with her in a basket.

'There!' she said, as she spread the table-cloth and put the sandwiches in a neat pile upon it. 'Don't they look tempting? I always think that food tastes better outdoors.'

'With that remark,' remarked Kismine, 'Jasmine enters the middle class.'

'Now,' said John eagerly, 'turn out your pocket and let's see what jewels you brought along. If you made a good selection we three ought to live comfortably all the rest of our lives.'

Obediently Kismine put her hand in her pocket and tossed two handfuls of glittering stones before him.

'Not so bad,' cried John, enthusiastically. 'They aren't very big, but – Hello!' His expression changed as he held one of them up to the declining sun. 'Why, these aren't diamonds! There's something the matter!'

'By golly!' exclaimed Kismine, with a startled look. 'What an idiot I am!'

'Why, these are rhinestones!' cried John.

'I know.' She broke into a laugh. 'I opened the wrong drawer. They belonged on the dress of a girl who visited Jasmine. I got her to give them to me in exchange for diamonds. I'd never seen anything but precious stones before.'

'And this is what you brought?'

'I'm afraid so.' She fingered the brilliants wistfully. 'I think I like these better. I'm a little tired of diamonds.'

'Very well,' said John gloomily. 'We'll have to live in Hades. And you will grow old telling incredulous women that you got the wrong drawer. Unfortunately your father's bank-books were consumed with him.'

'Well, what's the matter with Hades?'

'If I come home with a wife at my age my father is just as liable as not to cut me off with a hot coal, as they say down there.'

Jasmine spoke up.

'I love washing,' she said quietly. 'I have always washed my own handkerchiefs. I'll take in laundry and support you both.'

'Do they have washwomen in Hades?' asked Kismine innocently.

'Of course,' answered John. 'It's just like anywhere else.'

'I thought – perhaps it was too hot to wear any clothes.'

John laughed.

'Just try it!' he suggested. 'They'll run you out before you're half started.'

'Will father be there?' she asked.

John turned to her in astonishment.

'Your father is dead,' he replied somberly. 'Why should he go to Hades? You have it confused with another place that was abolished long ago.'

After supper they folded up the table-cloth and spread their blankets for the night.

'What a dream it was,' Kismine sighed, gazing up at the stars. 'How strange it seems to be here with one dress and a penniless fiancé!

'Under the stars,' she repeated. 'I never noticed the stars before. I always thought of them as great big diamonds that belonged to some one. Now they frighten me. They make me feel that it was all a dream, all my youth.'

'It *was* a dream,' said John quietly. 'Everybody's youth is a dream, a form of chemical madness.'

'How pleasant then to be insane!'

'So I'm told,' said John gloomily. 'I don't know any longer. At any rate, let us love for a while, for a year or so, you and me. That's a form of divine drunkenness that we can all try. There are only diamonds in the whole world, diamonds and perhaps the shabby gift of disillusion. Well, I have that last and I will make the usual nothing of it.' He shivered. 'Turn up your coat collar, little girl, the night's full of chill and you'll get pneumonia. His was a great sin who first invented consciousness. Let us lose it for a few hours.'

So wrapping himself in his blanket he fell off to sleep.

The Rich Boy
(1926)

Anson Hunter was based on Fitzgerald's school friend Ludlow Fowler:

> *I have written a fifteen thousand word story about you called 'The Rich Boy' – it is so disguised that no one except you and me and maybe two of the girls concerned would recognize, unless you give it away, but it is in a large measure the story of your life, toned down here and there and symplified. Also many gaps had to come out of my imagination. It is frank, unsparing but sympathetic and I think you will like it – it is one of the best things I have ever done.*

At Fowler's request two anecdotes about Hunter were cut from the magazine version when it was collected in All the Sad Young Men. *These passages have been restored in brackets here.*

His friend Ring Lardner's statement that 'The Rich Boy' should have been enlarged into a novel troubled Fitzgerald; and he explained to Maxwell Perkins that 'it would have been absolutely impossible for me to have stretched "The Rich Boy" into anything bigger than a novelette.'

Begin with an individual, and before you know it you find that you have created a type; begin with a type, and you find that you have created – nothing. That is because we are all queer fish, queerer behind our faces and voices than we want any one to know or than we know ourselves. When I hear a man proclaiming himself an 'average, honest, open fellow,' I feel pretty sure that he has some definite and perhaps terrible abnormality which he has agreed to conceal – and his protestation of being average and honest and open is his way of reminding himself of his misprision.

There are no types, no plurals. There is a rich boy, and this is his and not his brothers' story. All my life I have lived among his brothers but this one has been my friend. Besides, if I wrote about his brothers I should have to begin by attacking all the lies that the poor have told about the rich and the rich have told about themselves – such a wild structure they have erected that when we pick up a book about the rich, some instinct prepares us for unreality. Even the intelligent and impassioned reporters of life have made the country of the rich as unreal as fairy-land.

Let me tell you about the very rich. They are different from you and me. They possess and enjoy early, and it does something to them, makes them soft where we are hard, and cynical where we are trustful, in a way that, unless you were born rich, it is very difficult to understand. They think, deep in their hearts, that they are better than we are because we had to discover the compensations and refuges of life for ourselves. Even when they enter deep into our world or sink below us, they still think that they are better than we are. They are different. The only way I can describe young Anson Hunter is to approach him as if he were a foreigner and cling stubbornly to my point of view. If I accept his for a moment I am lost – I have nothing to show but a preposterous movie.

2

Anson was the eldest of six children who would some day divide a fortune of fifteen million dollars, and he reached the age of reason – is it seven? – at the beginning of the century when daring young women were already gliding along Fifth Avenue in electric 'mobiles.' In those days he and his brother had an English governess who spoke the language very clearly and crisply and well, so that the two boys grew to speak as she did – their words and sentences were all crisp and clear and not run together as ours are. They didn't talk exactly like English children but acquired an accent that is peculiar to fashionable people in the city of New York.

In the summer the six children were moved from the house on 71st Street to a big estate in northern Connecticut. It was not a fashionable locality – Anson's father wanted to delay as long as possible his children's knowledge of that side of life. He was a man somewhat superior to his class, which composed New York society, and to his period, which was the snobbish and formalized vulgarity of the Gilded Age, and he wanted his sons to learn habits of concentration and have sound constitutions and grow up into right-living and successful men. He and his wife kept an eye on them as well as they were able until the two older boys went away to school, but in huge establishments this is difficult – it was much simpler in the series of small and medium-sized houses in which my own youth was spent – I was never far out of the reach of my mother's voice, of the sense of her presence, her approval or disapproval.

Anson's first sense of his superiority came to him when he realized the half-grudging American deference that was paid to him in the Connecticut village. The parents of the boys he played with always inquired after his father and mother, and were vaguely excited when their own children were asked to the Hunters' house. He accepted this as the natural state of things, and a sort of impatience with all groups of which he was not the center – in money, in position, in authority – remained with him for the rest of his life. He disdained to struggle with other boys for precedence – he expected it to be given him freely, and when it wasn't he withdrew into his family. His family was sufficient, for in the East money is still a somewhat feudal thing, a clan-forming thing. In the snobbish West, money separates families to form 'sets.'

At eighteen, when he went to New Haven, Anson was tall and thick-set, with a clear complexion and a healthy color from the ordered life he had led in school. His hair was yellow and grew in a funny way on his head, his nose was beaked – these two things kept him from being handsome – but he had a confident charm and a certain brusque style, and the upper-class men who passed him on the street knew without being told that he was a rich boy and had gone to one of the best schools. Nevertheless, his very superiority kept him from being a success in college – the independence was mistaken for egotism, and the refusal to accept Yale standards with the proper awe seemed to belittle all those who had. So, long before he graduated, he began to shift the center of his life to New York.

He was at home in New York – there was his own house with 'the kind of servants you can't get any more' – and his own family, of which, because of his good humor and a certain ability to make things go, he was rapidly becoming the center, and the débutante parties, and the correct manly world of the men's clubs, and the occasional wild spree with the gallant girls whom New Haven only knew from the fifth row. His aspirations were conventional enough – they included even the irreproachable shadow he would some day marry, but they differed from the aspirations of the majority of young men in that there was no mist over them, none of that quality which is variously known as 'idealism' or 'illusion.' Anson accepted without reservation the world of high finance and high extravagance, of divorce and dissipation, of snobbery and of privilege. Most of our lives end as a compromise – it was as a compromise that his life began.

He and I first met in the late summer of 1917 when he was just out of Yale, and, like the rest of us, was swept up into the systematized hysteria of the war. In the blue-green uniform of the naval aviation he came down to Pensacola, where the hotel orchestras played 'I'm sorry, dear,' and we young officers danced with the girls. Every one liked him, and though he ran with the drinkers and wasn't an especially good pilot, even the instructors treated him with a certain respect. He was always having long talks with them in his confident, logical voice – talks which ended by his getting himself, or, more frequently, another officer, out of some impending trouble. He was convivial, bawdy, robustly avid for pleasure, and we were all surprised when he fell in love with a conservative and rather proper girl.

Her name was Paula Legendre, a dark, serious beauty from somewhere in California. Her family kept a winter residence just outside of town, and in spite of her primness she was enormously popular; there is a large class of men whose egotism can't endure humor in a woman. But Anson wasn't that sort, and I couldn't understand the attraction of her 'sincerity' – that was the thing to say about her – for his keen and somewhat sardonic mind.

Nevertheless, they fell in love – and on her terms. He no longer joined the twilight gathering at the De Sota bar, and whenever they were seen together they were engaged in a long, serious dialogue, which must have gone on several weeks. Long afterward he told me that it was not about anything in particular but was composed on both sides of immature and even meaningless statements – the emotional content that gradually came to fill it grew up not out of the words but out of its enormous seriousness. It was a sort of hypnosis. Often it was interrupted, giving way to that emasculated humor we call fun; when they were alone it was resumed again, solemn, low-keyed, and pitched so as to give each other a sense of unity in feeling and thought. They came to resent any interruptions of it, to be unresponsive to facetiousness about life, even to the mild cynicism of their contemporaries. They were only happy when the dialogue was going on, and its seriousness bathed them like the amber glow of an open fire. Toward the end there came an interruption they did not resent – it began to be interrupted by passion.

Oddly enough, Anson was as engrossed in the dialogue as she was and as profoundly affected by it, yet at the same time aware that on his side much was insincere, and on hers much was merely simple. At first, too, he despised her emotional simplicity as well, but with his love her nature deepened and blossomed, and he could despise it no longer. He felt that if he could enter into Paula's warm safe life he would be happy. The long preparation of the dialogue removed any constraint – he taught her some of what he had learned from more adventurous women, and she responded with a rapt holy intensity. One evening after a dance they agreed to marry, and he wrote a long letter about her to his mother. The next day Paula told him that she was rich, that she had a personal fortune of nearly a million dollars.

3

It was exactly as if they could say 'Neither of us has anything: we shall be poor together' – just as delightful that they should be rich instead. It gave them the same communion of adventure. Yet when Anson got leave in April, and Paula and her mother accompanied him North, she was impressed with the standing of his family in New York and with the scale on which they lived. Alone with Anson for the first time in the rooms where he had played as a boy, she was filled with a comfortable emotion, as though she were pre-eminently safe and taken care of. The pictures of Anson in a skull cap at his first school, of Anson on horseback with the sweetheart of a mysterious forgotten summer, of Anson in a gay group of ushers and bridesmaids at a wedding, made her jealous of his life apart from her in the past, and so completely did his authoritative person seem to sum up and typify these possessions of his that she was inspired with the idea of being married immediately and returning to Pensacola as his wife.

But an immediate marriage wasn't discussed – even the engagement was to be secret until after the war. When she realized that only two days of his leave remained, her dissatisfaction crystallized in the intention of making him as unwilling to wait as she was. They were driving to the country for dinner and she determined to force the issue that night.

Now a cousin of Paula's was staying with them at the Ritz, a severe, bitter girl who loved Paula but was somewhat jealous of her impressive engagement, and as Paula was late in dressing, the cousin, who wasn't going to the party, received Anson in the parlor of the suite.

Anson had met friends at five o'clock and drunk freely and indiscreetly with them for an hour. He left the Yale Club at a proper time, and his mother's chauffeur drove him to the Ritz, but his usual capacity was not in evidence, and the impact of the steam-heated sitting-room made him suddenly dizzy. He knew it, and he was both amused and sorry.

Paula's cousin was twenty-five, but she was exceptionally naïve, and at first failed to realize what was up. She had never met Anson before, and she was surprised when he mumbled strange information and nearly fell off his chair, but until Paula appeared it didn't occur to her that what she had taken for the odor of a dry-cleaned uniform was really whiskey. But Paula understood as soon as she appeared; her only thought was to get Anson away before her mother saw him, and at the look in her eyes the cousin understood too.

When Paula and Anson descended to the limousine they found two men inside, both asleep; they were the men with whom he had been drinking at the Yale Club, and they were also going to the party. He had entirely forgotten their presence in the car. On the way to Hempstead they awoke and sang. Some of the songs were rough, and though Paula tried to reconcile herself to the fact that Anson had few verbal inhibitions, her lips tightened with shame and distaste.

Back at the hotel the cousin, confused and agitated, considered the incident, and then walked into Mrs Legendre's bedroom, saying: 'Isn't he funny?'

'Who is funny?'

'Why – Mr Hunter. He seemed so funny.'

Mrs Legendre looked at her sharply.

'How is he funny?'

'Why, he said he was French. I didn't know he was French.'

'That's absurd. You must have misunderstood.' She smiled: 'It was a joke.'

The cousin shook her head stubbornly.

'No. He said he was brought up in France. He said he couldn't speak any English, and that's why he couldn't talk to me. And he couldn't!'

Mrs Legendre looked away with impatience just as the cousin added thoughtfully, 'Perhaps it was because he was so drunk,' and walked out of the room.

This curious report was true. Anson, finding his voice thick and uncontrollable, had taken the unusual refuge of announcing that he spoke no English. Years afterward he used to tell that part of the story, and he invariably communicated the uproarious laughter which the memory aroused in him.

Five times in the next hour Mrs Legendre tried to get Hempstead on the phone. When she succeeded, there was a ten-minute delay before she heard Paula's voice on the wire.

'Cousin Jo told me Anson was intoxicated.'

'Oh, no. . . .'

'Oh, yes. Cousin Jo says he was intoxicated. He told her he was French, and fell off his chair and behaved as if he was very intoxicated. I don't want you to come home with him.'

'Mother, he's all right! Please don't worry about—'

'But I do worry. I think it's dreadful. I want you to promise me not to come home with him.'

'I'll take care of it, mother. . . .'

'I don't want you to come home with him.'

'All right, mother. Good-by.'

'Be sure now, Paula. Ask some one to bring you.'

Deliberately Paula took the receiver from her ear and hung it up. Her face was flushed with helpless annoyance. Anson was stretched asleep out in a bedroom up-stairs, while the dinner-party below was proceeding lamely toward conclusion.

The hour's drive had sobered him somewhat – his arrival was merely hilarious – and Paula hoped that the evening was not spoiled, after all, but two imprudent cocktails before dinner completed the disaster. He talked boisterously and somewhat offensively to the party at large for fifteen minutes, and then slid silently under the table; like a man in an old print – but, unlike an old print, it was rather horrible without being at all quaint. None of the young girls present remarked upon the incident – it seemed to merit only silence. His uncle and two other men carried him up-stairs, and it was just after this that Paula was called to the phone.

An hour later Anson awoke in a fog of nervous agony, through which he perceived after a moment the figure of his uncle Robert standing by the door.

'. . . I said are you better?'

'What?'

'Do you feel better, old man?'

'Terrible,' said Anson.

'I'm going to try you on another bromo-seltzer. If you can hold it down, it'll do you good to sleep.'

With an effort Anson slid his legs from the bed and stood up.

'I'm all right,' he said dully.

'Take it easy.'

'I thin' if you gave me a glassbrandy I could go down-stairs.'

'Oh, no—'

'Yes, that's the only thin'. I'm all right now. . . . I suppose I'm in Dutch dow' there.'

'They know you're a little under the weather,' said his uncle deprecatingly. 'But don't worry about it. Schuyler didn't even get here. He passed away in the locker-room over at the Links.'

Indifferent to any opinion, except Paula's, Anson was nevertheless determined to save the débris of the evening, but when after a cold bath he made his appearance most of the party had already left. Paula got up immediately to go home.

In the limousine the old serious dialogue began. She had
known that he drank, she admitted, but she had never expected
anything like this – it seemed to her that perhaps they were not
suited to each other, after all. Their ideas about life were too
different, and so forth. When she finished speaking, Anson spoke
in turn, very soberly. Then Paula said she'd have to think it over;
she wouldn't decide to-night; she was not angry but she was
terribly sorry. Nor would she let him come into the hotel with
her, but just before she got out of the car she leaned and kissed
him unhappily on the cheek.

The next afternoon Anson had a long talk with Mrs Legendre
while Paula sat listening in silence. It was agreed that Paula was
to brood over the incident for a proper period and then, if mother
and daughter thought it best, they would follow Anson to
Pensacola. On his part he apologized with sincerity and dignity –
that was all; with every card in her hand Mrs Legendre was
unable to establish any advantage over him. He made no
promises, showed no humility, only delivered a few serious
comments on life which brought him off with rather a moral
superiority at the end. When they came South three weeks later,
neither Anson in his satisfaction nor Paula in her relief at the
reunion realized that the psychological moment had passed
forever.

4

He dominated and attracted her, and at the same time filled her
with anxiety. Confused by his mixture of solidity and self-
indulgence, of sentiment and cynicism – incongruities which her
gentle mind was unable to resolve – Paula grew to think of him
as two alternating personalities. When she saw him alone, or at a
formal party, or with his casual inferiors, she felt a tremendous
pride in his strong, attractive presence, the paternal, understanding stature of his mind. In other company she became uneasy
when what had been a fine imperviousness to mere gentility
showed its other face. The other face was gross, humorous,
reckless of everything but pleasure. It startled her mind temporarily away from him, even led her into a short covert experiment
with an old beau, but it was no use – after four months of

Anson's enveloping vitality there was an anæmic pallor in all other men.

In July he was ordered abroad, and their tenderness and desire reached a crescendo. Paula considered a last-minute marriage – decided against it only because there were always cocktails on his breath now, but the parting itself made her physically ill with grief. After his departure she wrote him long letters of regret for the days of love they had missed by waiting. In August Anson's plane slipped down into the North Sea. He was pulled onto a destroyer after a night in the water and sent to hospital with pneumonia; the armistice was signed before he was finally sent home.

Then, with every opportunity given back to them, with no material obstacle to overcome, the secret weavings of their temperaments came between them, drying up their kisses and their tears, making their voices less loud to one another, muffling the intimate chatter of their hearts until the old communication was only possible by letters, from far away. One afternoon a society reporter waited for two hours in the Hunters' house for a confirmation of their engagement. Anson denied it; nevertheless an early issue carried the report as a leading paragraph – they were 'constantly seen together at Southampton, Hot Springs, and Tuxedo Park.' But the serious dialogue had turned a corner into a long-sustained quarrel, and the affair was almost played out. Anson got drunk flagrantly and missed an engagement with her, whereupon Paula made certain behavioristic demands. His despair was helpless before his pride and his knowledge of himself: the engagement was definitely broken.

'Dearest,' said their letters now, 'Dearest, Dearest, when I wake up in the middle of the night and realize that after all it was not to be, I feel that I want to die. I can't go on living any more. Perhaps when we meet this summer we may talk things over and decide differently – we were so excited and sad that day, and I don't feel that I can live all my life without you. You speak of other people. Don't you know there are no other people for me, but only you. . . .'

But as Paula drifted here and there around the East she would sometimes mention her gaieties to make him wonder. Anson was too acute to wonder. When he saw a man's name in her letters

he felt more sure of her and a little disdainful – he was always
superior to such things. But he still hoped that they would some
day marry.

Meanwhile he plunged vigorously into all the movement and
glitter of post-bellum New York, entering a brokerage house,
joining half a dozen clubs, dancing late, and moving in three
worlds – his own world, the world of young Yale graduates, and
that section of the half-world which rests one end on Broadway.
But there was always a thorough and infractible eight hours
devoted to his work in Wall Street, where the combination of his
influential family connection, his sharp intelligence, and his
abundance of sheer physical energy brought him almost immediately forward. He had one of those invaluable minds with
partitions in it; sometimes he appeared at his office refreshed by
less than an hour's sleep, but such occurrences were rare. So
early as 1920 his income in salary and commissions exceeded
twelve thousand dollars.

As the Yale tradition slipped into the past he became more and
more of a popular figure among his classmates in New York,
more popular than he had ever been in college. He lived in a
great house, and had the means of introducing young men into
other great houses. Moreover, his life already seemed secure,
while theirs, for the most part, had arrived again at precarious
beginnings. They commenced to turn to him for amusement and
escape, and Anson responded readily, taking pleasure in helping
people and arranging their affairs.

There were no men in Paula's letters now, but a note of
tenderness ran through them that had not been there before.
From several sources he heard that she had 'a heavy beau,'
Lowell Thayer, a Bostonian of wealth and position, and though
he was sure she still loved him, it made him uneasy to think that
he might lose her, after all. Save for one unsatisfactory day she
had not been in New York for almost five months, and as the
rumors multiplied he became increasingly anxious to see her. In
February he took his vacation and went down to Florida.

Palm Beach sprawled plump and opulent between the spar-
kling sapphire of Lake Worth, flawed here and there by house-
boats at anchor, and the great turquoise bar of the Atlantic
Ocean. The huge bulks of the Breakers and the Royal Poinciana

rose as twin paunches from the bright level of the sand, and around them clustered the Dancing Glade, Bradley's House of Chance, and a dozen modistes and milliners with goods at triple prices from New York. Upon the trellissed veranda of the Breakers two hundred women stepped right, stepped left, wheeled, and slid in that then celebrated calisthenic known as the double-shuffle, while in half-time to the music two thousand bracelets clicked up and down on two hundred arms.

At the Everglades Club after dark Paula and Lowell Thayer and Anson and a casual fourth played bridge with hot cards. It seemed to Anson that her kind, serious face was wan and tired – she had been around now for four, five, years. He had known her for three.

'Two spades.'

'Cigarette?... Oh, I beg your pardon. By me.'

'By.'

'I'll double three spades.'

There were a dozen tables of bridge in the room, which was filling up with smoke. Anson's eyes met Paula's, held them persistently even when Thayer's glance fell between them....

'What was bid?' he asked abstractedly.

'Rose of Washington Square'

sang the young people in the corners:

> *'I'm withering there*
> *In basement air—'*

The smoke banked like fog, and the opening of a door filled the room with blown swirls of ectoplasm. Little Bright Eyes streaked past the tables seeking Mr Conan Doyle among the Englishmen who were posing as Englishmen about the lobby.

'You could cut it with a knife.'

'... cut it with a knife.'

'... a knife.'

At the end of the rubber Paula suddenly got up and spoke to Anson in a tense, low voice. With scarcely a glance at Lowell Thayer, they walked out the door and descended a long flight of stone steps – in a moment they were walking hand in hand along the moonlit beach.

'Darling, darling. . . .' They embraced recklessly, passionately, in a shadow. . . . Then Paula drew back her face to let his lips say what she wanted to hear – she could feel the words forming as they kissed again. . . . Again she broke away, listening, but as he pulled her close once more she realized that he had said nothing – only '*Darling! Darling!*' in that deep, sad whisper that always made her cry. Humbly, obediently, her emotions yielded to him and the tears streamed down her face, but her heart kept on crying: 'Ask me – oh, Anson, dearest, ask me!'

'Paula. . . . *Paula!*'

The words wrung her heart like hands, and Anson, feeling her tremble, knew that emotion was enough. He need say no more, commit their destinies to no practical enigma. Why should he, when he might hold her so, biding his own time, for another year – forever? He was considering them both, her more than himself. For a moment, when she said suddenly that she must go back to her hotel, he hesitated, thinking, first, 'This is the moment, after all,' and then: 'No, let it wait – she is mine. . . .'

He had forgotten that Paula too was worn away inside with the strain of three years. Her mood passed forever in the night.

He went back to New York next morning filled with a certain restless dissatisfaction. [There was a pretty débutante he knew in his car, and for two days they took their meals together. At first he told her a little about Paula and invented an esoteric incompatibility that was keeping them apart. The girl was of a wild, impulsive nature, and she was flattered by Anson's confidences. Like Kipling's soldier, he might have possessed himself of most of her before he reached New York, but luckily he was sober and kept control.] Late in April, without warning, he received a telegram from Bar Harbor in which Paula told him that she was engaged to Lowell Thayer, and that they would be married immediately in Boston. What he never really believed could happen had happened at last.

Anson filled himself with whiskey that morning, and going to the office, carried on his work without a break – rather with a fear of what would happen if he stopped. In the evening he went out as usual, saying nothing of what had occurred; he was cordial, humorous, unabstracted. But one thing he could not help

– for three days, in any place, in any company, he would suddenly bend his head into his hands and cry like a child.

5

In 1922 when Anson went abroad with the junior partner to investigate some London loans, the journey intimated that he was to be taken into the firm. He was twenty-seven now, a little heavy without being definitely stout, and with a manner older than his years. Old people and young people liked him and trusted him, and mothers felt safe when their daughters were in his charge, for he had a way, when he came into a room, of putting himself on a footing with the oldest and most conservative people there. 'You and I,' he seemed to say, 'we're solid. We understand.'

He had an instinctive and rather charitable knowledge of the weaknesses of men and women, and, like a priest, it made him the more concerned for the maintenance of outward forms. It was typical of him that every Sunday morning he taught in a fashionable Episcopal Sunday-school – even though a cold shower and a quick change into a cutaway coat were all that separated him from the wild night before. [Once, by some mutual instinct, several children got up from the front row and moved to the last. He told this story frequently, and it was usually greeted with hilarious laughter.]

After his father's death he was the practical head of his family, and, in effect, guided the destinies of the younger children. Through a complication his authority did not extend to his father's estate, which was administrated by his Uncle Robert, who was the horsey member of the family, a good-natured, hard-drinking member of that set which centers about Wheatley Hills.

Uncle Robert and his wife, Edna, had been great friends of Anson's youth, and the former was disappointed when his nephew's superiority failed to take a horsey form. He backed him for a city club which was the most difficult in America to enter – one could only join if one's family had 'helped to build up New York' (or, in other words, were rich before 1880) – and when Anson, after his election, neglected it for the Yale Club, Uncle Robert gave him a little talk on the subject. But when on top of that Anson declined to enter Robert Hunter's own conservative and somewhat neglected brokerage house, his manner grew cooler. Like a primary teacher who has taught all he knew, he slipped out of Anson's life.

There were so many friends in Anson's life – scarcely one for whom he had not done some unusual kindness and scarcely one whom he did not occasionally embarrass by his bursts of rough conversation or his habit of getting drunk whenever and however he liked. It annoyed him when any one else blundered in that regard – about his own lapses he was always humorous. Odd things happened to him and he told them with infectious laughter.

I was working in New York that spring, and I used to lunch with him at the Yale Club, which my university was sharing until the completion of our own. I had read of Paula's marriage, and one afternoon, when I asked him about her, something moved him to tell me the story. After that he frequently invited me to family dinners at his house and behaved as though there was a special relation between us, as though with his confidence a little of that consuming memory had passed into me.

I found that despite the trusting mothers, his attitude toward girls was not indiscriminately protective. It was up to the girl – if she showed an inclination toward looseness, she must take care of herself, even with him.

'Life,' he would explain sometimes, 'has made a cynic of me.'

By life he meant Paula. Sometimes, especially when he was drinking, it became a little twisted in his mind, and he thought that she had callously thrown him over.

This 'cynicism,' or rather his realization that naturally fast girls were not worth sparing, led to his affair with Dolly Karger. It wasn't his only affair in those years, but it came nearest to touching him deeply, and it had a profound effect upon his attitude toward life.

Dolly was the daughter of a notorious 'publicist' who had married into society. She herself grew up into the Junior League, came out at the Plaza, and went to the Assembly; and only a few old families like the Hunters could question whether or not she 'belonged,' for her picture was often in the papers, and she had more enviable attention than many girls who undoubtedly did.

She was dark-haired, with carmine lips and a high, lovely color, which she concealed under pinkish-gray powder all through the first year out, because high color was unfashionable – Victorian-pale was the thing to be. She wore black, severe suits and stood with her hands in her pockets leaning a little forward, with a humorous restraint on her face. She danced exquisitely – better than anything she liked to dance – better than anything except making love. Since she was ten she had always been in love, and, usually, with some boy who didn't respond to her. Those who did – and there were many – bored her after a brief encounter, but for her failures she reserved the warmest spot in her heart. When she met them she would always try once more – sometimes she succeeded, more often she failed.

It never occurred to this gypsy of the unattainable that there was a certain resemblance in those who refused to love her – they shared a hard intuition that saw through to her weakness, not a weakness of emotion but a weakness of rudder. Anson perceived this when he first met her, less than a month after Paula's marriage. He was drinking rather heavily, and he pretended for a week that he was falling in love with her. Then he dropped her abruptly and forgot – immediately he took up the commanding position in her heart.

Like so many girls of that day Dolly was slackly and indiscreetly wild. The unconventionality of a slightly older generation had been simply one facet of a post-war movement to discredit obsolete manners – Dolly's was both older and shabbier, and she saw in Anson the two extremes which the emotionally shiftless woman seeks, an abandon to indulgence alternating with a protective strength. In his character she felt both the sybarite and the solid rock, and these two satisfied every need of her nature.

She felt that it was going to be difficult, but she mistook the reason – she thought that Anson and his family expected a more spectacular marriage, but she guessed immediately that her advantage lay in his tendency to drink.

They met at the large débutante dances, but as her infatuation increased they managed to be more and more together. Like most mothers, Mrs Karger believed that Anson was exceptionally reliable, so she allowed Dolly to go with him to distant country clubs and suburban houses without inquiring closely into their activities or questioning her explanations when they came in late. At first these explanations might have been accurate, but Dolly's worldly ideas of capturing Anson were soon engulfed in the rising sweep of her emotion. Kisses in the back of taxis and motor-cars were no longer enough; they did a curious thing:

They dropped out of their world for a while and made another world just beneath it where Anson's tippling and Dolly's irregular hours would be less noticed and commented on. It was composed, this world, of varying elements – several of Anson's Yale friends and their wives, two or three young brokers and bond salesmen and a handful of unattached men, fresh from college, with money and a propensity to dissipation. What this world lacked in spaciousness and scale it made up for by allowing them a liberty that it scarcely permitted itself. Moreover, it centered around them and permitted Dolly the pleasure of a faint condescension – a pleasure which Anson, whose whole life was a condescension from the certitudes of his childhood, was unable to share.

He was not in love with her, and in the long feverish winter of their affair he frequently told her so. In the spring he was weary – he wanted to renew his life at some other source – moreover, he saw that either he must break with her now or accept the responsibility of a definite seduction. Her family's encouraging attitude precipitated his decision – one evening when Mr Karger knocked discreetly at the library door to announce that he had left a bottle of old brandy in the dining-room, Anson felt that life was hemming him in. That night he wrote her a short letter in which he told her that he was going on his vacation, and that in view of all the circumstances they had better meet no more.

It was June. His family had closed up the house and gone to the country, so he was living temporarily at the Yale Club. I had heard about his affair with Dolly as it developed – accounts salted with humor, for he despised unstable women, and granted them no place in the social edifice in which he believed – and when he told me that night that he was definitely breaking with her I was glad. I had seen Dolly here and there, and each time with a feeling of pity at the hopelessness of her struggle, and of shame at knowing so much about her that I had no right to know. She was what is known as 'a pretty little thing,' but there was a certain recklessness which rather fascinated me. Her dedication to the goddess of waste would have been less obvious had she been less spirited – she would most certainly throw herself away, but I was glad when I heard that the sacrifice would not be consummated in my sight.

Anson was going to leave the letter of farewell at her house next morning. It was one of the few houses left open in the Fifth Avenue district, and he knew that the Kargers, acting upon erroneous information from Dolly, had foregone a trip abroad to give their daughter her chance. As he stepped out the door of the Yale Club into Madison Avenue the postman passed him, and he followed back inside. The first letter that caught his eye was in Dolly's hand.

He knew what it would be – a lonely and tragic monologue, full of the reproaches he knew, the invoked memories, the 'I wonder if's' – all the immemorial intimacies that he had communicated to Paula Legendre in what seemed another age. Thumbing over some bills, he brought it on top again and opened it. To his surprise it was a short, somewhat formal note, which said that Dolly would be unable to go to the country with him for the weekend, because Perry Hull from Chicago had unexpectedly come to town. It added that Anson had brought this on himself: '– if I felt that you loved me as I love you I would go with you at any time, any place, but Perry is *so* nice, and he so much wants me to marry him–'

Anson smiled contemptuously – he had had experience with such decoy epistles. Moreover, he knew how Dolly had labored over this plan, probably sent for the faithful Perry and calculated the time of his arrival – even labored over the note so that it would make him jealous without driving him away. Like most compromises, it had neither force nor vitality but only a timorous despair.

Suddenly he was angry. He sat down in the lobby and read it again. Then he went to the phone, called Dolly and told her in his clear, compelling voice that he had received her note and would call for her at five o'clock as they had previously planned. Scarcely waiting for the pretended uncertainty of her 'Perhaps I can see you for an hour,' he hung up the receiver and went down to his office. On the way he tore his own letter into bits and dropped it in the street.

He was not jealous – she meant nothing to him – but at her pathetic ruse everything stubborn and self-indulgent in him came to the surface. It was a presumption from a mental inferior and it could not be overlooked. If she wanted to know to whom she belonged she would see.

He was on the door-step at quarter past five. Dolly was dressed for the street, and he listened in silence to the paragraph of 'I can only see you for an hour,' which she had begun on the phone.

'Put on your hat, Dolly,' he said, 'we'll take a walk.'

They strolled up Madison Avenue and over to Fifth while Anson's shirt dampened upon his portly body in the deep heat. He talked little, scolding her, making no love to her, but before they had walked six blocks she was his again, apologizing for the note, offering not to see Perry at all as an atonement, offering anything. She thought that he had come because he was beginning to love her.

'I'm hot,' he said when they reached 71st Street. 'This is a winter suit. If I stop by the house and change, would you mind waiting for me downstairs? I'll only be a minute.'

She was happy; the intimacy of his being hot, of any physical fact about him, thrilled her. When they came to the iron-grated door and Anson took out his key she experienced a sort of delight.

Down-stairs it was dark, and after he ascended in the lift Dolly raised a curtain and looked out through opaque lace at the houses over the way. She heard the lift machinery stop, and with the notion of teasing him pressed the button that brought it down. Then on what was more than an impulse she got into it and sent it up to what she guessed was his floor.

'Anson,' she called, laughing a little.

'Just a minute,' he answered from his bedroom . . . then after a brief delay: 'Now you can come in.'

He had changed and was buttoning his vest. 'This is my room,' he said lightly. 'How do you like it?'

She caught sight of Paula's picture on the wall and stared at it in fascination, just as Paula had stared at the pictures of Anson's childish sweethearts five years before. She knew something about

Paula – sometimes she tortured herself with fragments of the
story.

Suddenly she came close to Anson, raising her arms. They
embraced. Outside the area window a soft artificial twilight
already hovered, though the sun was still bright on a back roof
across the way. In half an hour the room would be quite dark.
The uncalculated opportunity overwhelmed them, made them
both breathless, and they clung more closely. It was eminent,
inevitable. Still holding one another, they raised their heads –
their eyes fell together upon Paula's picture, staring down at
them from the wall.

Suddenly Anson dropped his arms, and sitting down at his
desk tried the drawer with a bunch of keys.

'Like a drink?' he asked in a gruff voice.

'No, Anson.'

He poured himself half a tumbler of whiskey, swallowed it, and
then opened the door into the hall.

'Come on,' he said.

Dolly hesitated.

'Anson – I'm going to the country with you tonight, after all.
You understand that, don't you?'

'Of course,' he answered brusquely.

In Dolly's car they rode on to Long Island, closer in their
emotions than they had ever been before. They knew what would
happen – not with Paula's face to remind them that something
was lacking, but when they were alone in the still, hot Long
Island night they did not care.

The estate in Port Washington where they were to spend the
week-end belonged to a cousin of Anson's who had married a
Montana copper operator. An interminable drive began at the
lodge and twisted under imported poplar saplings toward a huge,
pink, Spanish house. Anson had often visited there before.

After dinner they danced at the Linx Club. About midnight
Anson assured himself that his cousins would not leave before
two – then he explained that Dolly was tired; he would take her
home and return to the dance later. Trembling a little with
excitement, they got into a borrowed car together and drove to
Port Washington. As they reached the lodge he stopped and
spoke to the night-watchman.

'When are you making a round, Carl?'

'Right away.'

'Then you'll be here till everybody's in?'

'Yes, sir.'

'All right. Listen: if any automobile, no matter whose it is, turns in at this gate, I want you to phone the house immediately.' He put a five-dollar bill into Carl's hand. 'Is that clear?'

'Yes, Mr Anson.' Being of the Old World, he neither winked nor smiled. Yet Dolly sat with her face turned slightly away.

Anson had a key. Once inside he poured a drink for both of them – Dolly left hers untouched – then he ascertained definitely the location of the phone, and found that it was within easy hearing distance of their rooms, both of which were on the first floor.

Five minutes later he knocked at the door of Dolly's room.

'Anson?' He went in, closing the door behind him. She was in bed leaning up anxiously with elbows on the pillow; sitting beside her he took her in his arms.

'Anson, darling.'

He didn't answer.

'Anson. . . . Anson! I love you. . . . Say you love me. Say it now – can't you say it now? Even if you don't mean it?'

He did not listen. Over her head he perceived that the picture of Paula was hanging here upon this wall.

He got up and went close to it. The frame gleamed faintly with thrice-reflected moonlight – within was a blurred shadow of a face that he saw he did not know. Almost sobbing, he turned around and stared with abomination at the little figure on the bed.

'This is all foolishness,' he said thickly. 'I don't know what I was thinking about. I don't love you and you'd better wait for somebody that loves you. I don't love you a bit, can't you understand?'

His voice broke, and he went hurriedly out. Back in the salon he was pouring himself a drink with uneasy fingers, when the front door opened suddenly, and his cousin came in.

'Why, Anson, I hear Dolly's sick,' she began solicitously. 'I hear she's sick. . . .'

'It was nothing,' he interrupted, raising his voice so that it would carry into Dolly's room. 'She was a little tired. She went to bed.'

For a long time afterward Anson believed that a protective God sometimes interfered in human affairs. But Dolly Karger, lying awake and staring at the ceiling, never again believed in anything at all.

6

When Dolly married during the following autumn, Anson was in London on business. Like Paula's marriage, it was sudden, but it affected him in a different way. At first he felt that it was funny, and had an inclination to laugh when he thought of it. Later it depressed him – it made him feel old.

There was something repetitive about it – why, Paula and Dolly had belonged to different generations. He had a foretaste of the sensation of a man of forty who hears that the daughter of an old flame has married. He wired congratulations and, as was not the case with Paula, they were sincere – he had never really hoped that Paula would be happy.

When he returned to New York, he was made a partner in the firm, and, as his responsibilities increased, he had less time on his hands. The refusal of a life-insurance company to issue him a policy made such an impression on him that he stopped drinking for a year, and claimed that he felt better physically, though I think he missed the convivial recounting of those Celliniesque adventures which, in his early twenties, had played such a part of his life. But he never abandoned the Yale Club. He was a figure there, a personality, and the tendency of his class, who were now seven years out of college, to drift away to more sober haunts was checked by his presence.

His day was never too full nor his mind too weary to give any sort of aid to any one who asked it. What had been done at first through pride and superiority had become a habit and a passion. And there was always something – a younger brother in trouble at New Haven, a quarrel to be patched up between a friend and his wife, a position to be found for this man, an investment for that. But his specialty was the solving of problems for young married people. Young married people fascinated him and their apartments were almost sacred to him – he knew the story of their love-affair, advised them where to live and how, and remembered their babies' names. Toward young wives his attitude was circumspect: he never abused the trust which their husbands – strangely enough in view of his unconcealed irregularities – invariably reposed in him.

He came to take a vicarious pleasure in happy marriages, and to be inspired to an almost equally pleasant melancholy by those that went astray. Not a season passed that he did not witness the collapse of an affair that perhaps he himself had fathered. When Paula was divorced and almost immediately remarried to another Bostonian, he talked about her to me all one afternoon. He would never love any one as he had loved Paula, but he insisted that he no longer cared.

'I'll never marry,' he came to say; 'I've seen too much of it, and I know a happy marriage is a very rare thing. Besides, I'm too old.'

But he did believe in marriage. Like all men who spring from a happy and successful marriage, he believed in it passionately – nothing he had seen would change his belief; his cynicism dissolved upon it like air. But he did really believe he was too old. At twenty-eight he began to accept with equanimity the prospect of marrying without romantic love; he resolutely chose a New York girl of his own class, pretty, intelligent, congenial, above reproach – and set about falling in love with her. The things he had said to Paula with sincerity, to other girls with grace, he could no longer say at all without smiling, or with the force necessary to convince.

'When I'm forty,' he told his friends, 'I'll be ripe. I'll fall for some chorus girl like the rest.'

Nevertheless, he persisted in his attempt. His mother wanted to see him married, and he could now well afford it – he had a seat on the Stock Exchange, and his earned income came to twenty-five thousand a year. The idea was agreeable: when his friends – he spent most of his time with the set he and Dolly had evolved – closed themselves in behind domestic doors at night, he no longer rejoiced in his freedom. He even wondered if he should have married Dolly. Not even Paula had loved him more, and he was learning the rarity, in a single life, of encountering true emotion.

Just as this mood began to creep over him a disquieting story reached his ear. His aunt Edna, a woman just this side of forty, was carrying on an open intrigue with a dissolute, hard-drinking young man named Cary Sloane. Every one knew of it except Anson's Uncle Robert, who for fifteen years had talked long in clubs and taken his wife for granted.

Anson heard the story again and again with increasing annoyance. Something of his old feeling for his uncle came back to him, a feeling that was more than personal, a reversion toward that family solidarity on which he had based his pride. His intuition singled out the essential point of the affair, which was that his uncle shouldn't be hurt. It was his first experiment in unsolicited meddling, but with his knowledge of Edna's character he felt that he could handle the matter better than a district judge or his uncle.

His uncle was in Hot Springs. Anson traced down the sources of the scandal so that there should be no possibility of mistake and then he called Edna and asked her to lunch with him at the Plaza next day. Something in his tone must have frightened her, for she was reluctant, but he insisted, putting off the date until she had no excuse for refusing.

She met him at the appointed time in the Plaza lobby, a lovely, faded, gray-eyed blonde in a coat of Russian sable. Five great rings, cold with diamonds and emeralds, sparkled on her slender hands. It occurred to Anson that it was his father's intelligence and not his uncle's that had earned the fur and the stones, the rich brilliance that buoyed up her passing beauty.

Though Edna scented his hostility, she was unprepared for the directness of his approach.

'Edna, I'm astonished at the way you've been acting,' he said in a strong, frank voice. 'At first I couldn't believe it.'

'Believe what?' she demanded sharply.

'You needn't pretend with me, Edna. I'm talking about Cary Sloane. Aside from any other consideration, I didn't think you could treat Uncle Robert—'

'Now look here, Anson –' she began angrily, but his peremptory voice broke through hers:

'– and your children in such a way. You've been married eighteen years, and you're old enough to know better.'

'You can't talk to me like that! You—'

'Yes, I can. Uncle Robert has always been my best friend.' He was tremendously moved. He felt a real distress about his uncle, about his three young cousins.

Edna stood up, leaving her crab-flake cocktail untasted.

'This is the silliest thing—'

'Very well, if you won't listen to me I'll go to Uncle Robert and tell him the whole story – he's bound to hear it sooner or later. And afterward I'll go to old Moses Sloane.'

Edna faltered back into her chair.

'Don't talk so loud,' she begged him. Her eyes blurred with tears. 'You have no idea how your voice carries. You might have chosen a less public place to make all these crazy accusations.'

He didn't answer.

'Oh, you never liked me, I know,' she went on. 'You're just taking advantage of some silly gossip to try and break up the only interesting friendship I've ever had. What did I ever do to make you hate me so?'

Still Anson waited. There would be the appeal to his chivalry, then to his pity, finally to his superior sophistication – when he had shouldered his way through all these there would be admissions, and he could come to grips with her. By being silent, by being impervious, by returning constantly to his main weapon, which was his own true emotion, he bullied her into frantic despair as the luncheon hour slipped away. At two o'clock she took out a mirror and a handkerchief, shined away the marks of her tears and powdered the slight hollows where they had lain. She had agreed to meet him at her own house at five.

When he arrived she was stretched on a chaise-longue which was covered with cretonne for the summer, and the tears he had called up at luncheon seemed still to be standing in her eyes. Then he was aware of Cary Sloane's dark anxious presence upon the cold hearth.

'What's this idea of yours?' broke out Sloane immediately. 'I understand you invited Edna to lunch and then threatened her on the basis of some cheap scandal.'

Anson sat down.

'I have no reason to think it's only scandal.'

'I hear you're going to take it to Robert Hunter, and to my father.'

Anson nodded.

'Either you break it off — or I will,' he said.

'What God damned business is it of yours, Hunter?'

'Don't lose your temper, Cary,' said Edna nervously. 'It's only a question of showing him how absurd—'

'For one thing, it's my name that's being handed around,' interrupted Anson. 'That's all that concerns you, Cary.'

'Edna isn't a member of your family.'

'She most certainly is!' His anger mounted. 'Why — she owes this house and the rings on her fingers to my father's brains. When Uncle Robert married her she didn't have a penny.'

They all looked at the rings as if they had a significant bearing on the situation. Edna made a gesture to take them from her hand.

'I guess they're not the only rings in the world,' said Sloane.

'Oh, this is absurd,' cried Edna. 'Anson, will you listen to me? I've found out how the silly story started. It was a maid I discharged who went right to the Chilicheffs — all these Russians pump things out of their servants and then put a false meaning on them.' She brought down her fist angrily on the table: 'And after Tom lent them the limousine for a whole month when we were South last winter—'

'Do you see?' demanded Sloane eagerly. 'This maid got hold of the wrong end of the thing. She knew that Edna and I were friends, and she carried it to the Chilicheffs. In Russia they assume that if a man and a woman—'

He enlarged the theme to a disquisition upon social relations in the Caucasus.

'If that's the case it better be explained to Uncle Robert,' said Anson dryly, 'so that when the rumors do reach him he'll know they're not true.'

Adopting the method he had followed with Edna at luncheon he let them explain it all away. He knew that they were guilty and that presently they would cross the line from explanation into justification and convict themselves more definitely than he could ever do. By seven they had taken the desperate step of telling him the truth — Robert Hunter's neglect, Edna's empty life,

the casual dalliance that had flamed up into passion – but like so
many true stories it had the misfortune of being old, and its
enfeebled body beat helplessly against the armor of Anson's will.
The threat to go to Sloane's father sealed their helplessness, for
the latter, a retired cotton broker out of Alabama, was a
notorious fundamentalist who controlled his son by a rigid
allowance and the promise that at his next vagary the allowance
would stop forever.

They dined at a small French restaurant, and the discussion
continued – at one time Sloane resorted to physical threats, a
little later they were both imploring him to give them time. But
Anson was obdurate. He saw that Edna was breaking up, and
that her spirit must not be refreshed by any renewal of their
passion.

At two o'clock in a small night-club on 53d Street, Edna's
nerves suddenly collapsed, and she cried to go home. Sloane had
been drinking heavily all evening, and he was faintly maudlin,
leaning on the table and weeping a little with his face in his
hands. Quickly Anson gave them his terms. Sloane was to leave
town for six months, and he must be gone within forty-eight
hours. When he returned there was to be no resumption of the
affair, but at the end of a year Edna might, if she wished, tell
Robert Hunter that she wanted a divorce and go about it in the
usual way.

He paused, gaining confidence from their faces for his final
word.

'Or there's another thing you can do,' he said slowly. 'If Edna
wants to leave her children, there's nothing I can do to prevent
your running off together.'

'I want to go home!' cried Edna again. 'Oh, haven't you done
enough to us for one day?'

Outside it was dark, save for a blurred glow from Sixth Avenue
down the street. In that light those two who had been lovers
looked for the last time into each other's tragic faces, realizing
that between them there was not enough youth and strength to
avert their eternal parting. Sloane walked suddenly off down the
street and Anson tapped a dozing taxi-driver on the arm.

It was almost four; there was a patient flow of cleaning water
along the ghostly pavement of Fifth Avenue, and the shadows of

two night women flitted over the dark façade of St Thomas's church. Then the desolate shrubbery of Central Park where Anson had often played as a child, and the mounting numbers, significant as names, of the marching streets. This was his city, he thought, where his name had flourished through five generations. No change could alter the permanence of its place here, for change itself was the essential substratum by which he and those of his name identified themselves with the spirit of New York. Resourcefulness and a powerful will – for his threats in weaker hands would have been less than nothing – had beaten the gathering dust from his uncle's name, from the name of his family, from even this shivering figure that sat beside him in the car.

Cary Sloane's body was found next morning on the lower shelf of a pillar of Queensboro Bridge. In the darkness and in his excitement he had thought that it was the water flowing black beneath him, but in less than a second it made no possible difference – unless he had planned to think one last thought of Edna, and call out her name as he struggled feebly in the water.

7

Anson never blamed himself for his part in this affair – the situation which brought it about had not been of his making. But the just suffer with the unjust, and he found that his oldest and somehow his most precious friendship was over. He never knew what distorted story Edna told, but he was welcome in his uncle's house no longer.

Just before Christmas Mrs Hunter retired to a select Episcopal heaven, and Anson became the responsible head of his family. An unmarried aunt who had lived with them for years ran the house, and attempted with helpless inefficiency to chaperone the younger girls. All the children were less self-reliant than Anson, more conventional both in their virtues and in their shortcomings. Mrs Hunter's death had postponed the début of one daughter and the wedding of another. Also it had taken something deeply material from all of them, for with her passing the quiet, expensive superiority of the Hunters came to an end.

For one thing, the estate, considerably diminished by two

inheritance taxes and soon to be divided among six children, was not a notable fortune any more. Anson saw a tendency in his youngest sisters to speak rather respectfully of families that hadn't 'existed' twenty years ago. His own feeling of precedence was not echoed in them – sometimes they were conventionally snobbish, that was all. For another thing, this was the last summer they would spend on the Connecticut estate; the clamor against it was too loud: 'Who wants to waste the best months of the year shut up in that dead old town?' Reluctantly he yielded – the house would go into the market in the fall, and next summer they would rent a smaller place in Westchester County. It was a step down from the expensive simplicity of his father's idea, and, while he sympathized with the revolt, it also annoyed him; during his mother's lifetime he had gone up there at least every other week-end – even in the gayest summers.

Yet he himself was part of this change, and his strong instinct for life had turned him in his twenties from the hollow obsequies of that abortive leisure class. He did not see this clearly – he still felt that there was a norm, a standard of society. But there was no norm; it was doubtful if there had ever been a true norm in New York. The few who still paid and fought to enter a particular set succeeded only to find that as a society it scarcely functioned – or, what was more alarming, that the Bohemia from which they fled sat above them at table.

At twenty-nine Anson's chief concern was his own growing loneliness. He was sure now that he would never marry. The number of weddings at which he had officiated as best man or usher was past all counting – there was a drawer at home that bulged with the official neckties of this or that wedding-party, neckties standing for romances that had not endured a year, for couples who had passed completely from his life. Scarf-pins, gold pencils, cuff-buttons, presents from a generation of grooms had passed through his jewel-box and been lost – and with every ceremony he was less and less able to imagine himself in the groom's place. Under his hearty good-will toward all those marriages there was despair about his own.

And as he neared thirty he became not a little depressed at the inroads that marriage, especially lately, had made upon his friendships. Groups of people had a disconcerting tendency to dissolve and disappear. The men from his own college – and it was upon them he had expended the most time and affection – were the most elusive of all. Most of them were drawn deep into domesticity, two were dead, one lived abroad, one was in Hollywood writing continuities for pictures that Anson went faithfully to see.

Most of them, however, were permanent commuters with an intricate family life centering around some suburban country club, and it was from these that he felt his estrangement most keenly.

In the early days of their married life they had all needed him; he gave them advice about their slim finances, he exorcised their doubts about the advisability of bringing a baby into two rooms and a bath, especially he stood for the great world outside. But now their financial troubles were in the past and the fearfully expected child had evolved into an absorbing family. They were always glad to see old Anson, but they dressed up for him and tried to impress him with their present importance, and kept their troubles to themselves. They needed him no longer.

A few weeks before his thirtieth birthday the last of his early and intimate friends was married. Anson acted in his usual rôle of best man, gave his usual silver tea-service, and went down to the usual *Homeric* to say good-by. It was a hot Friday afternoon in May, and as he walked from the pier he realized that Saturday closing had begun and he was free until Monday morning.

'Go where?' he asked himself.

The Yale Club, of course; bridge until dinner, then four or five raw cocktails in somebody's room and a pleasant confused evening. He regretted that this afternoon's groom wouldn't be along – they had always been able to cram so much into such nights: they knew how to attach women and how to get rid of them, how much consideration any girl deserved from their intelligent hedonism. A party was an adjusted thing – you took certain girls to certain places and spent just so much on their amusement; you drank a little, not much, more than you ought to drink, and at a certain time in the morning you stood up and said you were going home. You avoided college boys, sponges, future engagements, fights, sentiment, and indiscretions. That was the way it was done. All the rest was dissipation.

In the morning you were never violently sorry – you made no resolutions, but if you had overdone it and your heart was slightly out of order, you went on the wagon for a few days without saying anything about it, and waited until an accumulation of nervous boredom projected you into another party.

The lobby of the Yale Club was unpopulated. In the bar three very young alumni looked up at him, momentarily and without curiosity.

'Hello there, Oscar,' he said to the bartender. 'Mr Cahill been around this afternoon?'

'Mr Cahill's gone to New Haven.'

'Oh . . . that so?'

'Gone to the ball game. Lot of men gone up.'

Anson looked once again into the lobby, considered for a moment, and then walked out and over to Fifth Avenue. From the broad window of one of his clubs – one that he had scarcely visited in five years – a gray man with watery eyes stared down at him. Anson looked quickly away – that figure sitting in vacant resignation, in supercilious solitude, depressed him. He stopped and, retracing his steps, started over 47th Street toward Teak Warden's apartment. Teak and his wife had once been his most familiar friends – it was a household where he and Dolly Karger had been used to go in the days of their affair. But Teak had taken to drink, and his wife had remarked publicly that Anson was a bad influence on him. The remark reached Anson in an exaggerated form – when it was finally cleared up, the delicate spell of intimacy was broken, never to be renewed.

'Is Mr Warden at home?' he inquired.

'They've gone to the country.'

The fact unexpectedly cut at him. They were gone to the country and he hadn't known. Two years before he would have known the date, the hour, come up at the last moment for a final drink, and planned his first visit to them. Now they had gone without a word.

Anson looked at his watch and considered a week-end with his family, but the only train was a local that would jolt through the aggressive heat for three hours. And to-morrow in the country, and Sunday – he was in no mood for porch-bridge with polite undergraduates, and dancing after dinner at a rural roadhouse, a diminutive of gaiety which his father had estimated too well.

'Oh, no,' he said to himself. . . . 'No.'

He was a dignified, impressive young man, rather stout now, but otherwise unmarked by dissipation. He could have been cast for a pillar of something – at times you were sure it was not society, at others nothing else – for the law, for the church. He stood for a few minutes motionless on the sidewalk in front of a 47th Street apartment-house; for almost the first time in his life he had nothing whatever to do.

Then he began to walk briskly up Fifth Avenue, as if he had just been reminded of an important engagement there. The necessity of dissimulation is one of the few characteristics that we share with dogs, and I think of Anson on that day as some well-bred specimen who had been disappointed at a familiar back door. He was going to see Nick, once a fashionable bartender in demand at all private dances, and now employed in cooling non-alcoholic champagne among the labyrinthine cellars of the Plaza Hotel.

'Nick,' he said, 'what's happened to everything?'

'Dead,' Nick said.

'Make me a whiskey sour.' Anson handed a pint bottle over the counter. 'Nick, the girls are different; I had a little girl in Brooklyn and she got married last week without letting me know.'

'That a fact? Ha-ha-ha,' responded Nick diplomatically. 'Slipped it over on you.'

'Absolutely,' said Anson. 'And I was out with her the night before.'

'Ha-ha-ha,' said Nick, 'ha-ha-ha!'

'Do you remember the wedding, Nick, in Hot Springs where I had the waiters and the musicians singing "God save the King"?'

'Now where was that, Mr Hunter?' Nick concentrated doubtfully. 'Seems to me that was—'

'Next time they were back for more, and I began to wonder how much I'd paid them,' continued Anson.

'– seems to me that was at Mr Trenholm's wedding.'

'Don't know him,' said Anson decisively. He was offended that a strange name should intrude upon his reminiscences; Nick perceived this.

'Naw – aw –' he admitted, 'I ought to know that. It was one of *your* crowd – Brakins. . . . Baker—'

'Bicker Baker,' said Anson responsively. 'They put me in a hearse after it was over and covered me up with flowers and drove me away.'

'Ha-ha-ha,' said Nick. 'Ha-ha-ha.'

Nick's simulation of the old family servant paled presently and Anson went up-stairs to the lobby. He looked around – his eyes met the glance of an unfamiliar clerk at the desk, then fell upon a flower from the morning's marriage hesitating in the mouth of a brass cuspidor. He went out and walked slowly toward the blood-red sun over Columbus Circle. Suddenly he turned around and, retracing his steps to the Plaza, immured himself in a telephone-booth.

Later he said that he tried to get me three times that afternoon, that he tried every one who might be in New York – men and girls he had not seen for years, an artist's model of his college days whose faded number was still in his address book – Central told him that even the exchange existed no longer. At length his quest roved into the country, and he held brief disappointing conversations with emphatic butlers and maids. So-and-so was out, riding, swimming, playing golf, sailed to Europe last week. Who shall I say phoned?

It was intolerable that he should pass the evening alone – the private reckonings which one plans for a moment of leisure lose every charm when the solitude is enforced. There were always women of a sort, but the ones he knew had temporarily vanished, and to pass a New York evening in the hired company of a stranger never occurred to him – he would have considered that that was something shameful and secret, the diversion of a travelling salesman in a strange town.

Anson paid the telephone bill – the girl tried unsuccessfully to joke with him about its size – and for the second time that afternoon started to leave the Plaza and go he knew not where. Near the revolving door the figure of a woman, obviously with child, stood sideways to the light – a sheer beige cape fluttered at her shoulders when the door turned and, each time, she looked impatiently toward it as if she were weary of waiting. At the first sight of her a strong nervous thrill of familiarity went over him, but not until he was within five feet of her did he realize that it was Paula.

'Why, Anson Hunter!'

His heart turned over.

'Why, Paula—'

'Why, this is wonderful. I can't believe it, *Anson!*'

She took both his hands, and he saw in the freedom of the gesture that the memory of him had lost poignancy to her. But not to him – he felt that old mood that she evoked in him stealing over his brain, that gentleness with which he had always met her optimism as if afraid to mar its surface.

'We're at Rye for the summer. Pete had to come East on business – you know of course I'm Mrs Peter Hagerty now – so we brought the children and took a house. You've got to come out and see us.'

'Can I?' he asked directly. 'When?'

'When you like. Here's Pete.' The revolving door functioned, giving up a fine tall man of thirty with a tanned face and a trim mustache. His immaculate fitness made a sharp contrast with Anson's increasing bulk, which was obvious under the faintly tight cut-away coat.

'You oughtn't to be standing,' said Hagerty to his wife. 'Let's sit down here.' He indicated lobby chairs, but Paula hesitated.

'I've got to go right home,' she said. 'Anson, why don't you – why don't you come out and have dinner with us to-night? We're just getting settled, but if you can stand that—'

Hagerty confirmed the invitation cordially.

'Come out for the night.'

Their car waited in front of the hotel, and Paula with a tired gesture sank back against silk cushions in the corner.

'There's so much I want to talk to you about,' she said, 'it seems hopeless.'

'I want to hear about you.'

'Well' – she smiled at Hagerty – 'that would take a long time too. I have three children – by my first marriage. The oldest is five, then four, then three.' She smiled again. 'I didn't waste much time having them, did I?'

'Boys?'

'A boy and two girls. Then – oh, a lot of things happened, and I got a divorce in Paris a year ago and married Pete. That's all – except that I'm awfully happy.'

In Rye they drove up to a large house near the Beach Club, from which there issued presently three dark, slim children who broke from an English governess and approached them with an esoteric cry. Abstractedly and with difficulty Paula took each one into her arms, a caress which they accepted stiffly, as they had evidently been told not to bump into Mummy. Even against their fresh faces Paula's skin showed scarcely any weariness – for all her physical languor she seemed younger than when he had last seen her at Palm Beach seven years ago.

At dinner she was preoccupied, and afterward, during the homage to the radio, she lay with closed eyes on the sofa, until Anson wondered if his presence at this time were not an intrusion. But at nine o'clock, when Hagerty rose and said pleasantly that he was going to leave them by themselves for a while, she began to talk slowly about herself and the past.

'My first baby,' she said – 'the one we call Darling, the biggest little girl – I wanted to die when I knew I was going to have her, because Lowell was like a stranger to me. It didn't seem as though she could be my own. I wrote you a letter and tore it up. Oh, you were *so* bad to me, Anson.'

It was the dialogue again, rising and falling. Anson felt a sudden quickening of memory.

'Weren't you engaged once?' she asked – 'a girl named Dolly something?'

'I wasn't ever engaged. I tried to be engaged, but I never loved anybody but you, Paula.'

'Oh,' she said. Then after a moment: 'This baby is the first one I ever really wanted. You see, I'm in love now – at last.'

He didn't answer, shocked at the treachery of her remembrance. She must have seen that the 'at last' bruised him, for she continued:

'I was infatuated with you, Anson – you could make me do anything you liked. But we wouldn't have been happy. I'm not smart enough for you. I don't like things to be complicated like you do.' She paused. 'You'll never settle down,' she said.

The phrase struck at him from behind – it was an accusation that of all accusations he had never merited.

'I could settle down if women were different,' he said. 'If I didn't understand so much about them, if women didn't spoil you for other women, if they had only a little pride. If I could go to sleep for a while and wake up into a home that was really mine – why, that's what I'm made for, Paula, that's what women have seen in me and liked in me. It's only that I can't get through the preliminaries any more.'

Hagerty came in a little before eleven; after a whiskey Paula stood up and announced that she was going to bed. She went over and stood by her husband.

'Where did you go, dearest?' she demanded.

'I had a drink with Ed Saunders.'

'I was worried. I thought maybe you'd run away.'

She rested her head against his coat.

'He's sweet, isn't he, Anson?' she demanded.

'Absolutely,' said Anson, laughing.

She raised her face to her husband.

'Well, I'm ready,' she said. She turned to Anson: 'Do you want to see our family gymnastic stunt?'

'Yes,' he said in an interested voice.

'All right. Here we go!'

Hagerty picked her up easily in his arms.

'This is called the family acrobatic stunt,' said Paula. 'He carries me up-stairs. Isn't it sweet of him?'

'Yes,' said Anson.

Hagerty bent his head slightly until his face touched Paula's.

'And I love him,' she said. 'I've just been telling you, haven't I, Anson?'

'Yes,' he said.

'He's the dearest thing that ever lived in this world; aren't you, darling? . . . Well, good night. Here we go. Isn't he strong?'

'Yes,' Anson said.

'You'll find a pair of Pete's pajamas laid out for you. Sweet dreams – see you at breakfast.'

'Yes,' Anson said.

8

The older members of the firm insisted that Anson should go abroad for the summer. He had scarcely had a vacation in seven years, they said. He was stale and needed a change. Anson resisted.

'If I go,' he declared, 'I won't come back any more.'

'That's absurd, old man. You'll be back in three months with all this depression gone. Fit as ever.'

'No.' He shook his head stubbornly. 'If I stop, I won't go back to work. If I stop, that means I've given up – I'm through.'

'We'll take a chance on that. Stay six months if you like – we're not afraid you'll leave us. Why, you'd be miserable if you didn't work.'

They arranged his passage for him. They liked Anson – every one liked Anson – and the change that had been coming over him cast a sort of pall over the office. The enthusiasm that had invariably signalled up business, the consideration toward his equals and his inferiors, the lift of his vital presence – within the past four months his intense nervousness had melted down these qualities into the fussy pessimism of a man of forty. On every transaction in which he was involved he ached as a drag and a strain.

'If I go I'll never come back,' he said.

Three days before he sailed Paula Legendre Hagerty died in childbirth. I was with him a great deal then, for we were crossing together, but for the first time in our friendship he told me not a word of how he felt, nor did I see the slightest sign of emotion. His chief preoccupation was with the fact that he was thirty years old – he would turn the conversation to the point where he could remind you of it and then fall silent, as if he assumed that the statement would start a chain of thought sufficient to itself. Like his partners, I was amazed at the change in him, and I was glad when the *Paris* moved off into the wet space between the worlds, leaving his principality behind.

'How about a drink?' he suggested.

We walked into the bar with that defiant feeling that characterizes the day of departure and ordered four Martinis. After one cocktail a change came over him – he suddenly

reached across and slapped my knee with the first joviality I had
seen him exhibit for months.

'Did you see that girl in the red tam?' he demanded, 'the one
with the high color who had the two police dogs down to bid her
good-by.'

'She's pretty,' I agreed.

'I looked her up in the purser's office and found out that she's
alone. I'm going down to see the steward in a few minutes. We'll
have dinner with her to-night.'

After a while he left me, and within an hour he was walking
up and down the deck with her, talking to her in his strong, clear
voice. Her red tam was a bright spot of color against the steel-
green sea, and from time to time she looked up with a flashing
bob of her head, and smiled with amusement and interest, and
anticipation. At dinner we had champagne, and were very
joyous – afterward Anson ran the pool with infectious gusto, and
several people who had seen me with him asked me his name. He
and the girl were talking and laughing together on a lounge in
the bar when I went to bed.

I saw less of him on the trip than I had hoped. He wanted to
arrange a foursome, but there was no one available, so I saw him
only at meals. Sometimes, though, he would have a cocktail in
the bar, and he told me about the girl in the red tam, and his
adventures with her, making them all bizarre and amusing, as he
had a way of doing, and I was glad that he was himself again, or
at least the self that I knew, and with which I felt at home. I don't
think he was ever happy unless some one was in love with him,
responding to him like filings to a magnet, helping him to explain
himself, promising him something. What it was I do not know.
Perhaps they promised that there would always be women in the
world who would spend their brightest, freshest, rarest hours to
nurse and protect that superiority he cherished in his heart.

A Short Trip Home
(1927)

I was near her, for I had lingered behind in order to get the short walk with her from the living room to the front door. That was a lot, for she had flowered suddenly and I, being a man and only a year older, hadn't flowered at all, had scarcely dared to come near her in the week we'd been home. Nor was I going to say anything in that walk of ten feet, or touch her; but I had a vague hope she'd do something, give a gay little performance of some sort, personal only in so far as we were alone together.

She had bewitchment suddenly in the twinkle of short hairs on her neck, in the sure, clear confidence that at about eighteen begins to deepen and sing in attractive American girls. The lamp light shopped in the yellow strands of her hair.

Already she was sliding into another world – the world of Joe Jelke and Jim Cathcart waiting for us now in the car. In another year she would pass beyond me forever.

As I waited, feeling the others outside in the snowy night, feeling the excitement of Christmas week and the excitement of Ellen here, blooming away, filling the room with 'sex appeal' – a wretched phrase to express a quality that isn't like that at all – a maid came in from the dining room, spoke to Ellen quietly and handed her a note. Ellen read it and her eyes faded down, as when the current grows weak on rural circuits, and smouldered off into space. Then she gave me an odd look – in which I probably didn't show – and without a word, followed the maid into the dining room and beyond. I sat turning over the pages of a magazine for a quarter of an hour.

Author's Note: In a moment of hasty misjudgment a whole paragraph of description was lifted out of this tale where it originated, and properly belongs, and applied to quite a different character in a novel of mine. I have ventured nonetheless to leave it here, even at the risk of seeming to serve warmed-over fare.

Editor's Note: Fitzgerald's note above refers to the paragraph on p. 160 beginning 'Vaguely', which was used in *Tender Is the Night* (Book I, Chapter 21).

Joe Jelke came in, red-faced from the cold, his white silk muffler gleaming at the neck of his fur coat. He was a senior at New Haven, I was a sophomore. He was prominent, a member of Scroll and Keys, and, in my eyes, very distinguished and handsome.

'Isn't Ellen coming?'

'I don't know,' I answered discreetly. 'She was all ready.'

'Ellen!' he called. 'Ellen!'

He had left the front door open behind him and a great cloud of frosty air rolled in from outside. He went halfway up the stairs – he was a familiar in the house – and called again, till Mrs Baker came to the banister and said that Ellen was below. Then the maid, a little excited, appeared in the dining-room door.

'Mr Jelke,' she called in a low voice.

Joe's face fell as he turned toward her, sensing bad news.

'Miss Ellen says for you to go on to the party. She'll come later.'

'What's the matter?'

'She can't come now. She'll come later.'

He hesitated, confused. It was the last big dance of vacation, and he was mad about Ellen. He had tried to give her a ring for Christmas, and failing that, got her to accept a gold mesh bag that must have cost two hundred dollars. He wasn't the only one – there were three or four in the same wild condition, and all in the ten days she'd been home – but his chance came first, for he was rich and gracious and at that moment the 'desirable' boy of St Paul. To me it seemed impossible that she could prefer another, but the rumor was she'd described Joe as much too perfect. I suppose he lacked mystery for her, and when a man is up against that with a young girl who isn't thinking of the practical side of marriage yet – well –.

'She's in the kitchen,' Joe said angrily.

'No, she's not.' The maid was defiant and a little scared.

'She is.'

'She went out the back way, Mr Jelke.'

'I'm going to see.'

I followed him. The Swedish servants washing dishes looked up sideways at our approach and an interested crashing of pans marked our passage through. The storm door, unbolted, was flapping in the wind and as we walked out into the snowy yard we saw the tail light of a car turn the corner at the end of the back alley.

'I'm going after her,' Joe said slowly. 'I don't understand this at all.'

I was too awed by the calamity to argue. We hurried to his car and drove in a fruitless, despairing zigzag all over the residence section, peering into every machine on the streets. It was half an hour before the futility of the affair began to dawn upon him – St Paul is a city of almost three hundred thousand people – and Jim Cathcart reminded him that we had another girl to stop for. Like a wounded animal he sank into a melancholy mass of fur in the corner, from which position he jerked upright every few minutes and waved himself backward and forward a little in protest and despair.

Jim's girl was ready and impatient, but after what had happened her impatience didn't seem important. She looked lovely though. That's one thing about Christmas vacation – the excitement of growth and change and adventure in foreign parts transforming the people you've known all your life. Joe Jelke was polite to her in a daze – he indulged in one burst of short, loud, harsh laughter by way of conversation – and we drove to the hotel.

The chauffeur approached it on the wrong side – the side on which the line of cars was not putting forth guests – and because of that we came suddenly upon Ellen Baker just getting out of a small coupé. Even before we came to a stop, Joe Jelke had jumped excitedly from the car.

Ellen turned toward us, a faintly distracted look – perhaps of surprise, but certainly not of alarm – in her face; in fact, she didn't seem very aware of us. Joe approached her with a stern, dignified, injured and, I thought, just exactly correct reproof in his expression. I followed.

Seated in the coupé – he had not dismounted to help Ellen out – was a hard thin-faced man of about thirty-five with an air of being scarred, and a slight sinister smile. His eyes were a sort of taunt to the whole human family – they were the eyes of an animal, sleepy and quiescent in the presence of another species. They were helpless yet brutal, unhopeful yet confident. It was as if they felt themselves powerless to originate activity, but infinitely capable of profiting by a single gesture of weakness in another.

Vaguely I placed him as one of the sort of men whom I had been conscious of from my earliest youth as 'hanging around' – leaning with one elbow on the counters of tobacco stores, watching, through heaven knows what small chink of the mind, the people who hurried in and out. Intimate to garages, where he had vague business conducted in undertones, to barber shops and to the lobbies of theatres – in such places, anyhow, I placed the type, if type it was, that he reminded me of. Sometimes his face bobbed up in one of Tad's more savage cartoons, and I had always from earliest boyhood thrown a nervous glance toward the dim borderland where he stood, and seen him watching me and despising me. Once, in a dream, he had taken a few steps toward me, jerking his head back and muttering: 'Say, kid' in what was intended to be a reassuring voice, and I had broken for the door in terror. This was that sort of man.

Joe and Ellen faced each other silently; she seemed, as I have said, to be in a daze. It was cold, but she didn't notice that her coat had blown open; Joe reached out and pulled it together, and automatically she clutched it with her hand.

Suddenly the man in the coupé, who had been watching them silently, laughed. It was a bare laugh, done with the breath – just a noisy jerk of the head – but it was an insult if I had ever heard one; definite and not to be passed over. I wasn't surprised when Joe, who was quick tempered, turned to him angrily and said:

'What's your trouble?'

The man waited a moment, his eyes shifting and yet staring, and always seeing. Then he laughed again in the same way. Ellen stirred uneasily.

'Who is this – this –' Joe's voice trembled with annoyance.

'Look out now,' said the man slowly.

Joe turned to me.

'Eddie, take Ellen and Catherine in, will you?' he said quickly. . . . 'Ellen, go with Eddie.'

'Look out now,' the man repeated.

Ellen made a little sound with her tongue and teeth, but she didn't resist when I took her arm and moved her toward the side door of the hotel. It struck me as odd that she should be so helpless, even to the point of acquiescing by her silence in this imminent trouble.

'Let it go, Joe!' I called back over my shoulder. 'Come inside!'

Ellen, pulling against my arm, hurried us on. As we were caught up into the swinging doors I had the impression that the man was getting out of his coupé.

Ten minutes later, as I waited for the girls outside the women's dressing-room, Joe Jelke and Jim Cathcart stepped out of the elevator. Joe was very white; his eyes were heavy and glazed; there was a trickle of dark blood on his forehead and on his white muffler. Jim had both their hats in his hand.

'He hit Joe with brass knuckles,' Jim said in a low voice. 'Joe was out cold for a minute or so. I wish you'd send a bell boy for some witch-hazel and court-plaster.'

It was late and the hall was deserted; brassy fragments of the dance below reached us as if heavy curtains were being blown aside and dropping back into place. When Ellen came out I took her directly downstairs. We avoided the receiving line and went into a dim room set with scraggly hotel palms where couples sometimes sat out during the dance; there I told her what had happened.

'It was Joe's own fault,' she said, surprisingly. 'I told him not to interfere.'

This wasn't true. She had said nothing, only uttered one curious little click of impatience.

'You ran out the back door and disappeared for almost an hour,' I protested. 'Then you turned up with a hard-looking customer who laughed in Joe's face.'

'A hard-looking customer,' she repeated, as if tasting the sound of the words.

'Well, wasn't he? Where on earth did you get hold of him, Ellen?'

'On the train,' she answered. Immediately she seemed to regret this admission. 'You'd better stay out of things that aren't your business, Eddie. You see what happened to Joe.'

Literally I gasped. To watch her, seated beside me, immaculately glowing, her body giving off wave after wave of freshness and delicacy – and to hear her talk like that.

'But that man's a thug!' I cried. 'No girl could be safe with him. He used brass knuckles on Joe – brass knuckles!'

'Is that pretty bad?'

She asked this as she might have asked such a question a few years ago. She looked at me at last and really wanted an answer; for a moment it was as if she were trying to recapture an attitude that had almost departed; then she hardened again. I say 'hardened,' for I began to notice that when she was concerned with this man her eyelids fell a little, shutting other things – everything else – out of view.

That was a moment I might have said something, I suppose, but in spite of everything, I couldn't light into her. I was too much under the spell of her beauty and its success. I even began to find excuses for her – perhaps that man wasn't what he appeared to be; or perhaps – more romantically – she was involved with him against her will to shield some one else. At this point people began to drift into the room and come up to speak to us. We couldn't talk any more, so we went in and bowed to the chaperones. Then I gave her up to the bright restless sea of the dance, where she moved in an eddy of her own among the pleasant islands of colored favors set out on tables and the south winds from the brasses moaning across the hall. After a while I saw Joe Jelke sitting in a corner with a strip of court-plaster on his forehead watching Ellen as if she herself had struck him down, but I didn't go up to him. I felt queer myself – like I feel when I wake up after sleeping through an afternoon, strange and portentous, as if something had gone on in the interval that changed the values of everything and that I didn't see.

The night slipped on through successive phases of cardboard horns, amateur tableaux and flashlights for the morning papers. Then was the grand march and supper, and about two o'clock some of the committee dressed up as revenue agents pinched the party, and a facetious newspaper was distributed, burlesquing the events of the evening. And all the time out of the corner of my eye I watched the shining orchid on Ellen's shoulder as it moved like Stuart's plume about the room. I watched it with a definite foreboding until the last sleepy groups had crowded into the elevators, and then, bundled to the eyes in great shapeless fur coats, drifted out into the clear dry Minnesota night.

2

There is a sloping mid-section of our city which lies between the
residence quarter on the hill and the business district on the level
of the river. It is a vague part of town, broken by its climb into
triangles and odd shapes – there are names like Seven Corners –
and I don't believe a dozen people could draw an accurate map of
it, though every one traversed it by trolley, auto or shoe leather
twice a day. And though it was a busy section, it would be hard
for me to name the business that comprised its activity. There
were always long lines of trolley cars waiting to start somewhere;
there was a big movie theatre and many small ones with posters
of Hoot Gibson and Wonder Dogs and Wonder Horses outside;
there were small stores with 'Old King Brady' and 'The Liberty
Boys of '76' in the windows, and marbles, cigarettes and candy
inside; and – one definite place at least – a fancy costumer whom
we all visited at least once a year. Some time during boyhood I
became aware that one side of a certain obscure street there were
bawdy houses, and all through the district were pawnshops,
cheap jewellers, small athletic clubs and gymnasiums and
somewhat too blatantly run-down saloons.

The morning after the Cotillion Club party, I woke up late and
lazy, with the happy feeling that for a day or two more there was
no chapel, no classes – nothing to do but wait for another party
tonight. It was crisp and bright – one of those days when you
forget how cold it is until your cheek freezes – and the events of
the evening before seemed dim and far away. After luncheon I
started downtown on foot through a light, pleasant snow of small
flakes that would probably fall all afternoon, and I was about half
through that halfway section of town – so far as I know, there's
no inclusive name for it – when suddenly whatever idle thought
was in my head blew away like a hat and I began thinking hard
of Ellen Baker. I began worrying about her as I'd never worried
about anything outside myself before. I began to loiter, with an
instinct to go up on the hill again and find her and talk to her;
then I remembered that she was at a tea, and I went on again,
but still thinking of her, and harder than ever. Right then the
affair opened up again.

It was snowing, I said, and it was four o'clock on a December afternoon, when there is a promise of darkness in the air and the street lamps are just going on. I passed a combination pool parlor and restaurant, with a stove loaded with hot-dogs in the window, and a few loungers hanging around the door. The lights were on inside – not bright lights but just a few pale yellow high up on the ceiling – and the glow they threw out into the frosty dusk wasn't bright enough to tempt you to stare inside. As I went past, thinking hard of Ellen all this time, I took in the quartet of loafers out of the corner of my eye. I hadn't gone half a dozen steps down the street when one of them called to me, not by name but in a way clearly intended for my ear. I thought it was a tribute to my raccoon coat and paid no attention, but a moment later whoever it was called to me again in a peremptory voice. I was annoyed and turned around. There, standing in the group not ten feet away and looking at me with the half-sneer on his face with which he'd looked at Joe Jelke, was the scarred, thin-faced man of the night before.

He had on a black fancy-cut coat, buttoned up to his neck as if he were cold. His hands were deep in his pockets and he wore a derby and high button shoes. I was startled, and for a moment I hesitated, but I was most of all angry, and knowing that I was quicker with my hands than Joe Jelke, I took a tentative step back toward him. The other men weren't looking at me – I don't think they saw me at all – but I knew that this one recognized me; there was nothing casual about his look, no mistake.

'Here I am. What are you going to do about it?' his eyes seemed to say.

I took another step toward him and he laughed soundlessly, but with active contempt, and drew back into the group. I followed. I was going to speak to him – I wasn't sure what I was going to say – but when I came up he had either changed his mind and backed off, or else he wanted me to follow him inside, for he had slipped off and the three men watched my intent approach without curiosity. They were the same kind – sporty, but, unlike him, smooth rather than truculent; I didn't find any personal malice in their collective glance.

'Did he go inside?' I asked.

They looked at one another in that cagy way; a wink passed between them, and after a perceptible pause, one said:

'Who go inside?'

'I don't know his name.'

There was another wink. Annoyed and determined, I walked past them and into the pool room. There were a few people at a lunch counter along one side and a few more playing billiards, but he was not among them.

Again I hesitated. If his idea was to lead me into any blind part of the establishment – there were some half-open doors farther back – I wanted more support. I went up to the man at the desk.

'What became of the fellow who just walked in here?'

Was he on his guard immediately, or was that my imagination?

'What fellow?'

'Thin face – derby hat.'

'How long ago?'

'Oh – a minute.'

He shook his head again. 'Didn't see him,' he said.

I waited. The three men from outside had come in and were lined up beside me at the counter. I felt that all of them were looking at me in a peculiar way. Feeling helpless and increasingly uneasy, I turned suddenly and went out. A little way down the street I turned again and took a good look at the place, so I'd know it and could find it again. On the next corner I broke impulsively into a run, found a taxicab in front of the hotel and drove back up the hill.

Ellen wasn't home. Mrs Baker came downstairs and talked to me. She seemed entirely cheerful and proud of Ellen's beauty, and ignorant of anything being amiss or of anything unusual having taken place the night before. She was glad that vacation was almost over – it was a strain and Ellen wasn't very strong. Then she said something that relieved my mind enormously. She was glad that I had come in, for of course Ellen would want to see me, and the time was so short. She was going back at half-past eight tonight.

'Tonight!' I exclaimed. 'I thought it was the day after tomorrow.'

'She's going to visit the Brokaws in Chicago,' Mrs Baker said.

'They want her for some party. We just decided it today. She's leaving with the Ingersoll girls tonight.'

I was so glad I could barely restrain myself from shaking her hand. Ellen was safe. It had been nothing all along but a moment of the most casual adventure. I felt like an idiot, but I realized how much I cared about Ellen and how little I could endure anything terrible happening to her.

'She'll be in soon?'

'Any minute now. She just phoned from the University Club.'

I said I'd be over later – I lived almost next door and I wanted to be alone. Outside I remembered I didn't have a key, so I started up the Bakers' driveway to take the old cut we used in childhood through the intervening yard. It was still snowing, but the flakes were bigger now against the darkness, and trying to locate the buried walk I noticed that the Bakers' back door was ajar.

I scarcely know why I turned and walked into that kitchen. There was a time when I would have known the Bakers' servants by name. That wasn't true now, but they knew me, and I was aware of a sudden suspension as I came in – not only a suspension of talk but of some mood or expectation that had filled them. They began to go to work too quickly; they made unnecessary movements and clamor – those three. The parlor maid looked at me in a frightened way and I suddenly guessed she was waiting to deliver another message. I beckoned her into the pantry.

'I know all about this,' I said. 'It's a very serious business. Shall I go to Mrs Baker now, or will you shut and lock that back door?'

'Don't tell Mrs Baker, Mr Stinson!'

'Then I don't want Miss Ellen disturbed. If she is – and if she is I'll know of it –' I delivered some outrageous threat about going to all the employment agencies and seeing she never got another job in the city. She was thoroughly intimidated when I went out; it wasn't a minute before the back door was locked and bolted behind me.

Simultaneously I heard a big car drive up in front, chains crunching on the soft snow; it was bringing Ellen home, and I went in to say good-by.

Joe Jelke and two other boys were along, and none of the three could manage to take their eyes off her, even to say hello to me.

She had one of those exquisite rose skins frequent in our part of the country, and beautiful until the little veins begin to break at about forty; now, flushed with the cold, it was a riot of lovely delicate pinks like many carnations. She and Joe had reached some sort of reconciliation, or at least he was too far gone in love to remember last night; but I saw that though she laughed a lot she wasn't really paying any attention to him or any of them. She wanted them to go, so that there'd be a message from the kitchen, but I knew that the message wasn't coming – that she was safe. There was talk of the Pump and Slipper dance at New Haven and of the Princeton Prom, and then, in various moods, we four left and separated quickly outside. I walked home with a certain depression of spirit and lay for an hour in a hot bath thinking that vacation was all over for me now that she was gone; feeling, even more deeply than I had yesterday, that she was out of my life.

And something eluded me, some one more thing to do, something that I had lost amid the events of the afternoon, promising myself to go back and pick it up, only to find that it had escaped me. I associated it vaguely with Mrs Baker, and now I seemed to recall that it had poked up its head somewhere in the stream of conversation with her. In my relief about Ellen I had forgotten to ask her a question regarding something she had said.

The Brokaws – that was it – where Ellen was to visit. I knew Bill Brokaw well; he was in my class at Yale. Then I remembered and sat bolt upright in the tub – the Brokaws weren't in Chicago this Christmas; they were at Palm Beach!

Dripping I sprang out of the tub, threw an insufficient union suit around my shoulders and sprang for the phone in my room. I got the connection quick, but Miss Ellen had already started for the train.

Luckily our car was in, and while I squirmed, still damp, into my clothes, the chauffeur brought it around to the door. The night was cold and dry, and we made good time to the station through the hard, crusty snow. I felt queer and insecure starting out this way, but somehow more confident as the station loomed up bright and new against the dark, cold air. For fifty years my family had owned the land on which it was built and that made my temerity seem all right somehow. There was always a possibility that I was rushing in where angels feared to tread, but that sense of having a solid foothold in the past made me willing to make a fool of myself. This business was all wrong – terribly wrong. Any idea I had entertained that it was harmless dropped away now; between Ellen and some vague overwhelming catastrophe there stood me, or else the police and a scandal. I'm no moralist – there was another element here, dark and frightening, and I didn't want Ellen to go through it alone.

There are three competing trains from St Paul to Chicago that all leave within a few minutes of half-past eight. Hers was the Burlington, and as I ran across the station I saw the grating being pulled over and the light above it go out. I knew, though, that she had a drawing-room with the Ingersoll girls, because her mother had mentioned buying the ticket, so she was, literally speaking, tucked in until tomorrow.

The C., M. & St P. gate was down at the other end and I raced for it and made it. I had forgotten one thing, though, and that was enough to keep me awake and worried half the night. This train got into Chicago ten minutes after the other. Ellen had that much time to disappear into one of the largest cities in the world.

I gave the porter a wire to my family to send from Milwaukee, and at eight o'clock next morning I pushed violently by a whole line of passengers, clamoring over their bags parked in the vestibule, and shot out of the door with a sort of scramble over the porter's back. For a moment the confusion of a great station, the voluminous sounds and echoes and cross-currents of bells and smoke struck me helpless. Then I dashed for the exit and toward the only chance I knew of finding her.

I had guessed right. She was standing at the telegraph counter, sending off heaven knows what black lie to her mother, and her expression when she saw me had a sort of terror mixed up with its surprise. There was cunning in it too. She was thinking quickly – she would have liked to walk away from me as if I weren't there, and go about her own business, but she couldn't. I was too matter-of-fact a thing in her life. So we stood silently watching each other and each thinking hard.

'The Brokaws are in Florida,' I said after a minute.

'It was nice of you to take such a long trip to tell me that.'

'Since you've found it out, don't you think you'd better go on to school?'

'Please let me alone, Eddie,' she said.

'I'll go as far as New York with you. I've decided to go back early myself.'

'You'd better let me alone.' Her lovely eyes narrowed and her face took on a look of dumb-animal-like resistance. She made a visible effort, the cunning flickered back into it, then both were gone, and in their stead was a cheerful reassuring smile that all but convinced me.

'Eddie, you silly child, don't you think I'm old enough to take care of myself?' I didn't answer. 'I'm going to meet a man, you understand. I just want to see him today. I've got my ticket East on the five o'clock train. If you don't believe it, here it is in my bag.'

'I believe you.'

'The man isn't anybody that you know and – frankly, I think you're being awfully fresh and impossible.'

'I know who the man is.'

Again she lost control of her face. That terrible expression came back into it and she spoke with almost a snarl:

'You'd better let me alone.'

I took the blank out of her hand and wrote out an explanatory telegram to her mother. Then I turned to Ellen and said a little roughly:

'We'll take the five o'clock train East together. Meanwhile you're going to spend the day with me.'

The mere sound of my own voice saying this so emphatically encouraged me, and I think it impressed her too; at any rate, she submitted – at least temporarily – and came along without protest while I bought my ticket.

When I start to piece together the fragments of that day a sort of confusion begins, as if my memory didn't want to yield up any of it, or my consciousness let any of it pass through. There was a bright, fierce morning during which we rode about in a taxicab and went to a department store where Ellen said she wanted to buy something and then tried to slip away from me by a back way. I had the feeling, for an hour, that someone was following us along Lake Shore Drive in a taxicab, and I would try to catch them by turning quickly or looking suddenly into the chauffeur's mirror; but I could find no one, and when I turned back I could see that Ellen's face was contorted with mirthless, unnatural laughter.

All morning there was a raw, bleak wind off the lake, but when we went to the Blackstone for lunch a light snow came down past the windows and we talked almost naturally about our friends, and about casual things. Suddenly her tone changed; she grew serious and looked me in the eye, straight and sincere.

'Eddie, you're the oldest friend I have,' she said, 'and you oughtn't to find it too hard to trust me. If I promise you faithfully on my word of honor to catch that five o'clock train, will you let me alone a few hours this afternoon?'

'Why?'

'Well' – she hesitated and hung her head a little – 'I guess everybody has a right to say – good-by.'

'You want to say good-by to that—'

'Yes, yes,' she said hastily; 'just a few hours, Eddie, and I promise faithfully that I'll be on that train.'

'Well, I suppose no great harm could be done in two hours. If you really want to say good-by—'

I looked up suddenly, and surprised a look of such tense cunning in her face that I winced before it. Her lip was curled up and her eyes were slits again; there wasn't the faintest touch of fairness and sincerity in her whole face.

We argued. The argument was vague on her part and somewhat hard and reticent on mine. I wasn't going to be cajoled again into any weakness or be infected with any – and there was a contagion of evil in the air. She kept trying to imply, without any convincing evidence to bring forward, that everything was all right. Yet she was too full of the thing itself – whatever it was – to build up a real story, and she wanted to catch at any credulous and acquiescent train of thought that might start in my head, and work that for all it was worth. After every reassuring suggestion she threw out, she stared at me eagerly, as if she hoped I'd launch into a comfortable moral lecture with the customary sweet at the end – which in this case would be her liberty. But I was wearing her away a little. Two or three times it needed just a touch of pressure to bring her to the point of tears –

which, of course, was what I wanted – but I couldn't seem to manage it. Almost I had her – almost possessed her interior attention – then she would slip away.

I bullied her remorselessly into a taxi about four o'clock and started for the station. The wind was raw again, with a sting of snow in it, and the people in the streets, waiting for busses and street cars too small to take them all in, looked cold and disturbed and unhappy. I tried to think how lucky we were to be comfortably off and taken care of, but all the warm, respectable world I had been part of yesterday had dropped away from me. There was something we carried with us now that was the enemy and the opposite of all that; it was in the cabs beside us, the streets we passed through. With a touch of panic, I wondered if I wasn't slipping almost imperceptibly into Ellen's attitude of mind. The column of passengers waiting to go abroad the train were as remote from me as people from another world, but it was I that was drifting away and leaving them behind.

My lower was in the same car with her compartment. It was an old-fashioned car, its lights somewhat dim, its carpets and upholstery full of the dust of another generation. There were half a dozen other travellers, but they made no special impression on me, except that they shared the unreality that I was beginning to feel everywhere around me. We went into Ellen's compartment, shut the door and sat down.

Suddenly I put my arms around her and drew her over to me, just as tenderly as I knew how – as if she were a little girl – as she was. She resisted a little, but after a moment she submitted and lay tense and rigid in my arms.

'Ellen,' I said helplessly, 'you asked me to trust you. You have much more reason to trust me. Wouldn't it help to get rid of all this, if you told me a little?'

'I can't,' she said, very low – 'I mean, there's nothing to tell.'

'You met this man on the train coming home and you fell in love with him, isn't that true?'

'I don't know.'

'Tell me, Ellen. You fell in love with him?'

'I don't know. Please let me alone.'

'Call it anything you want,' I went on, 'he has some sort of hold over you. He's trying to use you; he's trying to get something from you. He's not in love with you.'

'What does that matter?' she said in a weak voice.

'It does matter. Instead of trying to fight this – this thing – you're trying to fight me. And I love you, Ellen. Do you hear? I'm telling you all of a sudden, but it isn't new with me. I love you.'

She looked at me with a sneer on her gentle face; it was an expression I had seen on men who were tight and didn't want to be taken home. But it was human. I was reaching her, faintly and from far away, but more than before.

'Ellen, I want you to answer me one question. Is he going to be on this train?'

She hesitated; then, an instant too late, she shook her head.

'Be careful, Ellen. Now I'm going to ask you one thing more, and I wish you'd try very hard to answer. Coming West, when did this man get on the train?'

'I don't know,' she said with an effort.

Just at that moment I became aware, with the unquestionable knowledge reserved for facts, that he was just outside the door. She knew it, too; the blood left her face and that expression of low-animal perspicacity came creeping back. I lowered my face into my hands and tried to think.

We must have sat there, with scarcely a word, for well over an hour. I was conscious that the lights of Chicago, then of Englewood and of endless suburbs, were moving by, and then there were no more lights and we were out on the dark flatness of Illinois. The train seemed to draw in upon itself; it took on an air of being alone. The porter knocked at the door and asked if he could make up the berth, but I said no and he went away.

After a while I convinced myself that the struggle inevitably coming wasn't beyond what remained of my sanity, my faith in the essential all-rightness of things and people. That this person's purpose was what we call 'criminal,' I took for granted, but there was no need of ascribing to him an intelligence that belonged to a higher plane of human, or inhuman, endeavor. It was still as a man that I considered him, and tried to get at his essence, his self-interest – what took the place in him of a comprehensible heart – but I suppose I more than half knew what I would find when I opened the door.

When I stood up Ellen didn't seem to see me at all. She was hunched into the corner staring straight ahead with a sort of film over her eyes, as if she were in a state of suspended animation of body and mind. I lifted her and put two pillows under her head and threw my fur coat over her knees. Then I knelt beside her and kissed her two hands, opened the door and went out into the hall.

I closed the door behind me and stood with my back against it for a minute. The car was dark save for the corridor lights at each end. There was no sound except the groaning of the couplers, the even click-a-click of the rails and someone's loud sleeping breath farther down the car. I became aware after a moment that the figure of a man was standing by the water cooler just outside the men's smoking room, his derby hat on his head, his coat collar turned up around his neck as if he were cold, his hands in his coat pockets. When I saw him, he turned and went into the smoking room, and I followed. He was sitting in the far corner of the long leather bench; I took the single armchair beside the door.

As I went in I nodded to him and he acknowledged my presence with one of those terrible soundless laughs of his. But this time it was prolonged, it seemed to go on forever, and mostly to cut it short, I asked: 'Where are you from?' in a voice I tried to make casual.

He stopped laughing and looked at me narrowly, wondering what my game was. When he decided to answer, his voice was muffled as though he were speaking through a silk scarf, and it seemed to come from a long way off.

'I'm from St Paul, Jack.'

'Been making a trip home?'

He nodded. Then he took a long breath and spoke in a hard, menacing voice:

'You better get off at Fort Wayne, Jack.'

He was dead. He was dead as hell – he had been dead all along, but what force had flowed through him, like blood in his veins, out to St Paul and back, was leaving him now. A new outline – the outline of him dead – was coming through the palpable figure that had knocked down Joe Jelke.

He spoke again, with a sort of jerking effort:

'You get off at Fort Wayne, Jack, or I'm going to wipe you out.' He moved his hand in his coat pocket and showed me the outline of a revolver.

I shook my head. 'You can't touch me,' I answered. 'You see, I know.' His terrible eyes shifted over me quickly, trying to determine whether or not I did know. Then he gave a snarl and made as though he were going to jump to his feet.

'You climb off here or else I'm going to get you, Jack!' he cried hoarsely. The train was slowing up for Fort Wayne and his voice rang loud in the comparative quiet, but he didn't move from his chair – he was too weak, I think – and we sat staring at each other while workmen passed up and down outside the window banging the brakes and wheels, and the engine gave out loud mournful pants up ahead. No one got into our car. After a while the porter closed the vestibule door and passed back along the corridor, and we slid out of the murky yellow station light and into the long darkness.

What I remember next must have extended over a space of five or six hours, though it comes back to me as something without any existence in time – something that might have taken five minutes or a year. There began a slow, calculated assault on me, wordless and terrible. I felt what I can only call a strangeness stealing over me – akin to the strangeness I had felt all afternoon, but deeper and more intensified. It was like nothing so much as the sensation of drifting away, and I gripped the arms of the chair convulsively, as if to hang onto a piece in the living world. Sometimes I felt myself going out with a rush. There would be almost a warm relief about it, a sense of not caring; then, with a violent wrench of the will, I'd pull myself back into the room.

Suddenly I realized that from a while back I had stopped hating him, stopped feeling violently alien to him, and with the realization, I went cold and sweat broke out all over my head. He was getting around my abhorrence, as he had got around Ellen coming West on the train; and it was just that strength he drew from preying on people that had brought him up to the point of concrete violence in St Paul, and that, fading and flickering out, still kept him fighting now.

He must have seen that faltering in my heart, for he spoke at once, in a low, even, almost gentle voice: 'You better go now.'

'Oh, I'm not going,' I forced myself to say.

'Suit yourself, Jack.'

He was my friend, he implied. He knew how it was with me and he wanted to help. He pitied me. I'd better go away before it was too late. The rhythm of his attack was soothing as a song: I'd better go away – *and let him get at Ellen*. With a little cry I sat bolt upright.

'What do you want of this girl?' I said, my voice shaking. 'To make a sort of walking hell of her.'

His glance held a quality of dumb surprise, as if I were punishing an animal for a fault of which he was not conscious. For an instant I faltered; then I went on blindly:

'You've lost her; she's put her trust in me.'

His countenance went suddenly black with evil, and he cried: 'You're a liar!' in a voice that was like cold hands.

'She trusts me,' I said. 'You can't touch her. She's safe!'

He controlled himself. His face grew bland, and I felt that curious weakness and indifference begin again inside me. What was the use of all this? What was the use?

'You haven't got much time left,' I forced myself to say, and then, in a flash of intuition, I jumped at the truth. 'You died, or you were killed, not far from here!' – Then I saw what I had not seen before – that his forehead was drilled with a small round hole like a larger picture nail leaves when it's pulled from a plaster wall. 'And now you're sinking. You've only got a few hours. The trip home is over!'

His face contorted, lost all semblance of humanity, living or dead. Simultaneously the room was full of cold air and with a noise that was something between a paroxysm of coughing and a burst of horrible laughter, he was on his feet, reeking of shame and blasphemy.

'Come and look!' he cried. 'I'll show you—'

He took a step toward me, then another and it was exactly as if a door stood open behind him, a door yawning out to an inconceivable abyss of darkness and corruption. There was a scream of mortal agony, from him or from somewhere behind, and abruptly the strength went out of him in a long husky sigh and he wilted to the floor . . .

How long I sat there, dazed with terror and exhaustion, I don't know. The next thing I remember is the sleepy porter shining shoes across the room from me, and outside the window the steel fires of Pittsburgh breaking the flat perspective also – something too faint for a man, too heavy for a shadow, of the night. There was something extended on the bench. Even as I perceived it it faded off and away.

Some minutes later I opened the door of Ellen's compartment. She was asleep where I had left her. Her lovely cheeks were white and wan, but she lay naturally – her hands relaxed and her breathing regular and clear. What had possessed her had gone out of her, leaving her exhausted but her own dear self again.

I made her a little more comfortable, tucked a blanket around her, extinguished the light and went out.

3

When I came home for Easter vacation, almost my first act was to go down to the billiard parlor near Seven Corners. The man at the cash register quite naturally didn't remember my hurried visit of three months before.

'I'm trying to locate a certain party who, I think, came here a lot some time ago.'

I described the man rather accurately, and when I had finished, the cashier called to a little jockeylike fellow who was sitting near with an air of having something very important to do that he couldn't quite remember.

'Hey, Shorty, talk to this guy, will you? I think he's looking for Joe Varland."

The little man gave me a tribal look of suspicion. I went and sat near him.

'Joe Varland's dead, fella,' he said grudgingly. 'He died last winter.'

I described him again – his overcoat, his laugh, the habitual expression of his eyes.

'That's Joe Varland you're looking for all right, but he's dead.'

'I want to find out something about him.'

'What you want to find out?'

'What did he do, for instance?'

'How should I know?'

'Look here! I'm not a policeman. I just want some kind of information about his habits. He's dead now and it can't hurt him. And it won't go beyond me.'

'Well' – he hesitated, looking me over – 'he was a great one for travelling. He got in a row in the station in Pittsburgh and a dick got him.'

I nodded. Broken pieces of the puzzle began to assemble in my head.

'Why was he a lot on trains?'

'How should I know, fella?'

'If you can use ten dollars, I'd like to know anything you may have heard on the subject.'

'Well,' said Shorty reluctantly, 'all I know is they used to say he worked the trains.'

'Worked the trains?'

'He had some racket of his own he'd never loosen up about. He used to work the girls travelling alone on the trains. Nobody ever knew much about it – he was a pretty smooth guy – but sometimes he'd turn up here with a lot of dough and he let 'em know it was the janes he got it off of.'

I thanked him and gave him the ten dollars and went out, very thoughtful, without mentioning that part of Joe Varland had made a last trip home.

Ellen wasn't West for Easter, and even if she had been I wouldn't have gone to her with the information, either – at least I've seen her almost every day this summer and we've managed to talk about everything else. Sometimes, though, she gets silent about nothing and wants to be very close to me, and I know what's in her mind.

Of course she's coming out this fall, and I have two more years at New Haven; still, things don't look so impossible as they did a few months ago. She belongs to me in a way – even if I lose her she belongs to me. Who knows? Anyhow, I'll always be there.

The Last of the Belles
(1929)

After Atlanta's elaborate and theatrical rendition of Southern charm, we all underestimated Tarleton. It was a little hotter than anywhere we'd been – a dozen rookies collapsed the first day in that Georgia sun – and when you saw herds of cows drifting through the business streets, hi-yaed by colored drovers, a trance stole down over you out of the hot light; you wanted to move a hand or foot to be sure you were alive.

So I stayed out at camp and let Lieutenant Warren tell me about the girls. This was fifteen years ago, and I've forgotten how I felt, except that the days went along, one after another, better than they do now, and I was empty-hearted, because up North she whose legend I had loved for three years was getting married. I saw the clippings and newspaper photographs. It was 'a romantic wartime wedding,' all very rich and sad. I felt vividly the dark radiance of the sky under which it took place, and as a young snob, was more envious than sorry.

A day came when I went into Tarleton for a haircut and ran into a nice fellow named Bill Knowles, who was in my time at Harvard. He'd been in the National Guard division that preceded us in camp; at the last moment he had transferred to aviation and been left behind.

'I'm glad I met you, Andy,' he said with undue seriousness. 'I'll hand you on all my information before I start for Texas. You see, there're really only three girls here—'

I was interested; there was something mystical about there being three girls.

'– and here's one of them now.'

We were in front of a drug store and he marched me in and introduced me to a lady I promptly detested.

'The other two are Ailie Calhoun and Sally Carrol Happer.'

I guessed from the way he pronounced her name, that he was interested in Ailie Calhoun. It was on his mind what she would be doing while he was gone; he wanted her to have a quiet, uninteresting time.

At my age I don't even hesitate to confess that entirely unchivalrous images of Ailie Calhoun – that lovely name – rushed into my mind. At twenty-three there is no such thing as a pre-empted beauty; though, had Bill asked me, I would doubtless have sworn in all sincerity to care for her like a sister. He didn't; he was just fretting out loud at having to go. Three days later he telephoned me that he was leaving next morning and he'd take me to her house that night.

We met at the hotel and walked uptown through the flowery, hot twilight. The four white pillars of the Calhoun house faced the street, and behind them the veranda was dark as a cave with hanging, weaving, climbing vines.

When we came up the walk a girl in a white dress tumbled out of the front door, crying, 'I'm so sorry I'm late!' and seeing us, added: 'Why, I thought I heard you come ten minutes—'

She broke off as a chair creaked and another man, an aviator from Camp Harry Lee, emerged from the obscurity of the veranda.

'Why, Canby!' she cried. 'How are you?'

He and Bill Knowles waited with the tenseness of open litigants.

'Canby, I want to whisper to you, honey,' she said, after just a second. 'You'll excuse us, Bill.'

They went aside. Presently Lieutenant Canby, immensely displeased, said in a grim voice, 'Then we'll make it Thursday, but that means sure.' Scarcely nodding to us, he went down the walk, the spurs with which he presumably urged on his aeroplane gleaming in the lamplight.

'Come in – I don't just know your name—'

There she was – the Southern type in all its purity. I would have recognized Ailie Calhoun if I'd never heard Ruth Draper or read Marse Chan. She had the adroitness sugar-coated with sweet, voluble simplicity, the suggested background of devoted fathers, brothers and admirers stretching back into the South's heroic age, the unfailing coolness acquired in the endless struggle with the heat. There were notes in her voice that ordered slaves around, that withered up Yankee captains, and then soft, wheedling notes that mingled in unfamiliar loveliness with the night.

I could scarcely see her in the darkness, but when I rose to go – it was plain that I was not to linger – she stood in the orange light from the doorway. She was small and very blond; there was too much fever-colored rouge on her face, accentuated by a nose dabbed clownish white, but she shone through that like a star.

'After Bill goes I'll be sitting here all alone night after night. Maybe you'll take me to the country-club dances.' The pathetic prophecy brought a laugh from Bill. 'Wait a minute,' Ailie murmured. 'Your guns are all crooked.'

She straightened my collar pin, looking up at me for a second with something more than curiosity. It was a seeking look, as if she asked, 'Could it be you?' Like Lieutenant Canby, I marched off unwillingly into the suddenly insufficient night.

Two weeks later I sat with her on the same veranda, or rather she half lay in my arms and yet scarcely touched me – how she managed that I don't remember. I was trying unsuccessfully to kiss her, and had been trying for the best part of an hour. We had a sort of joke about my not being sincere. My theory was that if she'd let me kiss her I'd fall in love with her. Her argument was that I was obviously insincere.

In a lull between two of these struggles she told me about her brother who had died in his senior year at Yale. She showed me his picture – it was a handsome, earnest face with a Leyendecker forelock – and told me that when she met someone who measured up to him she'd marry. I found this family idealism discouraging; even my brash confidence couldn't compete with the dead.

The evening and other evenings passed like that, and ended with my going back to camp with the remembered smell of magnolia flowers and a mood of vague dissatisfaction. I never kissed her. We went to the vaudeville and to the country club on Saturday nights, where she seldom took ten consecutive steps with one man, and she took me to barbecues and rowdy watermelon parties, and never thought it was worth while to change what I felt for her into love. I see now that it wouldn't have been hard, but she was a wise nineteen and she must have seen that we were emotionally incompatible. So I became her confidant instead.

We talked about Bill Knowles. She was considering Bill; for, though she wouldn't admit it, a winter at school in New York and a prom at Yale had turned her eyes North. She said she didn't think she'd marry a Southern man. And by degrees I saw that she was consciously and voluntarily different from these other girls who sang nigger songs and shot craps in the country-club bar. That's why Bill and I and others were drawn to her. We recognized her.

June and July, while the rumors reached us faintly, ineffectually, of battle and terror overseas, Ailie's eyes roved here and there about the country-club floor, seeking for something among the tall young officers. She attached several, choosing them with unfailing perspicacity – save in the case of Lieutenant Canby, whom she claimed to despise, but, nevertheless, gave dates to 'because he was so sincere' – and we apportioned her evenings among us all summer.

One day she broke all her dates – Bill Knowles had leave and was coming. We talked of the event with scientific impersonality – would he move her to a decision? Lieutenant Canby, on the contrary, wasn't impersonal at all; made a nuisance of himself. He told her that if she married Knowles he was going to climb up six thousand feet in his aeroplane, shut off the motor and let go. He frightened her – I had to yield him my last date before Bill came.

On Saturday night she and Bill Knowles came to the country club. They were very handsome together and once more I felt envious and sad. As they danced out on the floor the three-piece orchestra was playing After You've Gone, in a poignant incomplete way that I can hear yet, as if each bar were trickling off a precious minute of that time. I knew then that I had grown to love Tarleton, and I glanced about half in panic to see if some face wouldn't come in for me out of that warm, singing, outer darkness that yielded up couple after couple in organdie and olive drab. It was a time of youth and war, and there was never so much love around.

When I danced with Ailie she suddenly suggested that we go

outside to a car. She wanted to know why didn't people cut in on her tonight? Did they think she was already married?

'Are you going to be?'

'I don't know, Andy. Sometimes, when he treats me as if I were sacred, it thrills me.' Her voice was hushed and far away. 'And then—'

She laughed. Her body, so frail and tender, was touching mine, her face was turned up to me, and there, suddenly, with Bill Knowles ten yards off, I could have kissed her at last. Our lips just touched experimentally; then an aviation officer turned a corner of the veranda near us, peered into our darkness and hesitated.

'Ailie.'

'Yes.'

'You heard about this afternoon?'

'What?' She leaned forward, tenseness already in her voice.

'Horace Canby crashed. He was instantly killed.'

She got up slowly and stepped out of the car.

'You mean he was killed?' she said.

'Yes. They don't know what the trouble was. His motor—'

'Oh-h-h!' Her rasping whisper came through the hands suddenly covering her face. We watched her helplessly as she put her head on the side of the car, gagging dry tears. After a minute I went for Bill, who was standing in the stag line, searching anxiously about for her, and told him she wanted to go home.

I sat on the steps outside. I had disliked Canby, but his terrible, pointless death was more real to me then than the day's toll of thousands in France. In a few minutes Ailie and Bill came out. Ailie was whimpering a little, but when she saw me her eyes flexed and she came over swiftly.

'Andy' – she spoke in a quick, low voice – 'of course you must never tell anybody what I told you about Canby yesterday. What he said, I mean.'

'Of course not.'

She looked at me a second longer as if to be quite sure. Finally she was sure. Then she sighed in such a quaint little way that I could hardly believe my ears, and her brow went up in what can only be described as mock despair.

'An-dy!'

I looked uncomfortably at the ground, aware that she was

calling my attention to her involuntarily disastrous effect on men.

'Good night, Andy!' called Bill as they got into a taxi.

'Good night,' I said, and almost added: 'You poor fool.'

2

Of course I should have made one of those fine moral decisions that people make in books, and despised her. On the contrary, I don't doubt that she could still have had me by raising her hand.

A few days later she made it all right by saying wistfully, 'I know you think it was terrible of me to think of myself at a time like that, but it was such a shocking coincidence.'

At twenty-three I was entirely unconvinced about anything, except that some people were strong and attractive and could do what they wanted, and others were caught and disgraced. I hoped I was of the former. I was sure Ailie was.

I had to revise other ideas about her. In the course of a long discussion with some girl about kissing – in those days people still talked about kissing more than they kissed – I mentioned the fact that Ailie had only kissed two or three men, and only when she thought she was in love. To my considerable disconcertion the girl figuratively just lay on the floor and howled.

'But it's true,' I assured her, suddenly knowing it wasn't. 'She told me herself.'

'Ailie Calhoun! Oh, my heavens! Why, last year at the Tech spring house party—'

This was in September. We were going overseas any week now, and to bring us up to full strength a last batch of officers from the fourth training camp arrived. The fourth camp wasn't like the first three – the candidates were from the ranks; even from the drafted divisions. They had queer names without vowels in them, and save for a few young militiamen, you couldn't take it for granted that they came out of any background at all. The addition to our company was Lieutenant Earl Schoen from New Bedford, Massachusetts; as fine a physical specimen as I have ever seen. He was six-foot-three, with black hair, high color and glossy dark-brown eyes. He wasn't very smart and he was definitely illiterate, yet he was a good officer, high-tempered and commanding, and with that becoming touch of vanity that sits well on the military. I had an idea that New Bedford was a country town, and set down his bumptious qualities to that.

We were doubled up in living quarters and he came into my hut. Inside of a week there was a cabinet photograph of some Tarleton girl nailed brutally to the shack wall.

'She's no jane or anything like that. She's a society girl; goes with all the best people here.'

The following Sunday afternoon I met the lady at a semiprivate swimming pool in the country. When Ailie and I arrived, there was Schoen's muscular body rippling out of a bathing suit at the far end of the pool.

'Hey, lieutenant!'

When I waved back at him he grinned and winked, jerking his head toward the girl at his side. Then, digging her in the ribs, he jerked his head at me. It was a form of introduction.

'Who's that with Kitty Preston?' Ailie asked, and when I told her she said he looked like a street-car conductor, and pretended to look for her transfer.

A moment later he crawled powerfully and gracefully down the pool and pulled himself up at our side. I introduced him to Ailie.

'How do you like my girl, lieutenant?' he demanded. 'I told you she was all right, didn't I?' He jerked his head toward Ailie; this time to indicate that his girl and Ailie moved in the same circles. 'How about us all having dinner together down at the hotel some night?'

I left them in a moment, amused as I saw Ailie visibly making up her mind that here, anyhow, was not the ideal. But Lieutenant Earl Schoen was not to be dismissed so lightly. He ran his eyes cheerfully and inoffensively over her cute, slight figure, and decided that she would do even better than the other. Then minutes later I saw them in the water together, Ailie swimming away with a grim little stroke she had, and Schoen wallowing riotously around her and ahead of her, sometimes pausing and staring at her, fascinated, as a boy might look at a nautical doll.

While the afternoon passed he remained at her side. Finally Ailie came over to me and whispered, with a laugh: 'He's following me around. He thinks I haven't paid my carfare.'

She turned quickly. Miss Kitty Preston, her face curiously flustered, stood facing us.

'Ailie Calhoun, I didn't think it of you to go out and delib'ately try to take a man away from another girl.' – An expression of distress at the impending scene flitted over Ailie's face. – 'I thought you considered yourself above anything like that.'

Miss Preston's voice was low, but it held that tensity that can be felt farther than it can be heard, and I saw Ailie's clear lovely eyes glance about in panic. Luckily, Earl himself was ambling cheerfully and innocently toward us.

'If you care for him you certainly oughtn't to belittle yourself in front of him,' said Ailie in a flash, her head high.

It was her acquaintance with the traditional way of behaving against Kitty Preston's naïve and fierce possessiveness, or if you prefer it, Ailie's 'breeding' against the other's 'commonness.' She turned away.

'Wait a minute, kid!' cried Earl Schoen. 'How about your address? Maybe I'd like to give you a ring on the phone.'

She looked at him in a way that should have indicated to Kitty her entire lack of interest.

'I'm very busy at the Red Cross this month,' she said, her voice as cool as her slicked-back blond hair. 'Good-by.'

On the way home she laughed. Her air of having been unwittingly involved in a contemptible business vanished.

'She'll never hold that young man,' she said. 'He wants somebody new.'

'Apparently he wants Ailie Calhoun.'

The idea amused her.

'He could give me his ticket punch to wear, like a fraternity pin. What fun! If mother ever saw anybody like that come in the house, she'd just lie down and die.'

And to give Ailie credit, it was fully a fortnight before he did come in her house, although he rushed her until she pretended to be annoyed at the next country-club dance.

'He's the biggest tough, Andy,' she whispered to me. 'But he's so sincere.'

She used the word 'tough' without the conviction it would have carried had he been a Southern boy. She only knew it with her mind; her ear couldn't distinguish between one Yankee voice and another. And somehow Mrs Calhoun didn't expire at his appearance on the threshold. The supposedly ineradicable prejudices of Ailie's parents were a convenient phenomenon that disappeared at her wish. It was her friends who were astonished. Ailie, always a little above Tarleton, whose beaux had been very carefully the 'nicest' men of the camp – Ailie and Lieutenant Schoen! I grew tired of assuring people that she was merely distracting herself – and indeed every week or so there was someone new – an ensign from Pensacola, an old friend from New Orleans – but always, in between times, there was Earl Schoen.

Orders arrived for an advance party of officers and sergeants to proceed to the port of embarkation and take ship to France. My name was on the list. I had been on the range for a week and when I got back to camp, Earl Schoen buttonholed me immediately.

'We're giving a little farewell party in the mess. Just you and I and Captain Craker and three girls.'

Earl and I were to call for the girls. We picked up Sally Carrol Happer and Nancy Lamar, and went on to Ailie's house; to be met at the door by the butler with the announcement that she wasn't home.

'Isn't home?' Earl repeated blankly. 'Where is she?'

'Didn't leave no information about that; just said she wasn't home.'

'But this is a darn funny thing!' he exclaimed. He walked around the familiar dusky veranda while the butler waited at the door. Something occurred to him. 'Say,' he informed me – 'say, I think she's sore.'

I waited. He said sternly to the butler, 'You tell her I've got to speak to her a minute.'

'How'm I goin' tell her that when she ain't home?'

Again Earl walked musingly around the porch. Then he nodded several times and said:

'She's sore at something that happened downtown.'

In a few words he sketched out the matter to me.

'Look here; you wait in the car,' I said. 'Maybe I can fix this.' And when he reluctantly retreated: 'Oliver, you tell Miss Ailie I want to see her alone.'

After some argument he bore this message and in a moment returned with a reply:

'Miss Ailie say she don't want to see that other gentleman about nothing never. She say come in if you like.'

She was in the library. I had expected to see a picture of cool, outraged dignity, but her face was distraught, tumultuous, despairing. Her eyes were red-rimmed, as though she had been crying slowly and painfully, for hours.

'Oh, hello, Andy,' she said brokenly. 'I haven't seen you for so long. Has he gone?'

'Now, Ailie—'

'Now, Ailie!' she cried. 'Now, Ailie! He spoke to me, you see. He lifted his hat. He stood there ten feet from me with that horrible – that horrible woman – holding her arm and talking to her, and then when he saw me he raised his hat. Andy, I didn't know what to do. I had to go in the drug store and ask for a glass of water, and I was so afraid he'd follow in after me that I asked Mr Rich to let me go out the back way. I never want to see him or hear of him again.'

I talked. I said what one says in such cases. I said it for half an hour. I could not move her. Several times she answered by murmuring something about his not being 'sincere,' and for the fourth time I wondered what the word meant to her. Certainly not constancy; it was, I half suspected, some special way she wanted to be regarded.

I got up to go. And then, unbelievably, the automobile horn sounded three times impatiently outside. It was stupefying. It said as plainly as if Earl were in the room, 'All right; go to the devil then! I'm not going to wait here all night.'

Ailie looked at me aghast. And suddenly a peculiar look came into her face, spread, flickered, broke into a teary, hysterical smile.

'Isn't he awful?' she cried in helpless despair. 'Isn't he terrible?'

'Hurry up,' I said quickly. 'Get your cape. This is our last night.'

And I can still feel that last night vividly, the candlelight that flickered over the rough boards of the mess shack, over the frayed paper decorations left from the supply company's party, the sad mandolin down a company street that kept picking My Indiana

Home out of the universal nostalgia of the departing summer. The three girls lost in this mysterious men's city felt something, too – a bewitched impermanence as though they were on a magic carpet that had lighted on the Southern countryside, and any moment the wind would lift it and waft it away. We toasted ourselves and the South. Then we left our napkins and empty glasses and a little of the past on the table, and hand in hand went out into the moonlight itself. Taps had been played; there was no sound but the far-away whinny of a horse, and a loud persistent snore at which we laughed, and the leathery snap of a sentry coming to port over by the guardhouse. Craker was on duty; we others got into a waiting car, motored into Tarleton and left Craker's girl.

Then Ailie and Earl, Sally and I, two and two in the wide back seat, each couple turned from the other, absorbed and whispering, drove away into the wide, flat darkness.

We drove through pine woods heavy with lichen and Spanish moss, and between the fallow cotton fields along a road white as the rim of the world. We parked under the broken shadow of a mill where there was the sound of running water and restive squawky birds and over everything a brightness that tried to filter in anywhere – into the lost nigger cabins, the automobile, the fastnesses of the heart. The South sang to us – I wonder if they remember. I remember – the cool pale faces, the somnolent amorous eyes and the voices:

'Are you comfortable?'

'Yes; are you?'

'Are you sure you are?'

'Yes.'

Suddenly we knew it was late and there was nothing more. We turned home.

Our detachment started for Camp Mills next day, but I didn't go to France after all. We passed a cold month on Long Island, marched aboard a transport with steel helmets slung at our sides and then marched off again. There wasn't any more war. I had missed the war. When I came back to Tarleton I tried to get out of the Army, but I had a regular commission and it took most of the winter. But Earl Schoen was one of the first to be demobilized. He wanted to find a good job 'while the picking was good.' Ailie was noncommittal, but there was an understanding between them that he'd be back.

By January the camps, which for two years had dominated the little city, were already fading. There was only the persistent incinerator smell to remind one of all that activity and bustle. What life remained centered bitterly about divisional headquarters building, with the disgruntled regular officers who had also missed the war.

And now the young men of Tarleton began drifting back from the ends of the earth – some with Canadian uniforms, some with crutches or empty sleeves. A returned battalion of the National Guard paraded through the streets with open ranks for their dead, and then stepped down out of romance forever and sold you things over the counters of local stores. Only a few uniforms mingled with the dinner coats at the country-club dance.

Just before Christmas, Bill Knowles arrived unexpectedly one day and left the next – either he gave Ailie an ultimatum or she had made up her mind at last. I saw her sometimes when she wasn't busy with returned heroes from Savannah and Augusta, but I felt like an outmoded survival – and I was. She was waiting for Earl Schoen with such a vast uncertainty that she didn't like to talk about it. Three days before I got my final discharge he came.

I first happened upon them walking down Market Street together, and I don't think I've ever been so sorry for a couple in my life; though I suppose the same situation was repeating itself in every city where there had been camps. Exteriorly Earl had about everything wrong with him that could be imagined. His hat was green, with a radical feather; his suit was slashed and braided in a grotesque fashion that national advertising and the movies have put an end to. Evidently he had been to his old barber, for his hair bloused neatly on his pink, shaved neck. It wasn't as though he had been shiny and poor, but the background of mill-town dance halls and outing clubs flamed out at you – or rather flamed out at Ailie. For she had never quite imagined the reality; in these clothes even the natural grace of that magnificent body had departed. At first he boasted of his fine job; it would get them along all right until he could 'see some easy money.' But from the moment he came back into her world on its own terms he must have known it was hopeless. I don't know what Ailie said or how much her grief weighed against her stupefaction. She acted quickly – three days after his arrival, Earl and I went North together on the train.

'Well, that's the end of that,' he said moodily. 'She's a wonderful girl, but too much of a highbrow for me. I guess she's got to marry some rich guy that'll give her a great social position. I can't see that stuck-up sort of thing.' And then, later: 'She said to come back and see her in a year, but I'll never go back. This aristocrat stuff is all right if you got the money for it, but—'

'But it wasn't real,' he meant to finish. The provincial society in which he had moved with so much satisfaction for six months already appeared to him as affected, 'dudish' and artificial.

'Say, did you see what I saw getting on the train?' he asked me after a while. 'Two wonderful janes, all alone. What do you say we mosey into the next car and ask them to lunch? I'll take the one in blue.' Halfway down the car he turned around suddenly. 'Say, Andy,' he demanded, frowning; 'one thing – how do you suppose she knew I used to command a street car? I never told her that.'

'Search me.'

3

This narrative arrives now at one of the big gaps that stared me in the face when I began. For six years, while I finished at Harvard Law and built commercial aeroplanes and backed a pavement block that went gritty under trucks, Ailie Calhoun was scarcely more than a name on a Christmas card; something that blew a little in my mind on warm nights when I remembered the magnolia flowers. Occasionally an acquaintance of Army days would ask me, 'What became of that blond girl who was so popular?' but I didn't know. I ran into Nancy Lamar at the Montmartre in New York one evening and learned that Ailie had become engaged to a man in Cincinnati, had gone North to visit his family and then broken it off. She was lovely as ever and there was always a heavy beau or two. But neither Bill Knowles nor Earl Schoen had ever come back.

And somewhere about that time I heard that Bill Knowles had

married a girl he met on a boat. There you are – not much of a patch to mend six years with.

Oddly enough, a girl seen at twilight in a small Indiana station started me thinking about going South. The girl, in stiff pink organdie, threw her arms about a man who got off our train and hurried him to a waiting car, and I felt a sort of pang. It seemed to me that she was bearing him off into the lost midsummer world of my early twenties, where time had stood still and charming girls, dimly seen like the past itself, still loitered along the dusky streets. I suppose that poetry is a Northern man's dream of the South. But it was months later that I sent off a wire to Ailie, and immediately followed it to Tarleton.

It was July. The Jefferson Hotel seemed strangely shabby and stuffy – a boosters' club burst into intermittent song in the dining room that my memory had long dedicated to officers and girls. I recognized the taxi driver who took me up to Ailie's house, but his 'Sure, I do, lieutenant,' was unconvincing. I was only one of twenty thousand.

It was a curious three days. I suppose some of Ailie's first young lustre must have gone the way of such mortal shining, but I can't bear witness to it. She was still so physically appealing that you wanted to touch the personality that trembled on her lips. No – the change was more profound than that.

At once I saw she had a different line. The modulations of pride, the vocal hints that she knew the secrets of a brighter, finer ante-bellum day, were gone from her voice; there was no time for them now as it rambled on in the half-laughing, half-desperate banter of the newer South. And everything was swept into this banter in order to make it go on and leave no time for thinking – the present, the future, herself, me. We went to a rowdy party at the house of some young married people, and she was the nervous, glowing center of it. After all, she wasn't eighteen, and she was as attractive in her rôle of reckless clown as she had ever been in her life.

'Have you heard anything from Earl Schoen?' I asked her the second night, on our way to the country-club dance.

'No.' She was serious for a moment. 'I often think of him. He was the—' She hesitated.

'Go on.'

'I was going to say the man I loved most, but that wouldn't be true. I never exactly loved him, or I'd have married him any old how, wouldn't I?' She looked at me questioningly. 'At least I wouldn't have treated him like that.'

'It was impossible.'

'Of course,' she agreed uncertainly. Her mood changed; she became flippant: 'How the Yankees did deceive us poor little Southern girls. Ah, me!'

When we reached the country club she melted like a chameleon into the – to me – unfamiliar crowd. There was a new generation upon the floor, with less dignity than the ones I had known, but none of them were more a part of its lazy, feverish essence than Ailie. Possibly she had perceived that in her initial longing to escape from Tarleton's provincialism she had been walking alone, following a generation which was doomed to have no successors. Just where she lost the battle, waged behind the white pillars of her veranda, I don't know. But she had guessed wrong, missed out somewhere. Her wild animation, which even now called enough men around her to rival the entourage of the youngest and freshest, was an admission of defeat.

I left her house, as I had so often left it that vanished June, in a mood of vague dissatisfaction. It was hours later, tossing about my bed in the hotel, that I realized what was the matter, what had always been the matter – I was deeply and incurably in love with her. In spite of every incompatibility, she was still, she would always be to me, the most attractive girl I had ever known. I told her so next afternoon. It was one of those hot days I knew so well, and Ailie sat beside me on a couch in the darkened library.

'Oh, no, I couldn't marry you,' she said, almost frightened; 'I don't love you that way at all. . . . I never did. And you don't love me. I didn't mean to tell you now, but next month I'm going to marry another man. We're not even announcing it, because I've done that twice before.' Suddenly it occurred to her that I might be hurt: 'Andy, you just had a silly idea, didn't you? You know I couldn't ever marry a Northern man.'

'Who is he?' I demanded.

'A man from Savannah.'

'Are you in love with him?'

'Of course I am.' We both smiled. 'Of course I am! What are you trying to make me say?'

There were no doubts, as there had been with other men. She couldn't afford to let herself have doubts. I knew this because she had long ago stopped making any pretensions with me. This very naturalness, I realized, was because she didn't consider me as a suitor. Beneath her mask of an instinctive thoroughbred she had always been on to herself, and she couldn't believe that anyone not taken in to the point of uncritical worship could really love her. That was what she called being 'sincere'; she felt most security with men like Canby and Earl Schoen, who were incapable of passing judgments on the ostensibly aristocratic heart.

'All right,' I said, as if she had asked my permission to marry. 'Now, would you do something for me?'

'Anything.'

'Ride out to camp.'

'But there's nothing left there, honey.'

'I don't care.'

We walked downtown. The taxi driver in front of the hotel repeated her objection: 'Nothing there now, cap.'

'Never mind. Go there anyhow.'

Twenty minutes later he stopped on a wide unfamiliar plain powdered with new cotton fields and marked with isolated clumps of pine.

'Like to drive over yonder where you see the smoke?' asked the driver. 'That's the new state prison.'

'No. Just drive along this road. I want to find where I used to live.'

An old race course, inconspicuous in the camp's day of glory, had reared its dilapidated grandstand in the desolation. I tried in vain to orient myself.

'Go along this road past that clump of trees, and then turn right – no, turn left.'

He obeyed, with professional disgust.

'You won't find a single thing, darling,' said Ailie. 'The contractors took it all down.'

We rode slowly along the margin of the fields. It might have been here –

'All right. I want to get out,' I said suddenly.

I left Ailie sitting in the car, looking very beautiful with the warm breeze stirring her long, curly bob.

It might have been here. That would make the company streets down there and the mess shack, where we dined that night, just over the way.

The taxi driver regarded me indulgently while I stumbled here and there in the knee-deep underbrush, looking for my youth in a clapboard or a strip of roofing or a rusty tomato can. I tried to sight on a vaguely familiar clump of trees, but it was growing darker now and I couldn't be quite sure they were the right trees.

'They're going to fix up the old race course,' Ailie called from the car. 'Tarleton's getting quite doggy in its old age.'

No. Upon consideration they didn't look like the right trees. All I could be sure of was this place that had once been so full of life and effort was gone, as if it had never existed, and that in another month Ailie would be gone, and the South would be empty for me forever.

One Trip Abroad
(1930)

In the afternoon the air became black with locusts, and some of the women shrieked, sinking to the floor of the motorbus and covering their hair with traveling rugs. The locusts were coming north, eating everything in their path, which was not so much in that part of the world; they were flying silently and in straight lines, flakes of black snow. But none struck the windshield or tumbled into the car, and presently humorists began holding out their hands, trying to catch some. After ten minutes the cloud thinned out, passed, and the women emerged from the blankets, disheveled and feeling silly. And everyone talked together.

Everyone talked; it would have been absurd not to talk after having been through a swarm of locusts on the edge of the Sahara. The Smyrna-American talked to the British widow going down to Biskra to have one last fling with an as-yet-unencountered sheik. The member of the San Francisco Stock Exchange talked shyly to the author. 'Aren't you an author?' he said. The father and daughter from Wilmington talked to the cockney airman who was going to fly to Timbuctoo. Even the French chauffeur turned about and explained in a loud, clear voice: 'Bumblebees,' which sent the trained nurse from New York into shriek after shriek of hysterical laughter.

Amongst the unsubtle rushing together of the travelers there was one interchange more carefully considered. Mr and Mrs Liddell Miles, turning as one person, smiled and spoke to the young American couple in the seat behind:

'Didn't catch any in your hair?'

The young couple smiled back politely.

'No. We survived that plague.'

They were in their twenties, and there was still a pleasant touch of bride and groom upon them. A handsome couple; the man rather intense and sensitive, the girl arrestingly light of hue in eyes and hair, her face without shadows, its living freshness modulated by a lovely confident calm. Mr and Mrs Miles did not fail to notice their air of good breeding, of a specifically 'swell' background, expressed both by their unsophistication and by their ingrained reticence that was not stiffness. If they held aloof, it was because they were sufficient to each other, while Mr and Mrs Miles' aloofness toward the other passengers was a conscious mask, a social attitude, quite as public an affair in its essence as the ubiquitous advances of the Smyrna-American, who was snubbed by all.

The Mileses had, in fact, decided that the young couple were 'possible' and, bored with themselves, were frankly approaching them.

'Have you been to Africa before? It's been so utterly fascinating! Are you going on to Tunis?'

The Mileses, if somewhat worn away inside by fifteen years of a particular set in Paris, had undeniable style, even charm, and before the evening arrival at the little oasis town of Bou Saada they had all four become companionable. They uncovered mutual friends in New York and, meeting for a cocktail in the bar of the Hotel Transatlantique, decided to have dinner together.

As the young Kellys came downstairs later, Nicole was conscious of a certain regret that they had accepted, realizing that now they were probably committed to seeing a certain amount of their new acquaintances as far as Constantine, where their routes diverged.

In the eight months of their marriage she had been so very happy that it seemed like spoiling something. On the Italian liner that had brought them to Gibraltar they had not joined the groups that leaned desperately on one another in the bar; instead, they seriously studied French, and Nelson worked on business contingent on his recent inheritance of half a million dollars. Also he painted a picture of a smokestack. When one member of the gay crowd in the bar disappeared permanently into the Atlantic just this side of the Azores, the young Kellys were almost glad, for it justified their aloof attitude.

But there was another reason Nicole was sorry they had committed themselves. She spoke to Nelson about it: 'I passed that couple in the hall just now.'

'Who – the Mileses?'

'No, that young couple – about our age – the ones that were

on the other motorbus, that we thought looked so nice, in Bir Rabalou after lunch, in the camel market.'

'They did look nice.'

'Charming,' she said emphatically; 'the girl and man, both. I'm almost sure I've met the girl somewhere before.'

The couple referred to were sitting across the room at dinner, and Nicole found her eyes drawn irresistibly toward them. They, too, now had companions, and again Nicole, who had not talked to a girl of her own age for two months, felt a faint regret. The Mileses, being formally sophisticated and frankly snobbish, were a different matter. They had been to an alarming number of places and seemed to know all the flashing phantoms of the newspapers.

They dined on the hotel veranda under a sky that was low and full of the presence of a strange and watchful God; around the corners of the hotel the night already stirred with the sounds of which they had so often read but that were even so hysterically unfamiliar – drums from Senegal, a native flute, the selfish, effeminate whine of a camel, the Arabs pattering past in shoes made of old automobile tires, the wail of Magian prayer.

At the desk in the hotel, a fellow passenger was arguing monotonously with the clerk about the rate of exchange, and the inappropriateness added to the detachment which had increased steadily as they went south.

Mrs Miles was the first to break the lingering silence; with a sort of impatience she pulled them with her, in from the night and up to the table.

'We really should have dressed. Dinner's more amusing if people dress, because they feel differently in formal clothes. The English know that.'

'Dress here?' her husband objected. 'I'd feel like that man in the ragged dress suit we passed today, driving the flock of sheep.'

'I always feel like a tourist if I'm not dressed.'

'Well, we are, aren't we?' asked Nelson.

'I don't consider myself a tourist. A tourist is somebody who gets up early and goes to cathedrals and talks about scenery.'

Nicole and Nelson, having seen all the official sights from Fez to Algiers, and taken reels of moving pictures and felt improved, confessed themselves, but decided that their experiences on the trip would not interest Mrs Miles.

'Every place is the same,' Mrs Miles continued. 'The only thing that matters is who's there. New scenery is fine for half an hour, but after that you want your own kind to see. That's why some places have a certain vogue, and then the vogue changes and the people move on somewhere else. The place itself really never matters.'

'But doesn't somebody first decide that the place is nice?' objected Nelson. 'The first ones go there because they like the place.'

'Where were you going this spring?' Mrs Miles asked.

'We thought of San Remo, or maybe Sorrento. We've never been to Europe before.'

'My children, I know both Sorrento and San Remo, and you won't stand either of them for a week. They're full of the most awful English, reading the Daily Mail and waiting for letters and talking about the most incredibly dull things. You might as well go to Brighton or Bournemouth and buy a white poodle and a sunshade and walk on the pier. How long are you staying in Europe?'

'We don't know; perhaps several years.' Nicole hesitated. 'Nelson came into a little money, and we wanted a change. When I was young, my father had asthma and I had to live in the most depressing health resorts with him for years; and Nelson was in the fur business in Alaska and he loathed it; so when we were free we came abroad. Nelson's going to paint and I'm going to study singing.' She looked triumphantly at her husband. 'So far, it's been absolutely gorgeous.'

Mrs Miles decided, from the evidence of the younger woman's clothes, that it was quite a bit of money, and their enthusiasm was infectious.

'You really must go to Biarritz,' she advised them. 'Or else come to Monte Carlo.'

'They tell me there's a great show here,' said Miles, ordering champagne. 'The Ouled Naïls. The concierge says they're some kind of tribe of girls who come down from the mountains and learn to be dancers, and what not, till they've collected enough

gold to go back to their mountains and marry. Well, they give a
performance tonight.'

Walking over to the Café of the Ouled Naïls afterward, Nicole
regretted that she and Nelson were not strolling alone through
the ever-lower, ever-softer, ever-brighter night. Nelson had
reciprocated the bottle of champagne at dinner, and neither of
them was accustomed to so much. As they drew near the sad
flute she didn't want to go inside, but rather to climb to the top of
a low hill where a white mosque shone clear as a planet through
the night. Life was better than any show; closing in toward
Nelson, she pressed his hand.

The little cave of a café was filled with the passengers from the
two busses. The girls – light-brown, flat-nosed Berbers with fine,
deep-shaded eyes – were already doing each one her solo on the
platform. They wore cotton dresses, faintly reminiscent of
Southern mammies; under these their bodies writhed in a slow
nautch, culminating in a stomach dance, with silver belts
bobbing wildly and their strings of real gold coins tinkling on
their necks and arms. The flute player was also a comedian; he
danced, burlesquing the girls. The drummer, swathed in goat-
skins like a witch doctor, was a true black from the Sudan.

Through the smoke of cigarettes each girl went in turn
through the finger movement, like piano playing in the air –
outwardly facile, yet, after a few moments, so obviously exacting
– and then through the very simply languid yet equally precise
steps of the feet – these were but preparation to the wild
sensuality of the culminated dance.

Afterward there was a lull. Though the performance seemed
not quite over, most of the audience gradually got up to go, but
there was a whispering in the air.

'What is it?' Nicole asked her husband.

'Why, I believe – it appears that for a consideration the Ouled
Naïls dance in more or less – ah – Oriental style – in very little
except jewelry.'

'Oh.'

'We're all staying,' Mr Miles assured her jovially. 'After all,
we're here to see the real customs and manners of the country; a
little prudishness shouldn't stand in our way.'

Most of the men remained, and several of the women. Nicole stood up suddenly.

'I'll wait outside,' she said.

'Why not stay, Nicole? After all, Mrs Miles is staying.'

The flute player was making preliminary flourishes. Upon the raised dais two pale brown children of perhaps fourteen were taking off their cotton dresses. For an instant Nicole hesitated, torn between repulsion and the desire not to appear to be a prig. Then she saw another young American woman get up quickly and start for the door. Recognizing the attractive young wife from the other bus, her own decision came quickly and she followed.

Nelson hurried after her. 'I'm going if you go,' he said, but with evident reluctance.

'Please don't bother. I'll wait with the guide outside.'

'Well –' The drum was starting. He compromised: 'I'll only stay a minute. I want to see what it's like.'

Waiting in the fresh night, she found that the incident had hurt her – Nelson's not coming with her at once, giving as an argument the fact that Mrs Miles was staying. From being hurt, she grew angry and made signs to the guide that she wanted to return to the hotel.

Twenty minutes later, Nelson appeared, angry with the anxiety at finding her gone, as well as to hide his guilt at having left her. Incredulous with themselves, they were suddenly in a quarrel.

Much later, when there were no sounds at all in Bou Saada and the nomads in the market place were only motionless bundles rolled up in their burnouses, she was asleep upon his shoulder. Life is progressive, no matter what our intentions, but something was harmed, some precedent of possible nonagreement was set. It was a love match, though, and it could stand a great deal. She and Nelson had passed lonely youths, and now they wanted the taste and smell of the living world; for the present they were finding it in each other.

A month later they were in Sorrento, where Nicole took singing lessons and Nelson tried to paint something new into the Bay of Naples. It was the existence they had planned and often read about. But they found, as so many have found, that the charm of idyllic interludes depends upon one person's 'giving the party' – which is to say, furnishing the background, the experience, the patience, against which the other seems to enjoy again the spells of pastoral tranquillity recollected from childhood. Nicole and Nelson were at once too old and too young, and too American, to fall into immediate soft agreement with a strange land. Their vitality made them restless, for as yet his painting had no direction and her singing no immediate prospect of becoming serious. They said they were not 'getting anywhere' – the evenings were long, so they began to drink a lot of *vin de Capri* at dinner.

The English owned the hotel. They were aged, come South for good weather and tranquillity; Nelson and Nicole resented the mild tenor of their days. Could people be content to talk eternally about the weather, promenade the same walks, face the same variant of macaroni at dinner month after month? They grew bored, and Americans bored are already in sight of excitement. Things came to head all in one night.

Over a flask of wine at dinner they decided to go to Paris, settle in an apartment and work seriously. Paris promised metropolitan diversion, friends of their own age, a general intensity that Italy lacked. Eager with new hopes, they strolled into the salon after dinner, when, for the tenth time, Nelson noticed an ancient and enormous mechanical piano and was moved to try it.

Across the salon sat the only English people with whom they had had any connection – Gen. Sir Evelyne Fragelle and Lady Fragelle. The connection had been brief and unpleasant – seeing them walking out of the hotel in peignoirs to swim, she had announced, over quite a few yards of floor space, that it was disgusting and shouldn't be allowed.

But that was nothing compared with her response to the first terrific bursts of sound from the electric piano. As the dust of years trembled off the keyboard at the vibration, she shot galvanically forward with the sort of jerk associated with the electric chair. Somewhat stunned himself by the sudden din of Waiting for the Robert E. Lee, Nelson had scarcely sat down when she projected herself across the room, her train quivering behind her, and, without glancing at the Kellys, turned off the instrument.

It was one of those gestures that are either plainly justified, or else outrageous. For a moment Nelson hesitated uncertainly; then, remembering Lady Fragelle's arrogant remark about his bathing suit, he returned to the instrument in her still-billowing wake and turned it on again.

The incident had become international. The eyes of the entire salon fell eagerly upon the protagonists, watching for the next move. Nicole hurried after Nelson, urging him to let the matter pass, but it was too late. From the outraged English table there arose, joint by joint, Gen. Sir Evelyne Fragelle, faced with perhaps his most crucial situation since the relief of Ladysmith.

'T'lee outrageous! – 't'lee outrageous!'

'I beg your pardon,' said Nelson.

'Here for fifteen years!' screamed Sir Evelyne to himself. 'Never heard of anyone doing such a thing before!'

'I gathered that this was put here for the amusement of the guests.'

Scorning to answer, Sir Evelyne knelt, reached for the catch, pushed it the wrong way, whereupon the speed and volume of the instrument tripled until they stood in a wild pandemonium of sound; Sir Evelyne livid with military emotions, Nelson on the point of maniacal laughter.

In a moment the firm hand of the hotel manager settled the matter; the instrument gulped and stopped, trembling a little from its unaccustomed outburst, leaving behind it a great silence in which Sir Evelyne turned to the manager.

'Most outrageous affair ever heard of in my life. My wife turned it off once, and he' – this was his first acknowledgment of Nelson's identity as distinct from the instrument – 'he put it on again!'

'This is a public room in a hotel,' Nelson protested. 'The instrument is apparently here to be used.'

'Don't get in an argument,' Nicole whispered. 'They're old.'

But Nelson said, 'If there's any apology, it's certainly due to me.'

Sir Evelyne's eye was fixed menacingly upon the manager, waiting for him to do his duty. The latter thought of Sir Evelyne's fifteen years of residence, and cringed.

'It is not the habitude to play the instrument in the evening. The clients are each one quiet on his or her table.'

'American cheek!' snapped Sir Evelyne.

'Very well,' Nelson said; 'we'll relieve the hotel of our presence tomorrow.'

As a reaction from this incident, as a sort of protest against Sir Evelyne Fragelle, they went not to Paris but to Monte Carlo after all. They were through with being alone.

2

A little more than two years after the Kellys' first visit to Monte Carlo, Nicole woke up one morning into what, though it bore the same name, had become to her a different place altogether.

In spite of hurried months in Paris or Biarritz, it was now home to them. They had a villa, they had a large acquaintance among the spring and summer crowd – a crowd which, naturally, did not include people on charted trips or the shore parties from Mediterranean cruises; these latter had become for them 'tourists.'

They loved the Riviera in full summer with many friends there and the nights open and full of music. Before the maid drew the curtains this morning to shut out the glare, Nicole saw from her window the yacht of T. F. Golding, placid among the swells of the Monacan Bay, as if constantly bound on a romantic voyage not dependent upon actual motion.

The yacht had taken the slow tempo of the coast; it had gone no farther than to Cannes and back all summer, though it might have toured the world. The Kellys were dining on board that night.

Nicole spoke excellent French; she had five new evening dresses and four others that would do; she had her husband; she had two men in love with her, and she felt sad for one of them. She had her pretty face. At 10:30 she was meeting a third man, who was just beginning to be in love with her 'in a harmless way.' At one she was having a dozen charming people to luncheon. All that.

'I'm happy,' she brooded toward the bright blinds. 'I'm young and good-looking, and my name is often in the paper as having been here and there, but really I don't care about chi-chi. I think it's all awfully silly, but if you do want to see people, you might as well see the chic, amusing ones; and if people call you a snob, it's envy, and they know it and everybody knows it.'

She repeated the substance of this to Oscar Dane on the Mont Agel golf course two hours later, and he cursed her quietly.

'Not at all,' he said. 'You're just getting to be an old snob. Do you call that crowd of drunks you run with amusing people? Why, they're not even very swell. They're so hard that they've shifted down through Europe like nails in a sack of wheat, till they stick out of it a little into the Mediterranean Sea.'

Annoyed, Nicole fired a name at him, but he answered: 'Class C. A good solid article for beginners.'

'The Colbys – anyway, her.'

'Third flight.'

'Marquis and Marquise de Kalb.'

'If she didn't happen to take dope and he didn't have other peculiarities.'

'Well, then, where are the amusing people?' she demanded impatiently.

'Off by themselves somewhere. They don't hunt in herds, except occasionally.'

'How about you? You'd snap up an invitation from every person I named. I've heard stories about you wilder than any you can make up. There's not a man that's known you six months that would take your check for ten dollars. You're a sponge and a parasite and everything –'

'Shut up for a minute,' he interrupted. 'I don't want to spoil this drive. . . . I just don't like to see you kid yourself,' he continued. 'What passes with you for international society is just about as hard to enter nowadays as the public rooms at the Casino; and if I can make my living by sponging off it, I'm still giving twenty times more than I get. We dead beats are about the only people in it with any stuff, and we stay with it because we have to.'

She laughed, liking him immensely, wondering how angry Nelson would be when he found that Oscar had walked off with his nail scissors and his copy of the New York Herald this morning.

'Anyhow,' she thought afterward, as she drove home toward

luncheon, 'we're getting out of it all soon, and we'll be serious and have a baby. After this last summer.'

Stopping for a moment at a florist's, she saw a young woman coming out with an armful of flowers. The young woman glanced at her over the heap of color, and Nicole perceived that she was extremely smart, and then that her face was familiar. It was someone she had known once, but only slightly; the name had escaped her, so she did not nod, and forgot the incident until that afternoon.

They were twelve for luncheon: The Goldings' party from the yacht, Liddell and Cardine Miles, Mr Dane – seven different nationalities she counted; among them an exquisite young French-woman, Madame Delauney, whom Nicole referred to lightly as 'Nelson's girl.' Noel Delauney was perhaps her closest friend; when they made up foursomes for golf or for trips, she paired off with Nelson; but today, as Nicole introduced her to someone as 'Nelson's girl,' the bantering phrase filled Nicole with distaste.

She said aloud at luncheon: 'Nelson and I are going to get away from it all.'

Everybody agreed that they, too, were going to get away from it all.

'It's all right for the English,' someone said, 'because they're doing a sort of dance of death – you know, gayety in the doomed fort, with the Sepoys at the gate. You can see it by their faces when they dance – the intensity. They know it and they want it, and they don't see any future. But you Americans, you're having a rotten time. If you want to wear the green hat or the crushed hat, or whatever it is, you always have to get a little tipsy.'

'We're going to get away from it all,' Nicole said firmly, but something within her argued: 'What a pity – this lovely blue sea, this happy time.' What came afterward? Did one just accept a lessening of tension? It was somehow Nelson's business to answer that. His growing discontent that he wasn't getting anywhere ought to explode into a new life for both of them, or rather a new hope and content with life. That secret should be his masculine contribution.

'Well, children, good-by.'

'It was a great luncheon.'

'Don't forget about getting away from it all.'

'See you when –'

The guests walked down the path toward their cars. Only
Oscar, just faintly flushed on liqueurs, stood with Nicole on the
veranda, talking on and on about the girl he had invited up to see
his stamp collection. Momentarily tired of people, impatient to be
alone, Nicole listened for a moment and then, taking a glass vase
of flowers from the luncheon table, went through the French
windows into the dark, shadowy villa, his voice following her as
he talked on and on out there.

It was when she crossed the first salon, still hearing Oscar's
monologue on the veranda, that she began to hear another voice
in the next room, cutting sharply across Oscar's voice.

'Ah, but kiss me again,' it said, stopped; Nicole stopped, too,
rigid in the silence, now broken only by the voice on the porch.

'Be careful.' Nicole recognized the faint French accent of Noel
Delauney.

'I'm tired of being careful. Anyhow, they're on the veranda.'

'No, better the usual place.'

'Darling, sweet darling.'

The voice of Oscar Dane on the veranda grew weary and
stopped and, as if thereby released from her paralysis, Nicole took
a step – forward or backward, she did not know which. At the
sound of her heel on the floor, she heard the two people in the
next room breaking swiftly apart.

Then she went in. Nelson was lighting a cigarette; Noel, with
her back turned, was apparently hunting for hat or purse on a
chair. With blind horror rather than anger, Nicole threw, or
rather pushed away from her, the glass vase which she carried. If
at anyone, it was at Nelson she threw it, but the force of her
feeling had entered the inanimate thing; it flew past him, and
Noel Delauney, just turning about, was struck full on the side of
her head and face.

'Say, there!' Nelson cried. Noel sank slowly into the chair
before which she stood, her hand slowly rising to cover the side of
her face. The jar rolled unbroken on the thick carpet, scattering
its flowers.

'You look out!' Nelson was at Noel's side, trying to take the
hand away to see what had happened.

'*C'est liquide,*' gasped Noel in a whisper. '*Est-ce que c'est le sang?*'

He forced her hand away, and cried breathlessly, 'No, it's just water!' and then, to Oscar, who had appeared in the doorway: 'Get some cognac!' and to Nicole: 'You fool, you must be crazy!'

Nicole, breathing hard, said nothing. When the brandy arrived, there was a continuing silence, like that of people watching an operation, while Nelson poured a glass down Noel's throat. Nicole signaled to Oscar for a drink, and, as if afraid to break the silence without it, they all had a brandy. Then Noel and Nelson spoke at once:

'If you can find my hat –'

'This is the silliest –'

'– I shall go immediately.'

'– thing I ever saw; I –'

They all looked at Nicole, who said: 'Have her car drive right up to the door.' Oscar departed quickly.

'Are you sure you don't want to see a doctor?' asked Nelson anxiously.

'I want to go.'

A minute later, when the car had driven away, Nelson came in and poured himself another glass of brandy. A wave of subsiding tension flowed over him, showing in his face; Nicole saw it, and saw also his gathering will to make the best he could of it.

'I want to know just why you did that,' he demanded. 'No, don't go, Oscar.' He saw the story starting out into the world.

'What possible reason –'

'Oh, shut up!' snapped Nicole.

'If I kissed Noel, there's nothing so terrible about it. It's of absolutely no significance.'

She made a contemptuous sound. 'I heard what you said to her.'

'You're crazy.'

He said it as if she were crazy, and wild rage filled her.

'You liar! All this time pretending to be so square, and so particular what I did, and all the time behind my back you've been playing around with that little –'

She used a serious word, and as if maddened with the sound of it, she sprang toward his chair. In protection against this sudden attack, he flung up his arm quickly, and the knuckles of his open hand struck across the socket of her eye. Covering her face with her hand as Noel had done ten minutes previously, she fell sobbing to the floor.

'Hasn't this gone far enough?' Oscar cried.

'Yes,' admitted Nelson, 'I guess it has.'

'You go on out on the veranda and cool off.'

He got Nicole to a couch and sat beside her, holding her hand.

'Brace up – brace up, baby,' he said, over and over. 'What are you – Jack Dempsey? You can't go around hitting French women; they'll sue you.'

'He told her he loved her,' she gasped hysterically. 'She said she'd meet him at the same place. . . . Has he gone there now?'

'He's out on the porch, walking up and down, sorry as the devil that he accidentally hit you, and sorry he ever saw Noel Delauney.'

'Oh, yes!'

'You might have heard wrong, and it doesn't prove a thing, anyhow.'

After twenty minutes, Nelson came in suddenly and sank down on his knees by the side of his wife. Mr Oscar Dane, reënforced in his idea that he gave much more than he got, backed discreetly and far from unwillingly to the door.

In another hour, Nelson and Nicole, arm in arm, emerged from their villa and walked slowly down to the Café de Paris. They walked instead of driving, as if trying to return to the simplicity they had once possessed, as if they were trying to unwind something that had become visibly tangled. Nicole accepted his explanations, not because they were credible, but because she wanted passionately to believe them. They were both very quiet and sorry.

The Café de Paris was pleasant at that hour, with sunset drooping through the yellow awnings and the red parasols as through stained glass. Glancing about, Nicole saw the young woman she had encountered that morning. She was with a man now, and Nelson placed them immediately as the young couple they had seen in Algeria, almost three years ago.

'They've changed,' he commented. 'I suppose we have, too, but not so much. They're harder-looking and he looks dissipated. Dissipation always shows in light eyes rather than in dark ones.

The girl is *tout ce qu'il y a de chic*, as they say, but there's a hard look in her face too.'

'I like her.'

'Do you want me to go and ask them if they are that same couple?'

'No! That'd be like lonesome tourists do. They have their own friends.'

At that moment people were joining them at their table.

'Nelson, how about tonight?' Nicole asked a little later. 'Do you think we can appear at the Goldings' after what's happened?'

'We not only can but we've got to. If the story's around and we're not there, we'll just be handing them a nice juicy subject of conversation. . . . Hello! What on earth—'

Something strident and violent had happened across the café; a woman screamed and the people at one table were all on their feet, surging back and forth like one person. Then the people at the other tables were standing and crowding forward; for just a moment the Kellys saw the face of the girl they had been watching, pale now, and distorted with anger. Panic-stricken, Nicole plucked at Nelson's sleeve.

'I want to get out. I can't stand any more today. Take me home. Is everybody going crazy?'

On the way home, Nelson glanced at Nicole's face and perceived with a start that they were not going to dinner on the Goldings' yacht after all. For Nicole had the beginnings of a well-defined and unmistakable black eye – an eye that by eleven o'clock would be beyond the aid of all the cosmetics in the principality. His heart sank and he decided to say nothing about it until they reached home.

3

There is some wise advice in the catechism about avoiding the occasions of sin, and when the Kellys went up to Paris a month later they made a conscientious list of the places they wouldn't visit any more and the people they didn't want to see again. The places included several famous bars, all the night clubs except one or two that were highly decorous, all the early-morning clubs of every description, and all summer resorts that made whoopee for its own sake – whoopee triumphant and unrestrained – the main attraction of the season.

The people they were through with included three-fourths of those with whom they had passed the last two years. They did this not in snobbishness, but for self-preservation, and not without a certain fear in their hearts that they were cutting themselves off from human contacts forever.

But the world is always curious, and people become valuable merely for their inaccessibility. They found that there were others in Paris who were only interested in those who had separated from the many. The first crowd they had known was largely American, salted with Europeans; the second was largely European, peppered with Americans. This latter crowd was 'society,' and here and there it touched the ultimate *milieu*, made up of individuals of high position, of great fortune, very occasionally of genius, and always of power. Without being intimate with the great, they made new friends of a more conservative type. Moreover, Nelson began to paint again; he had a studio, and they visited the studios of Brancusi and Leger and Deschamps. It seemed that they were more part of something than before, and when certain gaudy rendezvous were mentioned, they felt a contempt for their first two years in Europe, speaking of their former acquaintances as 'that crowd' and as 'people who waste your time.'

So, although they kept their rules, they entertained frequently at home and they went out to the houses of others. They were young and handsome and intelligent; they came to know what did go and what did not go, and adapted themselves accordingly. Moreover, they were naturally generous and willing, within the limits of common sense, to pay.

When one went out one generally drank. This meant little to Nicole, who had a horror of losing her *soigné* air, losing a touch of bloom or a ray of admiration, but Nelson, thwarted somewhere, found himself quite as tempted to drink at these small dinners as in the more frankly rowdy world. He was not a drunk, he did nothing conspicuous or sodden, but he was no longer willing to go out socially without the stimulus of liquor. It was with the idea of bringing him to a serious and responsible attitude that

Nicole decided after a year in Paris, that the time had come to have a baby.

This was coincidental with their meeting Count Chiki Sarolai. He was an attractive relic of the Austrian court, with no fortune or pretense to any, but with solid social and financial connections in France. His sister was married to the Marquis de la Clos d'Hirondelle, who, in addition to being of the ancient noblesse, was a successful banker in Paris. Count Chiki roved here and there, frankly sponging, rather like Oscar Dane, but in a different sphere.

His penchant was Americans; he hung on their words with a pathetic eagerness, as if they would sooner or later let slip their mysterious formula for making money. After a casual meeting, his interest gravitated to the Kellys. During Nicole's months of waiting he was in the house continually, tirelessly interested in anything that concerned American crime, slang, finance or manners. He came in for a luncheon or dinner when he had no other place to go, and with tacit gratitude he persuaded his sister to call on Nicole, who was immensely flattered.

It was arranged that when Nicole went to the hospital he would stay at the *appartement* and keep Nelson company – an arrangement of which Nicole didn't approve, since they were inclined to drink together. But the day on which it was decided, he arrived with news of one of his brother-in-law's famous canal-boat parties on the Seine, to which the Kellys were to be invited and which, conveniently enough, was to occur three weeks after the arrival of the baby. So, when Nicole moved out to the American Hospital Count Chiki moved in.

The baby was a boy. For a while Nicole forgot all about people and their human status and their value. She even wondered at the fact that she had become such a snob, since everything seemed trivial compared with the new individual that, eight times a day, they carried to her breast.

After two weeks she and the baby went back to the apartment, but Chiki and his valet stayed on. It was understood, with that subtlety the Kellys had only recently begun to appreciate, that he was merely staying until after his brother-in-law's party, but the apartment was crowded and Nicole wished him gone. But her old idea, that if one had to see people they might as well be the best, was carried out in being invited to the de la Clos d'Hirondelles.

As she lay in her chaise longue the day before the event, Chiki explained the arrangements, in which he had evidently aided.

'Everyone who arrives must drink two cocktails in the American style before they can come aboard – as a ticket of admission.'

'But I thought that very fashionable French – Faubourg St Germain and all that – didn't drink cocktails.'

'Oh, but my family is very modern. We adopt many American customs.'

'Who'll be there?'

'Everyone! Everyone in Paris.'

Great names swam before her eyes. Next day she could not resist dragging the affair into conversation with her doctor. But she was rather offended at the look of astonishment and incredulity that came into his eyes.

'Did I understand you aright?' he demanded. 'Did I understand you to say that you were going to a ball tomorrow?'

'Why, yes,' she faltered. 'Why not?'

'My dear lady, you are not going to stir out of the house for two more weeks; you are not going to dance or do anything strenuous for two more after that.'

'That's ridiculous!' she cried. 'It's been three weeks already! Esther Sherman went to America after –'

'Never mind,' he interrupted. 'Every case is different. There is a complication which makes it positively necessary for you to follow my orders.'

'But the idea is that I'll just go for two hours, because of course I'll have to come home to Sonny –'

'You'll not go for two minutes.'

She knew, from the seriousness of his tone, that he was right, but, perversely, she did not mention the matter to Nelson. She said, instead, that she was tired, that possibly she might not go, and lay awake that night measuring her disappointment against her fear. She woke up for Sonny's first feeding, thinking to herself: 'But if I just take ten steps from a limousine to a chair and just sit half an hour –'

At the last minute the pale green evening dress from Callets, draped across a chair in her bedroom, decided her. She went.

Somewhere, during the shuffle and delay on the gangplank while the guests went aboard and were challenged and drank down their cocktails with attendant gayety, Nicole realized that she had made a mistake. There was, at any rate, no formal receiving line and, after greeting their hosts, Nelson found her a chair on deck, where presently her faintness disappeared.

Then she was glad she had come. The boat was hung with fragile lanterns, which blended with the pastels of the bridges and the reflected stars in the dark Seine, like a child's dream out of the Arabian Nights. A crowd of hungry-eyed spectators were gathered on the banks. Champagne moved past in platoons like a drill of bottles, while the music, instead of being loud and obtrusive, drifted down from the upper deck like frosting dripping over a cake. She became aware presently that they were not the only Americans there – across the deck were the Liddell Mileses, whom she had not seen for several years.

Other people from that crowd were present, and she felt a faint disappointment. What if this was not the marquis' best party? She remembered her mother's second days at home. She asked Chiki, who was at her side, to point out celebrities, but when she inquired about several people whom she associated with that set, he replied vaguely that they were away, or coming later, or could not be there. It seemed to her that she saw across the room the girl who had made the scene in the Café de Paris at Monte Carlo, but she could not be sure, for with the faint almost imperceptible movement of the boat, she realized that she was growing faint again. She sent for Nelson to take her home.

'You can come right back, of course. You needn't wait for me, because I'm going right to bed.'

He left her in the hands of the nurse, who helped her upstairs and aided her to undress quickly.

'I'm desperately tired,' Nicole said. 'Will you put my pearls away?'

'Where?'

'In the jewel box on the dressing table.'

'I don't see it,' said the nurse after a minute.

'Then it's in a drawer.'

There was a thorough rummaging of the dressing table, without result.

'But of course it's there.' Nicole attempted to rise, but fell back, exhausted. 'Look for it, please, again. Everything is in it – all my mother's things and my engagement things.'

'I'm sorry, Mrs Kelly. There's nothing in this room that answers to that description.'

'Wake up the maid.'

The maid knew nothing; then, after a persistent cross-examination, she did know something. Count Sarolai's valet had gone out, carrying his suitcase, half an hour after madame left the house.

Writhing in sharp and sudden pain, with a hastily summoned doctor at her side, it seemed to Nicole hours before Nelson came home. When he arrived, his face was deathly pale and his eyes were wild. He came directly into her room.

'What do you think?' he said savagely. Then he saw the doctor. 'Why, what's the matter?'

'Oh, Nelson, I'm sick as a dog and my jewel box is gone, and Chiki's valet has gone. I've told the police. . . . Perhaps Chiki would know where the man –'

'Chiki will never come in this house again,' he said slowly. 'Do you know whose party that was? Have you got any idea whose party that was?' He burst into wild laughter. 'It was our party – our party, do you understand? We gave it – we didn't know it, but we did.'

'*Maintenant, monsieur, il ne faut pas exciter madame –*' the doctor began.

'I thought it was odd when the marquis went home early, but I didn't suspect till the end. They were just guests – Chiki invited all the people. After it was over, the caterers and musicians began to come up and ask me where to send their bills. And that damn Chiki had the nerve to tell me he thought I knew all the time. He said that all he'd promised was that it would be his brother-in-law's sort of party, and that his sister would be there. He said perhaps I was drunk, or perhaps I didn't understand French – as if we'd ever talked anything but English to him.'

'Don't pay!' she said. 'I wouldn't think of paying.'

'So I said, but they're going to sue – the boat people and the others. They want twelve thousand dollars.'

She relaxed suddenly. 'Oh, go away!' she cried. 'I don't care! I've lost my jewels and I'm sick!'

4

This is the story of a trip abroad, and the geographical element must not be slighted. Having visited North Africa, Italy, the Riviera, Paris and points in between, it was not surprising that eventually the Kellys should go to Switzerland. Switzerland is a country where very few things begin, but many things end.

Though there was an element of choice in their other ports of call, the Kellys went to Switzerland because they had to. They had been married a little more than four years when they arrived one spring day at the lake that is the center of Europe – a placid, smiling spot with pastoral hillsides, a backdrop of mountains and waters of postcard blue, waters that are a little sinister beneath the surface with all the misery that has dragged itself here from every corner of Europe. Weariness to recuperate and death to die. There are schools, too, and young people splashing at the sunny plages; there is Bonivard's dungeon and Calvin's city, and the ghosts of Byron and Shelley still sail the dim shores by night; but the Lake Geneva that Nelson and Nicole came to was the dreary one of sanatoriums and rest hotels.

For, as if by some profound sympathy that had continued to exist beneath the unlucky destiny that had pursued their affairs, health had failed them both at the same time; Nicole lay on the balcony of a hotel coming slowly back to life after two successive operations, while Nelson fought for life against jaundice in a hospital two miles away. Even after the reserve force of twenty-nine years had pulled him through, there were months ahead during which he must live quietly. Often they wondered why, of all those who sought pleasure over the face of Europe, this misfortune should have come to them.

'There've been too many people in our lives,' Nelson said. 'We've never been able to resist people. We were so happy the first year when there weren't any people.'

Nicole agreed. 'If we could ever be alone – really alone – we could make up some kind of life for ourselves. We'll try, won't we, Nelson?'

But there were other days when they both wanted company desperately, concealing it from each other. Days when they eyed the obese, the wasted, the crippled and the broken of all nationalities who filled the hotel, seeking for one who might be amusing. It was a new life for them, turning on the daily visits of their two doctors, the arrival of the mail and newspapers from Paris, the little walk into the hillside village or occasionally the descent by funicular to the pale resort on the lake, with its *Kursaal*, its grass beach, its tennis clubs and sight-seeing busses. They read Tauchnitz editions and yellow-jacketed Edgar Walla- ces; at a certain hour each day they watched the baby being given its bath; three nights a week there was a tired and patient orchestra in the lounge after dinner, that was all.

And sometimes there was a booming from the vine-covered hills on the other side of the lake, which meant that cannons were shooting at hail-bearing clouds, to save the vineyard from an approaching storm; it came swiftly, first falling from the heavens and then falling again in torrents from the mountains, washing loudly down the roads and stone ditches; it came with a dark, frightening sky and savage filaments of lightning and crashing, world-splitting thunder, while ragged and destroyed clouds fled along before the wind past the hotel. The mountains and the lake disappeared completely; the hotel crouched alone amid tumult and chaos and darkness.

It was during such a storm, when the mere opening of a door admitted a tornado of rain and wind into the hall, that the Kellys for the first time in months saw someone they knew. Sitting downstairs with other victims of frayed nerves, they became aware of two new arrivals – a man and woman whom they recognized as the couple, first seen in Algiers, who had crossed their path several times since. A single unexpressed thought flashed through Nelson and Nicole. It seemed like destiny that at last here in this desolate place they should know them, and watching, they saw other couples eying them in the same tentative way. Yet something held the Kellys back. Had they not just been complaining that there were too many people in their lives?

Later, when the storm had dozed off into a quiet rain, Nicole found herself near the girl on the glass veranda. Under cover of reading a book, she inspected the face closely. It was an inquisitive face, she saw at once, possibly calculating; the eyes, intelligent enough, but with no peace in them, swept over people in a single quick glance as though estimating their value. 'Terrible egoist,' Nicole thought, with a certain distaste. For the rest, the cheeks were wan, and there were little pouches of ill health under the eyes; these combining with a certain flabbiness of arms and legs to give an impression of unwholesomeness. She was dressed expensively, but with a hint of slovenliness, as if she did not consider the people of the hotel important.

On the whole, Nicole decided she did not like her; she was glad that they had not spoken, but she was rather surprised that she had not noticed these things when the girl crossed her path before.

Telling Nelson her impression at dinner, he agreed with her.

'I ran into the man in the bar, and I noticed we both took nothing but mineral water, so I started to say something. But I got a good look at his face in the mirror and I decided not to. His face is so weak and self-indulgent that it's almost mean – the kind of face that needs half a dozen drinks really to open the eyes and stiffen the mouth up to normal.'

After dinner the rain stopped and the night was fine outside. Eager for the air, the Kellys wandered down into the dark garden; on their way they passed the subjects of their late discussion, who withdrew abruptly down a side path.

'I don't think they want to know us any more than we do them,' Nicole laughed.

They loitered among the wild rosebushes and the beds of damp-sweet, indistinguishable flowers. Below the hotel, where the terrace fell a thousand feet to the lake, stretched a necklace of lights that was Montreux and Vevey, and then, in a dim pendant, Lausanne; a blurred twinkling across the lake was Evian and France. From somewhere below – probably the *Kursaal* – came the sound of full-bodied dance music – American, they guessed, though now they heard American tunes months late, mere distant echoes of what was happening far away.

Over the Dent du Midi, over a black bank of clouds that was

the rearguard of the receding storm, the moon lifted itself and the lake brightened; the music and the far-away lights were like hope, like the enchanted distance from which children see things. In their separate hearts Nelson and Nicole gazed backward to a time when life was all like this. Her arm went through his quietly and drew him close.

'We can have it all again,' she whispered. 'Can't we try, Nelson?'

She paused as two dark forms came into the shadows nearby and stood looking down at the lake below.

Nelson put his arm around Nicole and pulled her closer.

'It's just that we don't understand what's the matter,' she said. 'Why did we lose peace and love and health, one after the other? If we knew, if there was anybody to tell us, I believe we could try. I'd try so hard.'

The last clouds were lifting themselves over the Bernese Alps. Suddenly, with a final intensity, the west flared with pale white lightning. Nelson and Nicole turned, and simultaneously the other couple turned, while for an instant the night was as bright as day. Then darkness and a last low peal of thunder, and from Nicole a sharp, terrified cry. She flung herself against Nelson; even in the darkness she saw that his face was as white and strained as her own.

'Did you see?' she cried in a whisper. 'Did you see them?'

'Yes!'

'They're us! They're us! Don't you see?'

Trembling, they clung together. The clouds merged into the dark mass of mountains; looking around after a moment, Nelson and Nicole saw that they were alone together in the tranquil moonlight.

Babylon Revisited
(1931)

'And where's Mr Campbell?' Charlie asked.

'Gone to Switzerland. Mr Campbell's a pretty sick man, Mr Wales.'

'I'm sorry to hear that. And George Hardt?' Charlie inquired.

'Back in America, gone to work.'

'And where is the Snow Bird?'

'He was in here last week. Anyway, his friend, Mr Schaeffer, is in Paris.'

Two familiar names from the long list of a year and a half ago. Charlie scribbled an address in his notebook and tore out the page.

'If you see Mr Schaeffer, give him this,' he said. 'It's my brother-in-law's address. I haven't settled on a hotel yet.'

He was not really disappointed to find Paris was so empty. But the stillness in the Ritz bar was strange and portentous. It was not an American bar any more – he felt polite in it, and not as if he owned it. It had gone back into France. He felt the stillness from the moment he got out of the taxi and saw the doorman, usually in a frenzy of activity at this hour, gossiping with a *chasseur* by the servants' entrance.

Passing through the corridor, he heard only a single, bored voice in the once-clamorous women's room. When he turned into the bar he travelled the twenty feet of green carpet with his eyes fixed straight ahead by old habit; and then, with his foot firmly on the rail, he turned and surveyed the room, encountering only a single pair of eyes that fluttered up from a newspaper in the corner. Charlie asked for the head barman, Paul, who in the latter days of the bull market had come to work in his own custom-built car – disembarking, however, with due nicety at the nearest corner. But Paul was at his country house today and Alix giving him information.

'No, no more,' Charlie said. 'I'm going slow these days.'

Alix congratulated him: 'You were going pretty strong a couple of years ago.'

'I'll stick to it all right,' Charlie assured him. 'I've stuck to it for over a year and a half now.'

'How do you find conditions in America?'

'I haven't been to America for months. I'm in business in Prague, representing a couple of concerns there. They don't know about me down there.'

Alix smiled.

'Remember the night of George Hardt's bachelor dinner here?' said Charlie. 'By the way, what's become of Claude Fessenden?'

Alix lowered his voice confidentially: 'He's in Paris, but he doesn't come here any more. Paul doesn't allow it. He ran up a bill of thirty thousand francs, charging all his drinks and his lunches, and usually his dinner, for more than a year. And when Paul finally told him he had to pay, he gave him a bad check.'

Alix shook his head sadly.

'I don't understand it, such a dandy fellow. Now he's all bloated up –' He made a plump apple of his hands.

Charlie watched a group of strident queens installing themselves in a corner.

'Nothing affects them,' he thought. 'Stocks rise and fall, people loaf or work, but they go on forever.' The place oppressed him. He called for the dice and shook with Alix for the drink.

'Here for long, Mr Wales?'

'I'm here for four or five days to see my little girl.'

'Oh-h! You have a little girl?'

Outside, the fire-red, gas-blue, ghost-green signs shone smokily through the tranquil rain. It was late afternoon and the streets were in movement; the *bistros* gleamed. At the corner of the Boulevard des Capucines he took a taxi. The Place de la Concorde moved by in pink majesty; they crossed the logical Seine, and Charlie felt the sudden provincial quality of the Left Bank.*

Charlie directed his taxi to the Avenue de l'Opera, which was out of his way. But he wanted to see the blue hour spread over

* Fitzgerald deleted this paragraph in a marked copy of *Taps at Reveille* because it was 'Used in *Tender*.' The excision solves the problem of Charlie's puzzling Right Bank-Left Bank-Right Bank-Left Bank itinerary.

the magnificent façade, and imagine that the cab horns, playing
endlessly the first few bars of *La Plus que Lent*, were the trumpets
of the Second Empire. They were closing the iron grill in front of
Brentano's Book-store, and people were already at dinner behind
the trim little bourgeois hedge of Duval's. He had never eaten at a
really cheap restaurant in Paris. Five-course dinner, four francs
fifty, eighteen cents, wine included. For some odd reason he
wished that he had.

As they rolled on to the Left Bank and he felt its sudden
provincialism, he thought, 'I spoiled this city for myself. I didn't
realize it, but the days came along one after another, and then
two years were gone, and everything was gone, and I was gone.'

He was thirty-five, and good to look at. The Irish mobility of his
face was sobered by a deep wrinkle between his eyes. As he rang
his brother-in-law's bell in the Rue Palatine, the wrinkle
deepened till it pulled down his brows; he felt a cramping
sensation in his belly. From behind the maid who opened the
door darted a lovely little girl of nine who shrieked 'Daddy!' and
flew up, struggling like a fish, into his arms. She pulled his head
around by one ear and set her cheek against his.

'My old pie,' he said.

'Oh, daddy, daddy, daddy, daddy, dads, dads, dads!'

She drew him into the salon, where the family waited, a boy
and girl his daughter's age, his sister-in-law and her husband. He
greeted Marion with his voice pitched carefully to avoid either
feigned enthusiasm or dislike, but her response was more frankly
tepid, though she minimized her expression of unalterable
distrust by directing her regard toward his child. The two men
clasped hands in a friendly way and Lincoln Peters rested his for
a moment on Charlie's shoulder.

The room was warm and comfortably American. The three
children moved intimately about, playing through the yellow
oblongs that led to other rooms; the cheer of six o'clock spoke in
the eager smacks of the fire and the sounds of French activity in
the kitchen. But Charlie did not relax; his heart sat up rigidly in
his body and he drew confidence from his daughter, who from
time to time came close to him, holding in her arms the doll he
had brought.

'Really extremely well,' he declared in answer to Lincoln's

question. 'There's a lot of business there that isn't moving at all, but we're doing even better than ever. In fact, damn well. I'm bringing my sister over from America next month to keep house for me. My income last year was bigger than it was when I had money. You see, the Czechs—'

His boasting was for a specific purpose; but after a moment, seeing a faint restiveness in Lincoln's eye, he changed the subject:

'Those are fine children of yours, well brought up, good manners.'

'We think Honoria's a great little girl too.'

Marion Peters came back from the kitchen. She was a tall woman with worried eyes, who had once possessed a fresh American loveliness. Charlie had never been sensitive to it and was always surprised when people spoke of how pretty she had been. From the first there had been an instinctive antipathy between them.

'Well, how do you find Honoria?' she asked.

'Wonderful. I was astonished how much she's grown in ten months. All the children are looking well.'

'We haven't had a doctor for a year. How do you like being back in Paris?'

'It seems very funny to see so few Americans around.'

'I'm delighted,' Marion said vehemently. 'Now at least you can go into a store without their assuming you're a millionaire. We've suffered like everybody, but on the whole it's a good deal pleasanter.'

'But it was nice while it lasted,' Charlie said. 'We were a sort of royalty, almost infallible, with a sort of magic around us. In the bar this afternoon' – he stumbled, seeing his mistake – 'there wasn't a man I knew.'

She looked at him keenly. 'I should think you'd have had enough of bars.'

'I only stayed a minute. I take one drink every afternoon, and no more.'

'Don't you want a cocktail before dinner?' Lincoln asked.

'I take only one drink every afternoon, and I've had that.'

'I hope you keep to it,' said Marion.

Her dislike was evident in the coldness with which she spoke, but Charlie only smiled; he had larger plans. Her very aggressiveness gave him an advantage, and he knew enough to wait. He wanted them to initiate the discussion of what they knew had brought him to Paris.

At dinner he couldn't decide whether Honoria was most like him or her mother. Fortunate if she didn't combine the traits of both that had brought them to disaster. A great wave of protectiveness went over him. He thought he knew what to do for her. He believed in character; he wanted to jump back a whole generation and trust in character again as the eternally valuable element. Everything wore out.

He left soon after dinner, but not to go home. He was curious to see Paris by night with clearer and more judicious eyes than those of other days. He bought a *strapontin* for the Casino and watched Josephine Baker go through her chocolate arabesques.

After an hour he left and strolled toward Montmartre, up the Rue Pigalle into the Place Blanche. The rain had stopped and there were a few people in evening clothes disembarking from taxis in front of cabarets, and *cocottes* prowling singly or in pairs, and many Negroes. He passed a lighted door from which issued music, and stopped with the sense of familiarity; it was Bricktop's, where he had parted with so many hours and so much money. A few doors farther on he found another ancient rendezvous and incautiously put his head inside. Immediately an eager orchestra burst into sound, a pair of professional dancers leaped to their feet and a maître d'hôtel swooped toward him, crying, 'Crowd just arriving, sir!' But he withdrew quickly.

'You have to be damn drunk,' he thought.

Zelli's was closed, the bleak and sinister cheap hotels surrounding it were dark; up in the Rue Blanche there was more light and a local, colloquial French crowd. The Poet's Cave had disappeared, but the two great mouths of the Café of Heaven and the Café of Hell still yawned – even devoured, as he watched, the meager contents of a tourist bus – a German, a Japanese, and an American couple who glanced at him with frightened eyes.

So much for the effort and ingenuity of Montmartre. All the catering to vice and waste was on an utterly childish scale, and he suddenly realized the meaning of the word 'dissipate' – to dissipate into thin air; to make nothing out of something. In the little hours of the night every move from place to place was an enormous human jump, an increase of paying for the privilege of slower and slower motion.

He remembered thousand-franc notes given to an orchestra for playing a single number, hundred-franc notes tossed to a doorman for calling a cab.

But it hadn't been given for nothing.

It had been given, even the most wildly squandered sum, as an offering to destiny that he might not remember the things most worth remembering, the things that now he would always remember – his child taken from his control, his wife escaped to a grave in Vermont.

In the glare of a *brasserie* a woman spoke to him. He bought her some eggs and coffee, and then, eluding her encouraging stare, gave her a twenty-franc note and took a taxi to his hotel.

2

He woke upon a fine fall day – football weather. The depression of yesterday was gone and he liked the people on the streets. At noon he sat opposite Honoria at Le Grand Vatel, the only restaurant he could think of not reminiscent of champagne dinners and long luncheons that began at two and ended in a blurred and vague twilight.

'Now, how about vegetables? Oughtn't you to have some vegetables?'

'Well, yes.'

'Here's *épinards* and *chou-fleur* and carrots and *haricots*.'

'I'd like *chou-fleur*.'

'Wouldn't you like to have two vegetables?'

'I usually only have one at lunch.'

The waiter was pretending to be inordinately fond of children. *'Qu'elle est mignonne la petite? Elle parle exactement comme une Française.'*

'How about dessert? Shall we wait and see?'

The waiter disappeared. Honoria looked at her father expectantly.

'What are we going to do?'

'First, we're going to that toy store in the Rue Saint-Honoré and buy you anything you like. And then we're going to the vaudeville at the Empire.'

She hesitated. 'I like it about the vaudeville, but not the toy store.'

'Why not?'

'Well, you brought me this doll.' She had it with her. 'And I've got lots of things. And we're not rich any more, are we?'

'We never were. But today you are to have anything you want.'

'All right,' she agreed resignedly.

When there had been her mother and a French nurse he had been inclined to be strict; now he extended himself, reached out for a new tolerance; he must be both parents to her and not shut any of her out of communication.

'I want to get to know you,' he said gravely. 'First let me introduce myself. My name is Charles J. Wales, of Prague.'

'Oh, daddy!' her voice cracked with laughter.

'And who are you, please?' he persisted, and she accepted a rôle immediately: 'Honoria Wales, Rue Palatine, Paris.'

'Married or single?'

'No, not married. Single.'

He indicated the doll. 'But I see you have a child, madame.'

Unwilling to disinherit it, she took it to her heart and thought quickly: 'Yes, I've been married, but I'm not married now. My husband is dead.'

He went on quickly, 'And the child's name?'

'Simone. That's after my best friend at school.'

'I'm very pleased that you're doing so well at school.'

'I'm third this month,' she boasted. 'Elsie' – that was her cousin – 'is only about eighteenth, and Richard is about at the bottom.'

'You like Richard and Elsie, don't you?'

'Oh, yes. I like Richard quite well and I like her all right.'

Cautiously and casually he asked: 'And Aunt Marion and Uncle Lincoln – which do you like best?'

'Oh, Uncle Lincoln, I guess.'

He was increasingly aware of her presence. As they came in, a murmur of '… adorable' followed them, and now the people at the next table bent all their silences upon her, staring as if she were something no more conscious than a flower.

'Why don't I live with you?' she asked suddenly. 'Because mamma's dead?'

'You must stay here and learn more French. It would have been hard for daddy to take care of you so well.'

'I don't really need much taking care of any more. I do everything for myself.'

Going out of the restaurant, a man and a woman unexpectedly hailed him.

'Well, the old Wales!'

'Hello there, Lorraine. . . . Dunc.'

Sudden ghosts out of the past: Duncan Schaeffer, a friend from college. Lorraine Quarrles, a lovely, pale blonde of thirty; one of a crowd who had helped them make months into days in the lavish times of three years ago.

'My husband couldn't come this year,' she said, in answer to his question. 'We're poor as hell. So he gave me two hundred a month and told me I could do my worst on that. . . . This your little girl?'

'What about coming back and sitting down?' Duncan asked.

'Can't do it.' He was glad for an excuse. As always, he felt Lorraine's passionate, provocative attraction, but his own rhythm was different now.

'Well, how about dinner?' she asked.

'I'm not free. Give me your address and let me call you.'

'Charlie, I believe you're sober,' she said judicially. 'I honestly believe he's sober, Dunc. Pinch him and see if he's sober.'

Charlie indicated Honoria with his head. They both laughed.

'What's your address?' said Duncan sceptically.

He hesitated, unwilling to give the name of his hotel.

'I'm not settled yet. I'd better call you. We're going to see the vaudeville at the Empire.'

'There! That's what I want to do,' Lorraine said. 'I want to see some clowns and acrobats and jugglers. That's just what we'll do, Dunc.'

'We've got to do an errand first,' said Charlie. 'Perhaps we'll see you there.'

'All right, you snob. . . . Good-by, beautiful little girl.'

'Good-by.'

Honoria bobbed politely.

Somehow, an unwelcome encounter. They liked him because he was functioning, because he was serious; they wanted to see him, because he was stronger than they were now, because they wanted to draw a certain sustenance from his strength.

At the Empire, Honoria proudly refused to sit upon her father's folded coat. She was already an individual with a code of her own, and Charlie was more and more absorbed by the desire of putting a little of himself into her before she crystallized utterly. It was hopeless to try to know her in so short a time.

Between the acts they came upon Duncan and Lorraine in the lobby where the band was playing.

'Have a drink?'

'All right, but not up at the bar. We'll take a table.'

'The perfect father.'

Listening abstractedly to Lorraine, Charlie watched Honoria's eyes leave their table, and he followed them wistfully about the room, wondering what they saw. He met her glance and she smiled.

'I liked that lemonade,' she said.

What had she said? What had he expected? Going home in a taxi afterward, he pulled her over until her head rested against his chest.

'Darling, do you ever think about your mother?'

'Yes, sometimes,' she answered vaguely.

'I don't want you to forget her. Have you got a picture of her?'

'Yes, I think so. Anyhow, Aunt Marion has. Why don't you want me to forget her?'

'She loved you very much.'

'I loved her too.'

They were silent for a moment.

'Daddy, I want to come and live with you,' she said suddenly.

His heart leaped; he had wanted it to come like this.

'Aren't you perfectly happy?'

'Yes, but I love you better than anybody. And you love me better than anybody, don't you, now that mummy's dead?'

'Of course I do. But you won't always like me best, honey.
You'll grow up and meet somebody your own age and go marry
him and forget you ever had a daddy.'

'Yes, that's true,' she agreed tranquilly.

He didn't go in. He was coming back at nine o'clock and he
wanted to keep himself fresh and new for the thing he must say
then.

'When you're safe inside, just show yourself in that window.'

'All right. Good-by, dads, dads, dads, dads.'

He waited in the dark street until she appeared, all warm and
glowing, in the window above and kissed her fingers out into the
night.

3

They were waiting. Marion sat behind the coffee service in a
dignified black dinner dress that just faintly suggested mourning.
Lincoln was walking up and down with the animation of one
who had already been talking. They were as anxious as he was to
get into the question. He opened it almost immediately:

'I suppose you know what I want to see you about – why I
really came to Paris.'

Marion played with the black stars on her necklace and
frowned.

'I'm awfully anxious to have a home,' he continued. 'And I'm
awfully anxious to have Honoria in it. I appreciate your taking in
Honoria for her mother's sake, but things have changed now' –
he hesitated and then continued more forcibly – 'changed
radically with me, and I want to ask you to reconsider the
matter. It would be silly for me to deny that about three years
ago I was acting badly—'

Marion looked up at him with hard eyes.

'– but all that's over. As I told you, I haven't had more than a
drink a day for over a year, and I take that drink deliberately, so
that the idea of alcohol won't get too big in my imagination. You
see the idea?'

'No,' said Marion succinctly.

'It's a sort of stunt I set myself. It keeps the matter in
proportion.'

'I get you,' said Lincoln. 'You don't want to admit it's got any attraction for you.'

'Something like that. Sometimes I forget and don't take it. But I try to take it. Anyhow, I couldn't afford to drink in my position. The people I represent are more than satisfied with what I've done, and I'm bringing my sister over from Burlington to keep house for me, and I want awfully to have Honoria too. You know that even when her mother and I weren't getting along well we never let anything that happened touch Honoria. I know she's fond of me and I know I'm able to take care of her and – well, there you are. How do you feel about it?'

He knew that now he would have to take a beating. It would last an hour or two hours, and it would be difficult, but if he modulated his inevitable resentment to the chastened attitude of the reformed sinner, he might win his point in the end.

Keep your temper, he told himself. You don't want to be justified. You want Honoria.

Lincoln spoke first: 'We've been talking it over ever since we got your letter last month. We're happy to have Honoria here. She's a dear little thing, and we're glad to be able to help her, but of course that isn't the question—'

Marion interrupted suddenly. 'How long are you going to stay sober, Charlie?' she asked.

'Permanently, I hope.'

'How can anybody count on that?'

'You know I never did drink heavily until I gave up business and came over here with nothing to do. Then Helen and I began to run around with—'

'Please leave Helen out of it. I can't bear to hear you talk about her like that.'

He stared at her grimly; he had never been certain how fond of each other the sisters were in life.

'My drinking only lasted about a year and a half – from the time we came over until I – collapsed.'

'It was time enough.'

'It was time enough,' he agreed.

'My duty is entirely to Helen,' she said. 'I try to think what she would have wanted me to do. Frankly, from the night you did

that terrible thing you haven't really existed for me. I can't help
that. She was my sister.'

'Yes.'

'When she was dying she asked me to look out for Honoria. If
you hadn't been in a sanitarium then, it might have helped
matters.'

He had no answer.

'I'll never in my life be able to forget the morning when Helen
knocked at my door, soaked to the skin and shivering, and said
you'd locked her out.'

Charlie gripped the sides of the chair. This was more difficult
than he expected; he wanted to launch out into a long
expostulation and explanation, but he only said: 'The night I
locked her out –' and she interrupted, 'I don't feel up to going
over that again.'

After a moment's silence Lincoln said: 'We're getting off the
subject. You want Marion to set aside her legal guardianship and
give you Honoria. I think the main point for her is whether she
has confidence in you or not.'

'I don't blame Marion,' Charlie said slowly, 'but I think she can
have entire confidence in me. I had a good record up to three
years ago. Of course, it's within human possibilities I might go
wrong any time. But if we wait much longer I'll lose Honoria's
childhood and my chance for a home.' He shook his head, 'I'll
simply lose her, don't you see?'

'Yes, I see,' said Lincoln.

'Why didn't you think of all this before?' Marion asked.

'I suppose I did, from time to time, but Helen and I were getting
along badly. When I consented to the guardianship, I was flat on
my back in a sanitarium and the market had cleaned me out. I
knew I'd acted badly, and I thought if it would bring any peace to
Helen, I'd agree to anything. But now it's different. I'm
functioning, I'm behaving damn well, so far as—'

'Please don't swear at me,' Marion said.

He looked at her, startled. With each remark the force of her
dislike became more and more apparent. She had built up all her
fear of life into one wall and faced it toward him. This trivial
reproof was possibly the result of some trouble with the cook
several hours before. Charlie became increasingly alarmed at

leaving Honoria in this atmosphere of hostility against himself; sooner or later it would come out, in a word here, a shake of the head there, and some of that distrust would be irrevocably implanted in Honoria. But he pulled his temper down out of his face and shut it up inside him; he had won a point, for Lincoln realized the absurdity of Marion's remark and asked her lightly since when she had objected to the word 'damn.'

'Another thing,' Charlie said: 'I'm able to give her certain advantages now. I'm going to take a French governess to Prague with me. I've got a lease on a new apartment—'

He stopped, realizing that he was blundering. They couldn't be expected to accept with equanimity the fact that his income was again twice as large as their own.

'I suppose you can give her more luxuries than we can,' said Marion. 'When you were throwing away money we were living along watching every ten francs. . . . I suppose you'll start doing it again.'

'Oh, no,' he said. 'I've learned. I worked hard for ten years, you know – until I got lucky in the market, like so many people. Terribly lucky. It didn't seem any use working any more, so I quit. It won't happen again.'

There was a long silence. All of them felt their nerves straining, and for the first time in a year Charlie wanted a drink. He was sure now that Lincoln Peters wanted him to have his child.

Marion shuddered suddenly; part of her saw that Charlie's feet were planted on the earth now, and her own maternal feeling recognized the naturalness of his desire; but she had lived for a long time with a prejudice – a prejudice founded on a curious disbelief in her sister's happiness, and which, in the shock of one terrible night, had turned to hatred for him. It had all happened at a point in her life where the discouragement of ill health and adverse circumstances made it necessary for her to believe in tangible villainy and a tangible villain.

'I can't help what I think!' she cried out suddenly. 'How much you were responsible for Helen's death, I don't know. It's something you'll have to square with your own conscience.'

An electric current of agony surged through him; for a moment he was almost on his feet, an unuttered sound echoing in his throat. He hung on to himself for a moment, another moment.

'Hold on there,' said Lincoln uncomfortably. 'I never thought you were responsible for that.'

'Helen died of heart trouble,' Charlie said dully.

'Yes, heart trouble.' Marion spoke as if the phrase had another meaning for her.

Then, in the flatness that followed her outburst, she saw him plainly and she knew he had somehow arrived at control over the situation. Glancing at her husband, she found no help from him, and as abruptly as if it were a matter of no importance, she threw up the sponge.

'Do what you like!' she cried, springing up from her chair. 'She's your child. I'm not the person to stand in your way. I think if it were my child I'd rather see her –' She managed to check herself. 'You two decide it. I can't stand this. I'm sick. I'm going to bed.'

She hurried from the room; after a moment Lincoln said:

'This has been a hard day for her. You know how strongly she feels –' His voice was almost apologetic: 'When a woman gets an idea in her head.'

'Of course.'

'It's going to be all right. I think she sees now that you – can provide for the child, and so we can't very well stand in your way or Honoria's way.'

'Thank you, Lincoln.'

'I'd better go along and see how she is.'

'I'm going.'

He was still trembling when he reached the street, but a walk down the Rue Bonaparte to the quais set him up, and as he crossed the Seine, fresh and new by the quai lamps, he felt exultant. But back in his room he couldn't sleep. The image of Helen haunted him. Helen whom he had loved so until they had senselessly begun to abuse each other's love, tear it into shreds. On that terrible February night that Marion remembered so vividly, a slow quarrel had gone on for hours. There was a scene at the Florida, and then he attempted to take her home, and then she kissed young Webb at a table; after that there was what she had hysterically said. When he arrived home alone he turned the key in the lock in wild anger. How could he know she would arrive an hour later alone, that there would be a snowstorm in which she wandered about in slippers, too confused to find a taxi? Then the aftermath, her escaping pneumonia by a miracle, and all the attendant horror. They were 'reconciled,' but that was the beginning of the end, and Marion, who had seen with her own eyes and who imagined it to be one of many scenes from her sister's martyrdom, never forgot.

Going over it again brought Helen nearer, and in the white, soft light that steals upon half sleep near morning he found himself talking to her again. She said that he was perfectly right about Honoria and that she wanted Honoria to be with him. She said she was glad he was being good and doing better. She said a lot of other things – very friendly things – but she was in a swing in a white dress, and swinging faster and faster all the time, so that at the end he could not hear clearly all that she said.

4

He woke up feeling happy. The door of the world was open again. He made plans, vistas, futures for Honoria and himself, but suddenly he grew sad, remembering all the plans he and Helen had made. She had not planned to die. The present was the thing – work to do and someone to love. But not to love too much, for he knew the injury that a father can do to a daughter or a mother to a son by attaching them too closely: afterward, out in the world, the child would seek in the marriage partner the same blind tenderness and, failing probably to find it, turn against love and life.

It was another bright, crisp day. He called Lincoln Peters at the bank where he worked and asked if he could count on taking Honoria when he left for Prague. Lincoln agreed that there was no reason for delay. One thing – the legal guardianship. Marion wanted to retain that a while longer. She was upset by the whole matter, and it would oil things if she felt that the situation was still in her control for another year. Charlie agreed, wanting only the tangible, visible child.

Then the question of a governess. Charlie sat in a gloomy agency and talked to a cross Béarnaise and to a buxom Breton peasant, neither of whom he could have endured. There were others whom he would see tomorrow.

He lunched with Lincoln Peters at Griffons, trying to keep down his exultation.

'There's nothing quite like your own child,' Lincoln said. 'But you understand how Marion feels too.'

'She's forgotten how hard I worked for seven years there,' Charlie said. 'She just remembers one night.'

'There's another thing.' Lincoln hesitated. 'While you and Helen were tearing around Europe throwing money away, we were just getting along. I didn't touch any of the prosperity because I never got ahead enough to carry anything but my insurance. I think Marion felt there was some kind of injustice in it – you not even working toward the end; and getting richer and richer.'

'It went just as quick as it came,' said Charlie.

'Yes, a lot of it stayed in the hands of *chasseurs* and saxophone players and maîtres d'hôtel – well, the big party's over now. I just said that to explain Marion's feeling about those crazy years. If you drop in about six o'clock tonight before Marion's too tired, we'll settle the details on the spot.'

Back at his hotel, Charlie found a *pneumatique* that had been redirected from the Ritz bar where Charlie had left his address for the purpose of finding a certain man.

Dear Charlie: You were so strange when we saw you the other day that I wondered if I did something to offend you. If so, I'm not conscious of it. In fact, I have thought about you too much for the last year, and it's always been in the back of my mind that I might see you if I came over here. We *did* have such good times that crazy spring, like the night you and I stole the butcher's tricycle, and the time we tried to call on the president and you had the old derby rim and the wire cane. Everybody seems so old lately, but I don't feel old a bit. Couldn't we get together some time today for old time's sake? I've got a vile hang-over for the moment, but will be feeling better this afternoon and will look for you about five in the sweat-shop at the Ritz.

Always devotedly,
LORRAINE

His first feeling was one of awe that he had actually, in his mature years, stolen a tricycle and pedalled Lorraine all over the Étoile between the small hours and dawn. In retrospect it was a nightmare. Locking out Helen didn't fit in with any other act of his life, but the tricycle incident did – it was one of many. How many weeks or months of dissipation to arrive at that condition of utter irresponsibility?

He tried to picture how Lorraine had appeared to him then – very attractive; Helen was unhappy about it, though she said nothing. Yesterday, in the restaurant, Lorraine had seemed trite, blurred, worn away. He emphatically did not want to see her, and he was glad Alix had not given away his hotel address. It was a relief to think, instead, of Honoria, to think of Sundays spent with her and of saying good morning to her and of knowing she was there in his house at night, drawing her breath in the darkness.

At five he took a taxi and bought presents for all the Peters – a piquant cloth doll, a box of Roman soldiers, flowers for Marion, big linen handkerchiefs for Lincoln.

He saw, when he arrived in the apartment, that Marion had accepted the inevitable. She greeted him now as though he were a recalcitrant member of the family, rather than a menacing outsider. Honoria had been told she was going; Charlie was glad to see that her tact made her conceal her excessive happiness. Only on his lap did she whisper her delight and the question 'When?' before she slipped away with the other children.

He and Marion were alone for a minute in the room, and on an impulse he spoke out boldly:

'Family quarrels are bitter things. They don't go according to any rules. They're not like aches or wounds; they're more like splits in the skin that won't heal because there's not enough material. I wish you and I could be on better terms.'

'Some things are hard to forget,' she answered. 'It's a question of confidence.' There was no answer to this and presently she asked, 'When do you propose to take her?'

'As soon as I can get a governess. I hoped the day after tomorrow.'

'That's impossible. I've got to get her things in shape. Not before Saturday.'

He yielded. Coming back into the room, Lincoln offered him a drink.

'I'll take my daily whisky,' he said.

It was warm here, it was a home, people together by a fire. The children felt very safe and important; the mother and father were serious, watchful. They had things to do for the children more important than his visit here. A spoonful of medicine was, after all, more important than the strained relations between Marion and himself. They were not dull people, but they were very much in the grip of life and circumstances. He wondered if he couldn't do something to get Lincoln out of his rut at the bank.

A long peal at the door-bell; the *bonne à tout faire* passed through and went down the corridor. The door opened upon another long ring, and then voices, and the three in the salon looked up expectantly; Lincoln moved to bring the corridor within his range of vision, and Marion rose. Then the maid came back along the corridor, closely followed by the voices, which developed under the light into Duncan Schaeffer and Lorraine Quarrles.

They were gay, they were hilarious, they were roaring with laughter. For a moment Charlie was astounded; unable to understand how they ferreted out the Peters' address.

'Ah-h-h!' Duncan wagged his finger roguishly at Charlie. 'Ah-h-h!'

They both slid down another cascade of laughter. Anxious and at a loss, Charlie shook hands with them quickly and presented them to Lincoln and Marion. Marion nodded, scarcely speaking. She had drawn back a step toward the fire; her little girl stood beside her, and Marion put an arm about her shoulder.

With growing annoyance at the intrusion, Charlie waited for them to explain themselves. After some concentration Duncan said:

'We came to invite you out to dinner. Lorraine and I insist that all this chi-chi, cagy business 'bout your address got to stop.'

Charlie came closer to them, as if to force them backward down the corridor.

'Sorry, but I can't. Tell me where you'll be and I'll phone you in half an hour.'

This made no impression. Lorraine sat down suddenly on the side of a chair, and focussing her eyes on Richard, cried, 'Oh, what a nice little boy! Come here, little boy.' Richard glanced at his mother, but did not move. With a perceptible shrug of her shoulders, Lorraine turned back to Charlie:

'Come and dine. Sure your cousins won' mine. See you so sel'om. Or solemn.'

'I can't,' said Charlie sharply. 'You two have dinner and I'll phone you.'

Her voice became suddenly unpleasant. 'All right, we'll go. But I remember once when you hammered on my door at four A.M. I was enough of a good sport to give you a drink. Come on, Dunc.'

Still in slow motion, with blurred, angry faces, with uncertain feet, they retired along the corridor.

'Good night,' Charlie said.

'Good night!' responded Lorraine emphatically.

When he went back into the salon Marion had not moved, only now her son was standing in the circle of her other arm. Lincoln was still swinging Honoria back and forth like a pendulum from side to side.

'What an outrage!' Charlie broke out. 'What an absolute outrage!'

Neither of them answered. Charlie dropped into an armchair, picked up his drink, set it down again and said:

'People I haven't seen for two years having the colossal nerve—'

He broke off. Marion had made the sound 'Oh!' in one swift, furious breath, turned her body from him with a jerk and left the room. Lincoln set down Honoria carefully.

'You children go in and start your soup,' he said, and when they obeyed, he said to Charlie:

'Marion's not well and she can't stand shocks. That kind of people make her really physically sick.'

'I didn't tell them to come here. They wormed your name out of somebody. They deliberately—'

'Well, it's too bad. It doesn't help matters. Excuse me a minute.'

Left alone, Charlie sat tense in his chair. In the next room he

could hear the children eating, talking in monosyllables, already
oblivious to the scene between their elders. He heard a murmur
of conversation from a farther room and then the ticking bell of a
telephone receiver picked up, and in a panic he moved to the
other side of the room and out of earshot.

In a minute Lincoln came back. 'Look here, Charlie. I think
we'd better call off dinner for tonight. Marion's in bad shape.'

'Is she angry with me?'

'Sort of,' he said, almost roughly. 'She's not strong and—'

'You mean she's changed her mind about Honoria?'

'She's pretty bitter right now. I don't know. You phone me at
the bank tomorrow.'

'I wish you'd explain to her I never dreamed these people
would come here. I'm just as sore as you are.'

'I couldn't explain anything to her now.'

Charlie got up. He took his coat and hat and started down the
corridor. Then he opened the door of the dining room and said in
a strange voice, 'Good night, children.'

Honoria rose and ran around the table to hug him.

'Good night, sweetheart,' he said vaguely, and then trying to
make his voice more tender, trying to conciliate something,
'Good night, dear children.'

5

Charlie went directly to the Ritz bar with the furious idea of
finding Lorraine and Duncan, but they were not there, and he
realized that in any case there was nothing he could do. He had
not touched his drink at the Peters', and now he ordered a
whisky-and-soda. Paul came over to say hello.

'It's a great change,' he said sadly. 'We do about half the
business we did. So many fellows I hear about back in the States
lost everything, maybe not in the first crash, but then in the
second. Your friend George Hardt lost every cent, I hear. Are you
back in the States?'

'No, I'm in business in Prague.'

'I heard that you lost a lot in the crash.'

'I did,' and he added grimly, 'but I lost everything I wanted in
the boom.'

'Selling short.'

'Something like that.'

Again the memory of those days swept over him like a nightmare – the people they had met travelling; then people who couldn't add a row of figures or speak a coherent sentence. The little man Helen had consented to dance with at the ship's party, who had insulted her ten feet from the table; the women and girls carried screaming with drink or drugs out of public places—

– The men who locked their wives out in the snow, because the snow of twenty-nine wasn't real snow. If you didn't want it to be snow, you just paid some money.

He went to the phone and called the Peters' apartment; Lincoln answered.

'I called up because this thing is on my mind. Has Marion said anything definite?'

'Marion's sick,' Lincoln answered shortly. 'I know this thing isn't altogether your fault, but I can't have her go to pieces about it. I'm afraid we'll have to let it slide for six months; I can't take the chance of working her up to this state again.'

'I see.'

'I'm sorry, Charlie.'

He went back to his table. His whisky glass was empty, but he shook his head when Alix looked at it questioningly. There wasn't much he could do now except send Honoria some things; he would send her a lot of things tomorrow. He thought rather angrily that this was just money – he had given so many people money. . . .

'No, no more,' he said to another waiter. 'What do I owe you?'

He would come back some day; they couldn't make him pay forever. But he wanted his child, and nothing was much good now, beside that fact. He wasn't young any more, with a lot of nice thoughts and dreams to have by himself. He was absolutely sure Helen wouldn't have wanted him to be so alone.

The Lost Decade
(1939)

All sorts of people came into the offices of the news-weekly and
Orrison Brown had all sorts of relations with them. Outside of
office hours he was 'one of the editors' – during work time he was
simply a curly-haired man who a year before had edited the
Dartmouth *Jack-O-Lantern* and was now only too glad to take the
undesirable assignments around the office, from straightening
out illegible copy to playing call boy without the title.

He had seen this visitor go into the editor's office – a pale, tall
man of forty with blond statuesque hair and a manner that was
neither shy nor timid, nor otherworldly like a monk, but
something of all three. The name on his card, Louis Trimble,
evoked some vague memory, but having nothing to start on,
Orrison did not puzzle over it – until a buzzer sounded on his
desk, and previous experience warned him that Mr Trimble was
to be his first course at lunch.

'Mr Trimble – Mr Brown,' said the Source of all luncheon
money. 'Orrison – Mr Trimble's been away a long time. Or he
feels it's a long time – almost twelve years. Some people would
consider themselves lucky to've missed the last decade.'

'That's so,' said Orrison.

'I can't lunch today,' continued his chief. 'Take him to Voisin
or 21 or anywhere he'd like. Mr Trimble feels there're lots of
things he hasn't seen.'

Trimble demurred politely.

'Oh, I can get around.'

'I know it, old boy. Nobody knew this place like you did once –
and if Brown tries to explain the horseless carriage just send him
back here to me. And you'll be back yourself by four, won't you?'

Orrison got his hat.

'You've been away ten years?' he asked while they went down
in the elevator.

'They'd begun the Empire State Building,' said Trimble. 'What
does that add up to?'

'About 1928. But as the chief said, you've been lucky to miss a lot.' As a feeler he added, 'Probably had more interesting things to look at.'

'Can't say I have.'

They reached the street and the way Trimble's face tightened at the roar of traffic made Orrison take one more guess.

'You've been out of civilization?'

'In a sense.' The words were spoken in such a measured way that Orrison concluded this man wouldn't talk unless he wanted to – and simultaneously wondered if he could have possibly spent the thirties in a prison or an insane asylum.

'This is the famous 21,' he said. 'Do you think you'd rather eat somewhere else?'

Trimble paused, looking carefully at the brownstone house.

'I can remember when the name 21 got to be famous,' he said, 'about the same year as Moriarty's.' Then he continued almost apologetically, 'I thought we might walk up Fifth Avenue about five minutes and eat wherever we happened to be. Some place with young people to look at.'

Orrison gave him a quick glance and once again thought of bars and gray walls and bars; he wondered if his duties included introducing Mr Trimble to complaisant girls. But Mr Trimble didn't look as if that was in his mind – the dominant expression was of absolute and deep-seated curiosity and Orrison attempted to connect the name with Admiral Byrd's hideout at the South Pole or flyers lost in Brazilian jungles. He was, or he had been, quite a fellow – that was obvious. But the only definite clue to his environment – and to Orrison the clue that led nowhere – was his countryman's obedience to the traffic lights and his predilection for walking on the side next to the shops and not the street. Once he stopped and gazed into a haberdasher's window.

'Crepe ties,' he said. 'I haven't seen one since I left college.'

'Where'd you go?'

'Massachusetts Tech.'

'Great place.'

'I'm going to take a look at it next week. Let's eat somewhere along here –' They were in the upper Fifties '– you choose.'

There was a good restaurant with a little awning just around the corner.

'What do you want to see most?' Orrison asked, as they sat down.

Trimble considered.

'Well – the back of people's heads,' he suggested. 'Their necks – how their heads are joined to their bodies. I'd like to hear what those two little girls are saying to their father. Not exactly what they're saying but whether the words float or submerge, how their mouths shut when they've finished speaking. Just a matter of rhythm – Cole Porter came back to the States in 1928 because he felt that there were new rhythms around.'

Orrison was sure he had his clue now, and with nice delicacy did not pursue it by a millimeter – even suppressing a sudden desire to say there was a fine concert in Carnegie Hall tonight.

'The weight of spoons,' said Trimble, 'so light. A little bowl with a stick attached. The cast in that waiter's eye. I knew him once but he wouldn't remember me.'

But as they left the restaurant the same waiter looked at Trimble rather puzzled as if he almost knew him. When they were outside Orrison laughed:

'After ten years people will forget.'

'Oh, I had dinner there last May –' He broke off in an abrupt manner.

It was all kind of nutsy, Orrison decided – and changed himself suddenly into a guide.

'From here you get a good candid focus on Rockefeller Center,' he pointed out with spirit '– and the Chrysler Building and the Armistead Building, the daddy of all the new ones.'

'The Armistead Building,' Trimble rubber-necked obediently. 'Yes – I designed it.'

Orrison shook his head cheerfully – he was used to going out with all kinds of people. But that stuff about having been in the restaurant last May. . . .

He paused by the brass entablature in the cornerstone of the building. 'Erected 1928,' it said.

Trimble nodded.

'But I was taken drunk that year – every-which-way drunk. So I never saw it before now.'

'Oh.' Orrison hesitated. 'Like to go in now?'

'I've been in it – lots of times. But I've never seen it. And now it isn't what I want to see. I wouldn't ever be able to see it now. I simply want to see how people walk and what their clothes and shoes and hats are made of. And their eyes and hands. Would you mind shaking hands with me?'

'Not at all, sir.'

'Thanks. Thanks. That's very kind. I suppose it looks strange – but people will think we're saying good-by. I'm going to walk up the avenue for awhile, so we *will* say good-by. Tell your office I'll be in at four.'

Orrison looked after him when he started out, half expecting him to turn into a bar. But there was nothing about him that suggested or ever had suggested drink.

'Jesus,' he said to himself. 'Drunk for ten years.'

He felt suddenly of the texture of his own coat and then he reached out and pressed his thumb against the granite of the building by his side.